IRISH
EYES

ALSO BY ANDREW M. GREELEY

All About Women
Angel Fire
Angel Light
Contract with an Angel
Faithful Attraction
The Final Planet
Furthermore! Memories of a Parish Priest
God Game
Irish Gold
Irish Lace
Irish Whiskey
A Midwinter's Tale
Star Bright!
Summer at the Lake
White Smoke
Younger than Springtime

Sacred Visions (editor with Michael Cassutt)

IRISH EYES

A Nuala Anne McGrail Novel

ANDREW M. GREELEY

DOUBLEDAY DIRECT LARGE PRINT EDITION

A TOM DOHERTY ASSOCIATES BOOK
NEW YORK

IRISH EYES

Copyright © 2000 by Andrew M. Greeley Enterprises, Ltd.

A Forge Book
Published by Tom Doherty Associates, LLC
175 Fifth Avenue
New York, NY 10010

Forge® is a registered trademark of Tom Doherty Associates, LLC.

ISBN 0-7394-0993-X

Printed in the United States of America

In honor of the men who made peace in
Northern Ireland

When Irish eyes are smiling,
'Tis like a day in spring.
In the lilt of Irish laughter,
You can hear the angels sing.

When Irish eyes are happy,
All the world is bright and gay,
But when Irish eyes are smiling,
Sure, they'll steal your heart away.

IRISH
EYES

1

The redhead with the green eyes continued to play with my wife's breast. She stared at me with what I thought was undisguised triumph. I had prior rights to that breast. The redhead was an interloper, a latecomer, a spoilsport.

"Had enough, had you now?" my wife said to her. "Want to go to himself, do you now?"

The myth was that this eating, defecating, sleeping machine loved me more than her ma. She supported the myth by stretching out her arms to me and gurgling, "Da."

It wasn't really "da." Everyone knows that going-on-seven-months-old children cannot pronounce words. But Nuala Anne had decreed that the gurgle meant "da" and there was no room for dispute.

"The child definitely likes you more than me, Dermot Michael," my wife said triumphantly, a view which was supposed to mitigate my unspoken anguish that the witch had intruded into our marriage and taken my wife away from me. Or at least destroyed my monopoly. "Ma for food, Da for love."

The bewitching little girl snuggled contentedly into my arms and promptly fell asleep, a characteristic she shared with her mother. Fiona, our pure white family wolfhound, watched me suspiciously, not at all sure that I was capable even of the minor task of holding the little redhead in my arms. In Fiona's eyes I was strictly number three. The intruder had taken not only my wife but my good dog away from me.

THIS IS ALL SILLY, the Adversary informed me. IT IS NOTHING MORE THAN A TYPICAL SUPERANNUATED ADOLESCENT MALE REACTION TO THE OBLIGATION OF SHARING ONE'S WIFE WITH ONE'S FIRST CHILD. ACTUALLY YOU ADORE THE LITTLE DEFECATING MACHINE.

I generally disagree with the Adversary, an inner voice which constantly criticizes me. However, I had to admit that the small creature sleeping in my arms was moderately adorable.

"She's a changeling," I replied to the Adversary. "At six months she shouldn't be trying to crawl and shouldn't be saying 'Da.' She's not altogether human. Didn't my mom say that most babies don't crawl till nine or ten months?"

AND YOU DIDN'T CRAWL TILL TWELVE MONTHS AND WALK TILL EIGHTEEN AND TALK UNTIL THREE AND ARE BARELY TOILET-TRAINED EVEN NOW.

Nuala Anne had tossed aside her robe and disclosed temporarily her spectacular naked body. I gasped inwardly. Fiona paced around anxiously, knowing that herself was dressing for her early morning run on the beach in the Indian summer sun. Breakfast for all of us, save the red-haired intruder, after her run and before my run.

A warning about my wife's name. It is definitely not Nuahla nor Nulla as in null and void. Nor is it "Null" like in "null and void" as some of my siblings call her, though not in my presence anymore. (She thinks my reaction to that nickname is "funny.") You might try "Noolah" with a touch of Galway fog in your voice or a bad cold and a long and soft emphasis on the "oo," as though you were negatively responding to an attractive invitation with a hesitant "no." I must warn you that she insists that it is impossible to pronounce it correctly unless you speak the Irish language, "and yourself with that terrible flat Chicago 'a'!"

"What was the matter with herself last night?" I asked as Nuala pulled on her running shorts.

Nelliecoyne is what is technically known as a "good baby," which means that she keeps regular hours and thus permits her parents to sleep through the night. It was unthinkable that any child of Nuala Anne McGrail, particularly a girl child, would be anything but a "good baby."

Last night, however, was another story. My wife and I are deep sleepers, particularly after a serious bout of lovemaking. Last night it had been mind-bending in its seriousness. Sometime in the depths of the early morning hours, I had heard as from a great distance an angry wail. I ignored it. Nelliecoyne was a good baby, wasn't she?

Fiona, however, was less easily persuaded by past performance, I felt her large snout nudge me.

"Go away," I told her.

Fiona thereupon barked loudly.

"What's wrong, Dermot Michael?" my wife demanded, her voice heavy with sleep.

"Your daughter is wailing."

"Is she now?"

"I'll go see what the trouble is," I said bravely.

"Ah, no. She's probably hungry and you can't feed her, can you?"

"I cannot," I said contentedly.

So Nuala bounded out of bed, and naked in the moonlight, dashed next door to the nursery, accompanied by the agitated Fiona.

Nuala always dashes. She also bounds. And slams doors.

The tyke continued to wail furiously, something had offended her sense of propriety and order. Her mother's nipple would not satisfy her.

We were spending time in my parents' home at Grand Beach in mid-October, when the place was deserted, to savor the color and the warmth of Indian summer before the arctic air imposed its winter penance on us and to celebrate the second anniversary of our marriage and the third of our chance encounter at O'Neill's Pub on College Green, just down the street from Trinity College. We would take turns each morning running on the beach, swim naked in the heated pool while Nelliecoyne would watch us under the careful supervision of good dog Fiona (who would chase squirrels for the fun of it but never run too far away), walk in the afternoon sunlight with our daughter in her traveling sack, and do our work, such as it was, in the time left over.

I would write a few desultory pages on the first novel of my new contract and Nuala Anne would practice the songs for her forthcoming disc *Nuala Anne Sings Lullabies.* She was far more serious in her work than I, but never pushed me to settle down and be as responsible as she was.

There were, however, two important reasons to escape Chicago during Indian summer—lovemaking and Nick Farmer, the "music critic" of *The Observer*, a Chicago magazine, who was grimly determined to wreck Nuala's career because he hated me. Without ever discussing it explicitly (the Irish are great at that) we both wanted to indulge ourselves in sexual abandon before winter came.

ORGY IS WHAT YOU MEAN, the Adversary sniffed puritanically.

I sleep with many different women: a shy, fragile, virginal creature, a sultry seducer, a playful child, an aggressive sexual demon, an outrageous tease, a warm and close friend. All of them are my wife. I am never sure which one I will encounter in our bedroom. I don't know whether she plays the game of being someone different every night with deliberate planning or whether it is mere random chance. I know her better than I know anyone else in the world. But I hardly know her at all.

Mind you, I'm not complaining.

As I heard her singing an Irish lullaby to our daughter, I imagined her naked in the moonlight, tenderly rocking Nelliecoyne in her arms against the background of the silver Lake.

"The October winds lament,
Around the castle of Dromore,
Yet peace lies in her lofty halls,
My loving treasure store.

Though autumn leaves may droop and die,
A bud of spring are you."

I sighed happily. 'Tis good to have a wife, particularly one like mine.

Normally Nuala Anne would not cross the bedroom without clutching some kind of protection for her modesty. But when the child wailed such concerns for modesty vanished.

Slowly, reluctantly, Nelliecoyne settled down. Her wail became a mild sniffle of protest. Then the only sound was yet another lullaby. Finally, my wife snuggled into bed next to me.

" 'Tis all right, Dermot," she said. "Something upset her. Fiona is staying with her."

Good dog, Fiona.

I extended my arm around her and we both slipped back into peaceful and compliant sleep.

The next morning, as she was tying her running shoes, Nuala Anne explained why our "really good" child had disrupted the serenity of our mid-October repose.

"Och, wasn't it most likely the boat that was offshore?"

She stood up and reached for her running bra, always the last garment to be put in place, at least when I was present. Deliberate? To taunt me, to tempt me, to promise me? What did I know?

"Boat?"

"That big five-masted schooner that was a hundred yards or so offshore."

"That one?" I said as an ominous shiver began at the base of my skull and ran down my spine. My wife is fey, you see. She *sees* things, usually from the past and, more often than not, things about which she and I must do something. Even the sight of her bare breasts, usually enough to cure me of any and all chills, didn't exorcise this shiver.

"Isn't it the one that is as long as your football fields?"

"That one?"

"You can put herself into the crib if you want, though like as not you'll want to hold her till I come back and tell yourself how much more beautiful she is than I am. . . . Come on, Fiona, girl, let's leave these slugabeds and get ourselves some *real* exercise!"

Nuala Anne and the dog thundered out of the house and bounded down the dune to the beach, two exuberant females liberated temporarily from their solemn duty to watch over Nelliecoyne and her inept and indulgent father.

Was unreal exercise what we did last night, exercise in which Nuala delighted in controlling the pace and action of our lovemaking?

I glanced out the window to watch them sprinting down the beach, a beach wider than it had ever been in my lifetime. My parents said that the March storms had swept in two mammoth sandbars that had lurked offshore for a couple of decades. There was debate in the community whether this meant greater hazard for houses on the Lake because the sandbars were better protection than sea walls. I was content with a better beach. But I've never been one with strong motivation to defer gratification.

The child stirred uneasily out of her sleep and whimpered a mild protest. I knew what that meant. So I changed her diaper, an exercise which the little monster seemed to think had been designed for amusement.

"You're a spoiled little brat," I informed her. "Your ma and your dog will spoil you altogether. It's lucky you have a stern father who will impose some discipline in your life."

THAT'S THE MOST RIDICULOUS THING I'VE

EVER HEARD YOU SAY, the Adversary informed me. YOU'RE COMPLETELY WITHOUT DISCIPLINE YOURSELF AND YOU'RE GOING TO TEACH IT TO THAT POOR CHILD?

I had been joking, but if the Adversary was too ignorant to know it I was not about to tell him.

Nelliecoyne gurgled happily as I replaced her in her crib. She was not old enough yet to distinguish the various caregivers who waited on her hand and foot. We were simply "the other one" whom she had to remind periodically of her needs. Even the snow-white hound was not distinct from the rest of us, though she seemed to be particularly happy when Fiona's ridiculously massive head loomed over her.

But what did I know?

I knew one thing, however, for sure as I began to prepare the waffles and bacon for our breakfast. There were no football-field-long five-masted schooners on Lake Michigan. There probably had not been any for a century. Save for those which were on the bottom of the Lake.

We were back to our old games. Nuala Anne McGrail was having one of her "interludes" during which the past and present combined into one eerie netherworld of mystery and pain.

That was bad enough. However, I knew that my wife was fey when I married her. Now I also knew that my daughter, the placidly sleeping Nelliecoyne, was also fey.

The chill ran down my spine again. This time it didn't go away.

2

Shrewd west of Ireland peasant that she is, Nuala Anne likes to keep life under control. That's why she was studying accounting at Trinity College when I first met her three years ago at O'Neill's Pub across from St. Anne's Church, a gorgeous nineteen-year-old in whose voice one heard the bells of music floating over the bogs of Connemara, a Celtic goddess in jeans and a sweatshirt.

The course of a pregnancy, however, was something she could not control. She was angry at herself for being sick almost all the time, for "spotting" intermittently, and for two near misses at miscarriages. She considered all of these natural inevitabilities to be signs of her own moral failure as both a wife and a potential mother.

Through a long and extremely difficult labor, she apologized to me and her mother—Annie McGrail, whom we had flown over for the event—for the inconvenience she was causing us. This is very Irish behavior and there was no point in trying to fight it. Did she mean it as literally true?

What do I know?

"Sure, doesn't she half believe it all?" Annie had whispered to me.

I have never been able to comprehend what the word *half* on the lips of an Irish person means.

"Didn't I half believe it meself?"

That settled nothing, save adding confirmation to the thesis that apples don't fall very far from their trees.

However, just as Jesus had wisely observed, all these feelings of guilt and responsibility had temporarily disappeared when a worn but radiant Nuala Anne had held the intolerably tiny redhead in her arms.

"Isn't she gorgeous, Dermot Michael?"

"She is," I agreed honestly enough.

"Now," she sighed, "won't I have to work very hard to be a good mother to her?"

What happens to me in all of that, I asked myself.

I said, however, "Nuala Anne, for you being a good mother will be as natural as breathing."

"Ah, no," she sighed.

I did not try to convince her. Try as I might, I had never persuaded her that she was as wonderful a wife as a young man could possibly hope for.

"Doesn't she look like your ma?"

"Ma" in our family meant my late grandmother, the indomitable Nell Pat Malone, with whom Nuala thought she had some weird psychic link.

"She does," I admitted.

"What will we call her, Dermot love?"

Long before the child had been conceived, indeed before we were married, Nuala had informed me that our first child would be a girl and that we would name her Mary Anne, which was my grandmother's real name.

"I thought we were going to call her Mary Anne."

"That will be her name," she said patiently, as though she had two infants on her hands, "but what will we *call* her?"

"Well," I said, "we can't call her Nell Pat."

"OF COURSE we can't call her that. Your name isn't Patrick like Nell Pat's father's was."

This was said in a tone that hinted it might well be my fault that I had not been named Patrick.

" 'Tis true," I said, half apologetically.

"We could call her Nell Derm?"

"Nuala, that sounds like some kind of body lotion."

We both giggled, happy that the agony of labor was over and that we had a new life in the family, even if I had some reservations in the back basement of my brain about playing second fiddle to this tiny intruder.

"WELL, what do you think we should call her, if you know so much?"

"Well," I said, feeling like I was already an old man, "I have this fantasy of our being at a Catholic League championship game in fifteen years or so and the announcer saying, 'And for St. Ignatius College Prep at forward, five-ten and All-State, Nellie Coyne!' "

No woman in her right mind would permit a daughter to be called Nellie, just because

her father wanted the child to be a basketball star.

"Five-ten, is it?"

"About her mother's height. And naturally
with her mother's figure. And her red hair in
a long ponytail. And a look of pure defiance
on her face."

"Sure, doesn't it have a certain ring to it?"

And she began to sing Victor Herbert's
"My Nellie's Blue Eyes."

Was it the name she had wanted all
along? Had she communicated this to me by
some weird psychic transfer?

I didn't want to think about that.

Oddly enough both families thought that
Nellie was a perfect name for our little rug
rat with the red hair and quickly adopted the
elision Nelliecoyne. As my brother George
the Priest, who knows nothing about such
matters, commented, "It fits her perfectly."
His boss, the little Bishop, observed more
realistically, "Nelliecoyne suggests what is
patent. She will be a handful, but a delightful
handful."

So Nelliecoyne she was.

None of them, however, had predicted
that she would be fey like her mother, that
at the age of six months she would see a

ghost ship, a ship that didn't exist and perhaps never existed, floating off the shore of
Grand Beach. Grand Beach, by the way, is
the last place on the planet one would have
expected a ghost ship to appear, especially
without the permission of the neo-au-
thoritarians in the Village Council and the
Michigan Department of Natural Resources.

The child remained in my arms.

"What are you up to, small girl child?" I
asked her.

She continued to sleep peacefully.

Nuala Anne was a good mother, tender,
gentle, but firm. Just as she was a good
wife, tender, gentle, but firm. She did not let
her compulsions about being inadequate interfere with her performance in either role.
They impeded (or perhaps half impeded)
only her self-image.

Nonetheless and paradoxically, marriage,
sexual self-possession (a long time in coming), and motherhood had in fact enhanced
her self-confidence. The persona of Nuala
Anne, the poised woman of the world,
emerged more often, though the ur-Nuala,
the shy, skittish child from the Irish Gaeltacht, still lurked.

That one, I add, without going into details,

is the most challenging and the most re-
warding of bedmates. When the Gaeltacht
lass was gently introduced to abandon, the
skies fell in on us.

She needed the resources of the poised
woman of the world when Nick Farmer began his "investigation" of her. By his own definition he was part of the Chicago literary
establishment, a combination of Nelson Al-
gren, Saul Bellow, and Mike Royko, a man
with impeccable taste who hung out at all
the right bars, knew all the right people, and
shared all the right opinions.

Worse luck for us, he and I, quite by
chance, published "Chicago" novels at the
same time. His was, according to his friends
who wrote the reviews, a "gritty, gutsy exposé of the phoniness of Chicago political
life." Mine was a "trashy potboiler." Mine
made the best-seller lists; his didn't go into
a second printing. Farmer told people that I
was a rich suburban scumbag and he would
get even with me. Naturally I heard about his
threats.

Farmer was, in my prejudiced opinion, an
overweight, untalented, mean-spirited slob.
Not good enough to become the music critic
of the major media outlets in Chicago, he

worked for one of the city's lesser alternative papers and a minor radio station and defined his role as "musical investigative reporter." Our least important and most sensationalist TV station gave him a few moments of airtime once a week. In both roles, he presented himself as a serious musical heavyweight, sternly upholding the highest of musical standards with righteous and crusading rigor.

He got even with me by going after Nuala. She was not part of the Chicago popular music establishment, just as I was not part of the local literary scene. She had achieved success and even a platinum disc (*Nuala Anne Goes to Church*). She was hardly a celebrity yet, but she was big enough, I guess, for a very small man to make his target.

"He's angry at her," I told my family, "because she's beautiful and Irish and a success."

"Naturally," George the Priest replied. "That's why he denounces her wonderful Celtic spirituality on the disc as 'Mystical Gobbledygook' and says that her 'pseudo-leprechaunish dialect' is a fake. The Irish are the only group in America that it is all right for his kind of person to hate."

"That's the way she talks," I protested.

"And the way you're beginning to talk."

Nick's attacks on my Nuala became feverish as her pregnancy continued. Her voice was untrained, not even pretty. Her "presence," both on the disc and on the video, was phony. Her "superstitious piety" should have been left behind in Ireland. Her success was the result of unscrupulous marketing and shameless self-promotion. She would never be a great singer or even a very good one. Once he had found his theme—"cheap Irish-Catholic kitsch"—he pushed it unremittingly.

At our first family conference on the subject, Nuala being excused "because of her condition" (she was at "Madam's" for one of her three times a week voice lessons), it was decided by our combination of lawyers, doctors, and public relations experts that the appropriate strategy was simply to ignore Nick Farmer.

The only dissenting voice was Mae Ellen (aka behind her back as Maybelline), my brother Jeff's wife, who announced in her usual tones of absolute certainty, "He's right, she should give up the brogue and talk like an American." We ignored Maybelline as we had become accustomed to doing. I clenched my fist, however, in pent-up rage. Maybelline was on Nuala's case all the time. As in such obiter dicta, "You have a cute figure, dear, but it's the kind that a few pregnancies will wipe out. So enjoy it while you can."

Nuala Anne hates but rarely, but when she does it is passionately. "At least I'll never be as fat and sloppy as you are."

That reply shocked the family, which likes to maintain peace among its disparate members. Only my dad suppressed a grin. To give him his due, George the Priest rolled his eyes appreciatively.

For the record, my wife's mother, of whom Nuala is a clone, a woman in her early fifties, has a perfectly presentable womanly body.

Nick Farmer's next ploy was to lament the "injustice" of the attention and success of an untrained and untalented Irish-Catholic singer while better and more deserving African-American singers were ignored. In other words he played the race card. None of us thought he would get away with it until

The New York Times featured a "report from Chicago" (a city which it views as a mixture of Kinshasa and Beirut) that reported Farmer's allegation as a serious matter and quoted a number of African-American singers as lamenting the "blatant racism" of Nuala's success. Then some of the African-American radio stations took up the battle which enabled the *Times* to report their protest as "racial controversy grows in Chicago."

(Ever notice how many times on a single page the *Times* reports something is either growing or declining, usually without any more evidence than selective interviews?)

As Jimmy Breslin remarked, it's not that *The New York Times* newspaper is anti–Irish Catholic, it's just the way things work out.

Nuala's recording company got cold feet. Something had to be done about the "bad publicity."

"They spelled her name right, didn't they?" my sister-in-law Tracy, our "in-house" public relations expert, asked. "The people who will buy herself's records don't read *The New York Times*."

Still, it was decided that I should write a

letter to the *Times* in my role as Nuala's "manager." In fact, I wasn't her manager. Nuala was her own manager. She had the good sense not to trust anything financial to me and I had the good sense not to want to manage anything.

So I drafted a letter which read, in part:

There was a time when *The New York Times* had yet to become a racist newspaper that it would check its facts, before printing falsehoods. The allegation that Ms. McGrail has had no vocal training is untrue, indeed it is repeated in reckless disregard of the truth. For several years she has studied under a woman who is universally regarded as one of the best voice teachers in the world. Moreover, apparently your reporter and editor have forgotten your popular music critic's view that "*Nuala Anne Goes to Church* is a rare treat by a rare talent, a festival of Celtic spirituality, ancient and modern." Finally it is absurd to suggest that Ms. McGrail is the only white singer who might be in competition with African-American singers or that she and she alone should end her vocal career to give more African Americans a chance for success. Indeed, even a cursory glance at the pop music charts would suggest that African-American women are doing very well indeed.

Mae Rosen, our "outside" media consultant, made me cut my final sentence: "Perhaps the editors of the *Times* are too obsessed with the President's sex life to treat fairly an Irish-Catholic woman from Chicago who by definition already has three strikes against her."

"Leave that to Cindy," she advised.

Cindy is my sister, Cynthia Coyne Hurley, as tough a litigator who has ever walked down LaSalle Street. She made a couple of calls to the *Times.* Their lawyers patronized her only once. After they got over the tsunami which hit them, they agreed to print my letter and to lay off Nuala.

Nuala herself was so sick that she really didn't much care. "Och, aren't you the fierce controversialist, Dermot Michael!" was her only comment on my letter.

Then Nick Farmer celebrated Nelliecoyne's birth by suggesting that it was a publicity trick timed to coincide with the recording of her third disc, *Nuala Anne Sings*

Lullabies. Moreover, he accused her of intending to exploit our "poor little tot" by putting her on the cover of the record and "dragging her before the camera" for the Christmas special in which herself was supposed to sing a few of her lullabies.

The council of war decided that someone should reply.

"You do it, Dermot," Mae Rosen said. "You're so good with the media."

I pretended that I didn't want to do it.

At Grand Beach on that morning in October after I had laid out the materials for breakfast and created my very own special blueberry pancake batter (bought at the supermarket in the Karwick Plaza), I went upstairs to begin my work for the day. Then, as I sat in front of my computer and stared vacantly out at the serene blue Lake, I changed my reveries from the encounter with Nick Farmer to the subject of the five-masted schooner.

I'll think of almost anything to put off work. I'm not lazy, well not in the ordinary sense of the word. I'd finish the novel about the Irish "Troubles" in County Limerick during the 1920s in time to meet the contract deadline and keep my publisher, Tim Donegan, and my editor, Henriette Murray, happy. But daydreams and distractions, reveries and reminiscences, are, I argue, necessary for a creative writer. Naturally, I must also spend some time recalling the delights of my romps ("rides" is what she calls them) with my wife.

I had set up my laptop in the room my father uses for his library at Grand Beach. His medical books are at the house in River Forest. At the Lake he stores fiction and his beloved collection of books on the Great Lakes and Great Lakes shipwrecks. Probably my fascination with airplane wrecks off the Chicago lakefront is somehow linked with his addiction to Great Lakes stories. I glanced at the books occasionally when I was growing up and listened to him talk about the Lakes, but, sonlike, had not permitted myself to succumb to the lure of shipping on the Lakes back in the days when Chicago was the busiest port in the world. I typed a few sentences of my novel (the only work I would do on it all day), rose from my makeshift desk, and began to browse through the "Old Fella's" (as Nuala called him, respectfully, of course) books.

After I opened the first book, however, I

wandered down the corridor to make sure my daughter was still breathing. Miraculously she still was sleeping the peace of a self-satisfied little angel.

I remembered George the Priest's comment shortly before Nelliecoyne had entered the world, "It will be a much more difficult adjustment than marriage, Little Bro."

I ignored George as I usually do. What did he know?

On that subject, it turned out he knew more than I thought he did.

Parent that I was, I could now put aside my adolescent rebellion against my father's obsession with the Lakes. As I paged through his books, I realized how many wonderful stories of tragedy, stupidity, and courage filled his collection.

ABOUT TIME YOU GREW UP, the Adversary sneered.

"Shut up," I told him. "I'm looking for a five-masted schooner."

THERE IT IS RIGHT IN FRONT OF YOU.

"How perceptive of you!"

The boat, a ship really, was the *Charles C. Campbell,* the only five-mast ever to sail the Lakes. She was a beautiful craft, sleek, smooth, shapely. And just a little sinister.

The note under the picture said that she really was a barkentine with fore and aft sails from her four rear masts and square-rigged sails from her foremast.

So the fore and aft rigging is what makes a schooner a schooner. Fair enough.

She was also one of the last schooners built on the Lakes. She was launched in 1885. By 1890, the windjammers were losing out to the steel-hulled steamers which carried iron and wheat and lumber more efficiently than the schooners. She had spent her final years, as had many other sailing craft, as a manned barge towed by a steam-powered ship. With her consort she disappeared in the famous Indian summer storm of 1901 on Lake Huron. No one ever found a trace of the wreckage.

I had never heard of the Indian summer storm. If I remembered Dad's tales, November was the month of terrible storms.

Uneasily I glanced out at the Lake. Still smooth as glass.

"Despite her elegance," said the last sentence of the note, "the *Charles C. Campbell* was always considered somewhat sinister after her tragic collision with the wooden paddle wheel passenger ship *City of Benton*

Harbor off Michigan City on a foggy night in October of 1898."

Oh, oh.

Before I could hunt for more information on the *City of Benton Harbor,* I saw my wife and my faithful hound dog racing madly down the beach. The goddess Maeve with the faithful wolfhound bitch Bran running ahead of her and then waiting for her to catch up and barking in protest that the goddess wasn't as fast as she was.

Maeve was blond, as I remember, and never did her long hair in a ponytail, and probably never ran on a beach. My own Irish deity was surely taller than the Passionate (which is what Maeve means) and her black ponytail trailed behind her like the trail of a dark comet. Also, Bran was Finn MacCool's dog and not Maeve's. But you can't expect a Yank to keep all his Irish mythology straight.

As I watched they stopped at the foot of the dune in front of our house. Nuala Anne kicked off her shoes and socks and dove into the Lake, Fiona right behind her. They frolicked in the water and splashed each other. They were both, as Nuala would have said, out of their friggin' minds. The water was no more than fifty-eight degrees, warm for October and warmer than the Gulf Stream off Galway, but still too cold altogether.

Fiona, white fur flat from the water, beat Nuala Anne to the beach and snatched up a piece of wood. She was doubtless playing some crazy wolfhound game.

I decided that I wanted to know as little as possible about the *City of Benton Harbor*. Maybe it would all go away. So I turned away from Dad's books and paid a visit to the nursery before I went downstairs to prepare breakfast for the tribe of Danu. All the ghost ships in the Lake would please go away.

The tyke from outer space was still alive, lightly breathing in and out. She was sleeping peacefully, as well she might. She was dry and well fed and adored, so all was right with the world.

"You're a sneaky little witch," I whispered to her. "Isn't it bad enough that you've taken my wife away from me? Now you turn out to be as fey as she is. I'm not sure why we let you in the house. You do nothing but eat and shit and sleep and wail when you know there's a ghost ship around. What good are you? You're nothing but trouble and you'll always be trouble, even if you do end up as an All-State point guard."

The witch slept on, utterly unperturbed by my denunciation.

BIG DEAL, said the Adversary.

"I'm just expressing my ambivalence."

YEAH. NOW KISS HER FOREHEAD AND GO COOK BREAKFAST.

So I did kiss her tiny forehead, as I always do when I check on her to see if she is still breathing.

3

As I walked down the stairs to finish my breakfast preparations I returned to my reveries about my battle with Nick Farmer.

For some reason I cannot understand, people think I'm a pushover. I'm a big blond guy whom Notre Dame wanted to play linebacker, but I didn't like football that much and didn't want to take steroids on the side. I guess I must look like a sweet but dumb innocent. Anyway, poor Nick thought he could cream me. So he was a sitting duck, a fat little sitting duck with a gravelly voice and a permanent sneer frozen on his botchy face.

"Don't you think, Dermot, that your wife is a woman without any musical talent?"

"I wouldn't be the one to judge, but Madam, her voice teacher, told her the first day she saw her that she would never be an opera star but that she had a light and lovely voice which would with practice serve well in the standards, musical comedy, and folk world. I accept that judgment. Ms. McGrail is no Dame Kiri, but she is good at what she does."

"You call a woman a dame?" he asked, befuddled. "Who is this Cleary person?"

Oh, my, it should not be this easy.

"Kiri Te Kanawa, Mr. Farmer. She's an opera singer from New Zealand who performs here at the Lyric often. She's a Dame of the British Empire, which is kind of like being a knight. To call her Dame Kiri is a sign of respect. She is, as I'm sure you know, half Maori, which is the native tribe in New Zealand."

"And the other half?" he snapped.

"The kind of person you don't like, Mr. Farmer. Irish Catholic."

"Your wife certainly doesn't believe all that mystical mumbo jumbo about the mountain behind the mountain, does she?"

"Certainly she does. It's age-old Irish spirituality. The Irish are very sensitive to the ultimate reality which lurks behind ordinary daily reality."

"And her brogue, that's fake too, isn't it?"

"Ms. McGrail speaks Irish as her first language. She prays in it and curses in it and sings in it. She speaks English just the way everyone from her part of Ireland speaks it, English enriched by a couple of thousand years of Gaelic poetry. On her records she is careful to keep the poetry under control."

There was one outright falsehood in that response. Nuala Anne does not curse in Irish, because the language lacks curse words. Poets that they all are, however, Irish speakers have skillfully adapted all those four-letter Anglo Saxon words to their language. They mean no harm by it.

"Don't you think that all the Irish stuff is very offensive to many Americans?"

"Probably no more than hip-hop. . . . Anyway, they don't have to listen to it."

"Why are you exploiting your baby to make money?"

"I am told that you really can't sing lullabies properly unless there is a baby around to hear them. Mary Anne loves to hear her mother sing lullabies. It won't make any difference to her that there's a television camera around. Besides, we're putting all the money from the disc into a fund for her college education, except for the twenty percent that Ms. McGrail always contributes to charity."

Not that Nelliecoyne would need money for college, because she was going to be an All-American point guard, wasn't she? Even if she was fey.

"When did you get the idea of using your kid as a prop?"

Sweat was pouring down Farmer's face, messing his makeup. He had expected me to be a dumb Irish Catholic who would be both furious and tongue-tied in the face of his attack on my wife.

Bingo!

"Actually we hadn't thought all that much about it until we heard that you were suggesting it. We thought it was kind of a good idea."

His face tightened in anger.

"Your wife is docile and passive like most Irishwomen, isn't she?"

Wry laugh from D. M. Coyne.

"You don't know many Irishwomen if you

think that, Mr. Farmer. Nor have you ever had to play tennis against that particular Irishwoman. You'd find it an enlightening experience."

The director, realizing that she had a fiasco on her hands, signaled us to wrap it up.

"Many people think her singing is like your fiction—exploitive kitsch."

Aha!

JUST BECAUSE HE'S ASKING FOR IT, YOU DON'T HAVE TO SAY IT.

"The hell I don't!"

"I'd rather think it's like my work which has been published in *Poetry* magazine."

ALL RIGHT, RUB IT IN!

"There are a lot of unanswered questions," Nick snarled, the journalist's final cliché.

"I'll be happy to answer them anytime," I said, with my most genial Dermot Michael Coyne smile. "We'll be listening to you for more suggestions."

That was not altogether true, but it was a nice ending.

"I'm going to drive her off the charts," he snarled at me as the floor director led me off the stage, fearful that I might demolish him physically.

"As herself would say, that will be as may be."

The people in the control booth rolled their eyes.

"You creamed him," the director said as she led me out of the studio.

"He's a larger-than-life Chicago character," I said, piously quoting a feature article on Farmer that had appeared in *Chicago* magazine.

Nuala's only comment that evening was, "The poor frigger never had a chance."

I was inordinately proud of myself.

Great reverie. I played it over and over.

Farmer's latest ploy was to insist that someone was making threats on his life, probably, he said, Irish terrorists.

I had just organized myself, as best as I ever can do that, in the kitchen when two M1A1 tanks roared into the house. The hound rushed upstairs to check on Nellie-coyne.

"Breakfast is it?" Nuala asked, frowning darkly.

" 'Tis."

"You've made a mess of me kitchen."

"Our kitchen."

"I don't suppose you've put the lass down?"

"She isn't here, where else would she be?"

My wife leaned against the doorjamb. She was soaking wet, her green (naturally) running bra and shorts looking like they had been pasted on, her shoes over her shoulder, her bare feet red from the cold. I gulped as I usually do when I see my wife. She's tall and lithe with a woman athlete's subtle but obvious figure and the pale white skin and deep blue eyes of your standard-issue Irish goddess. Her face is that of a model you'd see on a cover of an Irish fashion magazine and her jaw has the round firmness which is required of your normal Irish matriarch. Naturally her waist measured exactly what it had on the day she had married me. She had been sternly determined that pregnancy would not affect her figure, if only to prove Maybelline wrong.

She also bluntly refused to play tennis with me while she was nursing Nelliecoyne. Nursing mothers, she said, lacked athletic mobility. I learned that this assertion was a total falsehood. Moreover, she did battle with my sister Cindy a couple of times a week. The real reason is that she had not practiced during pregnancy and I had. She would be prepared to take me on again only when she knew she could beat me more than half the time.

Unlike me, er, my wife, I am perhaps the least competitive person in the world.

I absorbed her with a dangerous blend of desire, admiration, and love.

"And you didn't change her diaper, did you?"

"Certainly I did and hadn't, to quote you, she made a fine mess of shite for herself?"

You'll note that in this dialogue I had, perforce, adjusted to the Irish rules for such a conversation.

"And you haven't looked in on her at all, at all?"

"Woman, I've looked in three times. And wasn't she sleeping peacefully, as she should?"

Sometimes I'll have to interpret my Nuala Anne for you. Not only is it necessary for a man to hear what his wife means instead of what she says (wives should do the same thing, but the same rules don't apply), in the case of an Irish spouse the problem is more difficult. They never say what they mean or mean what they say.

Herself was begging me to reassure her that her beautiful little girl child had not died while she had neglected her to take a run on the beach.

"You shouldn't look at me that way, Dermot Michael Coyne."

A tinge of flush appeared on her cheeks. "What way?"

"Like you're more hungry for me than for your blueberry pancakes. . . ."

She lowered her eyes.

"Actually, I'll take the pancakes first. . . . But I'd be in serious trouble if I didn't look at you that way."

"You'll never learn, will you, Dermot Michael?" she said with an impish grin.

"What will I never learn?"

"That men can't win no matter what they do or say."

"I learned that long ago."

She leaned her body, now shivering a little from her unhealthy plunge in the Lake, against mine. I did not draw away from her, though she was cold and wet. I touched the firm flesh of her belly gently.

"You're a brilliant man altogether, Dermot

Michael Coyne," she whispered softly as her lips touched mine.

"Brilliant" was not a comment on my intelligence. Rather it is the superlative of a generic Irish adjective indicating approval; "grand" was followed by the comparative "super" on its way to "brilliant." If she had said that I was a "grand" man altogether, my feelings would have been hurt.

On the other hand, the fire in her kiss would have canceled out the moderation of being merely "grand."

"A good run?" I asked as she drew away from me.

"Wasn't it brilliant?" she said. "And the Lake like a little child that wants to play when she touches your toes and the sky as pure as a Blue Nun's veil and the beach all creamy soft and the trees watching like statues in a cathedral and the sun peeking up to see if it likes the day and God smiling down on all of us?"

"Celtic mumbo jumbo?"

" 'Tis not at all," she said with a laugh.

"There's a lake behind the Lake?"

"Why wouldn't there be? . . . Oh, and there is something wrong with your dog. Out on the beach she wouldn't give me back a piece of wood that I had thrown into the Lake."

"Shame on her!"

"You know how she wrestles with me for the stick? Well, this time she wouldn't let me have it after I'd thrown it into the Lake twice. Didn't she even come into the house with it in her teeth?"

" 'Tis strange."

I felt an uneasy twisting in my stomach. Did I have three fey females in the house with me? One human adult, one human infant, and one pushy pure-white Irish wolfhound?

"I'll go upstairs and change. I'll be right back down, save some of the breakfast for me. And only give herself one biscuit."

Nuala dashed up the stairs. She was so very beautiful and so very wonderful and the tension around her eyes scared the living daylights out of me. But what could I do? One of the reasons you marry is to have children. You agonize when you don't have a child. Then the child comes and you adore her. But she also turns out to be a demanding monster, even if she is a good baby. And what does the mother do who has to be practically perfect at everything? She goes tense and anxious.

My reverie was interrupted by a huge mass of wet white fur dashing into the kitchen. Sure enough, Fiona crunched a piece of driftwood in her teeth. Before noticing me, however, it was necessary for her to run around the kitchen sniffing all the corners and making sure that no objectionable smell had entered the kitchen since she had left the house. Then she approached me, tail wagging furiously, and dropped the driftwood in front of me.

"Good dog, Fiona," I said.

Rearing up on her hind legs, she put her forepaws on my shoulders and nuzzled my face. I'm six feet three inches tall and when Fiona puts her forepaws on my shoulders she's still an inch or so taller than I am. An enormous mass of wet white fur.

"Good dog, Fiona," I said.

She continued to nuzzle me affectionately, as if to assure me that even though I was the third most important person in the house, she still adored me.

"That won't get you any more than one doggie biscuit," I warned her.

Whereupon she removed her forepaws

from my shoulders, sank back to her normal position, and seriously shook the moisture out of her fur—in the process soaking me. This was standard procedure when Fiona came out of the water. She seemed to think that I liked the act.

"You good for nothing bitch!" I informed her.

She wagged her tail furiously, feeling that I'd paid her some kind of enormous compliment.

"Come on now," I said. "Don't tell herself but I'm going to sneak you an extra doggie biscuit because you're such a good doggie."

That comment was greeted with a bark of approval.

Surreptitiously, as if Nuala might be able to tell what I was doing, I opened the kitchen cabinet, removed a large doggie biscuit— wolfhounds only do large things—and slipped it into Fiona's open mouth. Delicately she removed the doggie biscuit from my hand and began to chomp on it.

"You'd better finish it before herself comes down," I warned her.

While Fiona disposed of the doggie biscuit I picked up the ancient piece of driftwood. It was a carving from a molding, arguably from a house but also from perhaps the dining room on a ship—ornate and elaborate. Why it had washed up on the beach this morning was an interesting question. Or maybe I was just imagining things.

I filled orange juice tumblers and poured the pancake batter on the frying pan. Nuala thundered down the stairs again and burst into the kitchen, a perfect picture of early morning vitality, in jean shorts and a dark red T-shirt which announced that she was a Galway Hooker. (A sailboat.)

"I want me tea!"

"Woman," I said, "can't you pour it yourself?"

"You're busy preparing the pancakes are you now?"

"Woman, I am. It's bad enough being the housewife around this cottage without having to make the pancakes and pour the tea at the same time—and while you're pouring it would you ever pour me a small cup of tea too?"

She poured the tea for the two of us, without polluting it with milk, a perverse Irish habit she had abandoned at my insistence.

"Hurry along with them pancakes," she ordered me. "Am I not perishing with the hunger? . . . You want a doggie biscuit, do you now, Fiona? Has himself given you one already?"

The wolfhound barked, wagged her tail, and rested a paw on Nuala's thigh. She knew what "doggie biscuit" meant and the appropriate behavior to obtain one from her mistress. Nuala did not ask me whether I had already rewarded the hound for her morning run. She knew that I had—Nuala tended to know everything I did or didn't do. But if she had asked and I had admitted my responsibility, then she would have been deprived of the pleasure of feeding her humongous pet. She reached up into the nearby cabinet, removed the box of biscuits, and said, "Say please."

Fiona whined, and then with even more delicacy than when she was accepting her prize from me, removed the cookie from my wife's fingers and retreated to the corner of the kitchen where, according to the rules, she was to remain while we ate our breakfast.

Good baby, good dog, good husband . . . sometimes even a brilliant husband!

I stacked up a half-dozen pancakes on Nuala's plate. She soaked them in maple syrup—pure Michigan maple syrup, of course, bought at the farmer's market in New Buffalo—and attacked them with vigor comparable to that of the wolfhound at suppertime. My wife displays perfect table manners in public situations when she puts on one of her public personae, of which she has many. In private, however, she consumes her food as if it might be going out of fashion.

"I want me bacon," she informed me with a mouth full of pancakes.

I brought her a paper towel loaded with crisp bacon. She jammed two pieces into her mouth.

"Aren't you a super cook!" she exclaimed. "Now eat your own breakfast, lest you perish with the hunger!"

Thereupon she poured maple syrup on her bacon. I winced—behind her back.

My wife takes nutrition seriously. Therefore, perforce, we eat healthy food. However, good Irish Catholic that she is, she is perfectly willing to grant dispensations from the rules, so long as we "don't do it too often." An Indian summer week at Grand Beach, I had argued, when proposing pancakes and bacon, was a good reason. She promptly agreed, adding for the sake of her virtue, "We mustn't do it too often."

"How's herself?" I asked, knowing that she had inspected the sleeping Nelliecoyne before she had discarded her running clothes.

"Brilliant!" she exclaimed. "Sleeping like the little angel that she is. . . . Och, Dermot, isn't she a beautiful little girl!"

"She is," I agreed solemnly, "though she does shite a lot!"

"That's what babies do, Dermot Michael Coyne!"

"So I have discovered."

"We must take very good care of her, so when she's grown up we can give her back to God as a healthy, happy adult. God only lends children to us, like me ma says."

"Somehow, I figure, Nelliecoyne will be able to take care of herself."

"It won't be me doing and meself a terrible mother altogether. Isn't she lucky to have you as her father?"

The tension around my wife's eyes deepened. My mother had consoled me with the thought that Nuala would stop worrying about her skills as a mother as soon as we had our second child. I shivered at the thought.

"Just as you're lucky to have me as a husband, and such a good cook too. . . . Have some more bacon!"

"Just one more piece. . . . Your overgrown bitch gave you that piece of wood, did she now?"

"She did." I picked the driftwood up off the floor. "It looks like a bit of fancy molding, maybe from a house or even a boat."

Nuala examined the molding carefully. If there were any psychic vibrations emanating from it, she didn't seem to notice them.

"From a boat?"

"Maybe something that was washed off in a storm."

"Boats don't sink out there, do they, Dermot Michael?"

I'd better tell her the truth.

"They do, Nuala Anne. The first ship ever built on the Great Lakes, La Salle's ship *Griffon,* disappeared maybe on Lake Huron, maybe on Lake Michigan, without a trace on her first voyage. Since then over ten thousand ships have sunk on the Great Lakes. Lake Superior, way up north, is supposed to be the most dangerous. A steel ore boat was torn in two up there not too many years ago by a couple of thirty-foot waves. However, more boats have sunk on Lake Michigan. The waves and the winds sweep down three hundred miles from the Soo in the November storms. You'll have to see one of them this year."

She glanced out of the window at the serene blue waters.

"And it looks so peaceful now. . . ."

"Those of us who have been around Michigan for all our lives know that you have to respect the Lake, Nuala. It's a lot more dangerous than Galway Bay."

She shivered. "I don't think I want to see one of them storms. I'll take your word about the Lake wanting respect."

"The bottom of the Lake is littered with wrecks," I went on, falling back on half-remembered stories from my father, "mostly from April or November storms. It's usually safe in the summer months and in the harbors. Sometimes the whole Lake is frozen for much of the winter, though some of the last ore boats were also icebreakers."

Nuala was suddenly very solemn. However, she did not look like one of her "spells" was coming on.

"People died out there?"

"Thousands I'm afraid. Most of the traffic was freight of one sort or another, grain, iron, gravel, lumber, beer, Christmas trees; but before the railroads there were a lot of passenger ships too. Chicago was the busiest port in the world in 1870 and the fourth busiest in 1900. In those days you could look out our window here and routinely see sailing craft and steamships, some with paddle wheels, just like we see cruisers now in the summer. All that's left now are a handful of massive boats which bring iron down from Minnesota or carry gravel and sand around the various Lake ports. No passenger ships at all, though there's talk of building a few luxury cruise ships. Dad says that it was quite a business before the war."

"I'd never get on one of them," she said firmly.

"They'd be as safe as any of the Atlantic or Caribbean cruise ships, though, like Dad says, the ports aren't all that interesting."

"I'll be afraid of sailing with you in the summer," she said somberly.

"No risk in the summer, Nuala Anne, especially if you keep your ear on the weather forecasts. I wouldn't think of sailing out this

time of the year, however. There were a
couple of disastrous storms around the turn
of the century right in the middle of Indian
summer, a foot of snow in Chicago."

I admit I was piling it on. However, veteran
of the hooker races in Galway Bay that she
was, herself tended to think of Lake Michigan as nothing but a big pond.

Before I could continue my lesson, she
and Fiona both heard a signal that was too
subtle for my male ear. They both dashed
for the stairs. The redhead from outer space
was awake. Since she wasn't screaming, I
figured there was no need for me to follow
them. I finished the pancakes and the bacon
and then ambled up to our temporary nursery.

Nelliecoyne was awake and smiling, content spinning the toys strung across her crib.
Mother and wolfhound watched her in mute
adoration.

She was, I had to admit, an absolute per-
fection of human offspring.

"Have you changed her diaper?" I asked.

"Give over, Dermot Michael Coyne," the
child's mother protested. "You know her delicacy. If she was carrying a load of shite,
wouldn't she be screaming her head off."

" 'Tis true," I admitted.

"Go along with you now and get your exercise. Won't I feed her when she gets hungry?"

"Do I have to?"

"Yes," Nuala said firmly, "I don't want a fat husband."

"Yes, ma'am," I replied docilely.

"You too, Fiona. I don't want any fat wolfhound bitches around my house."

Fat husband, I complained silently. I don't feel like running today. Why do I have to do everything the woman tells me to do?

BECAUSE YOU DON'T WANT TO PUT ON WEIGHT LIKE YOUR FRIENDS DO AFTER THEIR MARRIAGES, the Adversary informed me. WHEN YOU MARRIED HER YOU KNEW YOU WERE GOING TO HAVE TO ACT RIGHT FOR THE REST OF YOUR LIFE. DON'T BLAME ME. I WARNED YOU.

"Shut up," I told him.

It was, however, a splendid morning for a run on the beach. There was an astringent autumn smell in the air, decaying vegetation. Eliot was wrong. In Midwest America, October was the cruelest month of the year. The wolfhound and I raced each other and wrestled and played her game of rescuing sticks from the water. I absolutely refused to join her for a swim like my wife did. Then she brought me another piece of driftwood which she would not let me have.

"Good doggie," I said. "Now let me have the stick."

No way.

"Fiona!" I demanded. "Let it go!"

She wagged her huge tail but would not comply.

"I won't throw it back in . . . here, I'll throw another stick."

The bitch considered the implications, dropped the driftwood at my feet, and chased her new prey.

I picked up the piece of wood, perhaps nine inches long and three inches wide. Water and sand and time had bleached it almost white. However, at one end letters had been carved into it. I tried to read them in the bright sunlight: "bor."

As in "harbor"?

As perhaps in "Benton Harbor"?

4

A shocking surprise greeted me when I opened the door of the house—a typical eighty-year-old wooden summer home on which a score or so of additions had been built and as devoid of architectural style as it was filled with disordered but soothing warmth. "A house to live in," me wife had said when she first entered it.

"Would you ever look at your daughter, Dermot Michael Coyne!"

Nuala was sitting on a white wicker rocking chair with a comfortable old red pillow. She pointed in dismay at Nelliecoyne, clad only in a diaper. The future basketball great was sitting up, grinning happily. I had made Fiona shake out the Lake water before we entered, and now she carefully picked her way over to the human child and sniffed delicately.

"She's sitting up," I said cautiously.

"She shouldn't be sitting up, should she?"

"Maybe Father George will hear her confession."

I knelt beside our redhead. She waved clumsily at Fiona, then at me. She must have known that she'd done something remarkable, but wasn't all that sure what it was.

Nuala slipped between us and drew Nelliecoyne into her arms, hugging her fiercely.

"I won't let them make you take drugs, sweetheart! Never!"

Maybelline, having noted that as a neonate our daughter was active and curious, had warned us, "The doctors say that kids that are like that usually end up hyperactive. But don't worry about it. They have drugs for it now."

"At least she won't be a tub of lard, like your kids!" Nuala had fired back, her face taut with fury.

Such ripostes had no effect at all on my

sister-in-law. She seemed never to hear them, which is why the family had adopted the policy of ignoring her. "She's almost always in error," Cindy observed, "but never in doubt. Besides, she's a good soul. She means well."

I was sick of those two excuses. Maybelline was, it was argued, a good wife and a good mother even if a trifle overweight. She was involved in every good cause imaginable, from Rwandan orphans to monarch butterflies, though about all her causes she seemed to acquire only misinformation. She certainly worked hard on them, however, and Jeff seemed happy. She never thought much of me, however. "Dermot is just a good-looking oaf," she had commented when I was a teenager.

Ma, as I called my maternal grandmother, broke the family rules. "He's the smartest and best of all of them," she exploded, unfairly to my siblings it seemed to me, "and I'll not tolerate another word against him."

That had shut Maybelline up for a while. After Ma had followed Da home, she had started in on me again. Her most recent comment had been, "Face it, Dermot, your novel was just racy trash. No one with a taste for good literature could possibly approve of it."

"You've read it, have you now?" said the *bahn si* to whom I was married.

"I never read trash."

"Then you should keep your fat mouth shut about it."

The family froze and Maybelline just laughed.

"I called your mom," Nuala continued to hug our Nellie with the green eyes, "and she said that the child wasn't a changeling. She said some babies are just better coordinated than others."

She didn't seemed convinced.

"I think she is a changeling," I said with notable lack of consideration for my wife's worries. "A fairy queen from county Galway has taken her over."

"Och, Dermot, be serious," she replied as she put the green-eyed witch back on the floor, facedown. "Doesn't your mom say that she could be crawling in another couple of weeks and maybe walking in two months or so? How will we ever keep her out of trouble?"

Before I could answer that question, our little heroine rolled over and promptly sat up again. Fiona barked in approval. Nellie-coyne gurgled.

I realized I had better say something intelligent. And sensitive. So I put my arm around my wife.

"Come on, Nuala Anne, aren't we all proud of the little power forward? And herself already a great athlete like her ma? And don't we have to trust God and the angels and that overgrown wolfhound?"

Nuala laughed and said, "Isn't she ever a wonder altogether?"

Then she began to cry.

Which meant I had said the right thing.

LUCK, PURE BLIND DUMB LUCK, the Adversary remarked.

"That terrible woman was on the phone again," she said, sniffling.

"Maybelline?"

"Your man was on again last night she said."

That I knew. Cindy had called. Nick was talking about violation of the child labor laws and calling for a DCFS investigation of whether we were fit parents.

"Will they do it?"

"You can't tell what those assholes over there might do. But I'll have an injunction on them as quickly as I can walk into a court-room. Then we'll sue Farmer and his station. I'll talk to their general counsel tomorrow and warn him."

"That'll do the trick."

"You bet."

I hadn't felt all that reassured.

"And what advice did she offer?" I asked, waiting for the inevitable explosion.

"Didn't she say that Farmer had a good point. People would say we were exploiting the poor little tyke."

"And you said?"

"I said." Nuala hesitated. "Och, Dermot, wasn't I awful?"

"I'm sure your response was appropriate."

"I told her to keep her friggin' fat face out of our friggin' business or I'd scratch her eyes out."

"And she said?"

"She said I was being terribly selfish and not being a good mother. And I told her she was a nine-fingered shite hawk and hung up. . . . Dermot Michael Coyne, put down that telephone! Bad enough that I lost my temper!"

Reluctantly I hung up.

Our child distracted us by falling back on

the floor, an experience which seemed to amuse her. Then she kicked her legs and gurgled again.

"Doesn't she want to be fed again and then go to bed?" Nuala picked her up and pulled off her T-shirt. "You go upstairs, Dermot love, and change your clothes or you'll catch your death of cold."

I knew from long experience that there was no point in arguing that (a) viruses cause colds, not chills, and (b) during Indian summer there were no chills to be had. Like any dutiful Irish male I did what I was told.

Downstairs Nuala was singing as she nursed our future All-American. Before I went to our room, I peeked into my dad's study and consulted the listing in his big book under "*City of Benton Harbor.*" It had been rammed at night in October while returning to Chicago with an excursion party of Irish immigrants and their children. The *Charles C. Campbell* which rammed it pulled away without stopping to pick up survivors. The Life Guards from Michigan City had saved some of them.

Irish?

Somehow it figured.

Back in the parlor of the house, my wife,

naked to the waist, was sitting on the couch and crooning softly to our sleeping sports star.

"God and Mary will take care of her, won't they, Dermot love?"

"And Brigid and Patrick too," I said fervently, "and Ma too."

"That's what she says and Nellie being named after herself too."

I avoided all questions about Nuala Anne's relationship with my late grandmother. I didn't want to know about it. But I was pretty sure that in the World of Grace (as George the Priest called it) there was not a chance that Nell Pat Malone would not watch over her namesake.

"They're all so close to us, aren't they, Dermot Michael?"

Before Patrick and his crowd came, the Irish believed that the boundaries between the living and the dead were thin and permeable. The Catholic clergy never saw any good reason to disabuse them of that notion. On this particular Indian summer day at Grand Beach, I was hardly in a position to question the belief. Too damn close, I thought to myself.

I AGREE COMPLETELY.

"The very hairs of our heads are numbered," I said, figuring it was always safe to fall back on Jesus.

"I still have a little milk left, Dermot love, if yourself feels thirsty."

This was an invitation to an occasional intensely erotic sacrament.

I sat next to my wife, who was holding the child on her lap.

"Which faucet?"

"Isn't there some in both now?"

She drew my head to her nipple and sighed as I touched it with my tongue. Her skin was soft and smooth. She smelled of milk and springtime. The precious fluid was warm and sweet. For a moment I was a little boy again. She was now crooning over me. A brief taste of heaven.

"No wonder Nelliecoyne likes it," I said, shifting to the other breast.

"I love you, Dermot," she said with a loud, West of Ireland sigh, and then murmured some magic words in Irish.

I couldn't say anything at all.

"Well," she said, reaching for her bra, "there's tea in the kitchen and some soda bread I made last night. Don't spoil your lunch."

5

"Just kind of curious, Dad," I said to my father, trying to sound casual. "I was telling herself some of your stories about Great Lakes shipping. I wondered if there are any wrecks around here."

"I didn't think you listened to any of those stories," he said with a laugh.

"I remember some of them," I said defensively.

I was supposed to be working on my novel. Nelliecoyne was sound asleep, watched over by Fiona, who occasionally shuffled into the study to check on me, perhaps to find out if I was really working, which

I wasn't. Nuala was downstairs doing her voice exercises. Outside the window the Lake was serene under a light haze, a "curtain of gold to protect its privacy and ours," I had been told.

"You don't remember the story about the two-master which was buried under Sky High Dune?"

"I guess not."

I didn't even remember Sky High Dune.

"It was a really big dune about halfway to New Buffalo. Back in the days when I was a kid, long before the State of Michigan began to worry about the environment, a developer plowed away the top half of it and uncovered the remains of an old schooner called the *Mary Suzanne* which floundered off the beach back in the 1870s. A lot of us Grand Beach urchins walked on the deck. Most of the remnants were carted off to a museum somewhere."

"People on it?"

"She was carrying a load of Michigan timber from Sheboygan to Milwaukee. That was at the time that the timber barons were cutting down all the trees in the state. She got caught in an early winter storm. The New Buffalo papers said that the Life

Guards had removed the crew of eight on their surf boats. That was before the Life Guards were combined with the Revenue Cutter Service to form the Coast Guard. They were brave men."

"How did the schooner come ashore?"

"The Lake plays games endlessly with the shore and the dunes. We try to stop it by building our sea walls but eventually it rips out our puny protections. Before the developers put up these summer homes, the dunes literally traveled as the winds and the water shaped them and reshaped them. The sandbars came in and out, the beach expanded and contracted. The wreckage probably washed in and then was covered almost immediately by the sand and forgotten."

"I never realized that. Is there much wreckage under the sand?"

"If you consider the whole Lake, probably a lot. On our particular stretch of beach, hardly any. Still you never can tell."

"Our house might be over a shipwreck?"

"Dermot," he said with a laugh, "the West of Ireland influence is finally getting to you."

Dad did not know about Nuala's psychic kinks. George the Priest was the only one that did and he had enough sense to keep his mouth shut—on that subject anyway.

"They're never at a loss for stories, that's for sure."

"How is she and my red-haired grand-daughter?"

"Both flourishing. They even have a little time for me."

"To answer your question, which to tell the truth gives me a little shiver, I hardly think so. Yet our house was one of the first to be built up there. I gather from pictures from the old days, there was unspoiled dune all around. Too bad they didn't preserve some of it, but they didn't understand such things back at the turn of the century. I'm sure they leveled the dunes a bit to lay down the foundations. If they had found anything, we would have heard the legend, like the old—and false—one about U.S. 12 actually running along the lakeshore at one time."

I hadn't heard that one. Outside, the golden curtain seemed to be a bit thicker.

"So not very likely."

"But not impossible if you're thinking of making up a story. I think it would be a pretty good one."

Right! The remains of Irish immigrants buried beneath our house!

Suddenly I wanted to go home immediately.

"You don't mind if I call you and ask more questions?"

"You know how much I like to talk about the Lake."

I promised to give his love to the mother and child.

If there were remnants of the wreck anywhere around us, why hadn't Nuala noticed them before? The fey stuff was odd, however. We had driven by the site of Camp Douglas at 31st and the Lake several times before she heard the screams of the Confederate prisoners who were dying there.

When she heard them, however, it became essential that we solve the mystery of why she was hearing the cries. Nuala believed beyond doubt, beyond question, beyond discussion that when one of these incidents occurred she was supposed to discover why it was happening. It was her duty to put to rest the ghosts of the past.

As in so many other aspects of our relationship, I didn't argue. It would not have done any good. Besides, maybe she was right.

It could be that a critical mass of the fey was required because the vibrations of the past were stirred up. What if it required two witches to stir up the dead . . . who were, I had been told, not all that far away from us.

I shivered.

I read more about the wreck of the *City of Benton Harbor* in a thoroughly scary book called *Disasters on Lake Michigan*. She was an old wooden paddle wheel built in 1860 to move Union troops around the Lake. Later she was remodeled to serve as an "elegant" passenger ship with the "most modern" cabins and conveniences of her time. She was a funny-looking craft, stubby with two big paddle wheels and a single narrow smokestack. I personally would not have ventured on such a boat from New Buffalo to Michigan City, ten miles away. But reproductions of ads from her era referred to her as "Lake Michigan's Brightest Queen." In the years after the Civil War, she carried many immigrants from Buffalo to Cleveland and Chicago in "comfort which matched that of the most splendid ocean liners" without suffering a single loss of life. In her later years she was a "much prized" craft for weekend excursions from Chicago to ports on the opposite shore of the Lake such as Holland and Saugatuck.

Then, on a moonless Sunday evening, October 16 back in 1898, she was bringing back to Chicago some three hundred members of the Chicago Chapter of the Ancient Order of Hibernians from a weekend excursion to Saugatuck. The weather had been pleasant for two weeks and there was no hint of a storm. However, several hours out of Saugatuck the wind began to howl from the north, the Lake whipped up waves, and sheets of rain beat against the wooden decks. Captain Leonard Creamer apparently decided to try to stay close to the shore and take a long route to Chicago, perhaps so he could beach the ship if the storm became too bad.

According to survivors, lightning struck the ship several times. It was unable to make much headway against waves which were now at least fifteen feet high. Then the rain turned into snow. A rare October blizzard had swept down the Lake from the Soo.

The passengers had abandoned the deck

when it started to rain. However, they continued to sing and dance and drink as best they could in the crowded saloon. As a survivor later observed, "We lost a bit of the spirit of it, when someone said it was snowing. Then the saloon turned cold and suddenly we were all afraid."

The captain decided to try for Michigan City where Trail Creek provided the promise of some shelter. There was also a Life Guard Station at Michigan City which could perhaps fire a breeches buoy out to the ship to take off passengers or send out its surf boats to rescue survivors.

Although the ship was already leaking— its old oaken beams not able to stand the sudden pressures—it probably could have made it to Trail Creek. However, as Third Mate Ernest Roscoe would later report, suddenly a huge black shape loomed up out of the snow and plowed into the *Benton Harbor* just aft of her port paddle.

"It was like an earthquake. We had all our lights on. Even in the storm he should have been able to see us. I know it's harder for a schooner, especially one that big, to turn than for a steamship. He didn't seem interested in turning. Or even in coming back. He just kept on going, like a man who had stepped on a bug."

Hit-and-run driver.

Later, Hale Reed, captain of the *Campbell*, carrying "package goods," mostly whiskey and furniture from Sheboygan, brought his massive craft to the mouth of the Chicago River where a Revenue cutter tug appeared out of the snow and towed him in. The cutter had been waiting for the *Benton Harbor*, which was long overdue. Its skipper noticed that the ship's prow had been stoved in. Captain Reed didn't seem to know what had damaged it.

"Said he thought a big wave might have done it," the tug skipper later remarked at the Admiralty Court hearing. "I was a little suspicious. So I checked it out as we edged him into the dock at Wabash. I found a piece of wood which had 'Benton Harbor' painted on it hanging from the side of the prow. I asked him if he had seen an excursion boat on his way in. He said he had not."

If it had not been for the alert tug captain, Reed would have gotten away with his denial that he had rammed a ship off Michigan City and left it to sink. The author of the account in *Disasters on Lake Michigan* observed that although Hale Reed had a reputation for being an honest and upright man, it was hard to see how he could have been unaware of the impact of this crash with the *Benton Harbor.*

"Hale Reed," the author reported, "had a record of bringing his ships in on time, no matter what happened. The *Campbell* was filled with expensive cargo destined for shops in Chicago. He had promised to dock the boat on the crowded river by Monday morning. Despite the storm, he was determined to reach port on time, no matter what happened. His crew stood by him, though there were rumors that the first mate had pleaded with him to go back for survivors and several of the watchmen had whispered in the taverns along North Water Street that their captain had taken more than enough of the drink.

"The Admiralty Court conceded that the *Charles C. Campbell* had 'probably' rammed the *City of Benton Harbor,*" the author of *Disasters on Lake Michigan* wrote. "However, it ruled that Captain Hale Reed was not to blame for the accident because the snowstorm had caused visibility to deteriorate. Moreover, while he should have tried to pick up survivors, it was unlikely that in the storm he would have had any success. His master's certificate was suspended for six months. The Lake Michigan Transportation and Transfer Company was held liable only for the extent of its insurance, as was the customary decision in those days. Since its insurance was negligible, that meant no money for the survivors. Those who braved Lake Michigan, even in pleasant October weather, ran their own risks."

Meanwhile, somewhere near Michigan City, perhaps just off the shore of the barren dunes which would later become Grand Beach, the *City of Benton Harbor* lay mortally wounded.

"The Lake poured in through the hole," Third Mate Roscoe reported, "and into the engine room. The old boiler exploded and the ship began to sink. I told the captain that she was going under. He ignored me and ran towards the rail. I never saw him again. I tried to sound the abandon ship horn. But it didn't work. I struggled down to the saloon and pulled open the door. A mass of screaming people tumbled out and knocked me over. It was too late to organize anything, but I yelled 'abandon ship,' grabbed a woman with a baby in her arms, and pulled them with me as the boat tilted over. I found them a large plank and put them on it. I did my best to save some of the others, but I don't know how many of them made it. The water wasn't all that cold. Perhaps in the middle fifties. But the air was below freezing and the waves were huge. Everyone was screaming. We weren't very far from shore, but we could not swim through the surf. I had three people on my plank, two boys and the woman with the baby. She lost her child when a big wave rolled over us. She wanted to die, but I wouldn't let her. Later when she found her husband alive on the shore, she thanked me."

Not many survivors were that lucky.

Ernest Roscoe and his little band were finally picked up by a surf boat from Michigan City. A young woman had seen the explosion from the shore and had rushed through the falling snow to alert the Life Guards. Typical of their routine heroism, they launched their craft into the waves with only a faint idea of where the explosion had happened and even whether there in fact had been one.

"If it were not for the alert eyes of Miss

Elaine Manders and the quick courage of the Life Guards, there would have been very few survivors, save for the score or two whom the surf had deposited on the shore," the author summed up the story. "As it was, when the snow cleared the next morning, only a hundred and nine of the more than three hundred Irish Americans who had left Chicago on a hot Friday evening ever returned."

The book displayed photos of the Life Guard Station in Trail Creek, the two surf boats, and a group of very young men with very big muscles. I told myself I wouldn't ride out in one of those boats in three-foot waves.

BUT THEN, YOU'RE A COWARD.

I ignored him.

"Most of the bodies of the survivors were washed ashore along with large amounts of wreckage. Before the Michigan City Police could arrive, looters stripped the bodies. A few were arrested but later released for lack of evidence. Bodies were taken to the Michigan City morgue for identification. Twenty-three corpses were unclaimed and buried in the La Porte County potter's field. Most of the men and women who died were young, in their early and middle twenties. Every requiem mass at St. Gabriel's parish in Chicago was crowded with mourners."

No radar, no radio, no weather forecasts, no power cutters, no helicopters. How did anyone survive shipwrecks on the Lake in those days?

I closed the book, tears in my eyes. That poor woman who lost her child in the big wave certainly loved that baby as much as Nuala Anne loved Nelliecoyne. She had at least found her husband alive. How many young people had lost wives or husbands or sweethearts? I wanted to blame someone. One captain was a coward, the other a liar and a drunk. But even with the best skippers, the collision probably would have occurred anyway. The court of inquiry was perhaps right, the five-master probably couldn't have picked up many survivors. At least Hale Reed could have dropped anchor and tried. Elaine Manders and the brave and muscular young men from Trail Creek had saved many who would have otherwise drowned.

Looters, stealing from the bodies of the dead? Right out on the smooth sand at the foot of our dune? How evil could humans be?

Feeling that I may have missed something, I opened the book again, turned what I had thought was the last page of the story, and found a final paragraph:

Attempts made to find the remains of the *City of Benton Harbor* in the weeks after the wreck and then in the following spring were unsuccessful. After a brief interlude, the storm picked up fury and raged for three more days. It was assumed that the ship had been completely destroyed. The winter that year was colder than most. Long before Christmas the site of the wreck was covered with icy dunes. The *Charles C. Campbell,* reduced to the indignity of acting as a barge towed by a steamship, foundered with all hands three years later in a November storm on Lake Superior. It was an ignominious end for a graceful and tragic craft.

With no stomach for food, I went downstairs to prepare lunch. Nelliecoyne was sleeping again, the wolfhound at her side. Nuala had put aside her Irish harp and was poring over a sketch pad. I had no idea till the advent of our daughter that she could sketch. "I just draw now and then, Dermot Michael," she said, trying to hide the drawing of Nelliecoyne.

At first she wouldn't let me see it, then shyly she turned the pencil and paper drawing around. It portrayed Nellie with a goofy smile on her face. Naturally it was good. I insisted she should take art lessons. She replied that she had enough trouble with voice lessons. I argued that she should continue drawing at least while she was tied down by our daughter. To my surprise she admitted that it wasn't a bad idea, at all, at all.

"Whatcha drawing?" I asked.

"The schooner from last night, only it's not really a schooner. It's a barkentine."

"Because only the four rear masts are rigged fore and aft and the front mast is square-rigged?"

"Sure, Dermot Michael, don't you know everything?"

I didn't want to see the drawing, but she showed it to me anyway. If it wasn't the *Charles C. Campbell,* it was a dead ringer.

Oh.

IT'S CREEPY, the Adversary admitted.

"Tell me about it."

"Isn't she a lovely craft, Dermot? So sleek and graceful?"

"Looks a little sinister to me."

"Sinister?" She turned the sketch around and considered it. "I don't think so. . . . Have you ever seen her before?"

"I don't think so."

"I suppose she'd be from Chicago?"

"Maybe."

"Well," she said with a mild sigh, "we'll have to find out, won't we now?"

"I'm sure we will."

I shivered again.

"I didn't know there were ships like this on the Lake."

"Not very many," I said guardedly. " 'Tis a brilliant sketch though, considering you only saw it for a few moments."

"Thank you, Dermot love."

I escaped to the kitchen so she could not see my shivers.

6

I made a fusilli pasta with tomato sauce, mushrooms, and four cheeses (my own creation) for our lunch, which my bride devoured passionately ("I'm eating for two, am I not?"). She also informed me that I was the greatest husband cook in all the world. The truth is that it could have been served out of a can and she would have disposed of it with equal zest.

I didn't eat much of it, even though I was proud of my work.

We tried at lunch to feed Nelliecoyne some baby food, a process which she found amusing because it gave her an opportunity to spit the bright green-colored substance out of her mouth and throw it around. We laughed and she was very proud of herself until I said sternly, "Moire Ain Coyne, you will eat some of that food that your poor mother is trying to feed you."

She looked at me as though she were about to cry but slurped some of the stuff off the spoon Nuala held poised at her mouth.

"Aren't you the terrible stern da?" Nuala said, suppressing a giggle.

"Someone has to be."

FAKER.

Nuala giggled again.

The brat licked her lips and opened them for more.

"See, Daddy is always right," my wife said with yet a third giggle.

Then the four of us went for a walk, not on the beach but in the village, to soak up the warmth and revel in the red and gold and orange embroidery of the foliage. Despite the beauty and the color of the leaves, I felt kind of somber. Mother Nature was teasing us before she turned to her favorite season in our part of the world—endless winter.

I carried the small one in the harness.

Very early in her life, she refused to permit her face to be turned towards her parent's chest. Whichever one was carrying her must let her face out towards the wonderful world which she observed with the same wonder-filled curiosity that Fiona displayed when she explored the myriad smells of the village.

Nuala guided Fiona on a leash, lest she terrify a stranger who didn't realize how gentle wolfhounds were—until one or the other of us gave the commands "Get 'em!" or, God forbid, "Kill 'em!" that would bring the Garda dog out of retirement.

"Isn't it glorious, Dermot Michael! Everyone getting ready for winter—the squirrels collecting their nuts, the birds flying south, the trees showing off their fancy lingerie before they settle in for their long winter nap, the grass putting on its autumn suit, and God bathing us with His warm sunlight and His golden haze to promise that winter won't last forever."

"You've been through one Chicago winter, Nuala Anne, you know they do last forever."

"Go 'long with you, Dermot Michael, you're in a glum mood!"

I tried to deny it.

We walked in companionable silence for a few minutes. Soon winter would sweep away the foliage and many of the old homes in the side streets of the village would be exposed to what they were: one step above resort slums.

" 'Tain't frigging proper, Dermot Michael Coyne. That a mature matron like meself should be so addicted to a man."

"At twenty-two?"

"Going on twenty-three."

"True, but still . . ."

"In a few years I'll be turning thirty."

" 'Tis different altogether."

Obviously there had been a mood change since God was promising us that winter wouldn't last forever.

"Ah?"

"Promise me." The strain was lurking again around her radiant blue eyes.

"Anything."

"I don't mean anything."

"What do you mean?"

She hesitated. . . . "Well, that you won't ever leave us?"

"Who's us?"

"Me and me daughter."

"I thought she was my daughter."

"Only when she does bad things," she said, suddenly happy again. "You know the rules, Dermot Michael Coyne. All other times she's me daughter, not yours."

"Well, I'm not going to leave either of you," I said. "Didn't I promise that when we renewed our marriage vows in the presence of my brother the priest and your friend the little Bishop just these two weeks ago?"

"Didn't you just?" she said as she leaned over and brushed my lips with hers.

She was worried about something. No amount of probing would find out. I'd have to wait till she was ready to tell me.

As we climbed over the ancient dune which was Crescent Avenue, we encountered a young matron (which is to say at least eight years older than my wife) with two small children, both walking, so not as young as our small daughter.

"Doggie!" one of them announced, pointing at Fiona.

"Big doggie!" said her older sister cautiously.

"Pretty doggie!"

Fiona perked up her ears as she always did when kids drew near.

"Is the doggie friendly?" their mother, a small and slender blonde, asked anxiously.

There was strain around her eyes too. The advent of a second child had not cured it. Maybe nothing ever cured it for a mother.

"Is the Pope Catholic?" I asked.

"She adores little children." Nuala crouched next to the doggie who was wagging her big tail furiously. "Come here, dear, Fiona wants to meet you. . . . Fiona, shake hands with the little girl . . . what's your name, dear?"

"Siobhan," said the four-year-old cautiously.

"Is it Irish you are now. . . . Well, Fiona was born in Ireland too. . . . Fiona, shake hands with Siobhan!"

The dog raised her huge paw and the child touched it gingerly.

"Good doggie," she said tentatively.

"Very good doggie," Nuala agreed.

Without waiting for instructions our outsized pooch offered her paw to the two-year-old.

"She's Brigit," her mother said.

So Nuala introduced Brigit to Fiona, who sat on her haunches to await petting.

"You can pet her, girls, if you want," she assured them.

"Gently," their mother insisted.

Very gently, they petted Fiona, who positively beamed. Siobhan put on the ground a piece of charred driftwood. I picked it up and examined it. Very, very old.

All the while our daughter was watching the whole scene with considerable interest.

"There's a baby too," the mother pointed out.

"Her name is Moire Ain, but don't we call her Nellie?"

So there was the usual scene, kids alternating between admiration for "bebe" and "doggie," mothers exchanging names, Dermot keeping his big mouth shut. The woman's name was Rita O'Dwyer. Nothing wrong with that. Her husband was Neil O'Dwyer.

"My husband is a commodity trader," she confessed. "He's coming up on Friday for the weekend."

"Sure wasn't himself a trader too. But he didn't like it much, did you, Dermot?"

No answer was required or called for.

"My husband loves it! He seems to be

very good at it." She was choosing words carefully.

"I wasn't very good at it," I confessed, "only very lucky. . . . This is a very old piece of driftwood. Where did Siobhan find it?"

"On the beach by the stairs at the end of Willow Street. . . . What do you think it's from?"

Willow Street was right next to my parents' house. The spooks creeping around on this pre-Halloween day were really making a show of it.

MAYBE IT'S ONLY COINCIDENCE.

"Maybe."

"Probably a summer beach marshmallow roast," I said.

THAT'S A LIE!

"I'm supposed to say that it was a relic of a paddle wheel excursion boat which sank in a winter storm a hundred years ago today?"

"You're the young woman who sings, aren't you?"

"Is it a lullaby you want me to sing?"

"Would you ever, if it isn't too much of an imposition?"

"Would you ever" meant she was South

Side Irish. We more civilized West Siders never used the Irish polite subjunctive.

So Nuala lifted Nelliecoyne off my chest, knelt on the ground with her, and sang for the three little girls. Our daughter was so pleased that she closed her eyes. So did Fiona.

" 'Tis time to thrive, my ray of hope,
In the gardens of Dromore,
Take heed, young eaglet, the wings,
Are feathered, fit to soar.
A little rest and then the world,
Is filled with work to do.

"Sing hush a bye loo, lo loo lo lan,
Hushabye loo lo loo."

We promised to get together over the weekend.

Siobhan forgot her bit of driftwood.

"I sure wish I could get in a set of tennis with someone," I said, deliberately making trouble.

"Well, maybe Rita's husband plays. Besides, when you go back to Chicago you can play every day at the South Bank."

" 'Tis true."

"Anyway, don't we still have to do our swim?"

"I was hoping you'd remember!"

She snorted.

The haze thickened as we walked back to the house, but it was still warm, even hot. Somewhere nearby, someone was burning leaves, rather against the village regulations. I sensed impending doom all around us. Would it snow tonight?

Nuala had decreed at the beginning of our week that since there was hardly anyone around and since the wall was high and the gate was locked, we did not absolutely have to wear our swimsuits during our late afternoon swims. She dismissed my protests that this was a gross violation of modesty.

"You're having me on, Dermot Michael, and yourself staring at me all day like I don't have any clothes on anyway."

I couldn't quite figure out whether the reason for this dispensation from proper behavior was something she enjoyed—she claimed that she had done it in Galway Bay in the middle of winter—or for my entertainment. Nuala enjoyed sexual love but this week's orgy might well be designed for the ulterior purpose of making sure I never left them.

One did not merely throw off one's clothes at the side of the pool and dive in, nothing that simple. First of all, she had to feed the brat. Then she had to put on a white bikini and a vast terry-cloth robe. Next she had to strap the child into her car seat and fasten the seat in a chair as far away from the pool as possible and still be in the pool enclosure. Finally, Fiona must be introduced into the environs and stationed next to Nelliecoyne.

Only then would Nuala toss aside her robe, dive into the pool, and aggressively swim a couple of lengths. Finally the bits of fabric would appear on the side of the pool. However, we both had to exercise vigorously before she was willing to permit what she called "foolin' around."

I didn't mind the act at all even if herself's dive and crawl were far better than mine, indeed flawless. As I have said repeatedly, I'm not competitive.

I'm only working on my own tennis game to provide me wife with some challenge.

BULLSHIT.

"Shut up!"

While I was waiting in the parlor for the performance to progress, I flipped on the TV. I was greeted almost at once by the spokesperson for DCFS warning that her agency assumed responsibility for all children in the state of Illinois, no matter how famous or wealthy the parents might be, and that they would watch closely for any signs of exploitation by famous musical performers.

"Ms. Kenyon did not mention the name of folksinger Nuala Anne McGrail in response to our question," the reporter insisted, "but it was clear she had in mind the charges made by this station that she would be exploiting her six-month-old daughter by singing to her in a Christmas special on another network."

"Has anyone ever lost custody of a child for doing that before, Lulu?" the anchorperson asked, obviously setting up an answer.

"No, Jennie, but there's always a first time."

"Ms. McGrail and her husband Dermot Coyne, the novelist, are presently out of town. But Buddy Marshal caught up with Mr. Coyne's brother-in-law, Thomas Hurley, as

he came out of his law office late this afternoon."

"Mr. Hurley, do you think it likely that there
will be a custody battle concerning Mary
Anne Coyne?"

Tom, a big, handsome, Black Irish lug,
laughed pleasantly.

"Only if DCFS and Channel Three and Mr.
Farmer want a ton of lawsuits."

"How would you interpret Ms. Kenyon's
remark then?"

"Ms. Kenyon has never seen a television
camera that she hasn't wanted to talk to,"
he said, still grinning.

"So you don't anticipate any trouble, Mr.
Hurley?"

Tom turned solemn.

"That's entirely up to your station manager
and general counsel. You keep harassing
my brother-in-law and his family with these
absurd innuendos and we'll bury you. The
complaints are already drafted."

Aha. The clan was circling the wagons.
When would the government and the media
ever learn that it was unwise to trifle with the
Coynes?

Tom and Cindy had not even bothered to
call to warn us. Small-time stuff.

In fact, Tom had seemed altogether too ready to get into a fight.

Eventually everything was arranged in good order; Nelliecoyne, fed, reclothed, and content, slept in her car seat. Fiona rested next to her, eyes alert in case either of us needed help. The good wolfhound disdained the pool. Occasionally she would put a paw in it and sniff superciliously. It was too warm altogether. Nor did she pay any attention to our sexual high jinks which usually occurred after we had swum the prescribed laps. Fiona found human coupling uninteresting.

Nuala joined me in the pool, doffed her rags, and raced me for a couple of laps. Naturally she won.

In fact, Fiona did not seem much interested in canine coupling either. Wolfhound owners were seriously concerned about improving the gene pool, so that the wonderful pooches could live longer. Fiona had been carefully bred so that her life expectancy was now around ten years. So someone persuaded us to mate her with another snow-white hound named, appropriately, Fion. The two hounds became great friends on meeting. They bounded around the yard having a great old time with each other, like they were two pups rather than mature adults with procreative responsibilities, and herself being in heat as my wife put it.

Finally, the breeders worked the deed for them with firm but gentle skill. I will not go into the details, which I found revolting, but which Nuala, farm girl that she was, thought perfectly normal.

"Och, Dermot," she said, giggling, "no one has to do that with us, do they now?"

In due course Fiona gave birth to three snow-white pups, Fintan, Finbar, and Fionuala. We gave the first two away to delighted families and kept the bitch for ourselves because it was said that she had the makings of a show dog. However, since one wolfhound was more than enough for our family, we left her at the kennel for training.

My wife did not permit me to sentimentalize her separation from her mother or from us. "We just can't let her bond with us, Dermot Michael."

Still I liked to think that she remembered me when she greeted us warmly at the kennel.

However, wolfhounds greet everyone warmly.

We were about to turn to our romancing

when Fiona barked in protest and rose from her resting position. I knew what the bark meant. The hound's sensitive nostrils were affronted by the aroma of human excrement.

"Hasn't the little brat dumped another load!" my wife protested. "Isn't that just like her and meself giving her a clean diaper. . . . You stay here, Dermot love. . . . Haven't you changed her every time today? . . . Fiona, you take care of Dermot till I come back. . . ."

She vaulted out of the pool, threw her robe around her shoulders, snatched our daughter from her place of safety, and dashed into the house.

Obediently, Fiona came to the side of the pool and joined me.

"What the hell is going on, good doggie?" I asked her. "That little tyke couldn't see any ghost boat last night. There was no way she could look out the window from her crib. And what would a five-masted barkentine mean to her anyway? What does she know about collisions in Indian summer snowstorms anyway? And what does she know about 1898, she doesn't even know about 1998?"

The good doggie nuzzled me sympathetically, being very careful to stay away from the warm water.

"We do know that one baby girl died out there that night. Are her vibrations still around? Would they somehow affect a baby that happened to have a faint touch of the psychic in her makeup?"

Fiona had no answers.

I shivered once again, despite the warm water.

"I know you can't answer my questions, girl. You can distinguish a thousand different smells, but you can't quite think. Just now that makes me feel you're pretty lucky."

Nuala reappeared, clutching our daughter in her arms, like she was a newborn babe. The child was clad in a brand-new outfit, a T-shirt and overalls, and was grinning complacently. Very gently Nuala tied her back into the chair.

"Isn't she a glorious little urchin, Dermot Michael?"

"Shits a lot."

"Go 'long with you. So did you when you were a baby."

"I never did."

She threw aside her robe, poised a moment at the edge of the pool so that I might have a full view, and then dove in. Perfect swan dive. Naturally.

She swam to me, hugged me fiercely, and began to sob. I held her in my arms till her weeping stopped.

"Sure, now," she said brightly, "isn't it time for romance?"

"Is that what they call it?"

So it was romance we had.

Later we went to the Montana restaurant in New Buffalo for supper.

"Wouldn't you be after needing a rest from all the cooking, husband mine? I'll pay."

I didn't argue.

We brought Nelliecoyne along, of course. She was dressed in Gap denim overalls, a kelly green T-shirt, and a denim pointed cap which said "Bulls!" Nuala Anne disapproved of designer clothes for children. But a sale at the Gap didn't count.

We couldn't leave the child home, of course. But we did leave Fiona, who was none too happy about it. She curled up sullenly just inside the door of the house as if to say, "It really is a dog's life I lead."

Nelliecoyne was wide awake looking for fun. We put her in the high chair and gave her bits of bread and crackers to chew on and play with. She wanted no part of them. So she started throwing them at us and at the floor. When the waitress came to take our orders and cooed over her, Nelliecoyne was as good a little girl as you could imagine. But for her regular audience her name was still trouble.

"She's a terrible little bitch altogether," Nuala said darkly. "She's doing it just to embarrass us."

"Probably."

"Well, she's your daughter, isn't she, now?"

"She is."

So I put on my stern face, shook a warning finger at her, and said, "Nelliecoyne, stop that now. NO!"

She considered me thoughtfully and then apparently decided that she better find another game.

Nuala giggled.

"I shouldn't be the only authority figure in the family," I protested.

"Och, but, Dermot love, you're so good at it."

An older couple appeared at our table. They were friends of my parents but I couldn't quite remember their name.

"And who is this gorgeous little redhead?" the man asked.

"Och, Marty, isn't she Moire Ain Coyne? We call her Nellie."

Trust Nuala to remember their names.

Our daughter smiled and gurgled and reached out her arms. Mrs. Marty picked her up.

"She's a darling child, Nuala."

"Thanks, Teresa. . . . Doesn't she have a mind of her own though?"

"Can't imagine where she got that," I said.

We chatted for a few moments.

"Kind of a spooky day out on the Lake, isn't it, Dermot?" Marty said.

"Beautiful, but just a little sinister," I said. "Like a calm before a storm."

"I don't have to tell you how quickly the storms come up, do I? I remember once when we were racing to Mackinaw. It was a summer day just like this. Almost unbearably peaceful. Then a storm cell appeared over at Waukegan and drove the whole fleet over to this side of the Lake. The temperature fell twenty degrees, the rain was so thick that you couldn't see ten yards on either side. The wind just about tore off our sails. You could imagine that you could hear people screaming all around you."

"Oh."

Teresa had given the traitorous Nellie-coyne back to her mother. They were engaged in talk about babies, so thankfully Nuala didn't hear the conversation.

"A lot of people heard the screams or thought they did. Others didn't hear them at all. It stopped eventually."

"What were they screaming?"

"For help, I guess. I was convinced that we were losing boats all around us. Of course, we didn't lose any. . . . You know in the old days, in winter storms farther up the Lake, the watchmen said they heard men and women shouting, 'Mayday! Mayday!' "

"Really!"

"They thought there were vessels sinking all around them. Of course, there weren't any."

"Naturally not."

"Mayday is from the French *m'aidez*—help me! . . . Not that that means anything."

Well, at least we hadn't heard anyone shouting for help yet. At least I hadn't. No telling what our grinning little imp had heard last night.

That evening while we watched *Breaking the Waves* on videotape (accompanied by cries of outrage from Nuala Anne at the persecution of the Emily Watson character and cries of triumph when God vindicated her), I pondered what I had learned in the course of the day:

1) The *Charles C. Campbell* had appeared to my wife and child in the small hours of the morning, even though it had sunk with all hands in Lake Superior almost a hundred years ago.

2) Today was the hundredth anniversary of the sinking of the *City of Benton Harbor* somewhere off Michigan City when it was struggling for the Trail Creek Harbor in Michigan City. It had been rammed by the *Charles C. Campbell,* which did not stop to pick up survivors. At least two hundred Irish Americans, most of them from St. Gabriel's parish, had perished. Only a quick-witted young woman and brave Life Guards prevented the loss from being much worse.

3) Fiona, arguably also fey, had found two pieces of driftwood which were per-

haps part of the wreckage of the *City of Benton Harbor*. A small child had found what was perhaps another piece of wreckage on the steps up from the dunes to Lakeview Avenue.

4) No trace of the wreck of the *City of Benton Harbor* had ever been found, perhaps because the explosion of the ship's boiler had torn the ship apart and because of the severe ice pack that winter.

5) However, the action of wind and waves had on at least one occasion covered the remains of a wrecked schooner just down the beach from us. Therefore it was possible, not likely, but possible, that some or all of the wreckage of the ship and the bodies of some of the survivors had been buried in dunes on which the early village had been built.

THAT'S STRETCHING IT, BOYO.

"I know."

But I also knew that fewer psychic vibrations than those I had listed had been enough on prior occasions to touch my wife's complex sensitivity, Neanderthal vestiges as George the Priest called them.

I did not like it at all. Moreover, what were we supposed to do about a shipwreck a hundred years old?

TO THE DAY.

"I know."

I was not so distracted that I did not enjoy the pleasures of our complicated bedtime sexual rituals, however—rituals in which I discovered which of the many possible bed-mates would sleep with me that night.

The fragile Nuala, the sobbing girl in the pool, was my partner that night. Need I say, she was wonderful.

I must note that before the amusements began, herself would always kneel at the side of bed and say her night prayers. I had learned that they consisted mostly of lists of people for whom she was praying, both the living and the dead. She had said these prayers since she was a little girl, even dur-ing times at Trinity College when she had a hard time believing that God cared about humans.

When we were through, I resolved to sleep lightly because I was uncertain what might happen and I wanted to get into the nursery before my wife did.

7

The teenager with the red hair and the green eyes was wearing the maroon and gold uniform of St. Ignatius College Prep. She was bouncing a basketball up and down with practiced skill.

"Mom is pretty intense, isn't she?"

"Not unusually so for an Irishwoman."

"So our bond is pretty intense, huh?"

"I think I have noticed that."

"So I must be pretty intense too?"

"As the Cardinal says, arguably."

"You're not intense at all, Daddy."

"Uhm . . . well, maybe a little differently."

"No way. . . . Would it be better if I weren't so intense? Maybe I could change . . ."

"No way. You wouldn't be Nellie then. Besides, it's in your genes."

"I love Mom, like totally."

"Doesn't everyone."

"Sometimes I think we bond by fighting."

"That may be."

"But I don't want us ever to become enemies."

"For more than five minutes."

She grinned. "What do you mean?"

"I mean that you and herself stay angry at each other for no more than five minutes. Then you conspire against me."

"Would I do that?"

"Every day!"

"So you're not worried when Mom and I fight?"

"Only that I won't get out of the way."

"But, Daddy . . ."

Then the walls of the place where we were talking collapsed and the cold waters of the Lake rushed in. Somewhere there was an explosion. I was hurled out into the water and carried by an enormous breaker onto a beach. Nuala and Nellie were still out there. My wife was all right but my daughter, I knew, had drowned.

I sat up with a start! I was soaking wet. Lake water?

No, perspiration.

Only a dream? No, it was too real to be a dream!

Next to me, Nuala was sleeping soundly, her naked body glowing like polished silver in the moonlight.

Where was I?

My parents' house?

I slipped out of bed and into the room next door. Fiona looked up at me quizzically, then closed her eyes. Our redhead wasn't fifteen yet. She was only going on seven months. It had been a dream. But it had seemed so real!

As quietly as I could, I crept back into bed. I kissed Nuala's breast as I fell back to sleep. That was at least real. She murmured compliantly.

8

About three A.M. the little redhead began to wail angrily. Whatever had bothered her last night was bothering her again.

I jumped out of bed and dashed into the nursery before the wolfhound woke up and before Nuala heard the wailing. I was still soaking wet. The nursery was thick with humidity as if it were high August. The stench of dying nature permeated the air. Sure enough, in the moonlight my daughter's face was screwed up in an angry knot and she was shouting out her young lungs. So, I picked her up out of the bed, cuddled her in my arms. I decided that I had better sing a lullaby too. The only lullaby I know is the Brahms lullaby, and I have only the vaguest notion of what the words are. Still, under the circumstances, I began to sing it.

> Lullaby and good night
> With roses be delight
> With lilies be decked
> Is baby's sweet bed . . .

I hummed the next stanza. Nellycoyne's wailing diminished somewhat but she was still one very angry little six-month, going-on-seven-month-old child.

I looked out on the Lake, illuminated as it was in the glow of the moon, once more a silver plate on which little diamonds twinkled. No boat, not that I expected there to be one.

My third time through Brahms's lullaby, the child's wailing had diminished to soft weeping. Then Nuala Anne, accompanied by a fretful Fiona, appeared, this time clad modestly in her robe. She was sleepy-eyed and smelled of sex and springtime.

"Dermot Michael Coyne," she said impatiently. "Sure, isn't your voice enough to keep the baby awake for the rest of the night? Let me have the poor little tyke!"

"You should have heard her before I started to sing," I protested as I turned Nelliecoyne over to her mother. Nuala crooned an Irish song. The baby shut her eyes.

"Lullaby, lullaby,
Sweet little baby,
Don't you cry,
I'd rock my own little child to rest,
In a cradle of gold on the bough of a willow,
To the shoheen ho of the wind of the west,
And the lulla low of the soft sea billow.
Sleep, baby dear,
Sleep without fear,
Mother is here beside your pillow."

"Och, isn't it that boat out there again tonight?" Nuala whispered to me. "Sure, it's a strange one, isn't it now, one of them paddle-wheeled things? And what's the name on it?"

Fiona was, thank God, not staring at the Lake. Rather she sat on her haunches, content that Nelliecoyne was no longer wailing.

"Would it be something like the *City of Benton Harbor*?"

"Sure, that's what it is. It's a strange-looking boat, I've never seen one like that before in all me life."

I was silent for the moment because there was no paddle-wheeled steamer on the Lake, only the smooth water in the moonlight.

"You do see it, don't you, Dermot Michael?" she asked anxiously.

"Nuala, it's not there. The paddle-wheeled steamer the *City of Benton Harbor* sank in Lake Michigan one hundred years ago."

Nuala looked at the Lake, she looked at me, and then she looked at the little redhead now calm in her arms.

"Oh, Dermot Michael, whatever are we going to do?"

That was, I thought, a very good question. However, I knew that we would now have to figure out why the psychic vibrations were happening and how Nuala Anne was to bring peace to the ghosts which were haunting Grand Beach.

9

Well, Nuala Anne, my love. I've already told you the story of the *City of Benton Harbor* and the *Charles C. Campbell.* Since I know better than to try to talk you out of one of these adventures—though I personally think we should forget the whole thing—I herewith submit background information on Lake Michigan shipping for whatever good it may do.

The Great Lakes really ought not to be here, much less contain half the fresh water in the world. If it hadn't have been for a couple of ice ages, most of the ground covered by the Great Lakes would simply be prairie land, like the prairies that stretch west of Chicago. However, the Great Lakes were created by melting glaciers which completely modified the topography of North America. Only ten thousand years ago Lake Michigan was a glacier two miles high. The Lakes are in fact a mass of intrusion of nature into the normal geography of North America. Without them, however, our fair city of Chicago would not exist.

Chicago was originally a smelly swamp on the south side of Lake Michigan. The Native Americans were generally content to travel around it though occasionally in good weather they would venture out on it in big canoes, staying *very* close to shore. That's how Father Marquette, the Jesuit priest who was the first European to visit our city, traveled back and forth. There was no skyline then, only a smelly swamp. (I must insist, however, Nuala Anne, that there were signs which said "Richard M. Daley, Mayor.") The swamp was caused by the Chicago River, which was a switch-hitter in those days, a kind of drain pipe at the bottom of Lake Michigan (not to indulge in a more scatological metaphor). When the Lake was high, it would drain into the river and the excess water would flow south to the Gulf of Mexico. When the Lake was low, the river would drain into the Lake. Chicago is only 120 feet above sea level, but it sits on a continental divide. The Des Plaines River west of the city sends its waters to the Gulf while the Chicago River itself normally aims at the Atlantic Ocean. Now we've reversed it so that it flows always to the Gulf, lest sewage discharge into the Lake and cause typhoid fever.

The "smelly" part comes apparently from wild onions which used to grow in the swamp. It was not a spot on which any of the natives wanted to spend much time. However, when Europeans swarmed into America they began to establish the patterns of travel which shaped the future of what would become the United States and also the future of that smelly swamp. The first pattern was to travel west on land and eventually in wagons and then later on in railroads and finally today in planes. The earlier modes of transportation had to get around the Great Lakes and so they turned the corner at the southern end of Lake Michigan and came to the smelly swamp. Chicago became the "breaking point"—the place where cargoes were unloaded—for grain and cattle from the west and eventually iron ore and for people and lumber from the east. The Great Lakes themselves became the second major route for traveling west. I hope all these details are not boring you—you'd never tell me if they were, would you now?

Sailing and later steam vessels carried millions of tons of freight and hundreds of thousands of passengers from places like Oswego, Buffalo, Cleveland, and Detroit to Chicago and in return carried the produce of the prairies. In 1679 La Salle built the sailing ship *Griffon,* which sailed from Lake Huron to the Soo (Sault Sainte Marie) and then returned without La Salle. It sank in a storm on September 18 of that year, the first of perhaps the thousands of ships that sank on the Great Lakes in the last three hundred years. In 1832, just at the time Chicago was becoming a city, the first lighthouse was established at the mouth of the Chicago River, a harbinger of things to come. In 1839 there was a regular line of eight ships operating from Buffalo to Chicago and the first golden cargo of wheat was carried from Chicago back to Buffalo. In 1860 Chicago was already the busiest port in the world. Indeed, forty years later it was still the fourth busiest port in the world after London, Hamburg, and New York. In 1857 there were 107 side-wheeled steamers on the Lakes, 135 power steamers, and over one thousand sailing boats. At the end of the Civil War, the shipping of lumber from Michigan to Chicago and Milwaukee began. Soon there was a steady flow of lumber west across Lake Michigan as the lumber companies cleared the state of Michigan of its finest trees. At the end of the 1860s there were almost two thousand sailing vessels on the Great Lakes, many of them on Lake Michigan. The sailing vessels were almost entirely designed to carry freight—package freight, which meant everything that wasn't bulk, and bulk freight, such as lumber and iron ore and gravel and Christmas trees and grain. From 1890 on the sailing ships began to decline on the Lake as steamships replaced them.

The Lakes imposed certain serious constraints on the big bulk carriers: they had to be narrow so they could slip through the locks at the Soo (where St. Mary's River drains Lake Superior into the other four

Lakes); they had to be shallow so they could navigate the rivers which served as ports around the Lakes, and they had to be long to carry enough cargo to be profitable. So the ore boats that we used to see when we were young going by Chicago towards northern Indiana were eventually one thousand feet long. They were very strange-looking ships, but also very, very profitable.

In 1892 car ferries were introduced to carry railroad freight cars across the Lake from Muskegon, Michigan, to Sheboygan, Wisconsin, thus cutting the time passage to one-third of what it would have been if they had to go around the southern end of Lake Michigan and through Chicago.

You know, Nuala, I'm beginning to get an idea for a new novel about the Lake. Don't tell me I have to finish the present one first. I know that.

The Erie Canal connected central New York to Buffalo; the Welland Canal connected Lake Ontario and Lake Erie; the St. Lawrence Seaway connected the ocean to the Lakes; and finally the great Soo locks connected Lake Superior to Lake Huron and then Lake Michigan (which are in fact not two lakes but one since they have the same sea level and are the largest freshwater body in the world). Thus there were two continuous (though somewhat convoluted) water routes from Europe to the heart of North America—and back.

Passengers traveled for the most part on the steamships, paddle boats early on and then later power-driven boats. The shipping season was severely limited by Great Lakes weather. It began in early April and continued into early November. Between November and April, the storms were too dangerous and the Lake ice was too thick to permit shipping. This created considerable problems for the shipping companies. A lot of money could be made in a very brief time in Great Lakes shipping, a schooner for example could pay for itself within two years. But the problems with the weather and with business cycles made Great Lakes sailing a risky business for owners. Therefore, they were tempted to expand the shipping season into November and run risks of serious, even catastrophic losses. Though November first was a prudent time to stop Great Lakes shipping, most owners forced their skippers to stay out on the Lakes until middle and late November. Most of the great storms which destroyed ships were the ones of 1882, 1905, 1913 ("The Great Storm") that occurred in early November. Moreover, the *Edmund Fitzgerald,* the legendary ore boat that was torn apart by Lake Superior storms, went down on November 10, just a little too late to be out on the Lakes. The shipping business was ruthlessly capitalistic. The owners pushed the captains, the captains pushed the crews, and risks were taken with both weather and repairing ships that today would be against the law. There was some cursory inspection of ships, but safety regulations were minimal. Moreover, for most of the history of Great Lakes shipping, there was very little in the way of accurate weather forecasting and, of course, no radar, radio contact, or navigational aids like asdic which could tell a skipper where his ship was in the middle of a blinding snowstorm—and in our story where other ships were.

There were many elegant passenger ships on the Great Lakes, Nuala. Or at least people thought they were elegant. Sometimes they carried passengers from Buffalo to Chicago who were making the trip simply to get to Chicago. But some also, especially

later on, in cruise ships running as regularly
scheduled excursions from, let us say, Buffalo to Duluth, Minnesota, and back. In the
years just before the Second World War
there were two particularly large, elegant
vessels—*Seeandbee* and the *City of
Buffalo*—which were converted into aircraft
carriers during the Second World War for
training pilots from the Glenview Naval Air
Station just north of Chicago. Two graceful
vessels operated out of Chicago between
the two wars and for a time after the Second
World War, the *South American* and *North
American*. Then Great Lakes excursions became unfashionable when people could just
as easily sail to Alaska, or the Caribbean, or
even to the Mediterranean. There is some
talk now of a new era of Great Lakes excursions. Last summer a German cruise
ship visited Chicago. I can understand why
a cruise ship would want to come to Chicago, but why would the Germans want to
visit Buffalo or Erie or Cleveland or . . . But
then I'm not German!

Great Lakes shipping declined like everything else in the country during the Depression but became active again in the years
after the war. In the 1960s European motor

ships were coming through the St. Lawrence waterway through the Welland Canal, and docking at Navy Pier. However, these "canalers" were too small to be economical means of transportation to Midwest America. Some of them had managed to become involved in accidents on Lake Michigan and even to sink.

Eventually the Great Lakes shipping in the United States diminished to the carrying of bulk cargo via long (sometimes as long as one thousand feet) bulk carriers. Some are still out there on the Lakes, carrying sand and gravel and occasionally coal and iron ore. But I have only seen one in all my life go by Grand Beach. I hardly ever see one off the Chicago shoreline. The shipping of iron ore from the Mesabi Range in Minnesota has diminished, because the steel companies now import cheaper and richer iron ore from other countries. Where there were once thousands of vessels on the American Great Lakes now there are only forty and almost all of them self-unloading ore boats.

I've attached a picture I found in one of my dad's books on the Chicago Harbor in 1885. There are no locks and no jetties, only the mouth of the Chicago River with a tug pulling in a schooner. Notice that there is a traffic jam. Ships are crowded bow to stern on both sides of the river. The docks extended as far as 22nd Street, four miles up from the mouth of the river.

The major reasons why Chicago is hardly a port anymore is that other forms of transportation are cheaper and quicker and the limited season does not fit the needs of American industry. Some of the ore boats can operate all year round because their bows are as strong as those of icebreakers. But since the decline of the Mesabi there is not that much for them to do. I read somewhere or the other recently that there had been a slight increase in Great Lakes traffic last year. If the states and the two countries involved could get their acts together to improve the St. Lawrence waterway and the Welland Canal perhaps the story might be different. But the costs of such an improvement might be different. I said before that the two waterways from the Atlantic to the heart of America were complicated. The Erie Canal route is closed now and the St. Lawrence waterway is not very efficient because it can only accommodate ships with no larger than a twenty-six-foot draft.

So the fascinating history of Great Lakes transportation seems to have come almost to its end, though many stories remain for the nostalgia buffs of the wrecks and the ghost ships and the disasters which plagued the Lakes during the two hundred or so years when they were the most important water transportation in the world. The sinking of the *City of Benton Harbor* just off Michigan City a hundred years ago yesterday was only one of many disasters, and not even the worst.

Look out the window at Lake Michigan in the summertime. It's usually pretty calm. Sometimes there are three- or four-foot waves that challenge wind surfers and catamarans and ruin waterskiing. It's hard to believe that Lake Michigan and the other lakes are really inland seas and potentially enormous dangers to those who go out on them. Thousands of lives have been lost out there and hundreds, if not thousands, of ships sunk. Millions of dollars' worth of treasure are at the bottom of the Lake. At one time there was a suggestion that the Soo locks be closed so that the Lake could be drained and the treasure could be picked up. Needless to say the City of Chicago strongly opposed that suggestion which was, I think, more science fiction than serious proposal.

The books about Great Lakes shipping are filled with romantic nostalgia. Yet the work of an officer, an engineer, or a watchman on a Great Lakes ship, sail or steam, was difficult, dirty, and exhausting work with danger always lurking just at the edge. You were glad when you worked no matter how miserable the pay was and how dull and routine the work usually was. Working was better than not working. There was no union to protect your income during business cycles. There was little romance or adventure, most of the time. Usually it was no more exciting than driving a truck or a railroad train.

Your wife always worried when she saw your ship put out from Erie or Chicago or wherever that she might never see you again. Brave men certainly sailed the lakes: everybody that sails on a ship is brave—and usually bored out of their minds.

It is astonishing that we have so little memory of these men and their ships in Chicago. Occasionally we see a postcard of the Christmas tree ship which sailed from Wisconsin to Chicago and was sunk during a November storm. Some of us know a little bit about the worst Great Lakes tragedy of all, the sinking of the excursion ship *Eastland* in the Chicago River.

Yet when we look out now on the empty Lake, we see only the weekend cruisers and the offshore racers and the beach boats. We are oblivious to the danger and the harshness and the tragedy of working on a Great Lakes ship not so long ago. The first shipwreck on Lake Michigan was the sinking of the schooner *Hercules* in 1818, near what is now 63rd Street. All hands were lost. Indians in the vicinity found that bears and wolves had mutilated the bodies of most of the crew.

Of all the five lakes the danger was worst on Lake Michigan. Of the fifteen worst shipping accidents on the Great Lakes, eight happened on Lake Michigan and by far the highest number of casualties also happened on Lake Michigan. The worst of all occurred on July 24, 1915, in the Chicago River. The excursion ship *Eastland* capsized for reasons that still remain mysterious. Eight hundred and forty-four people, employees and families of the Western Electric Company, who had awakened that morning eagerly expecting a delightful summer cruise, died in the muddy waters of the river before the trip had a chance to begin.

On September 8, 1860, the *Lady Elgin,* with hundreds of Irish Americans on a weekend cruise, was rammed and sunk off Winnetka by the schooner *Augusta*; three hundred people died. On November 21, 1847, the passenger ship *Phoenix* was swept by fire on Lake Michigan and approximately two hundred people died. On October 15, 1898, the excursion boat *City of Benton Harbor* was sunk in a collision during a winter storm just off Michigan City, Indiana, with perhaps two hundred lives lost.

On April 9, 1868, the *Seabird* was destroyed by fire just off Chicago with the loss of perhaps one hundred lives. On October 16, 1880, the *Alpena* foundered in lower Lake Michigan with a loss of between sixty and one hundred lives. On September 24, 1856, the *Niagara* in upper Lake Michigan at a cost of sixty-five lives. On October 22, 1929, the car ferry *Milwaukee* disappeared in the middle of Lake Michigan with fifty on board. On October 22, 1856, the *Toledo* sank off Port Washington with the loss of at least fifty lives.

Most of these major Lake Michigan disasters did not occur during the storm season, only the *Milwaukee*, the *Alpena,* the *Toledo,* and the *City of Benton Harbor* sank in winter storms. The other losses were a result of either fire or collision or, in the case of the *Eastland* disaster, an inexplicable capsizing.

Since the *City of Benton Harbor* was probably not seaworthy and was rammed in the dark by a large schooner, it cannot really be counted as a casualty of a storm because it might have made it into Trail Creek, although in the absence of a breakwater off Michigan City at that time, such a refuge was problematic. If it had not been for the *Charles C. Campbell*, the skipper could have at least beached the ship and most of the passengers' lives been saved.

The ships lost in winter storms were almost entirely freight vessels like the ore carriers *Edmund Fitzgerald* or the *Carl D. Bradley* (the latter on Lake Michigan in 1958) which carried rather small crews. Hence while their loss was a tragedy to the families of the crews and frequently a disaster to the owners, they did not cause the major loss of life as did the sinking of the passenger ships.

Two footnotes, Nuala, about the *Eastland*; the United States Navy purchased the craft, salvaged it, and converted it into a naval training vessel USS *Wilmette*. Most people who years ago saw it moored in the Chicago harbor did not realize that it was a vessel associated with a tragedy, the worst tragedy in the history of the Lakes.

Finally, a quote from the Cleveland *Plain Dealer* of August 7, 1935:

Chicago August 7 (AP). The United States Circuit Court of Appeals today upheld the Circuit Court ruling that the St. Joseph Steamship Company, former owners of the steamer S. S. *Eastland*, which sank in the Chicago area July 24, 1915, was not liable for the 844 deaths in the disaster. The court held that the company was liable only to the extent of the salvage value of the vessel. That the boat was seaworthy, that the operators had taken proper precautions, and that the responsibility was traced to an engineer who had neglected to fill the ballast tanks properly.

That's the way it was on the Great Lakes in those days, Nuala love. If you died in a storm or a collision or a fire or an explosion or a capsizing, no one was to blame. It was your tough luck for going out on the Great Lakes.

10

TV clip.

Place: Daley Civic Center Plaza. Time: noon.

The Richard J. Daley Building looms in the background, the Picasso sculpture is off to one side. On a raised platform is a group of people—the Mayor, members of City Council, various important people, some of them in Roman collars. A large crowd fills the plaza, larger than most that come for a noon concert. Nuala Anne, Dermot, and Nelliecoyne are in the center of the platform. Fiona is not present. Since it is still Indian summer and quite warm, Nuala is wearing *a pink T-shirt dress with her long black hair tied back by a matching ribbon. Nellie, in Nuala's arms, is also wearing a pink T-shirt and her few strands of red hair are tied with a small pink ribbon. Dermot is carrying Nuala's harp case. They walk to the front of the platform, Dermot unpacks the harp case. They both remain standing in front of two chairs that have been placed there for them.*

Nuala: My name is Nuala Anne McGrail and this lovely child is my daughter Nellie. I'm supposed to sing lullabies for you today and I can't sing lullabies unless I have a baby to sing them to.

Nellie smiles at the crowd, laughs, gurgles, and seems very happy.

Nuala: You can see that Nellie loves you. That's because she's Irish and the Irish love people, the more the merrier. I think this is the largest crowd that Nellie has ever seen and she seems very happy to meet you all.

Crowd applauds loudly, Nellie grins even more.

While Nuala is talking Dermot unpacks the harp.

Dermot is a tall husky blond with a dimple in his chin and a sweet, sixth-grade altar-

boy smile, behind which one suspects lurks more than a touch of mischief.

Nuala: Now you needn't worry about disturbing me little tyke! (*Laughter from the crowd.*) I had to bring her along 'cause I'm nursing her. And she's just been fed and it's her naptime and she always sleeps when I sing lullabies to her, so she'll probably fall asleep and Dermot here will take good care of her. Dermot, by the way, is me first husband. He is also me only husband and he is not bad as a husband and he's pretty good as a father too. Doesn't he change herself's diapers at least twice as many times as I do!

Laughter from the crowd.

Both Dermot and Nuala sit on the chairs, Nuala holding her harp and Dermot holding the baby so Nuala can sing to her.

Nuala: Don't I think that God is always singing lullabies to us? Hasn't God brought us into the world just like mothers do? And hasn't He fallen in love with us? And don't mothers have to sing lullabies to their children? So I think when we mothers sing lullabies to our children we are imitating what God does all the time—and especially when

His children are loud and noisy and cantankerous!

More laughter from the crowd.

Nuala: The first lullaby I'm going to sing is a Choctaw Indian lullaby. I had to hunt pretty hard to find it because there's not that many Choctaw Indians left in America. I'll sing it first in the original—as best as I can pronounce it! And then I will sing my own translation. You know the story about the Choctaw Indians, don't you now? Way back when more than half the people in Ireland were starving to death, the Choctaws, who were in the Great Plains of this country and knew the meaning of famine themselves, heard about us and didn't they send us some of their own hard-earned money and some food to help us through the Famine? They were the only people in the world that sent food to Ireland during the Famine and the Brits shipping grain out of the country!

In Dublin under the Milltown bridge on the Dodder River there's a restaurant called The Dropping Well and back in the famine times it was a morgue. They used to fish people out of the stream and bring them in there before they would bury them. The Irish are a strange folk, it doesn't bother us at all, at all, to have a good dinner in a place that was once a morgue. Well, anyway right out in front of the former morgue by the river, always illumined at night, is this little shrine and itself being very graceful built by the people of Ireland in gratitude to the Choctaw Indians for helping us in the Famine.

Nuala sings a lullaby in Choctaw and then an English translation.

Nuala: It's a lovely melody, isn't it? Me friend Gary Whitedeer taught it to me. The mother tells the baby to go to sleep and they'll both go to pigtown together, which meant to her dream world.

The baby has closed her eyes and is sleeping peacefully.

Nuala: See didn't I tell you that me lass would fall right to sleep on us. She's really a very good little baby, she keeps regular hours and doesn't disturb me or her da at all, at all. Of course, when she's really angry she lets us know and that in no uncertain terms. But she's an Irishwoman now, isn't she?

More laughter from the crowd.

Nuala: Me next song isn't exactly a lullaby, though it sounds like one. It's a Choctaw song too, one about leaving your native land. It brings tears to me eyes every time I sing it. And doesn't it remind me how much the Irish and the Choctaw are like one another?

"Land where brightest waters flow,
Land where loveliest forests grow,
Where warriors drew the bow,
Native land farewell.

"He who made you stream and tree,
Made the White, the Red man free,
Gave the Indians' home to be,
Mid the forest's wilds.

"Have the waters ceased to flow?
Have the forests ceased to grow?
Why do our brothers bid us go,
From our native home?

"Here in infancy we played,
Here our happy wigwams made,
Here our fathers' bones are laid,
Must we leave them all?

"White men tell us of God on high.
So pure and bright in yonder sky,

Will not then His searching eye,
See the Indians' wrong?"

Nuala: Now I'm going to sing to you an Irish lullaby. This one is called the "Connemara Cradle Song" and meself being from Connemara, isn't it the first lullaby I ever heard. When Irish mothers sang lullabies not so long ago, they knew how many dangers would threaten their children—hunger, disease, storms, English bayonets. So they sang prayers for the protection of their little ones.

"On the wings of the wind, o'er the dark, rolling deep,
Angels are coming to watch o'er your sleep,
Angels are coming to watch over you,
So listen to the wind coming over the sea.

"Hear the wind blow, hear the wind blow,
Lean your head over, hear the wind blow."

Nuala sings several lullabies with commentaries on each one. Each one of them is cheered loudly and Dermot grins his mischievous smile. Nellie continues to sleep.

Nuala: Just to show you that I'm not a complete Irish bigot, I'm going to sing a song from the Isle of Man in Manx Gaelic, which I'm sure youse all understand!

Laughter.

Nuala: Well, all right I'll sing it in English. It's called the "Smuggler's Lullaby." Your Manx have been known to engage in smuggling, you see—something that we Irish Gaels would never do, would we now? Well, your Brits are raiding a smuggler's house and his wife is just singing a song for her child, minding her own business, you see? Now the Brits don't understand Gaelic but her man does.

"See the excise man coming,
Sleep, my little hero,
They'll be seeking wine and whiskey,
Ah me, child of mine.
Sleep, my little hero,
Daddy's late and we must warn him,
This time we'll have nothing illegal,
The Englishmen may board us,
They'll find nothing wrong.

Let them search the boat or house,
Nothing's in the hold but herrings!"

Applause! Cheers for the brave Manx woman!

Nuala: Did you like that now? Wasn't she the clever one? Since I'm running out of time, I'm going to sing one in Welsh Gaelic, one that you all know so you sing along with me in English.

She sings in Gaelic, crowd does fine on the first stanza, struggles through the second aided by Dermot's tenor.

"Sleep, my child, and peace attend thee,
All through the night.
Guardian angels God will send thee,
All through the night.
Soft the drowsy hours are creeping,
Hill and dale in slumber steeping,
I my loving vigil keeping,
All through the night."

Nuala: Now, before I leave youse, I'm going to sing an Irish-American song, one that your purists don't like although you sing it at every wedding, including me own. I love it!

She sings it as though it is a lullaby for her daughter.

"When Irish eyes are smiling,
'Tis like a day in spring.
In the lilt of Irish laughter,
You can hear the angels sing.

"When Irish eyes are happy,
All the world is bright and gay,
But when Irish eyes are smiling,
Sure, they'll steal your heart away."

She sings it a second time. Everyone joins in. Nelliecoyne opens her eyes and smiles.

Then the fifteen-minute concert is over, Nuala and Dermot stand up. Dermot puts the harp back in its case. Nuala takes the baby and then turns to the microphone again.

Nuala: Sure now wasn't it awful good of youse to come and listen to me singing here in the Daley Plaza. I'm glad you came and I'm delighted that your man (with a nod of her head to the Mayor) invited me and himself coming to listen too with all the terrible busy things he has to do to be Mayor. And

I'm also glad that the Bishop came and my husband Dermot's brother the priest, both of whom are very fine priests let me tell you!

Laughter and applause from the audience.

Nuala: So if you want to hear these songs again—and there's no reason at all, at all why you should—won't they be out on compact disc pretty soon and you've got to imagine that I'll be singing them for Nellie because that's the only way I can sing lullabies and really mean them but I promise you it will be at her naptime like this and you'll never hear a peep from her on the recording. She will be a perfectly proper young Irishwoman with her eyes closed and her big mouth shut! Just like her ma.

More laughter.

Nuala: And if it turns out that we're going to do a Christmas special, well I'll have to bring Nellie along too because what if she should get hungry?

Laughter and applause from the crowd.

Cut to another scene.

Farmer: Well, my friends, you have seen the clips so you know what I mean. If ever there has been a disgusting display of Chicago Irish-Catholic vulgarity complete with the politicians and the clergy sitting in the back, then it was Ms. McGrail's little concert in the Daley Civic Center Plaza today. As we all know her voice isn't even pretty. She claims only to be a folksinger, but most folksingers have better trained voices than she does. Moreover the little story she told of the Choctaw Indians was a shameless exploitation of the suffering of Native Americans. The Irish mystical mumbo jumbo was what we might expect from this very untalented young woman who makes up with lies and with phony charm for her absolute lack of talent. She is no more an artist than her goofy hack novelist husband.

But the most disgusting and disgraceful thing of all was to bring that poor little seven-month-old child along to entertain the crowd. One has to wonder whether the child was drugged because she slept so peacefully. Certainly no ordinary human baby can sleep through the noise of the crowd and the awkward, uneven, and sometimes off-key singing of her mother. I hope that the Department of Children and Family Services watches the clips of this concert very carefully. They have to insist that if Ms. McGrail and her husband wish to keep custody of their child, they must stop exploiting her in public in such a shameless ambitious fashion.

The Coynes can make all the threatening phone calls to me they want, I'm not going to back off. Ms. McGrail represents all that is wrong with Chicago Irish Catholicism, its vulgarity, its phoniness, its insincerity, and its absolute lack of talent, and I'm Nick Farmer.

Close-up of Nuala, Dermot, and Nellie walking off the platform. Nellie, cradled in her mother's arms, is sleeping the sleep of a just child. A cameraman descends upon them and the young reporter jabs a microphone at Nuala.

Reporter: Ms. McGrail, don't you think that you are exploiting the little baby terribly in this concert?

Nuala: Ah! Sure doesn't the poor little tyke look like she's exploited altogether and is herself sleeping just as though she knew the angels were looking down on her and taking care of her?

11

The young priest—with long black hair, pale
white skin, flashing blue eyes, and the demon smile of an Irish operator, perhaps
priest, perhaps politican, perhaps undertaker, perhaps bookmaker—welcomed us to
St. Gabriel's, the parish whose people had
drowned a hundred years before in the sinking of the *City of Benton Harbor*. Nuala—
who solves all our mysteries (I'm only a
Watson to her Holmes)—wanted to know
more about the people who had died in the
wreck. When she's sniffing her way through
a mystery I do what she wants.

"You were wonderful yesterday at the

Daley Plaza, Ms. McGrail," he said, enthusiastically shaking Nuala's hand and then
mine. "And so was this cute little tyke. I'm
happy that she has McGrail looks and not
Coyne looks. Wouldn't it be terrible for her
to grow up looking like Father Coyne?"

My brother, George the Priest, had arranged this interview with his classmate who
presided over the old Canaryville parish at
45th and Wallace.

"Johnny Devlin is a smooth one," he had
warned me. "Classmate of mine. Thinks he
knows everything."

"Takes one to know one," I replied since
herself was not around to remonstrate with
me about my deplorable lack of respect for
the clergy.

Nuala Ann knows very well when someone is "having her on."

"Ah well now, isn't His Reverence a grand
priest and himself so holy," she replied to
Johnny Devlin, "and wise and isn't me poor
little tyke of a daughter lucky to have such
a distinguished clergyman as her uncle?"

"In the immortal words of Sheridan White-
side in *The Man Who Came to Dinner*," I
murmured, "I may vomit!"

Nuala had done what she always does

with priests. She somehow or other gets them on her side against me. Except for the little Bishop, who treats me with enormous respect, doubtless for reasons of his own.

So I tried to change the subject as Johnny Devlin led us into an office with twelve-foot ceilings and ancient but elegant oak walls, a rectory office which would only have been possible in another era of Catholic history. Built a hundred years ago, it was supposed to be a witness to the immigrant population of the majesty and wisdom of the Catholic heritage and the wisdom and power of its clergy. Surprisingly, given the age of the rectory, the furniture inside the office was new and the office was neat and clean. A computer screen blinked in the background. Here the message was that the parish might be old and the church a historic landmark, but it was still an efficient and modern operation, just like its pastor in his gray slacks, blue blazer, and white shirt with an open neck.

"So this is the great parish of the South Side Irish?" I asked. "I must say that the church looks surprisingly modern even if this rectory is something right out of the 1860s."

"When old Father Dorney, who was the

pastor here, built the church, they said he was a hundred years ahead of his time and I really believe that's true." Johnny was repeating the archdiocesan line on St. Gabe's I had heard from George earlier in the day.

"He was a great man," Johnny continued. "After his funeral, the head of the cortege reached all the way to Mount Olivet Cemetery out on 111th Street while the hearse was still waiting here in front of the church. He was on the side of the unions and the workers against management, he was on the side of black people against oppression, he was for every good cause of his time and maybe the greatest priest in the history of the diocese. Now everyone has forgotten about him. There is, Dermot, as I'm sure your brother has told you, no one deader than a dead priest."

"I seem to remember hearing that."

In fact I had heard it from George that very morning. The little Bishop, Nelliecoyne resting comfortably in his arms as he presided over breakfast, made a wry face at this bit of clerical nonsense, but ignored it.

As we were leaving the Cathedral Rectory, he observed, "It is said that there are many ghosts lurking out there in St. Gabe's."

"Do you believe in ghosts?" I asked him.

He rolled his pale blue eyes behind his Coke-bottle glasses. "In theory, of course. In practice, I am profoundly skeptical. Your worthy brother and the inestimable Johnny Devlin believe just the opposite."

"In theory they reject ghosts but in practice they believe in them?"

"Patently."

Later I asked Nuala what she thought the little Bishop meant.

"Wasn't he saying we should be skeptical about all clerical stories about ghosts and such like?"

"And your stories?"

"Och, sure, there aren't any ghosts in my stories and besides, I'm not a priest."

I had no idea what she meant. If the ships she—and presumably our "bebe"—had seen on Lake Michigan were not ghosts, what were they?

I wisely kept my comment to myself.

"Are there still some Irish people living in the parish?" Nuala asked Johnny Devlin as we sat down in comfortable chairs around a coffee table in the rectory office. "Or have they moved out?"

"Oh, as long as Irish live in Chicago there

will be a few of them here in Canaryville as it's called. By the way, the name comes not from canaries singing here but from grackles which, as you folks may know, are the noisiest, ugliest, dirtiest birds in the world. One more example of Irish irony."

"Mostly Latino in the parish now, aren't there?" I asked, trying to sound well informed.

"We have four Masses on the weekend," said the priest, smiling happily. "Two are in English and two are in Spanish. Some of the old Turkey Birds come to the Spanish Masses because they say it reminds them of the Latin from the old days!"

Nuala Anne sighed loudly. "Sure aren't the Irish a terrible difficult people altogether?"

"Absolutely," the young priest said. "Could I be getting you a cup of coffee now?"

"Oh, no thanks, Father," I said quickly, too quickly. "We don't want to take up too much of your time."

"Well," Nuala said softly, "sure, couldn't I enjoy just a small cup of tea?"

Nellie, resting peacefully in her arms, sighed as if to echo her mother.

"I'll drink some of that to keep herself company."

"Any special kind of tea?" asked the young priest. "Nothing but the best for Father George's relatives!"

"Me husband drinks Earl Grey," Nuala informed him. "And I wouldn't mind a bit of Irish Breakfast tea if you have any around."

"Cream and sugar?"

"Ah, no, hasn't me husband cured me of the filthy habit of polluting me tea the way we do in Ireland?"

"Thank you, Father," I said respectfully, beating my wife to it.

"There's always hospitality here at St. Gabriel's," the priest said with a wave of his hand. "After all, we have a tradition to keep up, don't we now?"

There had been no more incidents at Grand Beach. My daughter did not wake up screaming the final two nights we were there. We went out to supper with our new friends the O'Dwyers on Saturday and Sunday nights. Our child was a perfect little angel, save for throwing crusts of bread on the floor. Neil O'Dwyer was a nice enough fellow, though a typical commodity trader, high on aggression, energetic, and just a little crazy. Fortunately Rita kept him in line.

They had left their two children at their cottage in the care of a thirteen-year-old baby-sitter. The tension around my wife's eyes deepened at the thought that someday she would have to leave our precious little Nelliecoyne in the care of some adolescent.

I did not particularly like that idea either, though I would have to be the voice of reason reassuring Nuala that there was no reason to worry.

The Indian summer weather continued as though it were going to last forever. There were no sudden winter storms as there had been in the middle of October a hundred years ago. I had given Nuala my "brief report" on Lake Michigan shipping, she had read it with considerable interest, her face solemn as she concentrated on the text. Then she had put the papers to the side and pondered silently for several minutes.

"I'll never, never go out sailing on that Lake again at all, at all," she informed me. "It's a dangerous, brutal, murdering Lake!"

"Only if you're not respectful of it," I said. "I'm not sure that it's any more dangerous than Galway Bay."

"That's neither here nor there," she said and so the question had been settled. By next summer she would change her mind and deny vigorously that she had ever vowed to avoid the Lake. She would insist on sailing and waterskiing with us on the Lake because most of the time in the summer it looks so peaceful.

"Well," she asked me after several more minutes of pondering, "what do you think we should do about all of this?"

"I'm not sure, Nuala," I replied. "Since the, er, phenomenon has stopped, maybe there is nothing at all for us to do about it, maybe it was just an incident from the past which generated strong vibrations particularly on the hundredth anniversary of the wreck. Maybe it's something we should just forget about."

YOU'RE DREAMING, BOYO, the Adversary warned me.

"Don't you know me better than that, Dermot Michael?" she asked indignantly. "Aren't we going to have to get to the bottom of it?"

"What bottom? The bottom of Lake Michigan?"

"If I knew that, Dermot Michael Coyne," she said tersely, "wouldn't I be after telling you right now? There's a mystery out there and we're supposed to solve it. Otherwise me and me daughter wouldn't have seen the two ships."

"But first of all we have to find out what the mystery is, don't we?"

"Isn't that the truth, Dermot Michael? We not only have to solve the mystery, we have to find out what it is."

Hence our visit to St. Gabriel's rectory on a chill gray day which said firmly that we had enjoyed Indian summer quite enough, thank you.

Father Devlin returned with three pots of tea, a plate of English raisin muffins, a nice American substitute for scones, butter, and strawberry jam. Nuala did the honors of pouring the tea. The priest dipped his finger in the strawberry jam, raised an eyebrow at my wife, who nodded with a smile, and offered the finger to our uneasy little daughter. She licked his finger eagerly and smiled contentedly.

"Better get your finger out quickly," I warned, "the lass is teething."

We all laughed, the child included. She continued to lick her lips lest she miss the smallest dab of precious sweetness.

Nuala buttered a muffin, soaked it in strawberry jam, not as good as raspberry, but still acceptable, and then placed it in my mouth, as priests did with Eucharist for those people who still want it on their tongues. She smiled at me, her smile a winsome mix of affection, love, and desire. My heart melted, my stomach became tight, my loins stirred.

"Would there be any memory in the parish," she asked cautiously, paying no attention to my abject surrender, "of a terrible shipwreck a hundred years ago on an Ancient Order of Hibernians excursion?"

The young priest frowned. "I'm not from the neighborhood, Nuala, and I haven't had time to read up on its history. I can't recall any story about a shipwreck. I do know that in those days some of the Hibernians, not all, were into things a little more violent than keeping gays and lesbians out of St. Patrick's Day parades in New York City."

"A touch of the nationalist in them?"

"The idea was that other Americans would accept us only when we had a country of our own. So Ireland had to be free before we would be respected."

"And Ireland is free," I added, "and they, whoever they are, still don't respect us."

We all laughed. So did Nelliecoyne, who thought she was part of the story. Which, come to think of it, she was.

"So some money from the people of the parish," the priest said, "undoubtedly went to the IRA or whatever they called themselves in those days."

Nuala plopped another muffin into my mouth, with the same alluring smile, which produced the same reaction. A beautiful woman and an English muffin dense with strawberry jam—who could ask for more? Well, it would be better with raspberry jam.

"That's all over now?" I asked.

He shrugged. "Pretty much. There are still some old-timers, immigrants from the 1920s or their children, who think that Gerry Adams is a traitor."

"It's easy to be a militant when the shooting is on the other side of the ocean."

"Over a hundred people from the parish died in the wreck," Nuala said softly. "Mostly young people."

"Really! Let me check our records. Everything is on microfilm now."

Nuala handed our daughter over to me

and peered over the priest's shoulder as he fit the microfiches into the viewer.

"Nope, that's 1899. . . . Let's see. . . . Here we are. 1898. Two kids killed in the Spanish-American War. . . . Gosh, look at all these names!"

He turned the viewer knob up.

"Look at that one!" Nuala exclaimed. "Agnes Mary Elizabeth Doolan! Born March 15, 1898. Seven months old!"

Nelliecoyne had taken possession of my finger and was biting on it. The name of the child who drowned in the Lake meant nothing to her, but then, why would it?

"4615 South Emerald! That's Bob Gomez's house . . . Dr. Robert Gomez, chairman of our parish finance committee and Chief of Service at Mercy Medical Center!"

"Can we learn the names of her parents?"

"Sure, if she was baptized in the parish. . . . Where's the Baptism records for that year? . . . March 1898 . . . Here she is—Father: Thomas Ignatius Doolan; Mother: Mary Louise Collins."

"Neither one of them was on the funeral list," Nuala said confidently, as if she had memorized the list. "They lost their daughter but both of them survived."

"With terrible guilt for the rest of their lives," the priest said with a heavy sigh. "Can't get away from that . . . Yep, here's their marriage record. March 15, 1897. Poor little Agnes was born exactly twelve months after their marriage."

"He was twenty-seven and she was twenty-two," Nuala observed.

"A little young for Irish marriages in those days," I mused.

"He must have been well-to-do to own that big house on Emerald. Best place in the neighborhood, even today. Bob did a lot of restoration on it."

"Both baptized here in the parish," I said.

"Anything more?" Father Devlin asked gently.

Nuala seemed thousands of miles away from Canaryville.

"Nuala?"

"What terrible heartache for them all," she said, taking our seven-month-old away from me.

Nelliecoyne was upset to lose my finger.

"By now God has long since wiped away all the tears," the priest said softly.

"We have to believe that, don't we, Father?" I said as I put my finger back into the little brat's mouth.

"Dermot Michael, isn't there a teething ring in me purse?"

We thanked Father Devlin for his help. He didn't seem to want to know what we were looking for. Perhaps George the Priest had conveyed the implication that I was working on a novel.

In the Mercedes I changed the little monster's diaper, a work which required some serious contortions. Nuala was deep in thought. Or deep into something. When I was finished with the kid's mess, Nuala strapped her into the car seat, checking three times to make sure everything was attached properly.

"Let's drive by that house," I suggested.

Since Nuala didn't object, I drove over to Emerald. As I turned off 45th Street onto Emerald, the child began to wail, just as she had at Grand Beach.

4615 was a big Victorian house with a vast front porch, turrets, bow windows, and stained glass on the third floor. The paint was light blue with dark blue trim. The lawns and bushes around it neat and trim. I reflected that it probably looked better than it had a hundred years ago.

There was not much time for reflection. Nelliecoyne went ballistic! She screamed, she cried, she shouted as if someone had stuck a pin into her.

"Dermot, let's get out of here!" Nuala begged.

We did.

> The sun is going down in the deep blue sea
> So close your eyes, go to sleep
> I'll wrap all the milk stars around you
> So dream and your dreams will come true
> You can ride past the winds as a champion
>   mare
> O'er the moors lighter than air
> You can fly to the moon as a great white
>   swan
> And back you will be before dawn.

Only when we passed the spires of Old St. Patrick's Church, looming over the Expressway like a mild and smiling angel, did Nelliecoyne calm down.

12

"You're interested in the ghosts in my house!" Dr. Roberto Gomez greeted me as I walked into his office at the Mercy Medical Center. "Well, if my grandmother is to be believed, there's a lot of them there!"

"I'm more interested in research on the history of Canaryville," I replied, wondering exactly what my father had told Gomez and how my old fellow knew that Nuala and I were out hunting ghosts.

"We are not experts in the spirits," Dr. Gomez said, waving me into a chair across the coffee table where he sat down. "My wife and I are actually skeptics on that subject, as are my kids, though I think my youngest daughter might be a little sensitive to them. Grandma, who lives with us, says the ghosts are there. Nobody argues with Grandma."

Roberto Gomez, MD, Chief of Staff at Mercy Hospital and Medical Center, was a handsome man with dark skin, neatly trimmed mustache, thick black hair, and gleaming white teeth. He looked more like an accomplished diplomat than a hotshot surgeon. He also talked a very diplomatic line.

"When your father said you've been doing research on our street, I told him I'd be happy to tell you the little I know. Your father was the best teacher I had in medical school and if it wasn't for him, I don't think I would ever have made it. And there's a hell of a lot of other people that would tell you the same thing."

"Even his children think the old fellow is special," I agreed. "It took us a long time to figure that out, however."

"We all owe him a lot and I am sure that there's a couple of dozen doctors in Chicago who would give you an interview on the strength of a phone call from Dr. Coyne."

"It's interesting, isn't it, Dr. Gomez," I said,

"that you live in Canaryville instead of Beverly, or Palos or Burr Ridge or one of those places?"

He laughed easily.

"I grew up in Canaryville," he said. "I always dreamed of coming back here and raising my children. It's a wonderful neighborhood and it's always been open to people that are different. I was one of the few Mexicans in St. Gabriel's when I was growing up, but nobody ever gave me any problem. We even have some African Americans in the parish now. Canaryville is what it always was, a mixture of many different social classes, and now we have the yuppies moving in too. It's a neighborhood, and it's a real neighborhood!"

"I'm especially interested in the Irish radicals who lived in Canaryville back in the turn of the century," I said, very pointedly pushing him to the subject of our investigation.

I had driven my wife and daughter home after our encounter with the spirits on Emerald Avenue. Nuala had crooned lullabies all the way home, but they had little effect. Nelliecoyne had stopped screaming, but she was still in an angry mood. Inside our house on Southport, she rejected her mother's nipple, a rare event. I had phoned my father about Dr. Gomez. He called back a few minutes later to tell me that I could see the doctor in about a half hour.

"Go see him, Dermot Michael. This little tiger will calm down when she's a mind to."

So I had driven back to the South Side.

"Supporters of the Irish Republican Army and other such groups?" Dr. Gomez asked me.

"The way I understand it there was a family named Doolan who lived in your house back at that time who were very active in the radical wing of the Ancient Order of Hibernians. It's their story I'd particularly like to unearth."

"The Doolans lived in that house for more than a hundred years," he replied. "I bought it from one of the great-grandchildren who was moving out to Beverly because he didn't like the class of people, as he put it, who were moving into the neighborhood. He and his parents had become conservative Republicans, which I suppose is what happens to Irish revolutionaries after a couple of generations."

"Are the ghosts in your house Irish?" I asked, changing the subject ever so slightly.

"What else would they be?" The doctor laughed. "They're benign ghosts, at least that's what Grandma says, very friendly, very nice to have around. One of them seems to be a bright little girl. I have been afraid to look up the family history to see who that bright little girl might be, although old Tom Doolan was always kind of a man of mystery. People seemed to be scared of him."

"I thought you didn't believe in ghosts?"

"I don't really believe in them but you never know, do you, Dermot?"

"No," I said flatly, "you never do know."

"How would you explain these phenomena?"

"Me? I don't know—maybe psychic vibrations that remain from the past, kind of hanging around the place where these experiences were originally felt."

That was the little Bishop's very reasonable explanation of the phenomena. It was as far as I wanted to go to try and explain any of the stuff that happens to my wife.

"Well," Dr. Gomez went on, "it is certainly true that the people that lived in the house for a couple of generations were ardent Irish patriots. They raised money for the Fenians and the Irish Republican Brotherhood and the Irish Volunteers and even up to the time Ireland finally won its independence—when was it . . . 1923, something like that?"

"About that," I agreed.

"Then they all kind of lost interest in it and like I say the family just got into becoming very conservative American Republicans."

"It's a very conservative neighborhood these days, isn't it?" I asked.

"It's a hard neighborhood to figure out, Dermot, but they vote Democratic in the local elections and I suspect most of us still vote Democratic in the national elections. Many of the folks are not too happy about the few African Americans that have moved in but as one old Mick said to me, I'd sooner have them than these damn smart-assed yuppies."

"People like me?"

"No son of Doc Coyne will ever be a smart-mouth yuppie!"

Like I said, the man was a diplomat.

"The family is all scattered now?" I asked.

"I suppose so. A lot of people moved out

of the neighborhood and we're into what, the fourth or fifth generation of that family."

"Is there anybody around Chicago that might have some of the documentation from the past?"

Dr. Gomez stirred uneasily. "Well, I suppose the best one would be Colleen Kavanagh, the daughter of the man I bought the house from, that is if she could find time to talk to you."

"Colleen Kavanagh?"

"She's the daughter of the last Doolan that lived in the house, the one I bought it from. Her husband is Dr. Kavanagh, who is quite famous as a neurologist out on the South Side. He's at Little Company of Mary Hospital."

"Seems to me that I've heard of the South Side. It's sort of anyplace south of Comisky Park, isn't it?"

Dr. Gomez laughed, a rich knowing laugh.

"I understand there are rivalries between the South Side Irish and the West Side Irish and if I had to choose I wouldn't. Colleen Kavanagh and her husband Patrick Kavanagh live in Beverly, for which I say God forgive them and that they could just as well have moved into Canaryville. She's a very busy woman and active in all kinds of boards and committees, Lyric Opera, Art Institute, Chicago Symphony, and doing much good around town. However, like I say, she is very, very busy."

"Somebody from Beverly that knows there's a Lyric Opera and an Art Institute and a Chicago Symphony?"

The doctor laughed again. "You are not going to get me into that argument, Dermot Coyne. I think if you call Colleen Kavanagh and ask her for an appointment she'd be happy to fit you into her schedule sometime next month. I suspect she might think any such thing as records from the past is not particularly important. She's not one of those Irish who have any sense of concern for history. If it's not good enough to be done in the present, she doesn't want to know anything about it. Still Patrick might be able to persuade her to talk to you because he's an admirer of your father too."

"Yes, I'll have to see if he's got clout," I said thoughtfully. "That house fascinates me."

"Well, it's a wonderful place to live. We've done quite a bit but maintained much of the old charm. We'd be delighted to have you and your wife, who is a wonderful singer by the way, over for dinner some night."

"That's an invitation I might take you up on."

I wondered as I said it what would happen if Nuala had one of her psychic experiences inside Roberto Gomez's house. Whatever the situation we would not bring Nellie along with us because she would certainly freak out and how would we explain that?

I thanked Dr. Gomez for his help and took my leave. In the Mercedes pulling out of the Mercy Hospital parking lot, I pondered over the whole crazy business. We were supposed to solve a mystery and we didn't even know what the mystery was. Well, I knew that would happen before I married the woman.

Nuala and I live a very low-key life financially. The Mercedes is fifteen years old. We live in an old house on Southport Avenue, a refurbished post–Civil War, two-story wooden "A" frame. Nuala buys all her clothes at marked-down prices—and with an unerring instinct about what will look good on her. We belong to a tennis club but not a golf club and we don't have a house at Grand Beach—although we use my parents' memberships in a couple of clubs for golf and we borrow their house at Grand Beach. I have money from my mistakes in the commodity markets and make something off my novels and Nuala makes a lot off her songs, but most of that we either stash away or invest in our children's future.

A lot of people are nervous that I don't seem to do much work and it looks like Nuala is supporting the family. We're both frugal, Nuala by disposition and background and myself because spending a lot of money or spending it conspicuously is just too exhausting for me to bother with it.

I had scarcely turned on the ignition when the phone rang. It was Nuala in tears.

"Oh, Dermot love, haven't I done a terrible thing. Won't you be angry at me for ever and ever! Am I not just the most awful woman in all the world!"

All this must be translated as saying, "I expect you, Dermot Michael Coyne, to agree with everything I've done."

"Maybelline call again?"

"So isn't she just the most horrible and didn't I tell her that I speak to her again and if I'd hang up and laughed and laughed and said I couldn't give up my curiosity to hang up on her!"

"What did she have to say this time?"

"Didn't she say that our poor little Nellie was almost an alcoholic!"

"What!" I said.

"She said that the Irish habit of giving kids a little bit of whiskey to calm them down was pernicious because recent studies had shown that children who are given alcohol for such purposes are much more likely to be alcoholics when they grow up!"

"Maybelline and her studies!"

"Dermot, that isn't true, is it?"

"I never knew Maybelline to have a study right and I'm sure, Nuala, she's got this one wrong too."

"Well ___ ___'s what I told her and I said I didn't ___ ___ ever talk to her again and she just laughed ___ hung up on me!"

"Whe___ ___ ___iness about giving Nellie whis___ ___ quiet?"

___ ___ ___ever did it, I never did ___ ___. My mother never ___ ___her!"

___ bsolutely sure ___ ___de her think

"Didn't your man put it in his column this week!"

"Farmer!"

"Sure, he said it was the way all the Irish kept their kids quiet at night and that's why there is so much Irish alcoholism. We're not a heavy drinking people, are we, Dermot Michael?"

"Ireland has the lowest per capita alcohol consumption in Europe. Nuala, you know that."

"Well, what am I going to do?" She was sobbing again.

"About Farmer?"

"No, Dermot Michael, about your poor sister-in-law. I was so terrible rude to her!"

"You do exactly what you said, every time she calls you hang up on her."

"Dermot love, I could never do that!"

"Of course you could."

Nuala was a very courteous young woman, she couldn't hang up on anybody. Unless she was told to.

"Nuala Anne, that's an order and you can blame me. The next time she tries to harass us about Nelliecoyne you tell her that I've told you that you should hang up on her and that you always do what I say."

Nuala's sobs turned into a giggle.

"Don't I always do what you tell me to do, Dermot Michael?"

"Well, you certainly do it when it suits your own plans as it does this time. You just tell her to go away and we don't want to have anything to do with her. Tell her that's what I've told you to say, which indeed is what I've just done."

"Haven't you now, Dermot Michael!"

Now laughing instead of crying, Nuala hung up. I turned off South Park onto the Stevenson absolutely furious. Something had to be done about this terrible woman. I simply could not permit her to harass my wife and my child the way she seemed bent on doing. I punched in the old fellow's number.

"Dr. Coyne."

The usual calm, cheerful, reassuring voice.

"Dermot," I said firmly.

"Did you have a nice interview with Dr. Gomez, Dermot?"

"Very nice, Dad. He was very helpful. And now it would appear that I have to talk for a while to a Colleen Kavanagh."

"Patrick Kavanagh's wife?"

"The very same."

"I'm not sure, Dermot," he said cautiously, "whether I have that kind of clout. With Patrick certainly, but with Colleen? She's so busy doing so many good things I don't know whether she has time to talk to anybody, even to her husband."

That was about as close to uncharitableness as my father or my mother ever came.

"Well, see what you can do. I really have to see her soon."

"I'll try," he said dubiously.

"And one more thing, Dad, something has to be done about Maybelline. She is harassing Nuala constantly. I don't like it and I want it to stop."

"Dermot," he said with a sigh, "she's done that to everybody else and we just got used to it. The woman has a good heart and she means well. Jeff loves her and she's wonderful with her children."

It was surely true that my brother loved her. The kids, however, were creeps, but perhaps not incorrigible creeps.

"Dad, she doesn't have a good heart and she doesn't mean well. She's a mean, vicious bitch and I am not going to tolerate her messing in my family life."

184 ANDREW M. GREELEY

"Dermot," he said reprovingly, "we've been through this with all the others and there's just no way to stop her. She's awfully good to Jeff and we have to support him."

"Dad, he's a psychiatrist, he should recognize the syndrome that he's dealing with."

"Psychiatrists can't deal with their own problems, Dermot, any more than surgeons can operate on themselves."

That was a wise statement, it was also irrelevant to the topic under discussion.

"Look, Dad, let me be blunt. Either the family finds some way to get Maybelline off Nuala's back or we're going to secede and I'll have nothing to do with her or anyone else in the family."

"Dermot!" Dad gasped.

Well he might gasp. His youngest son was a sweet, gentle young man who almost never lost his temper. Now he had lost it completely.

"It's just this simple, Dad. If the family has to choose between Maybelline and Nuala— and I'm saying it does—and it chooses Maybelline, then Nuala is out of the picture and so is her daughter and her husband. My mind is made up and I'm not prepared to compromise!"

The Adversary intervened.

YOU'RE OUT OF YOUR MIND, DERMOT. WHY IN THE WORLD ARE YOU CREATING A FAMILY CRISIS LIKE THAT? YOU DON'T HAVE THE GUTS TO STICK IT OUT.

I ignored the Adversary as I was doing, it seemed, with increasing frequency these days. "Dad, I'm sorry to create a crisis but I'm not going to put up with that woman. She damn well better leave my wife alone."

"Well," my father sighed sadly, "I'll have to talk to your mother and see what we can do about it. But, Dermot, this is a terrible thing to do to the family."

"Dad, Maybelline is doing terrible things to Nuala and it has to stop."

After we had hung up I thought about what the family would do next. Dad would call Mom and Mom would be more flustered and disturbed than he was, and then Mom would call Cindy, and Cindy would be assigned to call me to calm me down. Well, I'd make it clear to Cindy beforehand that I wasn't in a mood to be calmed down. So I pushed her number on the telephone as I worked my way north on the Dan Ryan. "Cynthia Hurley," she said brightly as though she were a switchboard operator at a very prestigious Loop law firm instead of a senior partner.

"Dermot," I said grimly.

"Oh, hi, Dermot, look, I don't think we should worry about Farmer. He's crazy, everybody knows he's crazy. He's like that guy who writes for the *Trib*, a professional hater. If we react to him we are just going to give him more publicity, he's going to wither on the vine of his own viciousness. The TV people are already uneasy about him. Just let him run his course and I don't think he's going to do us any harm."

That was sound legal advice but as it would turn out, however, it would not be that easy. Not at all, at all, as my wife would have said.

"I'm not talking about Nick Farmer," I said tersely. "I'm talking about that bitch Maybelline."

"Dermot!" Cynthia said in surprise. "What terrible language to use about your poor sister-in-law!"

"Poor sister-in-law be damned, Cindy, she's a bitch. She's making my wife's life miserable and I'm not going to tolerate it."

"Dermot!"

"I want to make my position clear to you,

Cindy, and to everybody else in the family. Either you folks get Maybelline out of our hair or I'm going to get Nuala out of the family. You can make your choice, it's Maybelline or Nuala. You can't have both."

"Dermot Michael Coyne, that's an outrageous statement. There's no way we can negotiate a compromise at all. You can't possibly take such a position. Moreover, I don't think you'd stick to such a position for long."

For a moment I seethed silently and then I said in the coldest tone of voice I could produce, "Cindy, listen very carefully to what I say. Unless Maybelline leaves Nuala alone we are going to secede from the family. I don't want to do that and Nuala doesn't want to either, but I don't want her sobbing every day when Maybelline makes one of her sickeningly vicious phone calls. Is that clear?"

Cindy hesitated.

"Dermot, she makes those phone calls to everyone."

"She may make them to everyone, Cindy. She's not going to make them to Nuala anymore. And Nuala and I aren't coming to any family gatherings where that woman is present. And don't look for room for negotiation because this isn't a legal matter. It's a matter of protecting my wife and my daughter and I am not prepared to negotiate that."

Again Cindy was silent. Good lawyer that she was, she was always looking for room for settlement. I had presented her with the kind of issue in which there didn't seem to be any room for settlement.

"Dermot, I'm going to have to think this over. But it's a very, very serious matter."

"Of course it's a serious matter. My wife's peace of mind is a serious matter. Nuala is a very fragile and vulnerable young woman, as you know, a shy, proud creature from the West of Ireland despite all the other masks she wears. Maybelline is trying to break her heart and I'm not going to let her do it."

"I'll have to think about it, Dermot, but I don't like ultimatums."

I drove by the Old St. Patrick's Church towering over the Expressway with the Loop towers standing respectfully behind it. Church! One more phone call to make. I pushed in another number.

"Holy Name Cathedral Rectory!" a teenage womanly voice announced cheerfully.

"Hi, Megan, it's Dermot."

"Oh, Mr. Coyne, how are you? How's Nuala? How's that gorgeous little daughter of yours?"

Megan was one of the porter persons who, with great charm and marvelous efficiency, managed access to the Cathedral Rectory after school hours. There were actually four Megans who worked at the rectory—an African-American Megan, a Korean-American Megan, a Latino-American Megan, and an Irish-American Megan. I couldn't distinguish among their voices but it was still safe to say hi to Megan. All the Megans, however, insisted on calling me Mr. Coyne and my wife Nuala. That was because I was real old and Nuala was still almost a teenager like themselves. Five years make that much difference?

"Do you want to talk to Father George? He's in and I'll buzz him, but he's terribly busy, Mr. Coyne, so don't take too much of his time."

"Yes, Megan."

Busy indeed!

"George Coyne," my brother the priest announced with brief, brisk efficiency.

"George, Dermot."

"You sound upset, Dermot," he replied.

"Not bad, George."

"I know you pretty well, Little Brother. Maybelline is it?"

Cindy could not have got to him so soon. George had guessed.

"She is a vicious, insensitive, nasty bitch."

"I quite agree."

"Something has to be done to stop her."

"You're absolutely right."

"I will not have her reducing my wife to tears every day."

"If I were in your position, I wouldn't either."

"Nor will I tolerate her saying nasty things about my daughter."

"How could anybody say nasty things about such a sweet little redhead."

"George, I'm serious. Unless the family can shut her up, Nuala and I are going to secede."

"Bravo! I'll secede with you."

"George, I am perfectly serious."

"Dermot, you're not listening to me. I've been telling you, or trying to tell you, that I'm on your side. For her own good Maybelline has to be stopped, but even if it doesn't help her, it's going to help not only Nuala but all the rest of us. She's getting worse every year."

"Are you saying you're on my side?"

George the Priest sighed loudly. "That's exactly what I'm saying, Dermot. Am I the first one you've talked to?"

"No, I talked to Dad first."

"That was inept."

"I guess so. There's no way he could deal with the problem."

"Then who did you call?"

"Cindy."

"Much wiser. She's the one who's going to have to drag the family into a solution on the subject of Maybelline. She'll want to come up with a negotiated settlement. We're not going to accept a negotiated settlement, Dermot. We're going to precipitate a full-scale family crisis and they're going to have to do something finally with their Maybelline problem. They've done nobody any favors by letting her get away with her little terrorist attacks on people."

Terrorist—that's what she was.

"So what do we do?"

"What you mean is what do you and I and Nuala do?"

So George had dealt himself into the con-flict. I felt that somehow or the other, he had edged off the top of the mountain.

"Exactly."

"We'll wait and see what happens, Little Brother. We'll let them worry about it for a while. Cindy will almost certainly be on the phone in a few minutes. I'll tell her that I'm on your side. That will really make the crisis serious."

"OK."

"Don't worry about it, Little Brother, we're going to win this one. And we're going to win it not because you and I are involved, they can do without us, but the family worships Nuala and they've already fallen in love with your daughter. They'll do anything to keep those two women in the fold."

I hadn't thought about it in those terms. But then I wouldn't think about it in those terms. Now all I had to do was to cool this crisis that I had created and which George was abetting.

It would, I suddenly realized, reduce Nuala to tears again. She wouldn't want to create problems in the family. Well, she hadn't.

TRY TELLING THAT TO HER.

When I turned off the Kennedy Expressway at Fullerton, rain was falling, a light rain at first but the kind of Chicago rain that you know is a harbinger of a major rainstorm, maybe even a thunderstorm. I drove east on Fullerton a few blocks and then turned south on Southport, the street on which we lived. Despite the rain it was like driving through a Gothic cathedral. The huge old trees still clung to most of their orange and red and gold leaves. Even without sunlight there was an air of reverence about the street. One sensed that holiness lurked just around the corner.

The homes on Southport were larger and more solid than the homes in Canaryville, a sometime dwelling place for different ethnic immigrants than Canaryville—Swedes, Germans, and Poles. Our own house was the rare wooden house in the street. Over 125 years old, it was in the area west of DePaul University, where Lincoln Park West petered out as it approached the Chicago River. The huge Polish Church of St. Josephat, across the street from us, presided over the block with aloof Slavic charm.

"Our house," Nuala always boasted, "is the prettiest house on the block, even if it is the oldest."

She could have added that it had the best electricity and plumbing on the street too. However, in its soft gray paint with white and blue trim, it was indeed the most attractive home on the street.

I pulled up to our parking place with a sigh of relief. I had been away from my wife and daughter for several hours and I missed them.

13

No one heard me come in. Four females, one canine and three human, were playing on the floor. The canine wore her usual white coat, the three humans were wearing the standard issue of jeans and sweatshirts, my daughter a red and black Chicago Bulls shirt, just like her mother's. Nessa's proclaimed that she was from DePaul University.

None of them paid any attention to me. The focus of attention rather was my daughter's attempts, sometimes more successful than others, to sit up. They laughed, herself included when she succeeded, and they laughed again, herself once more, when she failed. Only Fiona took notice of the return of the man of the house and then only perfunctorily. She ambled over to me for a quick pat on her huge head and then returned to the game.

"Oh, Mr. Coyne," Nessa exclaimed finally, "isn't your daughter the most darlin' baby in all the world, totally brilliant!"

Nessa, a graduate student in education at DePaul, was a combination mother's helper and baby-sitter. Like Nuala she was from County Galway and spoke Irish. A cute and very vivacious little blonde, she was studying for her Ph.D. in some kind of remedial education. She and Nuala always referred to it, as was proper in Irish English, as her P. Haitch D.

She was on retainer in her role because Nuala had insisted that the "poor child" (three years older than my wife) needed the money and she'd never earn enough money if she came only when we needed help or a baby-sitter. She was, I thought, worth all we paid her and more because she was a sounding board for my wife of the same gender and background. They had become thick as thieves and were constantly, I suspected, plotting against me.

Moreover, Nessa always insisted that I was either "Mr. Coyne" or "Sir."

" 'Tis because you're so solid and reliable," Nuala reassured me.

I doubted that.

"Nuala and I were just having some fun with your daughter, sir," Nessa said. "I think she's the happiest baby in all the world!"

"She apparently inherited that from her mother," I said with just a touch of irony in my voice.

I told everybody that I was an old man and Nuala was an only child.

My daughter rolled over and sat up as if to say, "See, I showed you what I could do."

Then she fell back on the floor, rolled over again, and tried desperately to crawl.

"She's going to make it, Dermot Michael, one of these days you're going to come home and your daughter is going to crawl across the floor to you, and then won't you have a grand feeling altogether!"

"The happiest baby in all the world."

"Isn't she now?"

Nobody asked me to sit down but I did. Moreover, I picked up my daughter and held her on my lap, a position in which she seemed quite content to lie.

"Nuala, would you ever like to visit a bar tonight for an hour or so?"

"The one down the street?" she asked.

"No, on 44th Street. It's called Michael's Bar and Tap."

"Why would I ever want to go there, Dermot Michael?" she asked suspiciously.

"I gather it's a bar where some of the old-time Irish revolutionaries gather at night. Perhaps we could pick up some of the folklore about our friends, the Doolans."

"Go on, Nuala," Nessa said. "It'd be good for you to get away for a couple of hours. It'd be good for your daughter too."

"You just want to play with her by yourself," Nuala said, somewhat petulantly.

"Give over," Nessa said with a laugh, "you need a night out and don't give me any new excuses."

"Well, maybe you're right."

"After I make a dish of pasta for supper," I said.

"I could bring over my homework and finish it off. Nelliecoyne won't be nearly as much a distraction as that amadon Seamus Lynch."

Seamus was an alleged boyfriend about whom we heard occasionally but never saw.

"I don't know." Nuala, eyes downcast, hesitated.

"Sure, won't it be good to get away for a little while?"

"If you think it would be all right, Dermot Michael?"

"I do indeed."

The tension around her eyes broke my heart.

"Well . . ."

" 'Tis all settled then. I'll come over right after supper."

"I'll ask Mr. Forest to pick you up."

"You don't have to do that, sir."

"Yes, I do."

Mr. Forest was our own personal taxi driver.

Fiona joined me and my daughter and rested her large muzzle on my knee.

My wife came over and kissed me on the forehead.

"All right, Dermot Michael, I'll go to your bar on 44th Street but only for an hour, no more than that, do you understand?"

"An hour and a half," I said.

YOU AND YOUR BROTHER ARE BOTH ASS-

HOLES, THERE'S NOTHING IN THE WORLD NU-
ALA CAN'T HANDLE. SHE CAN TAKE CARE OF
THAT CRAZY SISTER-IN-LAW OF YOURS WITH-
OUT YOU GUYS CREATING A FAMILY CRISIS.

"She's a fragile child."

BULLSHIT, DERMOT MICHAEL. SHE CAN BE
ANYBODY SHE WANTS TO BE. SHE CAN DEAL
WITH THAT WOMAN WITHOUT ANY OF YOUR
HELP.

The Adversary is usually wrong, but he
represents a dimension in myself or I
wouldn't be hearing him. This time I was
afraid he was right.

While I prepared our lasagna, I explained
to my wife what I had learned from Dr.
Gomez.

"I don't ever want to go into that house,
Dermot Michael," she said firmly.

"I don't know that we'll ever have to."

"That will be as may be," she said ominously.

After we had disposed of the pasta and
washed the dishes and Mr. Forest had
brought Nessa back, Nuala and I departed
for Canaryville. My wife was very tense at
the prospect of leaving our child alone—that
meant alone with Nessa. Nuala fed her
properly, indeed tried to force more of her

milk on the child than she wanted. Then, by using a torture instrument that I despised called a breast pump, we obtained a bottle of mother's milk and put it in the refrigerator. Finally my wife secreted in her purse a small portable phone so she could call home immediately without having to wait for me to dial the number on the car phone. So, prepared for all eventualities, off we went with the tension around Nuala's eyes as grim as I had ever seen it.

By now the rain was pouring, so she put a trench coat on over her Chicago Bulls jersey. The two of us looked like a pair of yuppies who might very well not be welcomed in Michael's Bar and Tap. So we'd have to play the game of being good yuppies. We had hardly turned off Fullerton and onto the Kennedy Expressway when Nuala pulled out her phone and, like E.T., called home. She babbled in Irish for some minutes, sighed, and closed the phone and returned it to her purse.

"Well, the little brat is sound asleep, Dermot," she said. "She doesn't seem to miss her mother and father at all."

"That's the way kids are."

She sighed in agreement.

Then after a long pause she shook her head and said, "Dermot Michael, you know something strange happened in front of that house on Emerald today."

"Oh?"

"I mean, why did our Nellie feel so angry?"

"I don't know. Did you sense anything there?"

"Only vague and distant emotions, Dermot. Conflict, tension, anger, terrible anger, and then it all kind of turned off, if you take my meaning."

"What was so strange about Nelliecoyne's anger—I mean strange even granted that she's fey on both sides of her family?"

"Well, it was just like the one at the Lake, wasn't it now?"

"It was."

"I thought the anger was at the death of poor little Agnes Mary Elizabeth Doolan, didn't you?"

"You mean at the Lake?"

"Yes, because the poor little tyke probably drowned right opposite your parents' house?"

"Probably."

"But then why would Nellie go into a rage at 4615 Emerald? Agnes Doolan wasn't there, Dermot, don't you see? I mean, she died on the Lake. So there would be no memory of her being at the house. Her mother's pain and her father's pain would be but not Agnes's."

I couldn't help myself—I shivered.

"Nuala, that's scary!"

"It's always scary, Dermot, but this one is more than just scary, it's odd."

As far as I was concerned the whole business was odd but I didn't think it wise to say that.

"And we don't even know the mystery we're supposed to solve, do we?" she went on.

"The only mystery we know about is the mystery of why Nelliecoyne grew angry those two nights at Grand Beach and even more angry when we passed the Doolan house this morning. And of course the mystery why both of you saw the ships that have been underneath the waters of Lake Michigan for one hundred years."

"Well, didn't the schooner survive a little longer?"

"That's true."

My conversation trailed off. Nuala made one more phone call and reported to me that the child was still asleep. I expressed some surprise at such good behavior.

"Isn't she the best baby in all the world?"

"You'll get no disagreement with me on that, Nuala dear."

Then she changed the subject abruptly.

"I'm worried about Nessa."

"Uh?"

I suspected that this was one of those times when it is the husband's role to listen very carefully, not to what his wife is saying, but to what she means. It was a knack that I was in the process of developing. I'd improved at it but I doubted I'd ever be adequate to the challenge.

"Well, isn't her young man Seamus the problem now?"

"Is she living with Seamus?"

"Dermot Michael Coyne, that's none of our business. But, no, she's not living with him. I won't go so far as to say that she doesn't sleep with him, however."

I waited for a further explanation of that. But none was forthcoming, so I asked, "Is she in love?"

"Oh, Dermot, she's in love with him all right, but isn't that the problem now?"

"She shouldn't be in love with him?"

"Don't be an eejit, Dermot Michael Coyne, of course she should be in love with him. Isn't she a wonderful girl and he a wonderful fella?"

"Indeed."

"The problem is that she is not in love with a painter, I mean a house painter, not one of your artist type painters."

"Ah," I said.

"Do you understand now, Dermot Michael?" she asked with a great show of patience.

I tried.

"Herself doesn't know whether she should marry somebody who has much less education than she has?"

"Haven't I been saying that all along? I wouldn't say she's a snob exactly. Because she's not, she's a very nice young woman. And she's very much in love. But she wonders about the social class difference between them. Isn't that a terrible thing to worry about, Dermot Michael Coyne?"

"It never bothered you to fall in love with a rich man's son!"

Nuala thought that was hilariously funny.

"And himself rich too. But only because he'd been lucky. You know, Dermot, I don't believe at all, at all in this social class stuff. Yet she has a very good point. It would be more of a point if Seamus wasn't so eager to read books and go to art museums and concerts and even operas. To tell you the truth, even though he doesn't have a Ph.D. and will never have one, he still has better taste than she does."

"Are they going to stay in Chicago?"

"Och, there's not a chance of that. They're both in love with the County Galway and doesn't he have to go back and take over his family's construction company? He's going to end up a rich man."

"And himself with no education other than from high school?"

"So that's the problem. Don't you see?"

"I do indeed."

But I didn't see what we were supposed to do about it.

"Well now, don't you think we ought to do something about it?"

Nuala Anne felt we'd better do something about it so that meant I ought to think we might do something about it.

"Like what?"

"Dermot Michael Coyne, don't be an eejit! Shouldn't we invite them both over for dinner one night so you and I can get to know Seamus better?"

"So we can judge whether he really is right for her?"

"You're still talking like an eejit, Dermot Michael Coyne!"

"I am?"

"We know he's good enough for her, we've just got to confirm that, Dermot, don't you see?"

Finally, yes indeed, I did see. Nuala was merely asking whether it would be all right to invite Seamus and Nessa over for supper one night.

"Won't I make my Hungarian goulash for them!"

"Ah, Dermot Michael Coyne, you're the most wonderful husband in all the world!"

I had to agree that I was.

After yet another call home as we turned off the Expressway at 43rd Street, Nuala began to relax a little bit.

"You know, Dermot Michael, the child doesn't seem to mind us going out at all, at all."

"As long as she has a full stomach and a dry diaper and Fiona and Nessa to adore her, why does she need us?"

Nuala giggled and slapped me very lightly on the arm as she might slap Fiona, if the wondrous canine had misbehaved slightly.

As bright and lively as Canaryville had seemed earlier in the day, it was now dark and strange. Most neighborhoods in Chicago look mysterious on rainy autumn nights with sheets of rain falling against the windshield of the car and the soggy tree branches hovering over our heads.

We managed to find a parking place near Michael's Bar and Tap and made a dash for the door. When we entered the bar, a dim and dingy place whose walls were lined with pictures of unfamiliar politicians and athletes, all conversation suddenly stopped and every eye in the tavern turned towards us. The room smelled of stale beer, indeed beer that had been stale for decades, maybe a century. My wife and I were the youngest people in the bar by a good thirty-five years.

We took off our raincoats, sat at a small, unstable table near the doorway, and began to chat softly. The bartender wandered over and asked us what we'd like to drink. Nuala ordered a diet cola—no alcohol in her mother's milk—and I asked for a pint of Guinness. The bartender nodded.

"You're newcomers around here, aren't you?"

"I guess so," I said as once more every eye in the place turned towards us.

"Me husband is a writer," Nuala said with her thickest Galaway accent. "And isn't he doing research on all the Chicago neighborhoods? And weren't we here in Canaryville this morning? And didn't we think it was one of the nicest places we'd ever seen—mind you outside of County Galway? And didn't I say to him why don't we come here tonight and find a nice cozy bar and see what the insides of the bars in Canaryville are like?"

"So you're not exactly yuppies?" said the bartender, beginning to warm to us.

"My husband used to work at the commodity exchanges and wasn't he a complete failure there, but like most Irishmen he's a grand storyteller and doesn't he write wonderful stories?"

Suspecting this was a cue for me, I said, "And doesn't herself sing beautiful songs?"

The man's eyes narrowed on us. "Aren't you the woman that sings on the television? Of course you are, what's your name again? Ah, I know, you're Nuala Anne!"

My wife blushed becomingly. "Well, it's

wonderful altogether that you recognize a poor child from the Gaeltacht in County Galway and yourself wearing a Chicago Bulls jacket on this cold, rainy night!"

No direct answer to the question, of course, that would indicate a lack of good manners, in County Galway—for cold, rainy nights are even more frequent there than in Chicago.

"Well," said the bartender, "we wouldn't dream of asking you to sing a song for us. Just a minute and I'll get your drinks."

Herself looked happy, knowing full well that once she turned on that kind of charm she was utterly irresistible. I knew it too because she turned it on me once in a bar on the street of Trinity College and periodically turned it on again. Like when she had given me the English muffin covered with strawberry jam earlier in the day.

The bartender brought back my pint of Guinness and her diet cola.

"Would you ever mind if I sing one of my husband's favorite Irish songs? It was the first one he ever heard me singing in a pub in Dublin and the poor man never had a chance after that!"

There was applause, discreet and quiet

applause, because this was a discreet and quiet bar.

So Nuala, her eyes filled with love, sang for us all "Molly Malone."

And after enthusiastic applause she sang a couple of lullabies. And then reached for the phone to call home again. It turned out that her daughter astonishingly was still sound asleep.

An elderly couple in their late seventies, tall, handsome people with silver hair and red faces, asked if they could join us. We said we'd be delighted. They were sweet old folks who had to show us pictures of their children, grandchildren, and their one little great-granddaughter. And of course, Nuala pulled out a whole wallet full of pictures of our Nellie. Both our new friends insisted that she was the most beautiful baby they'd ever seen. This was not a falsehood, though maybe a rhetorical exaggeration.

She was, however, one very pretty little girl, even if she had hardly any hair and was fey on both sides of her family.

"You folks are here from Galway are you?" asked the woman.

"Your man is from County Cook. I'm from

away out in Connemara," Nuala said. "You've heard of the town of Carraroe."

"Well, we've never been back to Ireland," the man said. "Our parents emigrated you see, they came over after the Troubles and we were born here. Our parents could never go back and didn't want to go back and of course we didn't want to go back either and still don't."

"Ah?" I said casually.

"You see," the man said, going a deep red, "we don't approve of the puppet Free State government in Dublin."

"It's run by a pack of traitors," the woman joined in. "Traitors like Michael Collins, and then after him didn't Eamon De Valera sell us out? And all those other fellows even up to the crowd that's there now."

"But it looks like it's all over," I said, "with the Good Friday Accord and all."

"Gerry Adams," said the man bitterly, "is the worst traitor of them all. That Good Friday agreement put the whole of Ireland once more on the cross of suffering and injustice. How could they possibly have given up a legitimate claim for the six counties under colonial occupation?"

"It'll be another fifty years," the woman

said, her lips thin with anger, "before there's a chance to unite all Ireland as God intended it to be united."

"The Republic is one and indivisible," her husband insisted loudly. "But nobody seems to realize that anymore even up in the occupied territories. It will take a lot more suffering and a lot more violence before the people in Ireland on both sides of the border can come to their senses."

Nuala nodded sympathetically though she thought the IRA were a bunch of eejits and disapproved of terrorists.

"This parish has always supported Irish freedom, hasn't it now?" she said so softly that I had to lean towards her to catch the words. "I can understand why that is, there were so many people leaving Ireland because of the oppression."

Almost every emigrant who came in the 1920s claimed to have a price on their head. Fortunately our new friends didn't make that claim.

"There has always been a lot of support for Ireland in this neighborhood, all the way back to the time of the Fenians," the man said, his voice becoming a little bit calmer. "Most of that died out a long time ago but there's still some of it around. There are still some true Irish patriots in the neighborhood, not very many but more than most people think."

I wouldn't have thought there were many Americans who would be that involved emotionally in a war of terrorism four thousand miles away in a country they had never visited.

Nuala smiled her most demure and charming smile. "It used to be said back in Galway that a long time ago back in the time of the Fenians, even before the Irish Volunteers, there was a lot of money from Chicago coming to support the cause of a free Ireland."

"Aye," said the old man, "there certainly was. The Ancient Order of Hibernians, which are now just a pale imitation of what they used to be, were deeply involved in raising money right here in this neighborhood for the cause of Ireland."

"If it hadn't been for American money, the lads would have never won all the battles against the Brits after the Easter Rising," his wife said bitterly. "Then the Free Staters lost it all for us."

"They collected a lot of money in St. Gabriel's parish," her husband sighed sadly. "It's a shame that our money and many lives were wasted when the Free State government in Dublin sold us out."

"Wasn't there a man named Thomas Doolan that was involved back in those times?" Nuala asked. "I seem to remember hearing his name now and again even out in Carraroe where I lived."

That wasn't altogether true, in fact it wasn't true at all, at all. Nuala had never heard of Thomas Doolan until this morning. But she heard of him during the day in St. Gabriel's rectory and that was probably enough to make her statement reasonably true. I was amazed at how hard she was pressing the angry couple without seeming to press them at all. I kept my mouth shut.

"He was a strange fella, that Tom Doolan," the man said slowly, "himself all puffed up because he was a lawyer and a judge and had a lot of money, most of which he inherited from his own father. He certainly talked a good revolutionary line. But I'm not sure that he was serious. There were a lot of strange rumors about him, let me tell you."

"And his wife," the woman went on. "She

was a stuck-up one, so pretty and so proud of herself and so filled with piety and holiness. But there was something a little wrong with her too."

"How awful," Nuala said sympathetically. "For people to pretend to be supporters of Ireland and still to be put up as an example for the rest of us."

"Now mind you, they were never turned out," the man went on, "they were too important and too influential and too rich for the supporters of Ireland to ignore. But a lot of the folks in my parents' generation said that we should never trust them. And so we never did."

"Old Tom Doolan died in 1947," the woman said abruptly, "right after my man came back from the Pacific. I don't quite remember when his wife died. I could never stand the woman."

"It was a few years later," her husband added. "They were both buried with all kinds of ceremony and every crooked Irish politician in Chicago at their wakes and funerals, and the Bishop himself preaching the sermon. It was enough to make one sick to one's stomach because there was something terribly wrong with them."

"Something about money I suppose?" Nuala said.

"It's always about money, isn't it?" the man replied. "But let's not talk about them anymore, let's talk more about the music and your writing and when your next record is coming out."

They were gentle, thoughtful, kindly old people who had a good life in America, who loved their children and their grandchildren greatly, even if some of the grandchildren had moved out to Beverly or even to Burr Ridge or even, God forgive them for it, to the North Side.

Nuala made yet another call home, babbled in Irish, and then said with a happy smile on her face, "Isn't the little girl still sound asleep?"

"Would you ever then sing one more song for us before you go home to her?" the woman asked.

The bartender brought me another glass of Guinness and Nuala another diet cola and she sang several more songs including the granddaddy of all Irish patriotic songs, "The Wearing of the Green."

Later in the car with the rain beating so fiercely against our windows it was hard to see more than three or four car lengths ahead of us, Nuala said, "Weren't they a lovely couple now, Dermot Michael?"

"Are you being ironic?"

"I'm never ironic, Dermot. You know that. They don't believe any of that revolutionary rhetoric and they wouldn't dare to imitate the real revolutionaries. It's just the slogans they learned when they were kids and they can't give them up. Deep down in their hearts they're as happy as anybody about the Good Friday Accord but they're sure it's not going to last."

"Ah," I said. They had seemed like strident, bitter people to me. Nuala Anne, however, was a better judge of people than I was. "We did learn something, however, didn't we now? We learned that the Doolans were leaders in the faction supporting the Fenians and the IRB and the Irish Volunteers and probably the IRA after the Easter Rising. We don't really know which side they were on during the civil war."

"Och, sure we do, Dermot Michael, they were on the side of Michael Collins and the government in Dublin. They were sensible people and they realized that the Brits had given the Irish just about all they could get away with. I don't think that the Doolans were idiots."

I might well have asked how she knew that. But one didn't ask Nuala how she knew things, I just assumed that she did.

"Well, we're making progress of a sort, we know that some kind of a problem is tied up with money?"

"As her man said, isn't it always money . . . I wonder if the cruise a hundred years ago was about money?"

"A benefit for the rebels?"

"It might have been, Dermot Michael."

We were quiet for a few minutes as I concentrated on navigating from the Dan Ryan into the Kennedy Expressway.

"Nuala, do you remember when you gave me the English muffin today in the rectory?"

"Dermot Michael Coyne, I gave you two English muffins!"

"And you did so with all the reverence of a priest putting a host on somebody's tongue."

"That is a pretty big host if you ask my opinion!"

"I have a pretty big mouth."

"Ah, there's that too, isn't it now?"

"And you smiled at me."

"Did I now?"

"And the smile was a mixture of love and affection and desire?"

"Dermot Michael Coyne," she protested, "would I ever look at you with desire inside a rectory with a holy priest around?"

"Nuala Anne McGrail, you would and you did and the priest never noticed."

"I knew he'd never notice. But you certainly noticed and you looked back at me like you wanted to fuck me then and there."

"And you liked that?"

"Of course I did."

"Sex and Eucharist," I said hesitantly, "an odd combination, isn't it?"

"Isn't it just like the little Bishop says, both are about the union of bodies in intimate love? And doesn't each of them remind us of the other?"

Her hand crept to my thigh.

"The little Bishop said that?"

"Didn't he say exactly that?"

Her fingers slipped up and down my leg and then over to more sensitive parts of my anatomy. I gasped audibly and she laughed, an amused seducer.

Thus encouraged, I thought it was safe to tell Nuala in some detail about the family crisis that I had created that afternoon. She listened silently as we crept northward on the rain-drenched expressway system with lightning crackling across the sky.

"Is that all you said?"

"'Tis," I replied.

"Well, now, aren't you and His Reverence a pair of friggin' eejits!"

Rarely, if ever, had I heard George the Priest called an eejit or indeed anything unfavorable by my wife.

"Something had to be done about it, Nuala," I said. "I'm afraid it wasn't a very Irish way. I know you prefer things to be indirect, but I don't know how to break out of a family neurosis on Maybelline without being direct."

"Hm," she snorted derisively. "Well, I suppose that's the most I can expect from a man whether he be Irish or American or a combination of both!"

"Nuala, I have the right to defend my wife and children from that she terrorist."

"You only have one child, Dermot Michael Coyne. And your wife can take care of herself and the child without any help from you."

Her fingers abandoned my loins.

"Nuala Anne!"

She sighed loudly. "Well, Dermot, I shouldn't have said that and I'm sorry. Our little girl and I DO need your protection. But not against Maybelline—I can handle that woman all by meself."

"She had you in tears this morning, didn't she?"

"Well, no, it was afternoon, wasn't it?"

I had learned very early in our relationship that one did not correct a woman when she insisted that one was inaccurate in a minor and irrelevant detail.

"Well, all right, this afternoon."

"That was different," she said dismissively. "From now on I can take care of her all by myself."

"Nuala, I don't doubt that for a moment. Still, I think I have to stand up to the family and to Maybelline. It's not that you can't take care of her. It's not your job to stop her. It's mine."

She thought about that for a minute. "Give over, Dermot Michael," she insisted. "You didn't have to make such a mess of taking care of her, now did you?"

"I don't know how you'd break through our collective neurosis other than by confrontation."

"I'm not a psychologist like you or His Reverence, but it would seem to me that's the last way to break through it!"

She was still angry at me and maybe she had reason to be. Still, something had to be done about Maybelline.

"I'm not sure it could be done any other way. The family has let this problem go on for so long and I don't see any other solution."

"Well, she's your problem, Dermot Michael Coyne, and His Reverence's and Cindy's and everybody else in the family's. And I suppose that youse have to do something about it. And you brought it upon yourselves by letting that poor unhappy woman take out her unhappiness on all of you. So, sure you have to stand up to her. I think you have to do it a lot more delicately and discreetly. But then, what do I know?"

"You know more about human nature, Nuala Anne, than anybody I've ever met."

Nuala opened her purse and took out the phone to make yet another call. She and Nessa exchanged the usual conversation in Irish. Nuala clicked the phone shut and put it in her purse with a sigh. "The little one is still sound asleep, which is what she ought to be doing, and it shows she has a lot better sense than her mother."

"In my observation her mother always shows sense," I said cautiously.

"No I don't, Dermot Michael, not at all, at all. I'm a worse eejit than you and His Reverence put together and I'm sorry for acting like one."

Her hand returned to my thigh.

"Oh?" I said, wondering what would come next.

"I like to pretend that I'm utterly self-sufficient and don't need anyone to take care of me. Of course, that's silly and I should have given that up when I married you, shouldn't I now?"

"Well, if you say so."

"I do say so. I knew you'd take care of me all the time, which is not to say that you don't need me to take care of you all the time, I hope that's clear, isn't it now?"

I imitated her sigh and said, "Sure, 'tis."

She had long since stopped objecting to my sigh and my use of the word *'tis*.

"And I do appreciate you and His Reverence trying to protect me from that poor unhappy woman. And I need your help. But still, Dermot Michael, I think I can pretty much take care of her myself. Now before you say I didn't this morning, that was this morning and now is now. Isn't it?"

I sighed again and repeated, " 'Tis."

I had no idea what the difference was, save that there would be a dramatic change of personae the next time Maybelline made one of her terrorist phone calls.

"All right, that's settled now. I'll fend the woman off when she calls me and you and His Reverence can worry about how you straighten things out in the family. Mind you, I'm not incapable of offering some advice now and then."

"I hardly thought you would be incapable, Nuala."

"Good." She squeezed my knee again. "So now we'd better think about our shower tonight, mind you after Mr. Forest takes Nessa home."

"How could I not want to think about that?"

Nuala loved joint hot showers. She said they were inexpensive entertainment and a lot more interesting than watching the telly. Naturally I agreed.

Her fingers found the most vulnerable part of me and played gently.

I decided to risk the delights of a shower

by asking her one more question, "And what happens if Maybelline goes after you at some other family gathering?"

"Och, Dermot Michael, she won't do it a second time, will she now?"

"I'm delighted to hear that."

"No, she won't go after me a second time at all, at all."

"I'd love to be there to see it."

"Oh, come on, Dermot Michael, you'll probably be there but afterward I'll feel terrible for hurting the poor unhappy woman. Just the same, like you say, it has to be done."

In the space of twelve hours on the subject of Maybelline my wife had changed from the fragile girl from Connemara into a sophisticated, tough-minded woman of the world. The latter was not as authentic as the former but it was authentic enough.

The lightning continued to crackle above us and thunder exploded as though it were following us down Southport Avenue. I turned off the ignition and crushed my wife into my arms, kissing her, caressing her, fondling her.

"I'd like to fuck you out here with the thunder crashing all around us."

For a moment she seemed afraid that I meant it.

"Dermot Michael," she said weakly, "not that it wouldn't be interesting, but we're not courting now and we don't have to make love in the front seat of a car, not mind you that we ever did. . . . And Nessa . . ."

"I'll get you some other time," I said in mock resignation. "But someday, woman, when you're teasing me, I'll just pull over to the side of the road and teach you a lesson or two."

She giggled.

"Won't I be waiting for that?"

YOU CAN'T MAKE LOVE IN THE FRONT SEAT OF A MERCEDES, the Adversary rebuked me.

"Someday I'll show you differently."

Despite our raincoats we both rushed for the door. While I fumbled with the keys, Nessa opened it inside and announced, "Come in quick! Glory be to God! Wasn't I crying every moment since your last call, Nuala Ann. It's such a terrible, terrible night out. No one should be out tonight on the streets of the city. You'd never know when lightning is going to strike one of these trees and knock it right over on top of your pretty car."

Nessa was patently an Irish matriarch in training. She might not go to church—Nuala told me she didn't—but she still had the Irishwoman's inclination to see grave danger in almost every possible situation and to turn to prayer against the danger. As though to confirm her fears, lightning sizzled right above us and almost instantly there was a mighty boom of thunder.

"Come on in, come on in," she ordered us. "You'll catch your death of cold in the rain and it sounded to me like that lightning had our names on it and ourselves in a wooden house as well."

I tried vainly to explain that the house was grounded so as to resist even a direct hit of lightning and completely fireproof. It did no good, both Nessa and Nuala cited the Chicago fire as evidence that fires happened in this city and worried that the next time it might spread farther west on Fullerton Avenue than it had the last time.

I didn't tell them that the Chicago fire was in October.

Our little princess with the few strands of red hair was still sound asleep. Our wolf-hound slept next to the crib in her standard guard dog position. She opened one eye somewhat contemptuously, I thought, as we came in, wondering where we'd been all night. Nelliecoyne was sound asleep and breathing, as far as I could see, normally.

Mr. Forest's cab pulled up and I escorted Nessa to the street under a big umbrella that informed the world that Chicago was a city that worked. As Nessa went out the door, I glanced back at my wife and noted that she was removing her sweatshirt.

Mr. Forest took Nessa home and Nuala and I settled in for our evening entertainment. Of course, we set up a monitor in the nursery and its counterpart in the bathroom right next to the shower so there was no danger that we would miss the slightest cry. Indeed a couple of times during our entertainments—about which I won't tell you in any detail except to remark that they were spectacular—Nuala had opened the shower door and listened to the monitor. At one time she even dashed into the nursery to make sure that the child wasn't crying. I can imagine Fiona's distress at a soaking wet human standing over her.

After the entertainments were over and I languished in bed Nuala, having donned a satin and lace gown with a matching robe (open of course!), was brushing her long black hair and looking very, very thoughtful as she carefully counted each stroke. Sometimes I was asked to brush her hair for her, at other times not. Tonight was one of those nights when she decided to do it herself. She'd shared enough of herself with me during our romp in the shower.

Fiona wandered into our bedroom from her post in the nursery and rolled over on her back for the night routine of belly scratching.

"No, I don't like it, Dermot Michael. I don't like it at all, at all. But I'm afraid we're going to have to take up your man's invitation."

"What don't you like? And which man and what invitation?"

She stopped brushing a moment to look at me in astonishment.

"Dr. Gomez's invitation, who else? That house is a scary place and I don't want to go into it, but still I think we'd better, don't you?"

"If you say so, Nuala, we will certainly do it. Do we bring herself?"

"Och, Dermot Michael, I wouldn't think of that. She'd carry on something terrible. And there would be too many questions we'd have to answer. No, it would be much better not to let Nelliecoyne near St. Gabriel's parish until we've solved the mystery."

"A mystery that the exact nature of which we don't know."

"I want to know a lot more about it, Dermot." She finished counting and put her hairbrush back on the table. "We know it's about money, we know it's about Irish revolutionaries. We know that it's something about which rumors circulated for the rest of their lives. And we know that it was somehow connected to what happened over in Michigan City. The more I know about it, Dermot Michael, the less I like it."

She climbed into bed next to me and snuggled up close. She reached for the bed lamp and flicked it off. "No, Dermot Michael, I don't like it one bit. But we're going to have to figure it out, aren't we?"

"If you say so, Nuala Anne," I murmured sleepily.

There was no answer to that, because my bride was already asleep.

Later in the night, or more likely early in the morning, we engaged in some activities which were to a certain extent a reprise of what happened in the shower. Our amusements might have gone on much longer had not Nelliecoyne exploded with another cry of outrage followed by terrified wailing. This time Nuala and I, both of us in what the newspapers call an advanced state of undress, charged into her nursery before Fiona could come drag us out of bed. Nuala snatched the little girl up in her arms and began singing her lovely lullabies once more. The wolfhound paced back and forth nervously in the nursery. She disapproved of this whole business of Nelliecoyne wailing in the middle of the night and of the child's human parents who were responsible for the disturbance.

I opened the drape on the window and looked out on Southport Avenue. The rain had stopped but the wet street glistened a shiny black, in the pale glow of the tree-shrouded streetlight. As far as I could see there was nothing outside. Nuala joined me at the window and looked out nervously and shook her head.

"No, Dermot Michael, there's nothing out there. No ships sailing down Southport Avenue. Nothing sinister at all, at all."

"What do you think happened?"

"Maybe she had a dream that recalled the

morning at the Lake. If we needed any more motivation to get to the bottom of this mystery, Dermot Michael Coyne, we have it now! Our little tyke wants us to."

There were some weaknesses in that reasoning, but I had enough sense not to dispute my wife.

14

The ghosts were gone the next morning. I decided that I would pretend that nothing had happened. It was not a morning for ghosts.

The day dawned sunny and cold, a clear blue sky, the temperature in the upper fifties, an acrid smell of real autumn—rotting leaves—in the air. It was autumn, it was time for autumn, so we may as well make our peace with it. After our morning exercise and breakfast, Nuala settled down to do her voice exercises and I went to my study and began to pound away on my computer. Is there any explanation why the writing demon (as distinct of course from the Adversary, who is someone else altogether) takes possession of me? I know of none. But for some reason or other, he did that morning. Still singing, Nuala stuck her head into the office. "Would you look at him," she exclaimed. "Isn't he acting just like he was a professional novelist?"

"Woman, you're a terrible distraction altogether! Can't you see that I'm hard at work!"

"Far be it from me, Dermot Michael Coyne, to distract a great writer when he's hard at work."

But she did distract me by leaning against me and pressing my head against her breasts.

"Sure," she went on, "won't a little bit of affection increase your productivity?"

"If there's much more of it," I said, "won't I be dragging you off to the shower again?"

"Och, wasn't I thinking to myself, Dermot Michael, that the next time we should use the bath instead of the shower? That will be more relaxing and yourself putting in a big bath just for that purpose."

"Away with you, woman," I ordered, not expecting her to go away at all. Then the phone rang. It was my father. He did not mention the ultimatum that I'd delivered yesterday.

"I talked to Dr. Kavanagh a couple of times, Dermot," he began uneasily. "At first his wife absolutely refused to see you. She doesn't think there could possibly be any interesting history in Canaryville. She's much more interested in late medieval England and its tapestries."

"Is she now?"

Dad laughed. "You know, you're beginning to sound more and more like that gorgeous young woman to whom you're married."

"Ah, isn't she a very influential person now? This Colleen Kavanagh person won't see us because she's not interested in Chicago history."

"I picked up a few markers from her husband and he tried again. She'll see you next Tuesday from eleven-thirty to eleven forty-five at her house on Hopkins Place in Beverly. You will only have fifteen minutes and not a second more. She also told her husband to tell me to tell you that she didn't think she had any useful documents about Canaryville. She said she didn't imagine that her father would have saved anything because he despised the neighborhood. The few times that she's driven through it she thought it was tacky."

"Tacky was the word she used?"

"It's the word her husband used—I presume he didn't make it up."

"I guess we'll just have to wait. Thanks much."

"Tacky is it?" Nuala said, an ominous look in her eyes.

This Colleen Kavanagh ought to beware. It's unlikely that she would encounter a shy child from Galway and much more likely that she will be seeing the serious determined woman of the world—the woman who would take care of Maybelline. And the woman who was adamant in her resistance to directors who try to make her sing songs that she didn't want to sing when she was doing her recording. Nuala could be as stubborn when she wanted to as anybody I've ever known. Rarely, thank God, was she stubborn with me.

"You remember, Dermot, that we were supposed to take poor Fiona up to the kennels this afternoon."

"I had forgotten it completely." Once a month we would take our dog up to Lake

County to the kennel that raised wolfhounds. They worried that the new popularity of the dogs might weaken the bloodlines of the species which the professional wolfhound breeders were trying to enhance. So they maintained a lofty standard of what the wolf-hound breed was.

Fiona loved to run with the other dogs. They don't recognize their mates or children I was told. I wasn't altogether sure I believed that. Wolfhounds are quite capable of deceiving us to protect their privacy.

"I'll let you work till noontime," Nuala said, "but then we'll have to go up to Lake County."

"Nelliecoyne?"

"Sure, Dermot Michael, we can't leave her all alone, can we now?"

YOU IDIOT. WHY DID YOU BOTHER TO ASK?

So we drove up to Lake Country and watched Fiona romp through the fresh pastures with the rest of her club. Some of them, including her daughter Fionulla and her sometime mate Finn, were as snow white as she was. They played, tumbled, and raced one another and had a glorious afternoon altogether. Our daughter, dressed in an orange and blue Chicago Bears sweatsuit, must have thought she was in paradise because there were so many dogs and some of them looked exactly like her own beloved Fiona.

As much as Fiona liked playing with her friends—dogs like to be with other dogs—she was not about to let us leave without her. As soon as we turned towards the car, she came charging up, jumped over the fence which was supposed to restrain the huge beasts—and dashed to the door of our car where she waited wagging her tail expectantly. Nuala embraced her. "We wouldn't go without you. We love you too much to leave you up here with all your friends but we'll come back next month."

I wondered about the separation anxieties which would occur when we left for Ireland at Christmastime. Nuala's parents would meet their new granddaughter and Nellie-coyne would get her first sight of the land of her ancestors. Dogs, I told myself, are not like humans. They don't like to see us going away but they enjoy themselves until we come back and then go crazy with joy when they see us again. As I reflected on this it occurred to me that it was a sensible way to deal with the uncertainties and the problems of life.

Cindy called as soon as we got back into the house.

"Dermot, where have you been all day?"

"We took Fiona up to Wolfhound Park in Lake County."

"If you decide to do something like that again when we have a situation on our hands, please leave word on your answering machine where you can be found. I called you in the car too but you must have been out cavorting around Lake County with your dog and her friends."

"Guilty as charged," I said, with a touch of asperity. We really didn't have a "situation." Only Nick Farmer.

"What's Farmer done now?"

"Farmer has lost his job at the television station. They received too many complaints from listeners about his anti-Irish bias. It plays in the taverns where he hangs out, places like Billygoat's and the Old Town Alehouse. Those folks seem to forget that there's an awful lot of Irish Catholics in the city."

"The way I heard it, we run it."

"More or less. Anyway, he's telling his

friends that you got him fired. He's talking the usual junk that he won't be censored and he won't be intimidated and he'll keep on speaking out against the misuse of art."

"He doesn't have an original line," I said.

"No, Dermot, he doesn't. He's a terribly insecure and inept man who is trying desperately to make a name for himself, probably for the last time since he's already in his early forties. It looks to me like his plans have backfired. I'm calling to warn you and Nuala that if anybody in the media calls to discuss his complaints about you, you just refer them to me and make no comment. Indeed, as Nuala would say, you make no comment at all, at all. Got it?"

"Anything you say, Counselor."

After Cindy hung up I wondered who my sister thought she was to tell me I should or should not talk to the media. No one was going to tell me when I should talk or when I shouldn't talk.

AREN'T YOU BECOMING THE FEISTY ONE WITH YOUR FAMILY? I WONDER HOW LONG IT WILL LAST.

I explained to Nuala the gist of the message.

"That poor unhappy man," she said. "We

really have to pray for him when we say our prayers tonight, Dermot."

"Is that before or after the bathtub?"

"Nobody ever said we were going to use the bathtub tonight, did they now?"

She was having me on.

The next day I continued the work on my book and Nuala put Nellie in her arms and went down for her singing lesson with Madam in the Fine Arts Building on South Michigan Avenue. Mr. Forest drove her down and then picked her up an hour later to bring her back. I busied myself in the afternoon with preparing the Hungarian goulash for our two possibly star-crossed Irish lovers who were coming to supper that night. Nuala wasted no time when she was involved in the matchmaking game.

"How did the lesson with Madam go?"

"Och, Dermot Michael, she says I'm getting terribly sloppy, that I'm not practicing hard enough or long enough, and I'll never get better, much less be a great singer, unless I put more time in practicing."

"And you said?"

"Didn't I say that I was a mother with a little daughter around the house?"

"To which Madam replied?"

"Madam replied by saying that such a lovely little girl could take care of herself enough while her mother practiced her singing, and that she would probably enjoy the singing a lot better if it was better done."

"Did she now?"

"It's one more judgment that I'm not good at anything, Dermot Michael. I'm not a very good mother or a very good wife or a very good singer."

Sometimes when Nuala says things like that she doesn't mean them, but today she meant them and the lines of tension around her eyes grew tighter.

"Nuala, I can't complain at all about the wife part and I haven't heard Nelliecoyne complain much about the mother part. As far as I can tell all Madam said was that you have to practice more carefully."

In answer, Nuala threw her arms around me and hugged me and cried again.

She had done a lot more crying, it seemed to me, since the advent of Nelliecoyne.

While I was preparing the Hungarian goulash for our supper that night, I had another idea, in fact the first good idea since Grand Beach. I washed my hands and picked up the phone to call the Michigan City Public

Library. Yes, of course, there were several newspapers in the city in 1898, of which the largest was the *Michigan City News.* Yes, that year was on microfiche. Yes, the records went back more than a hundred years. Yes, I could come up any time I wanted to look at them.

If Seamus wasn't the right young man for our Nessa (as we called her now), would she ever find the right one? Of medium height, slender, with sandy hair and freckled face, he was quiet at first, doubtless thinking that we were "gentry." When Nuala talked to him in Irish, however, he relaxed and smiled—a warm, wonderfully absorbing smile. His wit was deft and understated, as the best of Irish wit is. Moreover, his admiration for our daughter was unfeigned—as it had to be.

He examined our house with attention to minute details.

"Aye, they did a grand job, didn't they, and themselves putting up these homes in a short time?"

"This one took a little more time because it has two floors and because it was to be the first home of a lawyer who had returned from the Civil War and his young wife. Still, these houses were sturdily built. The construction people were an unsung proto School of Chicago Architecture."

"Ah," he said as he rubbed one of the walls, almost affectionately, "it's a shame to let a place like this just deteriorate, isn't it now, Mr. Coyne? Doesn't it take a lot of money to fix it up?"

"Nuala and I wanted a home that would be close to a church and a school with easy access to downtown. This seemed to be a real neighborhood with a wide variety of people, not as elegant perhaps as my home neighborhood out in River Forest, but much more interesting."

"And the outside staircase is because of the mud?"

"Right. People would enter on the second floor because there was so much mud on the ground. Chicago was still a swamp in those days. Later when they raised the street level, the first-floor entrance was right at ground level and the backyard, where Fiona runs, is a couple of feet below street level. We use the stairs now only as a kind of porch or balcony."

Fiona had decided promptly that she liked

Seamus and rolled over on her back to have her belly scratched.

"And your wife keeps her canogi stick in the parlor, does she now?"

"She claims it's her good luck sign. I won't let her have it in the bedroom."

Canogi is a woman's version of the Irish game of hurling, a dangerous form of field hockey in which several dozen young men (or women) are equipped with clubs and permitted, nay urged, to beat each other up. Nuala's team won the Galway championship when she was fourteen. Wherever she went, the stick, longer than a hockey stick with a twist on the end, went with her, just in case there was a chance for "the odd game."

She thought it was very funny that I had banned it from the bedroom because, "Sure, I'd never hit you with it, Dermot Michael." Nonetheless she had conveyed it to the parlor, decorated in all respects other than the television as it might have been in 1880.

I showed Seamus around the second floor while Nuala and Nessa gossiped in the kitchen.

"You've furnished the house in the fashion of the times, haven't you?" he said as we walked through the master bedroom.

"More or less, so long as it didn't cost too much."

"They wouldn't have a bathtub like that in the 1870s, would they?" he said, gesturing at the deep and wide tub in which my wife and I periodically frolicked.

"We have to adjust to the customs of the times," I said, feeling my face grow warm.

"Ah, you're a lucky man," he said.

It was a rather forward comment from one so reserved. I felt my face grow warmer.

"I wouldn't deny it," I agreed.

Although Seamus had no formal education after he had left secondary school, he was a very intelligent young man. In the booming Ireland of the present, he would indeed become a wealthy man. He was in every respect a good catch, even if I was Mr. Coyne and my wife was Nuala Anne.

He and our Nessa were very much in love although they rarely spoke to each other during the course of the evening. However, they certainly were not sleeping together. Looks of longing were on their faces that would be more discreet if they had become "partners."

"What do you think, Dermot Michael?" Nuala asked me later in the bath as she rubbed her big toe up and down my chest.

"What do I think about frolicking in the bathtub with a naked woman? I think it's wonderful."

"Don't be an eejit. I meant about Seamus and Nessa."

She reached for the monitor on the washstand next to the tub and listened to it carefully to make sure there was no noise coming from the nursery.

"Oh, are you talking about Seamus and Nessa? I didn't know that was the subject of conversation."

I reached down and tickled her.

"Don't change the subject, Dermot Michael!"

"I thought they were well matched. He's a very intelligent, serious young man and has a fine future. Perhaps a little too serious but that's not necessarily a fault in an Irish male."

"I never married one like that."

"Come to think of it, I've never heard anyone say I was too serious."

I continued to tickle her. She squealed and squirmed and giggled.

"He's a nice guy, she's a wonderful young

woman, and they're deeply in love. All this class stuff is nonsense!"

"That's what I hoped you'd say, Dermot. But still . . ."

"The way Ireland is building these days he'll make more money in the construction business than he would ever make teaching at University College Galway. My advice to Nessa would be to grab him while the grabbing is good."

YOU'RE JUST SAYING WHAT SHE WANTS YOU TO SAY.

"Don't I have a mind of my own?"

NO.

"So, you agree with me on that, do you now?"

"Have I ever been known to disagree with you, Mrs. Coyne?"

"Mrs. Coyne is your mother. I'm Nuala, OK?"

"That's right. . . . Hey, I almost forgot. I'm taking a ride up to Michigan City tomorrow morning. I'll be back in time for your singing lesson and then to get ready for the opera tomorrow night."

"I don't want to go to the opera, Dermot Michael. It would be terrible, wouldn't it now, to leave that poor child alone and ourselves over in luxury at the Lyric Opera listening to a bunch of Italians caterwauling all around the stage!"

"Nonetheless, you agreed that we're going to go to the opera. Nessa is all signed up to baby-sit and you can use your magical little telephone between each act."

"They won't let me use it during the opera!"

"Nuala Anne, don't be ridiculous!"

"All right, I'll do what I'm told but I won't enjoy it a single moment worrying about our daughter."

I wasn't sure whether she meant it or not. So before she could continue on that subject, I embraced her and pushed our two bodies together, chest against chest.

"You didn't say why you were going up to Michigan City?" she gasped.

"Oh, I was distracted by this naked woman that's cavorting around in the bathtub with me."

"Whom you're abusing something terrible!"

"Right!" I turned my attention to the most secret wonders of her body. She threw back her head and groaned.

"I called the library up there and asked

whether they had copies of newspapers from one hundred years ago. It turns out that they put them on microfilm back in the early nineties. They did a series of stories on the events of 1898, including the sinking of the *City of Benton Harbor*. I'll take a look at the records. Maybe I'll find something that we've missed."

"Aren't you the greatest detective in all the world!" she moaned.

"What you really mean is that I'm not a half-bad Dr. Watson."

She was in no condition to answer.

I stopped thinking about the mysteries we hadn't solved and concentrated on making the most of the mystery with which I was at the moment involved.

Later I was assigned to brush her hair. She wore a wrap, open of course, but this time without a gown.

INSATIABLE.

"You've noticed."

DON'T YOU THINK SHE'S DOING IT TO MAKE UP FOR THE INTRUSION OF THE CHILD INTO YOUR LIFE?

"So what if she is!"

The next day was clear and cold like the previous one, only much colder. Indeed the temperature when I got up in the morning about seven o'clock to go out to Michigan City was twenty-four degrees. When winter comes to the Midwest, it comes quickly, though not normally so quickly as it did on that October night of 1898.

The people at the Michigan City Library could not have been more helpful. They put me in a room with a viewer and microfiches that contained all the stories in 1898 and 1899 about the sinking of the *City of Benton Harbor* seven miles up the beach from Michigan City.

The journalistic media had advanced greatly in their technological skills in one hundred years. But the obsession with tragedy and heartache had not changed. The *News* contrasted the suffering and the tragedy of the disaster with the courage of the Life Guards in their surf boats and of the young woman who braved the storm to ride her bicycle into Michigan City to alert the Life Guards. Down the same road I presumed that now runs through Long Beach on the edge of the Lake.

The horror stories told by the survivors were heartbreaking. Those young men and women who had lost a lover, sweetheart, partner or spouse, or a child, were lacerated by agony which would last all their lives.

"I want to die. I want to go back and throw myself into the Lake."

"What's the point in going on in life if I've lost the woman I love? The Hibernians are guilty of a terrible crime."

The Hibernians? Why blame them? They were certainly not responsible for the ramming of the ship by a five-masted schooner in the midst of the storm. Nor for the poor maintenance of the ship itself. What was going on?

"I'll always blame the Hibernians for the shipwreck. If they weren't so eager to raise money they wouldn't have organized a cruise this late in the year."

"Thank God my wife and kids are still alive but it is not the Hibernians' fault they survived."

"Nobody in their right mind wants to go on an autumn cruise even if the weather is nice, nobody but your money-hungry AOH."

Oddly, none of these complaints against the Hibernians had appeared in any of the books in my father's library at Grand Beach. The people who wrote the books were probably not interested in Irish revolutionary organizations.

The rescue workers had found a little girl baby on the beach the next morning nearly dead from shock and exposure. They rushed her to the hospital in Michigan City and kept her alive. Nobody knew who she was or who her parents were. It was assumed that her parents died in the wreck. Several weeks later her name came up in a subsequent edition of the *News*. She was the daughter of a Mr. and Mrs. Hill from Detroit who had drowned. She had recovered from the trauma at the Lake. There were no known relatives.

Odd. What was that all about? How many people boarded the ship on the Michigan side at Saugatuck before it struggled back to Chicago? I pulled out of my briefcase a copy of the burials at St. Gabriel's which Father Devlin had printed out for us. Mr. and Mrs. Hill were not among the names of the people who were buried from the parish. They were probably buried in a potter's field in Michigan City. And their little girl? What had happened to her?

There are a few calm days in November before the winter storms. The southeast corner of the Lake usually turns to ice in late November or early December. Vast ice dunes appear offshore, created by the prevailing wind driving waves up against the beach. Salvage operations could not start normally until March or April, if then. An expert on salvage in Michigan City said that he very much doubted there would be anything to salvage because the ship had for all practical purposes broken its back. Only driftwood and small remnants of people's possessions were still out there.

Driftwood? Would there still be bits of driftwood around one hundred years after the wreck?

In the summer of 1899, there were, according to the news stories, major attempts at salvage. Salvage barges anchored off the Michigan/Indiana border searched for the relics of the *City of Benton Harbor*. The paper carried faded pictures of the barges taken from the beach, three of them strung out about one hundred yards offshore, with divers in old-fashioned diving gear going up and coming down. It didn't look from the pictures like they'd found very much.

Then came the show stopper.

"Thomas Doolan of Chicago, a survivor of

the wreck, was supervising the salvage work. He told the press, 'Many of us lost loved ones in the wreck. I myself lost a little girl. They found her body and we buried her in Mount Olivet Cemetery. We hope that maybe we'll find something else out there under the waters of the Lake that will help us to remember her.' "

Bullshit!

What the hell was going on?!

Whatever Tom Doolan was looking for, he must not have found it. The final article from the summer of 1899 about the salvage operation said it had been discontinued because remnants of the wreck had already been covered by large sandbars.

Or maybe he had found what he was looking for. Or didn't find what he hoped he would not find.

As the elderly man said in Michael's Bar and Tap, "It's always money, isn't it?"

It cost a lot of money to mount a salvage operation even for somebody who had a lot of money. What could have been worth poking around on the bottom of Lake Michigan if it wasn't money?

We were, I thought, beginning to get at

not a solution to the mystery but a definition of it.

I printed out copies of the relevant articles for Nuala.

On the way back to Chicago I stopped at the Chicago Historical Society and bought books by Louise Wade and Thomas Jablonski about Packingtown, as the area around the Union Stockyards was called. Perhaps they would contain something about the Hibernians and their activities in and at the end of the last century. I would read the books the next day, I promised myself. But the next day was a lot busier than we were expecting it would be.

Nuala was nursing our daughter when I returned, humming softly to her. Fiona was out in the yard running around and barking at falling leaves.

"If you're real good, Dermot Michael, I think there might be a tiny drop left for you."

"I'll be real good."

"Didn't your sister call me while you were away?"

"Which sister?"

"Wasn't it Cindy?"

"About Maybelline?"

"What else would she call me about?"

My temper flared. I jumped out of the chair and clutched my fists.

"Why the hell is she trying to go behind my back?"

"Will you sit down and stop acting like a shite hawk? Didn't I tell her that five or six times?"

I sat down.

"What did you tell her?"

"I told her that she should talk to you instead of me. Finally she heard what I was saying and apologized."

"Well . . ."

"She asked me if I thought Maybelline was a problem."

"And you said?"

"I said she was a terrorist, that no one should have to put up with her, that I could take care of myself and would in the future. Didn't I say she was Cindy's problem, not mine?"

"Wow," I said softly.

"She agreed, though I don't think she wanted to."

"Well done!"

"What else did you expect?"

There were indeed a few drops of milk left. I was offered some despite my poor performance on the subject of Cindy's phone call. There was enough milk to make me wish I were a baby again.

Nelliecoyne was consigned to her crib and promptly went to sleep.

"Poor little darlin' is not feeling all that well," her mother murmured. "Probably more teeth."

"She seems in a good mood."

"Some of the time."

I gave her the printouts. She read them carefully. Then, as is her custom in such matters, she read them again.

"I don't like it, Dermot Michael," she said as she put the sheets of paper aside.

"I don't either. But I think we have a clearer idea of the mystery, at least the lay of the land."

"I'll have to think about that."

So that evening it came time to go to the opera. While Nuala continued to insist that she did not want to go, she spent an inordinate amount of time preparing herself for the evening. Finally, all the preparations were in order.

Nuala had nursed Nelliecoyne and put her down. The kid's mood was fickle. She was both a bundle of energy who had expended much of her waking hours trying desperately to crawl and at the same time a sullen little brat who seemed to blame us for her discomfort. She cried in protest when we came close to her.

Nessa had arrived with her homework. A bottle of mother's milk was in the fridge. Nuala, dressed in a long black gown with a very high neck and very little back, a thigh-high slit, and a silver belt, was totally gorgeous, as Nessa and I repeated to her at least a dozen times. She had piled her long black hair up on the top of her head and tied it with a matching silver ribbon. She was indeed a perfect picture of a very elegant aristocratic young woman going off to town to weep at the sad story of Violeta.

She put her little telephone in her purse. "Dermot Michael, do you think they might possibly make an exception and let me use this phone while the singing is going on?"

"To quote something you might say to me, Nuala Anne, 'If you think that, you're out of your friggin' mind!' "

She smiled wryly.

"I didn't suppose they would. I really do have to get used to this separation anxiety, don't I, Dermot?" Tears sprang to her eyes.

"What will I ever do when the poor little kid goes off to university!?"

"We'll burn that bridge when we come to it. . . . Most likely sigh with relief."

Mr. Forest's cab pulled up outside and we set off for the opera. Nuala had donned a white cloak. I was wearing a cashmere topcoat that my wife had insisted on buying for me.

We called home twice from the cab and once sitting inside the Lyric before the music started. With a great show of reluctance, Nuala put the phone in my jacket pocket.

"Would you ever protect me from temptation, Dermot love?"

Despite herself, Nuala relaxed, took my hand in hers, and hummed very softly the opening lines of the "Drinking Song."

We were sitting next to a Ted and Florence Genovese, a couple from River Forest about my parents' age. They were quite dazzled by Nuala and impressed, naturally, by our wallet of pictures of Nuala's daughter. We invited them up to the Green Room for a drink between acts. They had white wine, I drank my Baileys, and Nuala was content with iced tea. She made only two calls home during intermission between the second and third acts, which was better than the three she had made between the first and the second acts.

Flo Genovese whispered in my ear, "Dermot, don't worry about her. Every mother is like that with her first child. She'll get over it."

"I'm not so sure I'd bet on that!"

Flo and Ted both laughed.

After the final act and the curtain call—Nuala would never let me leave anytime before the curtain calls were finished—the moment we entered the lobby, she grabbed the phone from my jacket pocket.

Nuala was dismayed, horrified after the exchange of Irish banter.

"You know what she's doing, Dermot Michael?"

"Nessa?"

"No, not poor Nessa. I mean your daughter!"

"She's my daughter so she must be doing something terrible."

"She's awake and she's playing and she refuses to go to sleep."

"Playing at this hour of the night! Nelliecoyne doesn't do that!"

"She's doing it now and I don't think it's

Nessa's fault. I think she knows we're out and she's just having a good time without us."

"Sounds like her."

"Ah," she sighed, "Dermot, we're going to have a terrible, terrible time with that young woman."

"I always said she took after her mother!"

"Amadon," she said, tapping my arm in reproof as I helped her into Mr. Forest's taxi.

On our way back to Southport Avenue, two more phone calls confirmed that indeed Nellie absolutely refused to go to bed and was having a great old time playing with Nessa and the ever cooperative Fiona.

Mr. Forest remained outside the house as Nuala and I went in. He would finish the day by taking Nessa back to her apartment. West Lincoln Park is a safe neighborhood but nobody in their right mind would let a young woman walk any street in Chicago at eleven-thirty at night by herself.

Nessa was at the door as I reached for the lock.

"You'll never believe what she's doing!"

"Is it something awful?"

"You gotta see it for yourself!"

She opened the door wide and there on

the far side of the room with Fiona in attendance, my daughter Mary Anne Coyne, aka Moire Ain Coyne, aka Nelliecoyne, began to crawl across the living-room floor towards us, an enormous grin on her face. Nuala moved as if to run to pick her up, then stopped and hung back.

"Let her show off!" I said.

So unsteadily but persistently, Nellie dragged herself across the floor in our direction, determined to complete her navigation of the room. When she got to Nuala's feet, her mother snapped her up into her arms and burst into tears.

"Nellie, darling," she said, "aren't you the grandest little baby in all the world! So clever, so determined, so happy! Aren't we the lucky ones to have someone like you?"

"I maintained that all along," Nessa informed us.

"Isn't going on eight months a little young to be crawling?" I asked.

"Don't be silly, Dermot Michael! It's early but not too early! Besides, we have a very gifted daughter, as you certainly ought to be able to see for yourself!"

"What you're saying is that your daughter is very gifted!"

"Didn't I just say that very thing?"

And then she began to cry and rock her daughter back and forth. Nellie cuddled in her arms and waited for the lullaby.

"O winds of the night, may your fury be
  crossed,
May no one that's dear to our island be lost,
Blow the winds lightly, calm be the foam,
Shine the light brightly to guide them back
  home.

"Hear the wind blow, hear the wind blow,
Lean your head over, hear the wind blow."

I walked Nessa down to the car and gave her two tickets for a performance of *Traviata* next week.

"Oh, Mr. Coyne, sir, you don't have to do that!"

"Yes, I do, Nessa, because tomorrow morning Nuala will have asked me if I'd got anything for you, especially since you were here with us to celebrate our daughter's creeping crawl. If I hadn't I'd be in deep trouble. Now take this envelope with the opera tickets and go on home."

"Yes, Mr. Coyne."

"Nessa?"

"Yes, sir?"

"If you let that young man get away, you're the worst eejit in the whole West of Ireland."

She giggled happily and climbed into the cab.

In the house my wife continued to weep, tears of sadness and joy, tears of fear and hope. Nelliecoyne fell asleep. Nuala put her in the crib. Then the two of us retired to our own bed, utterly exhausted. She turned off the light and cuddled in my arms. I understood that sex would be inappropriate that night. Anyway I'd had more than enough in the last couple of weeks. Then suddenly Nuala sat up in bed. "Oh, I am a terrible eejit altogether, Dermot Michael! Why didn't you tell me?"

"What didn't I tell you?"

"You didn't tell me to call me poor ma and tell her that her granddaughter was crawling and herself not eight months old."

She grabbed our bedside phone and punched in the numbers that would connect her with the lovely little town on the shore of Galway Bay three thousand miles away. I figured that it was about eight o'clock in the morning in Carraroe and her ma would be wide awake.

Nuala laughed and cried and shouted in Irish, but mostly laughed. She had to talk to her da too. Finally she said good-bye and hung up. Off went the light and she curled up in my arms and wept some more.

"You know what me ma said?"

"No, Nuala, what did your ma say?"

"Didn't she say I was crawling at the same age meself. So isn't Nelliecoyne perfectly normal?"

"Somehow the logic of that thought escapes me."

"Go to sleep, Dermot Michael Coyne, you're a terrible gobshite."

I did go to sleep with no expectations at all of the trouble we'd encounter the next morning.

15

The day started at three-thirty in the morning when Fiona appeared at our bedside barking loudly.

"What's the matter, girl?" I asked. She barked more loudly and then charged off back to the nursery. I followed after her and discovered that our world's champion crawler was crying her eyes out, not screaming angrily as she had done at Grand Beach or on Emerald Avenue, but rather crying steadily and consistently.

"Huh?" I said not too intelligently.

Nuala bounded into the nursery and got

the baby. "Glory be to God, Dermot, the child must be sick!"

"You don't think it's the teeth?"

"Not with the way she's crying—oh! what are we going to do?"

I put my hand on Nellie's forehead. It was quite warm.

"Nuala, I think she might have a fever!"

"A fever!" she shouted. "How could she ever get a fever!"

She ran to the bathroom and came back with a baby thermometer which confirmed that our little princess did indeed have a fever of 102.

Nuala wailed more loudly than her daughter. And the wolfhound, clearly distressed at the proceedings, barked anxiously.

"We might call a doctor."

"Wherever are we going to find a doctor at this time of night, Dermot Michael?"

"I'll call her pediatrician."

After some panicky stumbling around we got the man's answering service.

Nuala kind of lost it. She was moaning in Irish, prayers or curses or arguably both.

Then I had an idea.

"I think there's a pretty good chance we'll

find a doctor at the end of my parents' telephone line." I picked up the phone and punched in a code number for Dr. Patrick Coyne.

"Hello," my mom said sleepily. "This is Dr. Coyne's house."

"Mom, this is Dermot, we are looking for a doctor."

"A doctor?" she said in some surprise.

"My father, your husband. Our little daughter has a fever and her mother is terribly upset."

"Dermot, remember it's that way with the first child."

She handed her phone over to my dad and I gave ours to Nuala. I slipped into the nursery where, naturally, there was another phone and picked it up.

"It's 102," my wife moaned. "She's terrible sick, Dr. Coyne. Should we bring her over to the hospital?"

"You could probably give her better treatment than she'd receive in some of the emergency rooms around your part of the city."

"Whatever should we do!"

"I tell you what, Nuala, why don't you touch her ears and see how she reacts?"

"Do you think she's losing her hearing?"

My father suppressed a laugh, "No, but I suspect she probably has an ear infection. There's a lot of those going around just now."

That is the most frequent opinion doctors give. There is always something going around.

"I just touched her left ear," Nuala said cautiously. "And she didn't cry any worse."

"All right," my father said, "now try touching the other ear."

Nelliecoyne's wail shook the whole house. Fiona howled in protest.

"I heard that on the phone line," Dad observed. "Dermot, is that Osco pharmacy down at Webster Place open twenty-four hours?"

"It is, Dad," I said. "You call in a prescription and I'll go down and get it."

"That'll do it. It's an antibiotic that we use for children with ear infections. It works very effectively but sometimes it takes a day or two. Keep taking her temperature, see that she gets a lot of liquid. And call me later in the day or tomorrow whichever day today is."

Through her tears Nuala thanked my father from the bottom of her heart.

I wondered what would happen when the little girl really got sick.

I trotted down to the Osco, picked up the prescription that they had ready, trotted back, and gave the precious, lifesaving bottle to my wife, who carefully spooned two teaspoonfuls of it into Nelliecoyne's mouth.

Our daughter wanted no part of it. She waved the spoon off and spit the liquid out.

"Dermot, she won't take it! Whatever are we going to do!"

"Give me the bottle, Nuala," I said confidently. "They make this stuff sweet so babies like it once they get the first taste of it."

I bent over the kid with the spoon in my hand.

"Now listen here, young woman, you are going to take this stuff because it's going to make you better. I'll put up with none of your foolishness, do you hear?"

Nelliecoyne, surprised at the tone of my voice, looked up at me, her mouth open. I immediately poured the two spoonfuls into her mouth.

"Now swallow!"

She discovered that the liquid didn't taste bad at all and decided to do what I told her.

"See," I said to my wife, "your daughter knows who she has to really listen to in this house!"

"Och, Dermot Michael, she just got a taste of how sweet it is! Look at her licking her lips! She wants more!"

"She won't get more for three more hours."

We also gave her two teaspoons of the liquid aspirin which was waiting for me when I picked up the prescription. That also must have tasted sweet because Nelliecoyne managed a faint smile.

"There's no point in both of us losing a night's sleep," I said. "You and Fiona stay here for a couple of hours, I'll go back to bed. I'll spell the two of you about five o'clock."

I slept quickly enough, confident that Dr. Coyne knew what he was talking about.

When I awakened at a quarter to five, the child was sleeping restlessly.

"She seems better, Dermot Michael," Nuala informed me anxiously.

"She's at least not wailing. Fiona seems to think she's better because she has gone to sleep too. Now you take a nap. I'll wake you if there's any sign of her fever going back up."

Nuala hadn't taken the child's temperature for fear that it would be higher. So I took it and discovered that it was down under a hundred. I reflected briefly on how hard it must have been for parents of children in the days before antibiotics and children's aspirin.

Nuala woke up in an hour, checked out the child's temperature, which was now down to ninety-nine, and decided that it was now time to feed her.

"Best let her sleep for a while. Why don't you do your run and go to Mass. Then we'll see if she's hungry."

Nuala did as I suggested. I had established myself as an expert when dealing with sick little girls.

So as the sun popped up over the edge of the sky, something it was doing later each day now, much to my dismay, Nuala and Fiona departed for their sunrise run. Out of deference to the laws of the City of Chicago, Fiona was attached to a long leash. She didn't like it, but sensible canine that she was, she adapted herself to it, most of the time running at Nuala's speed.

I began to make breakfast—Mueslix, blueberries, orange juice, dry toast, and a strong pot of tea. Without milk, sugar, or lemon.

After I had set the table, I walked into the parlor and I looked out the window. My wife and my wolfhound were running back in our direction, two elegant and confident females. They paused at the door of St. Josephat's Church while Nuala debated whether it would be better for her to go into Mass and pray for Nelliecoyne or to dash into the house. Faith won. She chose the church. The wolfhound accompanied her as she always did.

The pastor of the parish and Nuala had not exactly hit it off. He could not figure her out and she thought he was a "gobshite." Nor did he like our snow-white wolfhound sitting at the back of his church during the first morning Mass. However, Fiona was very well behaved in church, curling up next to Nuala's pew and falling asleep. The priest knew that he would get absolutely nowhere by trying to forbid Nuala to take the dog into the church.

The phone rang.

"Dermot Michael Coyne."

"Cindy."

My sister was in her lawyer mode.

"Ah, Cindy, you heard about Nelliecoyne's sickness. She seems to be recovering."

"No, Dermot, I didn't hear about it. I'm glad she is getting better but I'm calling because . . . have you heard the news this morning?"

I confessed that I had not.

"Your good friend Nick Farmer was shot last night coming out of some bar in Evanston."

"That's too bad. Did he survive?"

"Apparently he did. They're saying at Evanston Hospital that he is in serious but stable condition. That means that he will live."

"I'll be a good Christian and say I'm glad of that."

"The problem, Dermot, is that he claims that you and Nuala are the ones that shot him."

"What!"

"Apparently when the patrons in the bar poured out to see what had happened he was screaming that the two of you were responsible. I suspect the Evanston Police will try to question you. Do you have an alibi?"

"Alibi?" I asked, astonished that I needed one.

"Dermot," Cindy said efficiently, "where were you and Nuala last night?"

"We went to the opera."

"*La Traviata,* wasn't it?"

"Yeah, it was superb."

"That's almost three and a half hours?"

"Something like that, it started at seven-thirty and we were out by eleven and home here by eleven-thirty."

Cindy sighed with relief.

"I suppose you saw people there that you know?"

"Sure, Ted and Flo Genovese sat right next to us. As a matter of fact, they joined us between the acts for a drink in the Green Room. Or the Graham Room as I guess we must call it now. They can testify to our presence at the Lyric Opera for the entire length of the performance. Mr. Forest picked us up and drove us home. We were back home I suppose a little before eleven-thirty."

"That's all we need, Dermot. Farmer was shot coming out of the bar at about ten o'clock. The Evanston Police will probably come after you. They'll figure they're under pressure to look like they're doing something because Farmer is a media figure, however lowly. You don't talk to them unless I'm present and unless somebody from the Chicago Police Department is present, and unless Mike Casey is present. Got it?"

Mike Casey presided over Reliable Security, a firm which I employed periodically to protect Nuala and myself from the real crazies, like renegade Irish revolutionaries. He was the former Acting Superintendent of the Chicago Police Department, an author of a standard textbook on criminal investigation procedures, and now a famous artist.

"I got it, Cindy. Do you think they'll show up, without Chicago cops?"

"Sure they will, the media are going to be all over there. They'll want to look like they're acting swiftly. Don't trust them."

"OK, I'll keep you informed."

I heard a lot of noise outside and walked from the kitchen into the parlor and glanced outside. It looked like every television channel in Chicago had camped on Southport Avenue with trucks, minicameras, and cars halfway to Webster. This we did not need, especially on a day when our little girl was sick.

Then as I watched, Nuala emerged from St. Josephat's. She stopped in dismay when she saw the crowd around her house. Fiona strained at her leash. She didn't like the crowd of people in front of her house.

Deftly Nuala walked across the street weaving her way among cameramen and reporters, the wolfhound now on a very short leash.

I ran to the door and threw it open. "There she is," someone shouted. The cameramen wheeled and journalists with their microphones in their hands rushed towards Nuala. This, I said to myself, was going to be very interesting.

Fiona barked, an angry bark that indicated she was not yet ready to start a fight. Several reporters, noting the dog's size, hesitated, but one bold woman jammed her microphone at Nuala's mouth and shouted, "Did you really shoot Nick Farmer last night, Nuala?"

That was too much for the dog. Her admonitory bark turned into a menacing growl followed by the wolfhound's favorite sound effect: a howl that suggested thousands of years of angry wolfhound bitches fighting off threats to somebody who was in their charge. The reporter retreated quickly. Our Fiona would have snatched the mike from her hand.

"No, Fiona, no," Nuala informed the wolfhound. "It's all right."

Fiona wasn't so sure. She went through the motions of struggling against the leash as if to chase the frightened young journalist.

"You'd better stay away from me," Nuala warned the members of the media, crusaders for the people's right to know in thirty-second sound bites. "Fiona is a very gentle dog. She likes people a lot but not when they seem to be threatening me. If you don't back off I can't promise you what she may do. She was a police guard dog in Ireland before we adopted her and she has some very strong instincts about what to do to people who seem to be attacking her friends."

That was a remarkably contained speech, I thought, from a woman who had a sick daughter in the house and now found herself surrounded by half-wits.

Calmly and confidently and not pulling on

the leash, she walked in the door to the house. I slammed it shut.

"Dermot Michael, whatever in the holy hell is going on? Why are all them gobshites out there?"

"Somebody took a shot at Nick Farmer last night. Cindy called me when you were in church. Farmer is blaming us for it. We are not to say anything to the Evanston Police until Cindy, a Chicago cop, probably John Culhane, and Mike Casey are here with us."

"But, Dermot, we didn't shoot the poor man!"

"He claimed we did. It's one more way for him to get publicity, perhaps a chance for him to get his television slot back."

"Whatever shall we do?"

"First thing we'll do is eat our breakfast, then we'll see if your troublesome daughter is well enough to have something to eat, and then we'll wait for the Evanston cops to show up. Maybe I'll get some time to write my report on Louise Wade's and Thomas Jablonski's books."

Nuala was nursing Nelliecoyne when the Evanston cops showed up. I opened the door cautiously, my hand firmly gripping Fiona's collar.

"Yes?" I said tentatively.

"I'm Lieutenant Knox of the Evanston Police," the taller cop said.

The shorter and fat one added, "And I'm Sergeant McKechnie. We're both in Evanston Homicide."

"Kind of out of your jurisdiction, aren't you?"

Fiona growled, a long plaintive and threatening growl.

"Is that dog dangerous?" Lieutenant Knox asked nervously.

"Sometimes. It depends on who she is growling at. She's a retired police dog from Ireland. She took a very early retirement. Now what can I do for you gentlemen?"

"We are here to ask you some questions regarding the shooting of a Mr. Nicholas Farmer on Chicago Avenue in Evanston last night."

"How interesting."

"Mr. Farmer asserts that you and your wife were the perpetrators of the shooting."

There must have been an especially sinister tone in his voice because Fiona's growl got louder and her strain against my hand more vigorous. She wouldn't break away unless I let her and she wouldn't leap on either of these two jerks unless I told her to do so. But the growl caused them both to back off a foot or two.

"I find it interesting that you are here outside of your own jurisdiction, as far as I can tell, without the presence of a Chicago police officer."

"It would be better for all concerned if we got to the bottom of this allegation of Mr. Farmer's quickly."

"I'm sure my lawyer wouldn't agree. Her name is Cynthia Hurley. You call her and she'll make arrangements for you to interview us at a time of her and our convenience."

Their faces both grew hard, like the cops on TV.

"You may regret this, Mr. Coyne," the sergeant said. "Regret it a lot."

"Good day, gentlemen, we will see you later when you follow the standards of appropriate police procedure in this kind of matter."

I closed the door firmly in their faces, an action which was followed by one of Fiona's loudest howls of protest. That would teach the Evanston cops a lesson.

Behind me Nuala was standing, holding a softly whining Nelliecoyne.

"Och, Dermot Michael, weren't you wonderful now!"

"I thought Fiona was more wonderful than I was. Did herself have anything to eat?"

"At first she wasn't interested but then she started to think 'oh milk again' and then, Dermot Michael, to tell you the truth, she's got something of her appetite back. What time is it? Oh, God, it's time for me to give her the medicine and hadn't I forgotten that altogether?"

So Nelliecoyne was given her medicine and put back in bed. After considerable unhappy protest, she decided maybe it would be a good thing to have a nap to make up for the sleep she had lost the night before.

I had one of my more insidious ideas. I opened the front door of the house and walked out to face the assembled media, a challenge which after a number of incidents I rather enjoy. I'm not very bright, but I'm brighter than they are.

"Dermot, do you and your wife have an alibi?" one of the half-wits demanded.

"An alibi?"

"Where were you last night when poor Nick Farmer was shot?"

"Is this gathering in honor of Nick Farmer?"

"He made certain allegations as he was taken off to the hospital."

"Allegations indeed?"

"Where were you last night at ten o'clock, Dermot?"

"I refused to answer that question to the police because they weren't following proper procedures. They should have come with a Chicago policeman since this neighborhood is out of their jurisdiction. I told them that they should talk to my attorney and find a Chicago cop to accompany them. When an appropriate time is agreed on, we'll be happy to answer their questions."

"Were you anywhere near Evanston last night?"

The young man must have thought he was Sam Donaldson.

"Only if the Lyric Opera of Chicago has been moved to Evanston."

"You were at the opera?"

"Indeed we were—from seven o'clock till eleven-thirty. And, yes, there were people there who could identify us, indeed the people we sat next to joined us in the Graham Room during intermissions. Any more questions?"

"What about Nick Farmer's allegations?"

I shrugged. "They are probably actionable, though I don't think we'll take any action."

I turned on my heel and, supremely satisfied with myself, walked back into the house.

Nuala had been standing close to the door listening to my performance.

"Sure, Dermot Michael, weren't you wonderful with them gobshites! We have our denial and our alibi on the record before them nine-fingered shite-hawk Evanston cops come back!"

"Piece of cake," I said as though I were an old hand in fending off the media.

"Dermot, isn't it terrible cold outside this morning? And them poor folks up so early? And doesn't it look like they have no coffee or tea or anything to eat? Why don't I make them some soda bread and some coffee and tea?"

That I thought would be a wonderful idea—ashes on their heads. It would also provide me with a chance to consume some of her world-class soda bread.

A half hour later, as the media folks shivered in the premature November cold, Nuala and I walked out with trays filled with soda bread. We returned to the house and came out again, this time with coffee and tea and paper cups. Nuala, against my strong advice, supplied butter and jam for the soda bread.

"Sure, they're only Yanks. They don't know you should never put jam on soda bread!"

Our visitors were astonished. They thanked us with something which, for media halfwits, came close to shamed faces.

"Isn't it what we should be giving to folks whose jobs get them up so early on a cold morning?" Nuala said, complacent in her virtue.

" 'Tis," I perforce agreed.

Generally reporters are not much into looking sheepish. However, when we arrived with their breakfasts they did look a little sheepish. Their mildly hangdog expressions were replaced by visages of pure delight when their teeth sank into Nuala Anne's soda bread, warm soda bread with butter and an extra layer of strawberry jam. Naturally, she put a piece into my mouth with her now expected alluring Eucharistic Minister smile.

We had left the door ajar when we came out with their breakfasts and who should parade out after us in all her canine glory but Fiona the wolfhound. She surveyed the crowd of media people, and having decided they couldn't be hostile or we wouldn't be feeding them, she ambled out to walk in her domain. At first they were frightened of her—who wouldn't be frightened of such a massive dog? They quickly discovered that all she wanted to do was be friends. So they patted her affectionately as she wandered about accepting their admiration and veneration.

"What would have happened," the young woman who had poked the microphone at Nuala asked me, "if I hadn't pulled back the mike when your dog growled at me?"

"If you were lucky she would have just taken the mike," I said.

"And if I wasn't lucky?"

"Then she might have taken your hand."

The young woman recoiled in horror. At that same moment Fiona chose to nudge her in a request for affection. The woman reached down and patted the dog's huge head.

Actually, I don't think Fiona would have chewed the woman's hand unless she'd been told to. Nonetheless, it is not wise to mess around with Irish wolfhounds, especially when they have been trained as police dogs.

The pastor of St. Josephat's emerged from his rectory to survey the scene. Fiona walked over to greet him. He did his best to ignore her, which is difficult when Fiona is determined that she wants to make friends with you.

"There always seems to be a lot of media activity around here, Mr. Coyne," he said. "We've had more since you moved in than we had in all the years before you arrived."

"Father," I said, "it must be nice to see a picture of your church on television."

He had a number of good reasons for not liking us. We went to Mass on Sunday at Old St. Patrick's because Nuala sang in the choir. We had a close relationship with the Cathedral, where my brother was on the staff and our friend the little Bishop presided. We were notoriously good friends with Cardinal Sean Cronin. However, we did contribute substantially to St. Josephat's and it would be most unlikely that our children would be barred from the school.

With a sniff of disapproval, he turned around and walked back into the rectory, the lord of the manor dismayed by the disorder in front of his castle.

The TV mob departed later in the morning. Their news directors must have decided that there was no more good footage on Southport Avenue.

16

After the media people left, disaster over-
took our family. Nuala became ill.

This was an absolutely unique event, because, save for morning sickness, Nuala
protested that she had never been sick a
day in her life. This day she, however,
was really sick. She had caught whatever
bug was affecting our daughter and was
promptly laid low by it.

"I feel dizzy, Dermot Michael," she said as
we returned to the house with the remnants
of our take-out breakfasts. "I feel like I'm
gonna collapse."

She did just that in my arms. I helped her

lie down on the couch in our parlor and felt her forehead. It wasn't as warm as the child's had been the night before but it was still warmer than it should be.

"I'm very much afraid that my daughter has infected you," I concluded.

"Then we'll just have to give her away to somebody who has more immunities than I do!"

"Do you want me to call the doctor?"

"Oh, please do, Dermot Michael, before I perish with the bug, sure, I'm not long for this world!"

When Nuala was sick, even with morning sickness, she also became very funny. There would be a lot of laughing in the next couple of days. I didn't care, I wanted my healthy Nuala back.

I called her internist and her OB doctor. Neither of them was available. Naturally. So I called my father.

"Couldn't find her real doctors, huh, Dermot?"

"Yup."

"I figured I'd hear from you this morning. That's the way these family epidemics start. One of the kids gets it, then the other kids get it, then the mother gets it, and then finally the father gets it."

"You'd better order prescriptions or whatever for me too."

"It's something they never warn you about when you decide to have children. You just have to take it for granted that you are going to be sick about half the time. I'll call the prescriptions in to your local Osco."

So I trotted down to the drugstore again, collected two bottles of each, and brought them back to the house. Nuala had not stirred from the couch on which she had collapsed. Fiona, anxious about the mysterious behavior of her mistress, stood next to her, feeling perhaps it would be more useful to watch her this morning than to watch the child.

"How is Nelliecoyne doing, girl?" I asked the dog.

At the word *Nelliecoyne* she bounded up the stairs, at about the same speed Nuala would bound, and with the same amount of noise, to check on the baby.

"Are you awake, Nuala Anne?"

"I'm not awake, Dermot Michael. Haven't I died and gone to heaven? Promise you'll take good care of me daughter and me dog."

"I brought the medicine."

" 'Tis too late altogether for medicine. I'm not long for this world."

I made her take medicine just the same.

"Nuala, you'd better come upstairs and go to bed. You're not doing yourself or anybody else any good down here. You have to get as much rest as you can."

"Dermot Michael, would you ever make me a hot toddy with Irish whiskey and lemonade?"

I helped her up and led her to the stairs.

"Nuala, there is no medical evidence that such concoctions can heal viral infections."

"Och, sure, Dermot Michael, I know that. But it kills the pain. You don't notice how sick you really are!"

So I walked her upstairs and put her to bed.

"I should be nursing your baby, shouldn't I, and meself on me last legs?"

"When she wakes up, I'll bring her in."

"She is responsible for it all. Why didn't they warn me that babies do this kind of thing to you!"

"Weren't you after doing it to your own ma?"

"Och, Dermot," she confessed, "I did indeed. 'Tis a wonder the poor woman didn't throw me out into the bog!"

"I don't think there is any danger of us taking Nelliecoyne over to the Chicago River and dumping her in."

"You know, Dermot Michael, at a time like this, that doesn't seem to me to be a half-bad idea! Now would you ever please go off and make me a hot toddy."

I was leaving the bedroom when she shouted after me, "Dermot, unless I'm delirious, more so than usual, didn't your sister Cindy call and say that the police were going to be here at two o'clock this afternoon?"

"Two o'clock this afternoon. We'll get it over with and settle back to healing whatever ails you."

I glanced in the nursery. Our daughter was awake and not in a particularly happy mood but she didn't seem to be hungry.

"All that will have to happen, Fiona girl," I said to our wolfhound, "is for you to get sick. I'd be taking care of all three of you!"

So I made a hot toddy—which broke all of Nuala's rules about what she should drink when she was nursing—and brought it up to her.

"Hadn't I better feed the little monster before I drink this, Dermot?"

So I went to the nursery, picked up Nellie,
who was not happy at my disturbing her,
and carried her into the bedroom. She drank
her late morning's milk, however, with her
accustomed vigor.

"She seems to be on the mend, Nuala," I
observed.

"I hope she's happy that she's getting better and her mother all but half dead. I don't
care about what this kid will do for her next
feeding. Maybe she'll have to go hungry
and, sure, won't that serve her right!"

"Drink your hot toddy, woman, and go to
sleep."

Before she went to sleep she muttered,
"Dermot Michael, what will I ever do when
them constables come?"

"What you'll do, Nuala Anne, is get up and
answer their questions and go right back to
bed."

Cindy and Mike Casey appeared promptly
at two o'clock.

"I saw on the twelve o'clock news that
you'd got your alibi out on the record, Dermot," my sister said. "That was very clever."

Cindy, a slender, blond, good-looking

woman in her early forties, had to go into the nursery and investigate Nellie's condition. Fiona, who adored Cindy, insisted on licking her face before she went up the stairs.

"Is your little girl sick, Fiona?" she said, hugging the dog. "She'll be well in a little while."

Mike Casey, a tall, slim man, just turned seventy, sat down in one of our Victorian chairs and accepted my offer of a cup of tea. He was impeccably dressed in a blue Italian suit which set off his silver hair and his lean, handsome face. He looked like the late Basil Rathbone playing Sherlock Holmes in the old movies.

"A lot of cops will try to do what those two guys tried to do this morning, Dermot," he said. "They know they shouldn't but they always hope they can get away with it."

"They might have, if Cindy hadn't called us. They don't have a thing on us. We have the perfect excuse."

"Still, they'll want to come and question you if only to give the impression that they're seriously searching for the would-be assassin, if there is a would-be assassin. It should only take a couple of minutes."

Our doorbell rang. I opened it and the two Evanston cops stood there, both doing their best to look stern and responsible.

"You have time for us now, Mr. Coyne?"

"The lawyers are both here but we'll have to wait for a representative of the Chicago Police Department."

"May we come in?"

I looked back at Cindy, who had just come down the stairs from the nursery. She nodded.

"You may," I said.

Cindy began the conversation by remarking on the elementary professional standards that cops are supposed to follow when they go out of their jurisdiction. The two cops said nothing in response. What could they say? They knew the rules. Their boss had told them to forget the rules.

I introduced Mike as Mr. Casey, so they didn't know that they were facing one of the most influential cops in America.

A blue and white Chicago police car rolled up to the door. John Culhane, Area Six Commander, emerged briskly. I opened our door and let him in.

"Dermot Coyne," he said with a big grin, "what are you and that beautiful wife getting yourself into now? We haven't had any trouble from you for almost a year. I was beginning to wonder if you'd moved back to Ireland."

"Hi, Superintendent," John said to Mike Casey. "Nice to see you again. You're looking as fit and happy as ever."

"So do you, my friend. Glad to see you're still working out every day."

"There are days I don't work out. Like when I get involved with this dangerous duo."

John was about fifty, trim, muscular, good-looking, with rimless glasses and sandy hair closely trimmed, very much the ex-Marine that he was. And one of the finest cops in Chicago.

He turned to the two Evaston policemen who were standing awkwardly.

"Lieutenant Knox," said the tall cop.

"Sergeant McKechnie," said the short one nervously.

"It would have been better if you'd called us first," John said, as he declined their handshakes.

"It's a murder investigation," said Knox. "We thought that it might be appropriate to question the Coynes because of our haste to resolve the problem. Sorry to have offended you."

"Attempted murder," Cindy corrected him.

"Next time, call," John said tersely.

"I suppose we can begin our discussion," Cindy took charge of the gathering. "You might as well ask your questions, Lieutenant Knox."

"Now, Mr. Coyne, we are here to ask if you know anything about the shooting last night of the music critic, Mr. Nicholas Farmer."

"Lieutenant," Cindy interrupted, "I can't imagine a more amateurish way of beginning an interview. I instruct my clients to ignore the question."

Nessa was in the nursery with Nellie. Fiona was out in the yard chasing falling leaves and barking at them. Nuala sat in the old rocking chair, perhaps in the same place Laetitia Walsh often occupied back in the nineteenth century. She was wearing jeans and her beloved Marquette University sweatshirt and looking very, very pale.

"Next question, Lieutenant," Cindy demanded.

"Mr. Coyne, would you account for your

movements last night, say between seven
o'clock and eleven o'clock?"

"I would be happy to."

Casting myself as the hero in one of my
novels, I recited our story and provided the
names of Flo and Ted Genovese, Peter Forest, and Nessa O'Toole.

"What are their phone numbers?" Mc-
Kechnie asked as he jotted rapidly in his
notebook.

"You don't expect, do you, Lieutenant, to
get that kind of information from my client?"
Cindy scoffed. "Do your police work and find
out the phone numbers for yourself."

"Mrs. Coyne, you carried a handheld telephone with you at the opera last night, did
you not?"

Nuala stared blankly out in space.

"Mrs. Coyne?" he said again.

"Nuala Anne," I said, "he means you."

"Och, are you talking to me now?" Nuala
Anne stirred a bit in the rocker. "Don't I always think of Dermot's mother when someone says that name? What were you
asking?"

"You are reported as having a handheld
telephone in the opera last night."

Big deal discovery. Someone had called

that in to him after seeing me on the noon news. Were we supposed to be frightened?

"Sure, but I only used it during the intermissions!" Nuala strongly protested. "I didn't break any laws, I didn't disturb the concert with the phone!"

I couldn't tell whether she was serious or whether she was just having them on. Probably both.

"May I ask who you were calling that often on your portable phone?"

"Is eight times often, Lieutenant?" I asked.

"We will return to that, Mr. Coyne."

"Why can't Mrs. Coyne use her telephone at intermissions during an opera?" Cindy cut in. "Are you implying that she might have been in touch with someone involved in the shooting of Mr. Farmer?"

"We have to investigate every possibility, Counselor."

"Anyway, it was nine phone calls, Dermot, not eight."

Wrong again!

"And who were those phone calls to?"

"Wasn't I calling our baby-sitter to see how our little girl was doing while we were at the opera?"

"Nine times?"

"That's enough, Officer," Cindy said impersonally. "It is no business of yours how many times Mrs. Coyne checks on her daughter's health."

"It does seem to be a lot of phone calls."

"Do you have children, Officer?"

He ignored the cross-exam.

"Would you tell us your phone numbers, both here and on your portable phone, so that we could check that out, Mrs. Coyne?"

"She certainly will not, Officer," Cindy exploded. "Do your own police work and find out the numbers yourself. When you check the records, I'm sure you will discover that all of Mrs. Coyne's phone calls were indeed to this house."

The lieutenant squirmed. He wasn't getting anyplace and didn't have any idea where he wanted to go.

"Mr. Coyne, are you acquainted with any persons involved in organized crime?"

"Officer, do you really have to think I'm such an incompetent attorney that I would permit you to ask such a question? What do you mean by 'involved with' and what do you mean by 'organized crime' and what do you mean by 'acquainted with'?"

"I'll try to be clear."

"Mr. Coyne, do you know any Mafia hit men?"

"We call them Outfit here in the big city," John Culhane murmured.

"One more question like that, Officer, and I'll terminate this interview," Cindy said with icy menace in her voice.

"Counselor, the injured man alleges that Mr. and Mrs. Coyne were involved in the attempt on his life. They have supplied us with information that would lead us to suspect that they were not physically present at the time of the shooting . . ."

"Leads you to suspect," Cindy snorted. "Officer, you have got to be kidding!"

"Therefore we must pursue other possibilities. Mr. Farmer must certainly have reasons to suspect your clients' involvement or he would not have made the accusation."

"Officer, I'm not going to take that issue seriously."

"I will change the question, Counselor. Mr. Coyne, do you know of any reasons why Mr. Farmer would make these allegations against you?"

"None whatever."

"Yet he has made these allegations?"

"Instead of asking Mr. Coyne for Mr. Farmer's reasons, Lieutenant, you might ask Mr. Farmer. If he doesn't have any evidence, then he may be guilty of defamation."

"Mr. Farmer insists that your clients are responsible for his dismissal from his television job."

"He better have something more than an allegation like that, Officer. Dermot, you may answer that if you want."

"The implied question being whether we tried to get Nicholas Farmer fired from his television slot?"

"Yes, something like that."

"We did not," I replied, trying to suppress my grin.

"He thinks you did."

"He thinks wrong."

"Do you know anything about the attempt on Mr. Farmer's life?"

I was becoming more angry than I should have.

"All that I know I've heard on television. It makes no sense to me at all. I have no idea who might have wounded him last night or why they might."

"And if I could add a word," Cindy interjected, "you would be much better advised to spend your time trying to find out who the people were that drove up in the car and fired the actual shot at Mr. Farmer."

"Shots, Counselor."

"From what distance?" Mike Casey joined the conversation for the first time.

Lieutenant Knox glared at him.

"Who the hell are you anyway?"

Mike ignored him.

Knox gritted his teeth and answered the question.

"Maybe ten feet. The car pulled up right along the curb."

"And how many shots?"

"Three."

Mike sighed, "Lieutenant Knox, have you ever had any experience investigating possible contract killings?"

Knox shifted uneasily.

"We don't have many such in Evanston, sir."

"Let me tell you two things about Outfit contract killers. They don't miss. And they don't fire shots recklessly. If this was indeed an Outfit hit, it was very unprofessional. The hit man will wait a long time for another contract."

"I see," said the lieutenant, not altogether sure whether he should take Mike seriously.

"Were other people standing around?" Mike continued.

"Farmer was standing outside with three friends, a man and two women."

"The car, a late-model Saab according to the press, simply pulled up and apparently someone fired three shots?"

"That is what the witnesses say."

"It has none of the marks at all of a contract killing," Mike Casey said, shaking his head and sitting back on his chair. "It was an amateur job, almost as amateur as this investigation is. Besides, the Outfit doesn't drive Saabs."

"What did you say your name was, sir?" Sergeant McKechnie asked. "So we can have your full name for our records."

"Michael Patrick Vincent Casey." Mike gave his name slowly with emphasis on each word.

Sergeant McKechnie looked up from his notes, pencil in hand. "The man who wrote the book?"

"Indeed, Sergeant, the man who wrote the book. I would recommend to you that you might reread it sometime soon."

"Och," my wife spoke up. "Things are never what they seem, are they now?"

308 ANDREW M. GREELEY

"What do you mean, Nuala dear?" Cindy asked.

"Isn't it clear what happened? Things never are what they seem to most people."

"And why is that?" Lieutenant Knox asked, baffled by the pale oracle.

"The shots weren't supposed to hit poor Mr. Farmer. The shots were supposed to miss him. The man with the gun made a mistake. It's a lucky thing that he didn't kill poor Mr. Farmer or somebody else who was standing nearby. The story is not about an assassination or an attempted assassination. This story is a fake assassination that was bungled. Isn't it clear as the nose on all your faces that the whole thing was a fake? Then go into the hospital room and ask Mr. Farmer why he tried to fake his own assassination and he'll break down and admit it."

John Culhane glanced at Mike Casey. Mike smiled back.

"Any time she wants to stop singing she can have a job at Reliable Security."

"Not if the Chicago P.D. gets there first."

Nuala was staring blankly off into space.

"You're all out of your friggin' minds," she said.

Cindy intervened.

"I think I'm going to call this interview to an end. It is a pointless waste of time for the Coynes and for the rest of us. I'm going to notify the ethics board at the Evanston Police Department that this was an utterly unprofessional interview."

"And I will call your Chief of Police and tell him that he shouldn't have sent boys to do a man's job," Mike Casey added.

The two cops left quietly.

"They should follow up on Nuala's suggestion," I said.

"They will," John Culhane replied. "It's too good an idea to pass up."

Mike Casey stood up to leave with the Commander.

"Your guys, John, could clean this up in no time. Nuala is absolutely right that it smells of a fake. All they have to do is find out who Nick Farmer knows that might agree to a trick like this."

"Why were they so dumb?" Nuala asked as John and Mike were leaving the house.

Mike turned and smiled gently.

"When you are as old as I am, Nuala Anne, you'll realize that there are a lot of dumb people around."

"Is it over, Dermot Michael?" Nuala asked.

"I must go back to my bed and prepare for the end with one last hot toddy . . . would you ever bring me one, please?"

"You certainly helped to solve another problem," Cindy said softly.

"Which problem?"

"Maybelline."

"What!" I cried in disbelief.

"Apparently she called here to harass Nuala about something."

"Terrorize."

"I grant you the word. And Nuala told her off."

"Twice," my darling wife, obsessed with precision even in her sickness, corrected Cindy. "I was terrible altogether."

"And very effective. She was hysterical when your brother came home and asked him whether he thought she might need psychiatric help."

"Impossible!"

"Impossible, Dermot, but true. So I guess you and George are not going to have to secede from the family."

"They never would," Nuala remarked.

"It's too early to predict what's going to happen but it's a beginning. She called all the women in the family and told them that she's going to try to straighten out her life."

"I'll be damned," I said in astonishment.

"No you won't, Dermot Michael, I'll be up there right next to St. Peter's computer defending you against all the charges just like Cindy defended us this afternoon."

SEE, said the Adversary. WHAT DID I TELL YOU? THAT ONE CAN TAKE CARE OF HERSELF.

17

It was fun to minister to Nuala while she was sick. I didn't enjoy the sickness and I didn't enjoy her dependency but I did enjoy the opportunity to be nice to her. I enjoyed bringing her hot soup and her pot of tea and her hot whiskey toddy.

"Sure, Dermot Michael Coyne, aren't you spoiling me rotten altogether!"

"What else can I do when my poor wife is at death's door?"

"I know that and I enjoy your attention, but I'm not sure I deserve it!"

"Spoken like a true Irishwoman."

"Besides, you'll turn me into a terrible alcoholic with all this whiskey toddy you're giving me."

"You're the one that's demanding it, woman."

"Sure, it doesn't make my cold any better but, as I said, Dermot Michael, doesn't it help to kill the pain?"

My daughter had recovered from the infection she'd brought to the house and was her usual happy self though she hadn't yet tried to repeat her crawling feat. Fiona kept a close eye on her while I was being nice to Nuala.

My wife was so "destroyed" by her cold that she wasn't able to sing at Old Saint Patrick's on Sunday or to walk across the street to Mass. Nonetheless, she insisted that I attend and bring the baby along because didn't she have to get in the habit of going to church on Sunday?

Nessa was absolutely banned from the house for fear she too would be infected. "The poor young woman has to study for her Ph.D. exam. She can't afford to be sick."

My wife looked pale and haggard, utterly exhausted by the nasty virus which had taken possession of her. I suspected myself that all the strain and tension of motherhood had also caught up with her and she was in no position to resist any wandering bug.

Nick Farmer had been restored to his job but apparently warned to lay off us because the Lyric Opera was now his target, though it seemed to go beyond his popular music venue. He appeared on camera ostentatiously wrapped up with a bandage around his arm looking like a returned war veteran, probably trying to win sympathy. He was a desperate, desperate man.

I heard from George the Priest that Maybelline had regressed from her decision to see a therapist. She had come back from her first treatment wailing that there was nothing wrong with her and called all the women in the family, except my wife, to tell them that it was a waste of time. However, a number of people responded that she should stick at it because it might help her to relax a little. Whether she would respond positively to this advice still was in doubt.

I tried to find more information about Canaryville and the wreck and the Town of Lake. I phoned the Chicago Historical Society but they didn't seem to have much information other than the standard literature. So I sat down when I wasn't waiting on Nuala and keeping an eye on Nellie to write a report on Louise Wade's fine book *Chicago's Pride* and Thomas Jablonski's book *Pride in the Jungle.*

Picture hell, Nuala Anne. Then you will know what the Stockyards and the neighborhood around them were like a hundred years ago.

The sky is dark and filled with clouds of dirt and dust, fires burn fiercely. An unbearable stench permeates the air. Drunken men stagger out of the long rows of taverns. Garbage lies everywhere. The streets are seas of mud. The sewage system doesn't work, water is available only intermittently. Nearby streams are filled with offal and pieces, large and small, of dead animals. The people who live there are shabby, dull, discouraged, overwhelmed. As you ride through the area dismayed by the stench and misery and suffering, you think it would be good if the whole area could be obliterated from the face of the earth.

For the people living on the inside of the environs of the Union Stockyards it was another matter. The Union Stockyards and the neighborhoods surrounding them were sites from which they were wrestling for a better living than they would have dreamed possible before they migrated to America, the first step on the ladder to success and affluence in America. The dark gloom of the malodorous streets to them was not hell but perhaps an antechamber to heaven, purgatory at worst.

The most infuriating thing, Nuala, about reading the literature on "Packingtown," as they called it, is the snobbery of the University of Chicago graduate students who snooped around it looking down their long elite noses at the masses of immigrants. The same for Upton Sinclair, whose novel, *The Jungle,* was a marvelous example of elite left-wing snobbery.

Consider this particular passage, from a certain Charles Bushnell who was writing his doctoral dissertation at the university: "With our cities growing much more rapidly than our country districts, many hordes of population, of diverse languages, customs, and habits, are being crowded annually into congested city wards where life becomes a wild, saddened, sickening, inhuman, and infinitely tragic struggle; not only a menace to those finer dreams of noble, joyous and beautiful national life but a threat to the very essentials of common and decent civilization it-self."

Another outsider said that "Packingtown begins to seem like a world in itself. You feel that there is a great mass of humanity, the kind that is hardest to manage, the easiest to inflame, the slowest to understand."

The University of Chicago do-gooders swarmed all over the neighborhood. They saw the externals but did not really understand what was happening. Many of them thought that it would be wonderful if the whole residential district could be swept away with its muddy streets, its poor lighting, its inadequate water supply, its dubious sewage, its irregular garbage removal, its dirt, its filth, and its foreigners.

Especially the foreigners.

Yet they missed the fact that by the turn of the century more than half of the people in the area around the Union Stockyards owned their own homes and that they and their elected representatives were struggling to improve the water, the lighting, the garbage disposal, the sewage, and the streets. Moreover, through the years they would convert the neighborhoods into decent, comfortable, and attractive places to live.

The story of the preservation of "Packing-town" is part of the great American secret of immigrants who survived and succeeded in American life. Moreover, if the Union Stock-yards were dirty, smelly, ugly, horrible places, the workers still earned more money than people in the steel mills or other indus-trial jobs, worked more regular hours, and had better chances for promotion. The "Yards" were an appalling place to work but also a good place to work if you were first- or second-generation American struggling to find your way in the world.

There were a number of immigrant com-munities that circled the Yards. On the north from the Canal to 31st Street was Bridge-port, the village where the Irish canal work-ers had lived. Just south of them was the German village of Hamburg running from 31st Street to 39th Street. When the Irish migrated in great numbers through Bridge-port they pretty much took over Hamburg, though there were always a lot of German immigrants in the area. From 39th Street, the border of Chicago until just before the time of our story, to 47th Street was Cana-ryville, which was also called North East

Corners and was supposed to be "a notorious hangout of Irish toughs."

From 49th Street to 55th was Englewood, the neighborhood to which some of the more successful immigrants moved. Englewood's pride and joy was Cook County Normal School. (They now call it Chicago State University.) Englewood looked down on its neighbors to the north. West of Canaryville (part of which was also called "Car Shops" because there were so many railroad yards and repair facilities along the east end of the district) was New City, the major German immigrant settlement neighborhood, which engaged in constant political infighting with the Irish. The Germans usually lost—because the Irish were too tricky for them. West of New City, the section around Ashland and back up to 39th Street, was a neighborhood called "Stockyards" or eventually "Back o' the Yards." Here the immigrants after the Irish and the Germans settled—Bohemians, Poles, Lithuanians, and eventually some Italians. So the Yards were surrounded by diverse communities which often fought with one another and which also often united, sometimes in labor unions, to resist the imperialism of the meat packers.

Religiously the center of Canaryville was St. Gabriel's. While other parishes were cut off from it, like St. Rose of Lima and Visitation, and there were Lithuanian and German and Polish parishes, Maurice Dorney, the pastor of St. Gabriel's, was the towering religious figure of the district.

There were several strikes in the late part of the nineteenth century at the Yards. They were not, however, as violent as the railroad strikes would be later on. The packers were robber barons, but they were more generous with their workers than many of the other barons. They could afford to be because meat packing was an enormously successful industry. It went through a revolution in technology every ten years as assembly line and mass production techniques were applied to the slaughter—a horrible scene that I would not want to witness. I wonder how the men that worked there could go home at night and sleep. Apparently they became inured to the savagery of the whole business and slept soundly. Perhaps they dreamed of the prosperity and respectability for which they were striving and

which the Canaryville Irish had come reasonably close to achieving. Some of them,
of course, like the Doolans, had already arrived.

I pondered as I read the books why the
Doolans hadn't moved south to Englewood
where there were more homes like the kind
in which they lived on Emerald Avenue and
where they could have been free of the ag-
gravations of Canaryville. Perhaps they
thought that they would rather be closer to
their Irish friends and, if Tom was involved
in politics, constituents. Moreover, Canaryville was itself a hotbed of Irish nationalism
of which Father Dorney himself was one of
the leaders—the Clan'a Gael, the Ancient
Order of Hibernians, and the Irish Rifles. After one of the strikes (which the unions lost,
mostly because of the stupidity of Terence
Powderly, the head of the Knights of Labor),
the various ethnic groups established their
own militias in case it was necessary to fight
a war against the Pinkerton agents who had
killed a couple of Irish workers during the
strike. The state passed a law forbidding
these rifle companies from putting bayonets
on their guns but they still wore uniforms
and drilled with their rifles, much to the dis-

may of the more affluent people living nearby in Hyde Park and Englewood.

Politics, Irish nationalism, and the Church were all tied up in one twisted tangle. As Mr. Dooley, about whom I've told you, said to his close friend Hennessey, "Did you ever see a man who wanted a free Ireland the day after tomorrow that didn't run for Alderman sooner or later?"

Ashland and Halsted had been paved with large granite blocks. The side streets were mud, thick mud, much of the year. When the Doolans came down the steps of their house to step aboard their carriage and eventually their Stanley Steamer—I imagine they must have had one—they would wear boots and tread very carefully. In their fine clothes they were in constant danger of being spattered with the thick mud that was a reminder that Chicago was built on a swamp.

We must picture the Canaryville Irish, Nuala, living in a world of mud, terrible odors, darkness at night, and unruly people even if they were struggling up America's economic ladder. The unruly people carried rifles when they drilled in front of St. Gabriel's Church. Moreover, both Ashland and Halsted were little more than long rows of saloons. There was no rule against drinking on the job, so there was a steady stream of men across the two streets at all hours of the day to fetch buckets of beer to bring back into the Yards.

One can imagine that young Tom carried a gun and marched in the Irish Rifles and perhaps he belonged to the Clan or the Land League as well as the Ancient Order of Hibernians. Canaryville then was not merely a center for Irish nationalism at the time of our mystery, it was a contentious and on occasion dangerous hotbed of Irish nationalist politics.

The homes must have some memories of conflicts within families. Perhaps the Doolans, father and son, were split on the issue. Perhaps husband and wife disagreed. However, it's hard to imagine that both of them did not respect Father Dorney. I can't suppress some images of that zealous, fierce, magnanimous parish priest meeting the two of them when they came back from Michigan City and sobbing with them over the death of their little girl.

That's about it, Nuala, make of this whatever you can.

Nuala was sitting up in a robe in the parlor

when I gave her my report. As usual she read it twice and put it aside, her face locked in a deep frown—and looking very attractive despite its unnatural pallor.

"A grand bunch of friggin' eejits, weren't they, Dermot Michael?"

"They were, Nuala Anne."

"What brave people too, to work in such a horrible place and themselves owning their own homes and improving their neighborhood and their life."

"They were that too."

"And they'd already begun to go to college?"

"Not all of them surely but enough of them to pass the national average. By the turn of the century the Irish, including Canaryville Irish, had already become successful Americans, and being Irish they didn't care who they told about it."

"And themselves taking over the City of Chicago. Sure, that shouldn't have surprised anyone, should it?"

"Not anyone who knows the Irish."

"Is that where your man is from?"

"The clan hails from Hamburg. It's all in the Eleventh Ward now."

"That just goes to show you, doesn't it?"

I agreed that it did, though I wasn't sure what it showed us.

"Does this report of mine throw any light on our problem?" I then asked.

"Dermot Michael, it suggests there must have still been a lot of conflicts going on in 1898, perhaps not openly but still strongly felt. Our kind of people, as I don't have to tell you, have long, long memories."

Nuala pondered my report again and put it aside on my part of the bed.

"Things are never what they seem, are they, Dermot Michael?"

"You've been saying that a lot lately."

"There seems to be a story here. Maybe your Ancient Order of Hibernians is split. It's late October, not exactly a time for an excursion, but the weather is wonderful and the Hibernians are trying to raise money for the Cause. So they charter this old ship to go across the Lake. Everybody is looking forward to a grand time. Some folk say, 'Isn't it too late?' but they are overruled and the boat goes off. Unbeknown to them, however, there is going to be a rendezvous between a man, maybe named Hill, who somehow represents the revolutionaries in Ireland, and young Tom Doolan. Mary Louise Collins Doolan does not want to go but he insists, everybody else is bringing their wives and, if they have any, their children. It will be a pleasant weekend, no great trouble for anyone. A man from Detroit gets on the ship in Saugatuck, perhaps your man Hill. The ship heads back for Chicago. Whatever mysterious exchange is supposed to happen takes place between him and Tom Doolan. Then the ship is rammed and sunk. Doolan and his wife escape. Their poor little girl dies. The man from Detroit and his wife, whatever their real name might have been, also die. People blame Doolan for organizing a cruise at the wrong time of the year. He has to live with that guilt for the rest of his life. He can never forgive himself for all the deaths, including the death of his daughter. His wife refuses to forgive him. Their marriage is blighted, their love is destroyed, their lives are ruined. Still, Doolan, an Irish patriot no matter what, comes back the next summer and tries to find whatever it was that went down with the ship. Apparently he fails. End of the story. Doesn't that seem likely, Dermot Michael?"

"That's what I thought."

Nuala Anne sighed.

"Sure, it looks plausible, doesn't it? A bunch of eejits—and Irish eejits at that—doing eejit things and risking the lives of their wives and children. But we don't know if any of that's true, it's all something that we pieced together from a few clues. And, to tell you the truth, it doesn't fit. Who needs a cruise boat to exchange something from Ireland? And if it's money going to Ireland, then why couldn't it have been given to the man in Chicago? And if it's something coming from Ireland, wouldn't it have been a lot simpler in 1898 to take one of your trains around the south side of the Lake? Why risk a dubious excursion at the wrong time of the year?"

"Yet something strange happened, something besides a random accident, an unexpected collision in the dark. You're right: every incident in the story could somehow point in the opposite direction."

"And the biggest question of all, Dermot Michael, is why are we involved?"

"Because you and Nelliecoyne saw the ships on the Lake and herself went crazy when we drove by the house in which the Doolans once lived!"

"These things always happen to me for

some kind of purpose, Dermot. Why wouldn't the same thing be true for poor little Nelliecoyne? There is something from the past that we're supposed to straighten out. But what could it be? We can't bring little Agnes Mary Elizabeth Doolan back to life, can we? Even if she hadn't drowned in Lake Michigan, she'd now probably be dead."

"Or a hundred years old."

"Something needs to be straightened out," my wife announced firmly. "And ourselves not knowing what the mystery is."

"Let's hope this Ms. Colleen Doolan Kavanagh is able to give us a few more pieces next week."

"Dermot Michael," she sighed, lying back on her pillow, "I wouldn't count on that very much if I were you. Now would you ever bring me another one of your brilliant hot toddies?"

18

Monday was not exactly a brilliant day. The two women in my life were recovering, my wife much more slowly than my daughter. Nuala spent half the day in bed with a touch of fever. I began to wonder whether we had to really take her to see a doctor. I called my father, however, and he assured me that what Nuala had, had been going around a lot lately.

Naturally.

Things started out badly in the morning when I decided that I ought to take the wolfhound for her morning run, since Nuala now had missed two days. For some reason

Fiona was in a contentious mood. She objected to my putting the flexi-leash on her collar, she objected to going outside, though it was a nice enough if bitter cold morning. Then, when we were outside, sensing that the situation might be different with me, she ran faster than I did, tugged on her leash, almost pulled me over, and generally misbehaved like a very bad dog. In the struggle for dominance between her and me, I emerged at best a close second. A squad car came by as we were running down Webster and the cop rolled down the window to warn me that I should be very careful to keep that dangerous-looking dog on the leash. He added that it looked to him that she was about to break free.

I thanked him politely. Fiona barked loudly at him as if to tell him he had absolutely no business at all, at all, interfering with her morning run.

Back on Southport I decided that perhaps I ought to replace Nuala at Mass too. So I walked into church just as the pastor was beginning the liturgy, and ordered Fiona to sit down next to the last pew. She absolutely refused to do so and continued to strain on the leash as though she wanted to dash up to the altar and smother the priest with affection. Finally I tapped her on the nose and said, "Fiona, you are a very bad dog today—stop it, and stop it now!"

She yiped in protest. The priest winced as though somebody had stuck a knife in his back. I felt that it would be nice if temporarily the ground opened and swallowed me up.

"Fiona," I said ominously, "bad dog."

She looked surprised and then guilty and curled up at my feet in a solid, sullen knot.

"Miserable bitch," I whispered to her.

We went back to the house and I let her out in the yard where she could continue her recreation of chasing what was left of the leaves falling from the tree.

Nuala was making breakfast, pale and tired and discouraged.

"Dermot Michael Coyne, I'm never going to get better. Why don't you just take me to the home for the incurables and leave me there for the rest of my life."

"We don't have homes for incurables anymore, Nuala, and Ireland doesn't either."

She poured me my morning shot of Earl Grey tea.

"Maybe they could start one for me because I'm not ever going to get better, not ever, ever, ever, at all, at all, at all!"

"Your dog was misbehaving this morning," I told her.

She sank into a chair across the kitchen table from me and brushed her disorderly hair away from her face.

"Kind of pushed you as far as she could to see what she could get away with?"

"That seems a fair description of it."

"Och, the poor thing, she must miss me on her morning runs."

That was one explanation.

Finally, we let the wolfhound back into the house. She sort of sulked by me, avoiding my accusing stare. Nuala went back up to bed and I went into the nursery to investigate Nellie. She glared at me too, not at all ready to be pleasant on a day on which the blue sky now was rapidly turning gray and the wind suggested that it was getting colder and colder.

It was time for a diaper change. So I put her on the diaper table and wiped her off. That improved her disposition considerably. She waved her arms, kicked her legs, and gurgled.

I folded the smelly diaper and stuck it in

the diaper genie. I noted that I had better empty the genie before Nuala was well enough to inspect it. I lifted my laughing daughter off the table and put her on the floor for a moment so I could remove the bag inside the can. She rolled over and tried to sit up, but failed in her attempts. Still weak from the infection I thought. The phone rang, Nuala picked it up in the bedroom. Very cautiously Fiona thrust herself into the bedroom and nuzzled me. I patted her on the head very briefly.

"We're not making peace yet, girl. You were a bad dog in church this morning."

She hung her massive head in shame.

Why do dogs show shame so easily?

"Dermot Michael," Nuala cried from the bedroom.

"Coming."

I walked out of the door of the nursery, which was only a few feet down the corridor from the bedroom. I'd walked maybe half those feet when suddenly Fiona went berserk, barking like she were the hound of heaven.

"What's the matter with you now?" I demanded and then I looked at my feet. Scooting around me at full speed was a going-on-eight-months-old baby, crawling straight for the staircase. I snatched her up and carried her back to the bedroom and put her in the crib. Her dignity had been badly violated. She shouted in protest.

"Shut up, you little brat," I told her. "Before this day is over I'm going to get a gate put at the top of that stairway so you won't ever risk your life doing a crazy thing like that again."

Fiona nuzzled me as I turned to go to Nuala's room.

"Yes, Fiona, you're a very good dog. We're good friends now. Don't ever let Nelliecoyne do that again."

As I went into Nuala's room I thought to myself that it might be a good idea for me to get the hell out of the house and go back to working in the Board of Trade, a far more peaceful place. Thank God my wife had not caught me in that moment of carelessness.

"What's the matter with herself?" she demanded as I entered the bedroom, a warning frown on her face.

"She tried to crawl out of the bedroom and Fiona and I stopped her. She was most upset when I put her back in the crib."

"Och, Dermot Michael, won't that child be the death of all of us!"

"We're going to have to keep a pretty close eye on her from now on. I guess she's discovering the world and has found out that it's a very big place."

"And doesn't she want to know everything about it? Och, Dermot Michael, what a shame it is that I'm never going to recover to be able to take care of her."

I sat down in the chair next to the bed and felt her forehead, still a touch of fever.

"I hope you get better soon, Nuala Anne."

"So you can get back into the habit of fucking me?"

"Nuala!"

"Don't tell me you're not thinking about it now because I know you are!"

"The thought had occurred to me."

She sighed loudly.

"I guess we'll just have to make up for lost time, if I ever do recover, which I know I won't."

"I suppose I could manage that."

"I just had a call from poor Nessa," Nuala changed the subject. "Hasn't the little eejit broken up with her Seamus?"

"Why did she do that?"

"She had him out with some of her fancy friends from the University last night and they had some big argument and he disagreed with all the rest of them and embarrassed her something terrible."

"How did he do that?"

"Faith, Dermot Michael, I don't know. They were arguing about the Church and all of them were your kind of fallen away Catholics who felt the Church was terrible, and your poor man had the radical notion that people are the Church and it's crazy to leave it."

"That's what the little Bishop says, isn't it?"

"Sure is," she said, sighing. "But these friends of hers like to stand on the outside and criticize."

"So she was ashamed of him?"

"Didn't she say that very thing? She said he was a nice young man and he was going to make a lot of money when he went back to Galway. They had different interests and they would have different kinds of friends and she simply couldn't trust him in a room with a bunch of intellectuals."

"How many intellectuals do they have at DePaul?"

"I don't know, Dermot. Most of them are probably pretend intellectuals instead of real intellectuals like your man the little Bishop. But your pretend intellectuals are worse than your real intellectuals."

The next blow came in midmorning when we had a call from a very officious woman who informed us that she was Ms. Kavanagh's administrative assistant. Ms. Kavanagh, she said superciliously, had an emergency board meeting and would not be able to see us on Tuesday morning. She was rescheduling our conversation for Thursday morning at the same time. I hardly had a chance to say "thank you" to her for the message.

Then at noontime Cindy called to report on Maybelline.

"She went ballistic after her first session with the new psychiatrist this morning, Dermot. She screamed and ranted and insisted there was nothing wrong with her and she was never going to go into the psychiatrist's office again, that all psychiatrists were charlatans."

"Her husband is a psychiatrist, isn't he?"

"I'm afraid that Maybelline has been on the edge for a long time. The rest of us simply haven't noticed because she doesn't seem very different than in years gone by. Maybe she's been right on the edge as long as we've known her. Her confrontation with Nuala might have pushed her over the edge. I'm not sure whether that's good or bad, but it's going to be hell on her husband and probably on the rest of us."

"Oh, great!"

I told Nuala only a little about that phone call.

She felt better as the day went on and found enough strength to get out of bed and put on her jeans and her Bulls sweatshirt and walk downstairs into the television room.

I joined her.

"Is it because of your Stockyards, Dermot Michael, that they call the basketball team the Bulls?"

" 'Tis, though the Yards are gone."

"I keep learning about this strange city. . . . Strange and wonderful. . . . I should really be practicing me songs, shouldn't I, Dermot? And doing the voice exercises? Won't Madam be furious at me when she finds out that I have missed three whole days of exercises?"

"You can tell Madam that you were sick, can't you?"

"Madam's pupils are not permitted to get sick, Dermot Michael, you ought to know that."

She did work up enough energy towards suppertime to sing a little bit. When Nellie-coyne heard her, she cried in protest.

"Would you ever bring her downstairs, Dermot Michael?"

Our daughter was standing up and hanging on the side of the crib when I entered the bedroom. She scowled at me and shook the crib angrily. I better let her mother discover this new trick for herself.

I removed her from the crib and brought her down to the television room so she could rest contentedly in her mother's arms while the singing went on.

Nuala turned on the five o'clock news to see if Nick Farmer would appear. He was only supposed to have one slot a week but now that he had made himself into a celebrity, perhaps they would give him more.

The lead story on the news was about Nick Farmer.

"Chicago journalism," the artificial blonde began solemnly, "has lost one of its most vivid and controversial commentators. Nicholas Herman Farmer's dead body was found late today in an alley in the Uptown neighborhood. According to Area Six Commander John Culhane, he probably died last night and his body was only discovered behind a clump of bushes late this morning."

The camera cut to John Culhane at his usual station behind a podium in Area Six headquarters.

"We have no report on the cause of death yet. Mr. Farmer does not seem to be a victim of foul play. We are investigating further."

Then there was a shot of a covered body being brought into Ravenswood Hospital.

"Farmer had a distinguished career in Chicago journalism," the blonde went on. "He had worked for the *Chicago Tribune*, the *Chicago Sun-Times, Chicago Magazine*, WMAQ Radio, *The Reader*, and a number of other journals. Most recently, he had also been a commentator on this station. He also contributed many articles to culture reviews. His voice was always clear, firm, and honest. Jody Clough, station manager of Channel Three, said in a statement this afternoon, 'Nick Farmer was the last of an old breed of Chicago journalists. A man of total integrity and gutsy honesty. We will miss him, we will not see his like again.' "

"Bullshit."

"Dermot Michael Coyne!" Nuala said in shock. "The poor man is dead!"

"Indeed he is."

"Funeral details are not confirmed yet," the anchorperson continued. "Mr. Farmer is survived by his wife Martha and two teenage children."

"I never knew that the man had a wife and kids," Nuala said. "Poor dear people!"

The phone rang. I picked it up.

"Dermot Michael Coyne!"

"John Joseph Culhane here, Dermot. You've seen the five o'clock news?"

"Yeah, quite by chance we turned it on."

"I wanted to get to you before it broke. We haven't told them yet that Farmer was almost certainly murdered. He was given a huge overdose of heroin while his hands and feet were bound. After he was dead, his killers dumped the body in an alley behind Ashland Avenue and just north of Wilson in Uptown. The irony is that someone came forward in Evanston this morning and admitted that the assassination last week was, just as Nuala thought, fake. Farmer was hoping to get enough publicity so that somebody would give him a slot on television again. Evanston didn't call us until the news broke this afternoon that this time he was really dead. I'll try to keep you informed. By the way, there's a wake tomorrow afternoon and evening up on Clark Street and the funeral Mass at St. Gregory's on Wednesday morning."

"St. Gregory's?"

"Yeah, Dermot, I guess the poor man was one of us."

There was mystery aplenty in the world.

"Dermot Michael," my wife said to me, "you look stricken! Aren't you at least as pale as I am?"

"He was murdered, Nuala, it wasn't a heart attack, it wasn't a stroke, it was a massive overdose of heroin administered hours before his body was thrown into the alley in Uptown. The wake is tomorrow afternoon and evening and the Mass is at St. Gregory's Church up in Summerdale on Wednesday morning."

"Dermot Michael," she said firmly, "we're going to have to go, aren't we? The poor man was a Catholic, it is the only thing for us to do."

Catholics, especially Irish Catholics, have a dangerous habit of being ready to forgive everything at the time of death—however temporary that forgiveness is.

"Nuala, he tried to destroy your career, he tried to frame us for attempted murder, he was a mean, nasty, vicious man. I don't see why we should pay any attention to his death other than to breathe a sigh of relief."

"Dermot! You should be ashamed of yourself! The poor man is dead. We have to go up there and offer our sympathies to his wife and children! We are Catholics after all, are we not, Dermot Michael?"

"I guess so."

"Besides, now we have another mystery to solve, don't we?"

"Why is this our mystery, Nuala? Can't we leave it to John Culhane and Area Six?"

"It's our mystery, Dermot, because if it isn't solved there's always going to be a suspicion that somehow or the other we did it."

"Culhane doesn't believe that for a moment. The Chicago Police Department isn't going to put us on its list of suspects."

"It isn't the Chicago Police Department

that we have to worry about, Dermot, it's public opinion. The poor man attacked us on television. He said that we were making threats against him. Someone wounded him in front of a bar. Then he turns up dead. Though they'll never have any proof that we were involved—because of course we weren't—the suspicion will still linger. I don't want our poor little Nelliecoyne growing up with that kind of suspicion around her family."

"Now that you put it that way, Nuala, I can see your point. We do indeed have two mysteries."

"And both of them, Dermot, are mysteries in which we really don't know what the mystery is and a mystery in which what things seem to be is probably not what they are at all."

"We have a pretty clear idea of what happened to Nicholas Farmer, don't we? He was a mean, nasty man who made a lot of enemies and his enemies finally caught up with him."

"That's what it looks like, Dermot, but we should know by now that often things aren't what they look like."

The following afternoon Nuala announced

that she was well enough to go to the wake. Irishwoman that she was, she would pull herself out of bed with a 103 fever to make it to a wake.

"What does His Reverence's book say about St. Gregory's, Dermot Michael?"

There was no point in denying that I had looked the parish up in George the Priest's two-volume history of Chicago parishes.

"It was a German national parish founded in 1904, two decades after St. Gabe's. Germans were a major component of the population of Chicago, more of them, in fact, than there were Irish. They were moving up from the near North Side to a district which people tend to call Lakeview or Edgewater but which, across Clark Street, is really Summerdale, because once there were summer homes up there. The Germans built lovely churches while, with the exception of Father Dorney, the Irish put up school buildings and used the auditoriums as churches. They also were much more serious about church music and liturgy than we were. The day the parish was founded, they chose eight men to be their choir."

"Not wild men from the bogs, were they now?"

"More civilized and more literate than we were, but not nearly as clever when it came to politics."

At the wake we met Nick Farmer's estranged wife, Martha. She was a tall, attractive, and somewhat haggard but extremely pleasant woman in her early forties. She introduced us to her son and daughter, two somber but presentable teenagers who both attended St. Gregory's High School.

"It was so very nice of you to come," she said sweetly. "Poor Nicholas was a deeply troubled man but he had so many good qualities and so much talent. Though we haven't been together for many years, I still will miss him. Every once in a while he would feel terribly guilty about what he had done and would try to patch together our marriage. It never worked. His ambition was too strong and the sense that his great talent had been frustrated always burdened him."

"How very sad," Nuala said sympathetically.

"I know that he gave you a very hard time, Ms. McGrail. I don't think there was any personal animosity in it. He had a hot temper but it cooled down very quickly. His vitriolic attacks on people were sudden bursts of anger which he knew called attention to himself and his work. He meant no harm by it."

He may not have meant any harm by it, I thought to myself, but he surely did a lot of harm.

"Och," Nuala said, "we weren't thinking about that at all, at all. We just feel sorry for the poor man and for all your own sufferings."

Martha nodded solemnly. "It's very strange. I received a letter from him just yesterday, it must have been mailed right before he died. There was no hint in it that he expected to die. He pleaded for my forgiveness more strongly than he had ever pleaded before. Of course I forgave him, I had always forgiven him. I'm only sorry I didn't have a chance to tell him that one last time."

"He asked for forgiveness?" Nuala whispered.

"Forgiveness, Ms. McGrail. Here, let me read the paragraph."

She opened her purse and removed a much worn sheet of paper.

" 'Martha, I have been a rotten husband and a rotten father and I'm not much of a music critic either. I don't know what's happened to my life. I'm terribly sorry for having let you down so many times. I hope you will forgive me. I know that it is impossible for us ever to get together again. How did you and the kids put up with me at the times we were together? I'm a slob, a phony, a faker, and also a burnt-out case. I always will be that. On this day, when I feel a little guilt for the bad things I've done to people, I want to tell you how sorry I am.' "

Tears poured down the woman's cheeks. Behind her, her daughter was weeping too and her son was struggling with his emotions.

"Daddy was not a bad man," the daughter said. "Things simply never seemed to go right for him."

Nuala was crying too when we left the funeral hone.

John Culhane greeted us as we emerged.

"I saw the ancient Mercedes," he said, "and I thought I would stop to have a word with you."

"It's all so terrible," Nuala said, dabbing her eyes with a tissue. "The poor dead man, the poor woman, the poor kids."

"You see it every day in police work," John replied. "Wasted lives. This man was apparently talented and he didn't have the character to use his abilities."

Too simple, I thought.

"Who might have killed him?" I asked. "What kind of enemies did he have?"

These are the kind of bread-and-butter questions that I am permitted to ask. It's only the questions about ultimate meetings and stories that Nuala bothers herself with.

"A long, long list of enemies, Dermot. Lots of people disliked him. He had very few friends. The crowd he hung out with in the bar on Chicago Avenue up in Evanston were celebrity worshipers, would-be intellectuals and would-be liberals who cluster around Northwestern University like vultures. In Chicago he hung out at the Old Town Alehouse which, as you know, is a dingy place for dingy journalists. I'm not sure that he had friends there. He has offended just about every editor and news director in Chicago and most of the journalists too. There won't be a very big crowd here at his wake."

"What did he do to offend editors and other journalists?"

"What didn't he do! He stole other people's work, he faked scoops, he plagiarized,

he betrayed confidences, he attacked the innocent, he took advantage of young reporters. He didn't destroy people but it wasn't
for want of trying. He seemed to think that
he could succeed only if other people failed.
For him all other Chicago media people
were miserable fakes. He might have been
right, but you can't be too obvious about
your contempt for your colleagues. He was
smart and charming when he wanted to be
and had a way with words. However, he usually destroyed himself before he achieved
any real success."

"That's pretty sad."

"Yeah, and he drank too much and he
was always overweight and he pumped all
kinds of chemicals into his system."

"How did he get the job at Channel
Three?"

"Doug Jurgens, the news director there,
was an old friend. Went to high school with
him. Figured he owed him a couple of favors. There weren't very many markers out
there for Farmer to pick up."

As we angled over to Lake Shore Drive,
Nuala said, "Dermot Michael, don't you think
it's time you check with your friends out on
the West Side?"

"I hadn't thought of that at all."

When Lieutenant Knox asked the question about contacts with people who are involved in organized crime I completely forgot that Nuala Anne and I both knew the top leader of the Outfit. I had gone to grammar school with his grandson. He was terrified of Nuala because he realized that she was one of the dark ones.

"I could find out whether this was an outside job."

"And maybe find out who did it."

"As you know, that has to be an indirect approach. I'll see what I can do as soon as we get home."

"We're really going to have to go to the funeral mass tomorrow, aren't we, Dermot Michael?"

Did I have any choice? No.

"Certainly."

"And to the cemetery afterward. There is bound to be only a handful of people there."

"I quite agree."

I agreed, mind you, but I would never have thought of doing it myself.

Nuala flipped open her tiny phone and called Nessa.

She shook her head after the usual brisk exchange in Irish.

"I think, Dermot Michael, that we better get gates at the top and the bottom of the stairs. This little monster is trouble."

"Seamus?"

"Not a thing."

Later, when Nuala was nursing Nellie after we returned to the house, she informed me, "That young woman is not only an eejit, she's a fookin' onchuck!"

"Nuala, I thought you'd given up such language!"

"Give over, Dermot Michael, sometimes only that type of language expresses the reality of things."

"I suppose it does."

"She didn't say anything to you about Seamus?"

"If she wouldn't say anything to you, she wouldn't say it to me."

"You're right, Dermot Michael, as always you're right."

As always, huh?

"In two days," Nuala predicted, "she'll be missing him and then it might be too late, poor little thing."

I wondered how often I was poor little Dermot when she was talking to Nessa.

I called my friend out on the West Side to see what he could do for me.

"My friend out on the West Side" didn't necessarily mean that the man in question lived on the West Side, though in fact in this case he did. Or that he was necessarily a friend. It merely meant that he was "connected" with the Outfit and sometimes acted as a go-between.

"Hey! Dermot my friend, how are you? It's been a while since I have seen you!"

"Hey! I don't get downtown too much these days. I stay home and I work on my stories."

"I don't blame you, Dermot. There's nothing much going on downtown."

We chatted for a few moments for the sake of professional courtesy.

"I wonder if we could find out something from some friends of friends of yours?"

Instantly he became uneasy.

"Dermot, I'll be happy to talk to some of my friends to see if their friends can provide anything for you."

"There was a certain business operation in Uptown the other night. I've been wondering if you could learn from any of your friends whether it was a legitimate business operation."

"Gotcha, Dermot."

"Sounds like something crazies out in South Chicago might try."

I meant the Latino drug gangs who made the Outfit in its present elderly manifestations look benign.

"I'll see what I can do. I'll be back to you, Dermot, as soon as I can talk to some of my friends who have friends."

I was asking whether the mob was involved in putting down Farmer. It didn't sound like the kind of thing they would go after. He was far too small a target for the cautious old men who now ran it. Some hits went down without authorization, which they knew about but did not stop because it was not worth their effort to do so. Rarely did the Outfit use anything so crude as heroin overdoses. I wanted to be able to exclude them from our considerations and perhaps open the possibility that they might be our allies.

There was only a small group of people at the funeral mass the next day at St. Gregory's, a delicately beautiful church of the sort the Germans tended to build in Chicago.

The Catholic funeral liturgy, done properly as it would be in a church whose origins were German, is an extraordinary experience. Restrained sadness and serene joy invade the souls of the participants. The service dulls the pain and lifts the spirit.

Hope is not a bad idea.

The elderly priest who had known Farmer as a student in high school thirty years before talked about his earnestness and enthusiasms and especially about the hungers in his heart.

"Nicholas hungered for the infinite," the priest concluded, "we all hunger for the infinite. His hunger was stronger than that of most of us. I don't think he came very close to the infinite during his life, though on occasion he seemed to know what he was seeking. Now he has it all and we rejoice he's gone home to the peace and love for which he was always hungering."

Several pews in front of us his wife was crying. Naturally Nuala Anne was crying next to me.

Then we rode up to All Saints Cemetery on the edge of the city. The same elderly priest said the prayers at the graveside and offered his sympathy to the family. Nuala and I shook hands with the widow and her children. Nuala and Martha embraced.

A strikingly handsome man, with a shock of iron gray hair and big sad eyes, one of a dozen or so mourners around the graveside, extended his hand to me.

"Dermot Coyne?"

"That's me."

"I'm Rog Conrad. I went to St. Gregory's with Nicholas. It was very graceful of you and your wife to come to the funeral. Not many people cared about him."

"My wife insisted."

"I would like to buy you both lunch, as a sign of my gratitude."

"Sure . . . Nuala, this is Rog Conrad. He wants to buy us lunch."

"Sure, we never turn down a free meal, do we, Dermot Michael?" Nuala said, turning on all her charm.

Nuala's eyes flickered at me as we turned to walk to our cars. The flicker meant, "We ought to talk to this man."

I was improving at the art of reading her signals.

He was a freelance writer, a sometime reporter for *The Wall Street Journal* who had specialized in business scandals. He had written several books on the subject and was, he seemed to hint, very successful at that trade. I vaguely remembered reviews of a prizewinner about American oil companies in Africa.

He took us to an elegant restaurant in downtown Evanston—rich green wall hangings, daylight filtering in through skylights, crisp white linen tablecloths, shining silverware, attentive waiters, and a fascinating menu. In French.

Big deal.

Nuala made another phone call home. Apparently reassured by Nessa, she continued to charm our host.

"This is a brilliant restaurant altogether, Mr. Conrad," she said. "Isn't it, Dermot Michael?"

I agreed that it was.

"I owe you two something for being so generous to Nicholas. He didn't deserve it, but it was still good of you to be concerned about him and especially his family."

"Your man must have been terribly unhappy."

Sure, wasn't she on the case and wasn't I therefore advised to keep my mouth shut?

"And himself with a very nice wife and two beautiful children," Nuala continued.

"He had lots of talent, as Father Reinhard said at Mass. As a high school kid he was magic. Pure charisma. Enormously popular. What he lacked, I think, was patience. He had to have instant success. When he left college to go to work for the City News Bureau, an apprenticeship for many of us in those days, he charged in with supreme confidence that he was better than anyone else in the shop. Naturally, the veterans—guys a couple of years older than he was—found ways to make him look ridiculous. He was furious. He set out to get even with them and he did, but he made a lot of enemies."

"Poor man."

"Nick was too brash, too ambitious. He wasn't able to keep his mouth shut, you see, and wait for the next time. And there would have been next times. Then later on he had to pick on younger guys just as older guys picked on him. He couldn't help himself. When he wasn't stirring up trouble against the boss, whoever the boss might be, he was feuding with his colleagues."

We were served a mild red wine. Nuala ordered tournedos Rossini. So did I.

"I don't want to get involved with this," Conrad continued. "I don't want to dig into his life and his past to get a story. There are enough stories going around as it is. I know you two are close to Culhane and I think you might want to pass something on to him."

Aha, now we get down to business.

"I'm sure John would be happy if we passed something useful on to him," Nuala said easily.

"Nick was working on a big story. A really big story. Or so he told me. He was always on to something big. This time he was more excited than usual. It'll knock your socks off, Rog, he said several times."

"Were any of his other stories really big?"

"Some weren't, but some were. He'd always blow it."

"Did it have anything to do with the music industry?" Nuala asked as she destroyed altogether an oil and vinegar salad.

"It might have. I think so. He was very vague about it. Nick was always vague about his top stories because he was afraid someone was trying to steal them. A couple of times his stories were stolen. Other times he tried to steal stories himself. I suspect that it was music. It was the beat he had chosen for himself."

"Any idea what kind of music?"

"Gangsta Rap."

"Bad business," I said, tasting the wine and then tasting it again.

"Did he seem to think his investigation was dangerous?" Nuala asked, sipping delicately from her glass.

"Things were always dangerous for Nick. To hear him tell it, he never moved onto something that was safe. It was always a big story that people were trying to prevent him from telling. Danger, even if it was imaginary danger, turned him on."

"How horrible!"

"Yes, indeed, Ms. McGrail."

"That's me mother. I'm Nuala or, if someone is wanting to say something special to me, Nuala Anne."

Conrad, who did not seem much into smiling, smiled.

"All right, Nuala Anne. When we were all back in St. Gregory's twenty-five years ago, he didn't seem crazy. Ambitious, yes, a little ruthless, yes. But lots of fun. He was the leader of our little group who ran the school paper, a bunch of kids who wanted to grow up and be like Woodward and Bernstein. He was a charmer too. Martha Grimm was the prettiest girl in the class. She fell totally in love with him and never really stopped loving him."

"She's free now though," Nuala said.

"Free indeed but really not free and she might never be."

"Poor woman," Nuala said with the barest hint of a flicker of an eye in my direction.

"I don't really know what he was working on. He certainly had lots of contacts around the city. And a nose for dirt. Sometimes he made up the dirt as he did about you folks. . . . He trusted me more than anyone else, but not by any means one hundred percent. I think he was a little scared. He made me promise to try to take care of Martha and the kids if anything happened to him. He had never done that before."

"And would they be needing someone to take care of them?"

He shrugged indifferently.

"She doesn't need anyone to take care of her or the kids, at least not financially. And I'm happily married so that's not a route I'd be inclined to go."

There was a faint hint in his voice that at one time he might have been inclined to go that route. Was Nick an old rival who had won in the contest for Martha?

"Tell us more about that darlin' little parish. Did you all go through school there?"

My wife was up to something. I didn't know exactly what she was up to but she was up to it.

"From first grade to high school senior year."

His eyes clouded over and a quick spasm of pain raced across his face.

"And you all wanted to be journalists, did you now?"

She attacked the beef with a savagery that astonished me. Yep, she was getting better.

"Everything was clear during the time after the Watergate crisis. We wanted to make money, become famous, and perhaps improve the world. Since the Northwestern Journalism school was up here in Evanston, we figured we would go there and become the Pulitzer Prize winners of our generation. Martha, Nicholas, Johnny Quinn, Doug Jurgens, Robin Cleary, and I. Nick dropped out after his sophomore year because he said they had nothing more to teach him. Johnny and Robin married each other and gave up on journalism. Johnny is an investment banker downtown and she has her own PR firm. Very power people. Martha heads up a small but well-respected market research firm. Doug is news director at Channel Three. Only Nicholas and I stayed in reporting."

The facts in his narrative did not seem to justify the deep sadness with which he told the story.

"Ah, sure, don't we all have great dreams when we're young and we settle down and accept whatever happens."

"You and Dermot seem to have done all right in your professional careers, Nuala Anne."

"I never thought I was going to be a singer and Dermot never thought he was going to be a writer. I was going to be an accountant and he was going to be a commodity trader. And we were both going to be huge successes. Dermot was a failure as a trader, but made a lot of money at the exchange by mistake and got out while he could. And I had a good job at Arthur Anderson, but I liked singing better. So our dreams didn't come true and ourselves being lucky that they didn't."

I didn't like Nuala's comment that I had failed in my chosen career. Still, it was the absolute truth, wasn't it now? I had no idea what she was talking about. Neither, I suspected, did Rog Conrad.

"I've made it, I guess," he said. "I've become the kind of journalist I wanted to be back in the days at St. Gregory. Sometimes I think it's better if your dreams don't come true. Today I wish we were all juniors again, just taking over the school paper."

"Isn't that the truth about dreams?"

"I never feel safe in Evanston," I said to my wife as we drove home in the rain. "It's where they started Prohibition."

"It's no wonder I was uneasy the whole time . . . what a terrible thing to do!"

"It was indeed. I expected any moment that someone from the Women's Christian Temperance Union would come in and take the wine away from us."

There was a silence, then Nuala said, "Dermot Michael, whatever did you make of that man?"

"I'm not sure, Nuala. I remembered who he was during lunch. He's a very famous writer. His book on Nigeria will probably win the nonfiction Pulitzer this year. The reviews were ecstatic. He managed to break through the protection around the military government and find out how they live. He reported in detail the corrupt relationship between the government and the oil companies. Somehow he was present at a number of embarrassing conversations in which the oil people bought off government leaders and later defended their actions to him on the grounds that America had to have oil and that's the way business is done in the third world. Vivid, searing, scary stuff."

"Doesn't seem like the kind of man who could do that, does he?"

"His earlier books were pretty good too. Some people say he's the best journalist in America. . . . What did you make of him?"

That was the question I was supposed to ask.

"Dermot," she said thoughtfully, "he's an awful nice fellow and very charming and he's always been in love with Martha and he can't wait to get rid of his own wife and pursue her, but he doesn't have the courage or the passion to do it. And he really never liked poor Nicholas, especially since he stole Martha. Yet he came to the funeral. And himself trying to throw dust in our eyes, which I found most unusual, didn't you now, Dermot?"

"Oh, yes, most unusual," I said, not having noticed any dust at all. "Why would he want to throw dust in our eyes?"

"Now isn't that the real question. Why would he tell us so much that he didn't need to tell us without any good reason?"

"Because he had a good reason."

"I think, Dermot, someday before the week is over we're gonna have to pay a visit to Martha Farmer. Did they really think that journalism would be exciting when all it means is standing around outside a house on Southport Avenue on a cold morning waiting for something to happen, and knowing all along that nothing was going to happen?"

We turned off Sheridan Road and onto Lake Shore Drive. The skyline of Chicago loomed in front of us, a silver etching against the dark gray sky.

"Maybe he knew a little bit about your detective record and wanted to steer you down a wrong track."

"Isn't it clear that he wanted to do that?

He didn't need us to pass on a hint to your man."

"Didn't he take a risk by talking to us?"

"He was afraid of us, Dermot Michael."

"Oh."

"Don't we now have two mysteries in which we don't know what the mystery is?"

"In this mystery isn't the puzzle who killed Nick Farmer?"

"No, Dermot Michael. It's what happened to those poor people when they were back at St. Gregory's High School."

19

We only consumed ten minutes of Colleen
Kavanagh's precious fifteen minutes of time.
She took an instant dislike to Nuala, which
reduced my ordinarily feisty wife to silence.
Moreover, she didn't have much to tell us
and gave the impression that if she did she
wouldn't have told it to us.

On Thursday morning we drove out to
Beverly, which Nuala thought was a darling
neighborhood but not as darling as River
Forest. As we drove through the valleys and
the hills and the curving streets with gra-
cious old homes, I told her stories about the

neighborhood as a onetime hideout for cattle rustlers.

"You're having me on, Dermot Michael. This grand little neighborhood isn't the wild west."

She particularly liked the dazzling modern parish church.

"You have to admit, Dermot, that it's almost as lovely as Old St. Pat's."

Forest Preserve woods on three sides shield the massive Kavanagh house at 2020 Hopkins Place from the rest of the world. We were admitted into the house by a supercilious maid who looked down her nose at us. Apparently she did not realize that West Side Irish are more refined and more sensitive than refugees from the Yards.

We were conducted into a small sitting room and told that Mrs. Kavanagh would be with us as soon as was convenient.

Promptly at eleven forty-five we were shown into her office; a large, flawlessly neat room overlooking a carefully tended backyard in which the rosebushes were already covered for winter protection.

Mrs. Kavanagh did not stand to greet us but at least she asked us to sit down. She was a slender woman in her middle forties who would have been attractive, perhaps, if she ever smiled. In our ten minutes in her office she didn't begin to smile. Moreover, her eyes were hostile and her tone of voice contemptuous. She was obviously a very important person and we weren't important at all.

I introduced myself and Nuala as my wife.

Some women don't like Nuala on sight— her beauty is too perfect and too patently durable to be tolerable to women who are prone to envy about physical appearances. I don't know whether Nuala has ever understood or recognized this envy, but it was impossible to avoid Colleen Kavanagh's antipathy.

"You don't have any children yet, do you?" was the first question she fired.

Nuala's technique when she encounters hostile women has always been to revert to the simple pleasant lass from the wilds of Connemara who needs mothering and protection. In that role she does need protection, but it is by no means her only role.

"Oh, indeed I do, Mrs. Kavanagh," she said, beaming proudly, and pulled the wallet with Nelliecoyne's pictures out of her purse.

Colleen Kavanagh barely glanced at the pictures.

"Yes, very pretty, I'm sure."

"Thank you, ma'am," said Nuala, putting the wallet back into the purse.

"Now let's get down to business. I have two board meetings this afternoon and I must be punctual for both of them. I believe you are interested in the house our family used to occupy on Emerald Avenue?"

"We are," I said.

"I must confess I'm not much concerned about history. The experience of our family living in such a terrible neighborhood was something that I have no reason to be proud of. I do not want to remember it. While I am perfectly prepared to accept the notion that the immigrants had to struggle to escape poverty, it does seem to me that the very fact that the community remains is proof that there is very little in the way of work ethic or ambition among the Irish in this city."

"Yes, ma'am," Nuala said, cutting off effectively the outburst of temper she anticipated from me.

I was about to comment on the fact that Chicago's Mayor was from that neighborhood, more or less.

"You are particularly interested in my great-grandparents, the Doolans, who lived there at the turn of the century?"

"Yes, ma'am," Nuala said.

"I can't understand why anybody would be interested in them. My great-grandfather was not a particularly attractive man, a cheap lawyer and politician, and deeply involved in the violence of Irish nationalism from what I understand. We don't have much in the way of documents."

She reached into a folder on her desk and pulled out some photographs and a number of papers.

"Here is the family of Mr. and Mrs. Thomas Doolan in 1916. You can see they have five children—two daughters and three sons. The second oldest"—she pointed at a young man who was in his early teens—"is my grandfather. For reasons that escape me, when his parents died in the time after the Second World War, he moved into the house and raised my father there. They had lived on the North Shore before that time and you can imagine what a shock it was to my father as a young lad to move into the Stockyards area."

"Yes, ma'am."

"Do you keep in contact with your cousins, who are also descendants of the Doolans?" I asked cautiously.

"Generally I don't find it convenient to do so," she said. "There is just so much time in life and I have enough obligations with my own family and my brother's family not to want to extend the boundaries of intimacy any further."

"Do you know where they live?"

"Vaguely." She waved her hand negligently. "I believe we send Christmas cards to them but I have very little other contact with them. Only a few of them still live in the Chicago area."

"What about the descendants of this child, the pretty daughter?" Nuala asked.

"Oh, my dear, do you consider her pretty? I'm afraid I wouldn't think so. I don't really remember what her name was."

"Ellen," Nuala said, turning over the picture to read the names on the back.

"I do know that one of her grandchildren does live in a western suburb, Oak Brook perhaps. Her name I believe is Ellen Hegarty. Her husband is some sort of commodity broker. They may have better records than we have. I encounter her occasionally at important Chicago civic functions and generally find that the two of us have nothing in common."

This woman, I said to myself, is a classic snob. She knows something about her predecessors, enough to be ashamed of them. Still she's only a generation removed from the Yards and acts like she might be a first cousin of the Queen of England. Her husband is a respectable doctor with a nice income, but they are not exactly aristocrats. Certainly no more than the Coyne clan.

"Hegarty," I said. "Perhaps we'll look her up."

"Tell me, ma'am, do you have any recollections of the house itself? Didn't you live there before your father sold it?"

Colleen Kavanagh lost her composure. She shuddered briefly; I watched her fingers tremble slightly and saw the enormous struggle on her face not to show any emotion.

"I . . . I try to think of it as little as possible," she said. "It was a horrid house; old, dirty, decrepit, dismal, discouraging."

Nuala's eyes became wide, an expression of quite believable but to me phony Irish surprise.

"It sounds like you found the house frightening, Ms. Kavanagh?" she said.

"Frightening! Well, dear, I wouldn't go so far as to say that. It was simply unpleasant and I was very happy when we moved out."

We took the pictures and the clippings and departed with as much dignity as we could muster under the circumstances.

"Bitch with a capital B," I observed in the driveway.

"Dermot Michael! We must be charitable, mustn't we now? She's a very insecure and unhappy woman and all her activity isn't able to fill up the hollow inside of her. And herself a dark one like me."

"A dark one?"

"Didn't she feel the vibrations in the house!"

"Dr. Gomez says that his grandmother finds the vibrations pleasant."

"His grandmother isn't Colleen Doolan Kavanagh. Canaryville isn't what she's trying to forget. It's that terrible, terrible house! I don't want to do it but I'm afraid we are going to have to dine there with your friend, Dr. Gomez."

Nuala flipped open her little telephone and pushed the magic button to give her almost instant contact with her daughter. She talked for a few quick moments with the virtuous Nessa and then stopped. She closed the phone with a gesture of impatience.

"The little bitch really is just not going to grow up!"

"My daughter?"

If the child were a bitch she certainly couldn't be Nuala's daughter!

"Of course not, Dermot Michael Coyne, what in the world is the matter with you? No, I meant Nessa, she still doesn't want to talk to me about herself and Seamus. We have got to put a stop to that, do you understand, we have to put a stop to it!"

"Oh. And how are we going to do that?"

"I have a scheme in my head and I might have to activate that scheme pretty soon."

"And what is the scheme?"

"Och, I won't be telling you that, Dermot Michael, till it's clearer in my mind than it is now. I think you'll love it, no, I know you'll love it!"

"Oh. . . . Would it be too much to ask how our daughter is doing?"

"You mean Nelliecoyne? Why, she's doing fine, how else would she be doing, Dermot? She's playing with Nessa and with the dog and crawling all around the floor and drinking milk out of the bottle I left in the fridge and slurping up carrot baby food. What else would she be doing?"

So all right, what do I know!

In the car Nuala flipped through the pictures and documents while I steered us down 87th Street.

"Dermot, they are a fine-looking bunch of kids. Five of them. That means that whatever happened between Mary Louise and Tom Doolan they at least didn't stop sleeping with one another."

"Did people do that in those days?"

"How should I be knowing? I wasn't there, was I now? Sure wouldn't losing a child that way break up lots of marriages. The woman might just have moved into another bedroom and stayed there for a half a year or so. Still, she doesn't look like the kind that would do that. In fact, she looks very pretty and very sweet and very nice. Also, despite that terrible corset thing she's wearing, she was a very sexy woman. Tom Doolan was lucky to have a wife like her . . . and, Dermot Michael, don't you be looking at the picture . . . you're driving the car. Let us just get out of this terrible neighborhood and back home where we belong!"

I obeyed. Naturally.

However, the blond woman certainly did look sexy.

"Now, let's see," she went on, "there's five kids and on the back here they have written their names: Ellen, Tom, named after his father I suppose, John, Joseph, and Mary Louise. None of your Tiffanys or your Taylors or your Traceys or any of them other weird names, are there now?"

"Should you ever want to burden one of our children with a name like that, Nuala Anne, I'd be the one sleeping in another room!"

She found that very funny. My wife, still a little pale, was her feisty self again.

"So the woman we have to look for now would be the granddaughter of Miss Ellen. Did you know anybody named Hegarty when you were working on the Board of Trade?"

"I think so, Nuala," I said. "A very nice guy, good-looking, friendly, and as smart as they come. Crazy, like they all are. I wouldn't be surprised that he is able to afford a new home in Oak Brook these days."

"Not as successful as your lucky traders or your young novelists, is he now?"

"I mean not everybody marries a successful singer either."

"Somebody in your family must know them. You'll have to give them a ring and find out what they can tell us."

"Yes, ma'am."

"Dermot, will you ever drive north on the Lake Shore Drive instead of on this terrible Dan Ryan thing?"

"Sure, why do you want the Drive today?"

"It's such a wonderful day with the wind blowing and the waves dancing along the shore. Doesn't it take me back to Galway when I watch the waves dancing on the shore!"

So I turned off the Ryan onto the Stevenson and then onto Lake Shore Drive heading north by McCormick Place. Sure enough, the Lake was raging and dancing all along the shore with ranks of whitecaps radiant under the bright sun attacking like an army besieging a city.

"Does it really remind you of Galway Bay?" I asked.

"Oh, Dermot, not really. Galway Bay never gets that angry and besides it doesn't wash up such big waves into Galway City either, does it now?"

"I guess not."

"Isn't it a beautiful lake, Dermot Michael? It's hard to imagine it is as dangerous as you say it is and them terrible stories about the ships sinking."

"Let me tell you a story, Nuala, one I haven't told you before. Sometimes I tell it to people who are new to Lake Michigan so they'll be careful when they go swimming in it. I never told it to you because you're a very careful swimmer."

"It sounds like a scary story, Dermot Michael."

"No, it's a tragic story. Many years ago when I was a kid, I mean a little kid like eleven or twelve, one of the families down the beach imported an Irish seminarian to kind of baby-sit for their two boys during the summer. They figured that a young male would be a much better role model for their two sons, who were effeminate punks as I remember them. The young man turned out to be a fine lad. It was his first time out of Ireland and he was excited by the trip and excited by the United States and Lake Michigan and Grand Beach. He sang songs and told stories and all the little kids my age at Grand Beach fell in love with him. One day, when the Lake was really bad and the surf was washing, and the kids shouldn't have been swimming, the lifeguard wasn't there, we dove into the Lake anyhow. One of the boys he was in charge of went out too far and he was caught in the undertow. The seminarian couldn't swim but tried to save him. He grabbed him and shoved him towards the shore where someone else who could swim grabbed the lad. The current caught the seminarian, pulled him under, and sent him out into the Lake. He disappeared like he'd never been there. The fire alarms went off, the police cars pulled up, and the Coast Guard came by in their search boat. No sign of the poor seminarian at all. Three days later I was walking down the beach by myself feeling very sad for this lad: he was such a nice young man and he sang such wonderful songs and he seemed so happy. And I came upon his body, purple and twisted and lying lifeless on the shore."

"Glory to God!" said Nuala, grabbing my arm as though to protect me from the sight.

"I was scared. I'd never seen a dead body before. It was horrible. Once he'd been so alive and so vigorous and so happy and filled with so many plans for the priesthood. He wanted to be a missionary in Africa. And now he was this lifeless thing, like an old, rotten dead fish on the beach. I ran back to the house and told my father. He and my mother came down to the beach. I trailed after them, hoping that my father, who was such a wonderful doctor, could revive him. It was too late, several days too late. Lake Michigan had claimed one more life."

"Dermot, what a horrible thing to happen to a little boy!"

"No more horrible than a lot of things that have happened to many twelve-year-olds through the centuries, Nuala. Maybe we twelve-year-olds on Grand Beach had been protected too much from the sight of death. I'll never forget that twisted, purple face that had once been so vibrant and so handsome. I can't figure out why God let it happen. He would have made a wonderful priest. He would have done good things for many people. He would have been a credit to the Church and Ireland. Instead he died in a foreign country, thousands of miles from his family and friends. As I remember the story the people who had recruited him were not all that interested in paying the money to send his body back to Ireland. It was said they wouldn't call the undertaker. My father and mother took charge of it."

"A lot of death all around us these days, isn't there, Dermot Michael?"

"Indeed, Nuala, it's sad and scary. But we all must die, I guess. And there are no good ways to die."

"No, Dermot Michael, there are not, although some are worse than others."

We were silent for a minute as we drove by Grant Park with the skyscrapers standing watch behind the park. We continued north along the Gold Coast and Lincoln Park.

"It makes me feel more sorry," Nuala said, "for poor Mr. Farmer and his family."

"It makes me feel sorry, Nuala, for everybody. Those that die and those who mourn the ones who die."

"You know, Dermot Michael," she said as we turned off the Drive at Fullerton, "there's something wrong with this picture."

"Something wrong with it, Nuala?"

"This picture of Tom and Mary Louise Doolan and their five children—there's something wrong with it altogether and I'm not quite sure what it is. If I can figure out what's wrong with it, then a lot of the pieces of our puzzle might fit together."

I concentrated on the Fullerton traffic.

"We drink our water from that Lake, don't we, Dermot?"

"Life and death, Nuala? Like Baptism . . . I'm really sounding like a philosopher this afternoon, am I not?"

"Sure, Dermot, aren't you talking like a storyteller?"

Fullerton was designed for carriages. With cars parked on either side and other cars constantly moving in and out of the Lincoln Park neighborhood, it is permanent rush hour. I like the Drive better than the Expressway, but I try to avoid the intersection of Fullerton and Sheridan Road as though it were a permanent crime site.

We pulled up to our parking spot in front of the house. Inside the wolfhound was barking, apparently welcoming us home. This was a new trick. Perhaps she had decided to appease my anger of the other morning.

I opened the front door and walked in and there was the barking wolfhound and Nessa and our daughter pulling herself up on the coffee table with a grin of pure delight on her tiny face.

"Isn't she the terrible one altogether?" Nessa said approvingly. "She's been doing that all morning and she just won't give up." Whereupon Nellie fell back on her rear end with a bump. She looked startled and then grinned and began attacking the coffee table once more.

"Och, haven't I warned you, Dermot Michael, this one's going to be the death of us!"

"She'll never give you a moment's peace, that's for sure," Nessa agreed.

Nessa sped off immediately before either one of us could talk about Seamus and their sometime relationship.

"Isn't she a sneak?" Nuala asked me. "She knows if she gives us a chance we will tell her what an eejit she really is!"

By the telephone there was a note that Nessa had scrawled.

"A Mrs. Martha Farmer called. Unless she hears from you she'll come by to visit you about seven o'clock."

"Look at this, Nuala!"

Nuala read the note and shook her head.

"Dermot, we're getting deeper and deeper into the mystery."

"Isn't that what you want?"

"There's just a little bit too much mystery going on now, if you take me meaning."

The phone rang—it was John Culhane.

"Dermot, the word is out that the assassination up in Evanston was faked. It's probably going to be on television this evening. Maybe some of them will come by to see if you have any comment. We now have the fascinating puzzle of why a man should fake his own assassination and then a couple of days later actually be assassinated. I don't see any connection between the two of them except coincidence. See what your wife thinks and let me know."

"Is your man asking me questions?" Nuala said as she began to nurse our daughter. "Isn't he the Commander of detectives in Area Six? Does he expect me to be solving his mysteries for him?"

It had been several days since I had fondled that lovely breast. I wanted it.

"In a word, Nuala Anne, yes!"

"If they ask me and I guess he did, I think there is a close connection between the fake assassination and the real one and that it goes back a long time and I have no idea what it is."

"Uh-huh."

"That woman is coming this evening to tell us something more about poor Mr. Farmer. There's too many people wanting to whisper in our ears about poor Nicholas Farmer."

"Should I call him back and tell him that?"

Nuala pondered it.

"Not today, Dermot Michael, we're going to have to wait awhile to see what happens . . . and I wish I could figure out what's wrong with this picture!"

We looked over the picture and the few newspaper clippings that came with it. They were death notices for both Mary Louise Collins Doolan and for Thomas Patrick Doolan. He had served as a colonel in the United States Army in the First World War. One of his sons, John Doolan, was killed in the Second World War. Their family history looked like a history of Irish Catholics in the twentieth century—eager to serve in defense of America because America had done so much for them. A later generation would be much less patriotic and much more cynical.

"So it all looks like ordinary family stuff,

doesn't it?" my wife asked me. "How bright and hardworking men and women make the most of the opportunities in America. It is a wonder, isn't it, that they didn't have a house at Grand Beach, just like your folks. . . . Oh, Dermot, what an eejit I am! They wouldn't want to rent a house at Grand Beach, not Tom and Mary Louise anyway. And if they told their children any of the story, then they wouldn't want a house there either."

"Maybe they spent their summers at South Shore Country Club, which was right along the Lake a couple of miles farther south."

"Isn't that the place that you told me that the people that were members sold it to the city instead of letting black and Jewish people join?"

"The very same."

"I wonder how the Doolans would have voted."

It was a fair question. There were strong racist tendencies in some of the South Side Irish. Were the Doolans the kind who would give in or the kind that would resist? That was probably irrelevant to our attempts to solve the mystery.

The phone rang again—this time it was

Mrs. Kavanagh's assistant. Mrs. Kavanagh had discovered, quite by chance, another document similar to the ones she had given us. She only glanced at it but it seemed to be a family diary. She saw no reason to withhold the diary from us. When we were finished with the materials we could pass them on to the Chicago Historical Society. She could not understand why anybody would be interested in a story of a family who lived in St. Gabriel's one hundred years ago. Could I send a messenger to pick it up?

I explained her message to my wife, whose daughter was now sound asleep in her arms.

"Dermot Michael, would you ever call the messenger service and have them pick it up for us. We should have it in a couple of hours."

Nuala finally tossed the picture aside. "Dermot, give a call to your brothers and sisters and find out where them Hegarty folks live. Your wife and your daughter are going to have themselves a nice little nap."

"I'll see to it, Nuala."

20

Before I could make my phone calls, my friend from the West Side called me.

"Hey, Dermot!"

"Hey!" I responded.

This is the proper password when dealing with friends from the West Side.

"I looked into that business matter you asked me about. My friends and their friends were very interested in what you were interested in. They wanted to tell you the truth because they didn't want anybody to misunderstand. They had nothing to do with that business arrangement. They hoped that the people who did were not successful in it."

"Uh-huh."

"They said it was a foreign firm that was involved."

"Foreign?"

"Yeah, hired Eastern European, Dermot. You know what they're like."

"No respect?"

"And no ethics."

"A Russian firm?"

"Naw, Balkan. Located up there in Lakeview. Not very ethical businesspeople, though they have a wide range of interests."

"Indeed!"

"My friends think they're dangerous. They firmly believe that the Chicago Police Department ought to do something about them."

"I can only agree with them."

"Yeah, Dermot, it's been nice talking to you. Stay in touch. I'll deliver your message back to my friends to pass to their friends."

Anybody tapping the phone would hardly suspect that he was telling me that the hit that went down on Nick Farmer came from a Balkan Mafia-style gang located in Lakeview just across Clark Street from Summerdale. Nor would a listener suspect that the wise guys out on the West Side didn't like the Balkan gangs. They wanted me to pass on the word to John Culhane. What a marvelous Chicago way of doing things!

I called John promptly.

"John, I have information that the group responsible for the Nick Farmer business is a Balkan gang up at Lakeview."

"Really! They're mean, mean guys. The sort of thing they might do. I don't suppose you have any evidence?"

"Not a bit. But I thought the hint might be of some help to you."

"So, you just talked to friends about it?"

"Me have friends? John, don't be ridiculous!"

He laughed.

He too understood that the word had come through a chain of friends for me to pass on to him to go after the Balkan mob in Lakeview. The Outfit leaders didn't like "foreign" groups imitating the style that was theirs when they were young.

I then called Mike Casey.

"Mike, I think you'd better put some of your people around us again."

"What!"

"I don't want to go into detail. I don't think we're in any real danger. But I don't want to take any chances."

"Twenty-four hours?"

"Yeah, for a few days anyhow."

I then called the messenger service to pick up the package waiting for us at 2020 Hopkins Place.

This was a lot of work for me, a busy day, all these phone calls. Not much time for writing novels, was there?

The final call was to Liam Hegarty at his office at the Board of Trade.

"Dermot Coyne! I haven't heard from you for ages. How does it feel to be a famous novelist married to a famous singer!"

"Being married to a famous singer is wonderful!"

"I can believe that!"

"Liam, I have a strange question for you. I'd like to meet with your wife someday to talk about her great-grandparents."

"Ellen's great-grandparents?"

"Yeah, her great-grandparents the Doolans who lived in St. Gabriel's."

"That's before her family became civilized and moved to the West Side. I'm sure Ellen would like nothing more than to talk to you about her grandmother who was also an Ellen as was her mother. They were quite a bunch of people. Hey, how about lunch at the Trader's Inn tomorrow? Ellen works down here too. She thinks she is a better trader than I am."

"She's Irish, isn't she?"

He laughed, "You know all about it, huh, Dermot?"

"Maybe I'll bring my own wife around."

"Hey, we'd really like to meet her!"

I decided that I had done everything I was supposed to do. Maybe it was time for me to take a nap too.

The phone wouldn't leave me alone. This time it was Cindy.

"Maybelline is in a psychiatric hospital, Dermot. It's supposed to be a secret, so I can't tell anyone where she is. The doctors have given her tranquilizers to calm her down. It should only be a week or so and she'll be at least able to get back to the family and settle down to serious therapy."

"Wow!"

"This hospitalization, Dermot, comes as a tremendous shock. And we shouldn't be surprised, should we? We knew there was something hyper about her, we just didn't know how deep it went. Poor woman, she's now at least got a chance to straighten out her life if she wants to."

"I sure hope she does."

I hung up the phone and there was something like a shout from upstairs. It was a baby shout so it had to be my daughter instead of my wife. The wolfhound, whose belly I had been scratching, rolled over and jumped up and charged the stairs in two or three bounds. I followed her almost as quickly.

Nellie was standing up in her bed hanging on to the rails of the crib and shouting. She wasn't crying, she wasn't wailing, she was shouting. Almost like a gorilla pounding on his chest. She swayed back and forth, and then began to throw her toys out of the bed, probably at me.

I took her off the rail of the crib. She kept right on shouting. An exuberant little brat.

I picked her up, she squirmed. That was unusual, normally in somebody's arms Nellie settled back. But this time she squirmed. She was having too much fun demonstrating in the crib. She didn't want out of the crib yet. She wanted to raise a little hell.

"Shush, Nellie, isn't your mother trying to get a nap and herself worn out from her virus?"

Her diaper was undisturbed and she didn't seem particularly hungry. All she wanted was to make noise. And throw things.

"I'm going to leave you in here," I told her. "You can shout your heart out and that's fine, it's good exercise for your lungs. But I don't want you waking up your mother so I'm gonna close the door. Okay?"

Her next shout did not at any rate indicate disapproval of my plan. So I tiptoed out of the room and closed the door. The wolfhound showed no intention of accompanying me. I started downstairs. I hesitated and opened the door to Nuala's room to see how she was doing.

"Is it you, Dermot Michael?"

" 'Tis."

"What took you so long and meself up here waiting for you?"

"Were you expecting me, woman?"

"Wasn't I now?"

How could I refuse an invitation like that? My rival in the nursery could shout all she wanted. Now I had my woman to myself.

Later, after our exertions, I was half-asleep and pondering the mystery of love between a man and a woman. We were at the age in our marriage where the wonder was supposed to be wearing off. For me the love between myself and my wife seemed to grow each time we were together. My desire for her, after a session of love, was almost unbearable. The intensity of our romance was entirely her doing. She was determined that our romance would never fade. I was one very lucky guy.

"Dermot Michael!" my wife shrieked, "I know what's wrong with the picture!"

I rolled over. She was sitting straight up in bed, one arm and a hand covering, ineffectively, her bare breasts.

"What's wrong with the picture, Nuala?"

"Ellen, the oldest daughter!"

"What's wrong with her?"

"In the death notice when she died in 1975 it said that she was seventy-seven years old. Dermot Michael, what happens if you subtract seventy-seven from seventy-five?"

I calculated quickly.

"You get minus two!"

She pounded on the bed.

"Not if you die in 1975. You get 1898!"

"So?"

"So, Dermot Michael, Ellen Doolan could not have been born in 1898."

"Why not?"

"Because that was the year that Agnes Mary Elizabeth was born and later died. They couldn't have had another daughter the same age, unless they were twins, and if you remember the records at St. Gabriel's there weren't any twins."

I tried to think about it but the excitement of our nap had temporarily dulled what passes through my Dr. Watson mind.

"So, Nuala, what does that mean?"

"I don't know what it means yet, Dermot. But it means somehow or the other they acquired a baby to replace Agnes Mary Elizabeth. They integrated her into the family, perhaps didn't tell her of her origins. And she became a regular member of the family, the oldest child. Don't you see, she was a replacement child in the strict sense of that word. How many families would do something like that?"

"Families that are trying to forget something."

"At least that, at least that." She pulled the sheet over and snuggled down next to me.

"I don't see how that solves things for us."

"It doesn't solve anything at all, at all, Dermot. But I have a hunch that it's going to solve everything."

After supper Martha Grimm Farmer appeared at our front door. She was dressed in black, a neatly tailored suit with a long skirt. Properly made up as a career woman should be, she seemed much less haggard than she had at the wake. Yet there was an expression of deep sorrow in her gray eyes.

"I'm sorry to disturb you after you being so kind and coming to Nicholas's wake and funeral. I heard that Roger Conrad has talked with you. I don't know what lies he might have told you. I wanted to clarify things a little."

I invited her in. She declined a drink but accepted a cup of tea. Fiona rumbled downstairs from the nursery, sniffed Martha approvingly, and then curled up at her feet.

"She's a pretty fierce watchdog, isn't she?" she said with a smile.

"Mostly she's just a good dog and responds positively to that title. Still, she checks everyone out. You are obviously a person approved so she adopts you as one of her friends."

"Rog Conrad is a very nice man. I've always been fond of him. Though he does some strange things every once in a while. My late husband was too predictable. Roger is just the opposite, too unpredictable. I don't know why he told you those stories about Nicholas working on some big scoop."

"He wasn't working at a big scoop?" Nuala asked her.

"He was always working at a big scoop, Nuala. It was an obsession with him. He was going to win the Pulitzer Prize eventually no matter how many people he had to ruin. For some reason he always undercut himself. I have no idea what this particular story was supposed to be about but I'm sure the same thing would have happened. It just isn't important."

"However," Nuala said gently, "it may be what led to his murder."

"I don't want revenge. I hope the police find out who they are and why they killed him. That won't bring Nicholas back to us. I don't think he told anybody about the story, if there was one. Not even Doug Jurgens at Channel Three who went to school with us."

I had forgotten that he was part of the group that had gone to St. Gregory's.

"And not Johnny Quinn or Robin Cleary, his wife, either?"

"We never see them. Rog's trouble is that he lives in the past. Although he's been very successful and made a lot of money, he thinks that the best days of his life were at the newspaper at St. Gregory's High School. I don't think those were such happy days at all. Roger is covering over the unhappiness and rivalry with nostalgia."

"He seems to have been fond of your late husband?" Nuala murmured.

"We all were," she sighed. "I don't know when Roger turned melancholy. It was probably after the marriage, but I don't blame the marriage. His wife is a lovely woman. He has no grounds for complaint against her."

"It's also very sad," Nuala said, leaving the way open for Martha to tell us more.

"Very, very sad. Nicholas was such a wonderful young man. Everybody adored him. He got away with everything. The priests and the nuns and most of the kids loved him. I suppose he had too many successes too early. That was the way it was in those days. Investigative reporters were the folk heroes. I thought they were snoops and that's why I went into market research instead of reporting. I suppose that market research is a kind of snooping too but it doesn't try to destroy individual people. I'm afraid Nicholas believed that a good journalist was somebody who destroyed famous people. Like he tried to destroy you two, which was really crazy of him. . . . He was so desperate to get back on television."

"Poor man."

"It was a shame that Nicholas had to grow up. He thought that the whole world would be like our high school in that little room where we edited the newspaper. When he found out that it wasn't, he was disillusioned, shattered, and furious. I fell in love with him when we were juniors. I joined the newspaper staff so I could be with him more. I never did fall out of love, despite all the terrible things that happened later, because I remembered who he had been. At first, I didn't notice the change in him after he dropped out of college. I didn't notice when we were courting and after we were married. It was only after he was fired from the *Tribune* that I began to realize that he wasn't the same old sweet, gentle Nick. He was a raging, bitterly angry man. He drank too much, smoked too much, ate too much, and fought too much. After a while, much as I loved him, it was impossible to have him in the same house, especially with the kids."

"St. Gregory's must have been a very nice place to grow up," Nuala said softly.

"It was really quite wonderful, it's kind of a small neighborhood, actually called Summerdale to distinguish it from Lakeview, squeezed between Rosehill Cemetery on the west and Clark Street on the east. Twenty-five years ago it was still very German. Not all the people were German like Nicholas and I were. There were a lot of us around and Germans kind of set the tone of the parish—music, drama, celebrations of national events. We managed to protect it from you Irish. Mind you, the Irish didn't seem to object. They liked the neighborhood too and were willing to concede that it wasn't theirs, at least until they became a majority. Which they never did. We all got along very well together."

"And you still live there?"

"I do and I still love it. The neighborhood's changed, we still have the Germans and the Irish and we also have Filipinos and Palestinians and Koreans and some Albanians. Yet Summerdale's still a nice, quiet, friendly place and kids in the high school, like my son and daughter, get along with each other just fine."

"Even the people from the Balkans?" I asked.

Nuala Ann looked at me surprised. I hadn't had the chance to tell her what was said to me; that folks from the Balkans were now part of our story.

"I think there's only one or two Balkan children in our school. Most of them are passionately loyal to the Orthodox Church. Some of them are Catholic like the ones at St. Gregory's. My kids tell me they're more Balkan than they are Catholic."

"Och, sure," Nuala sighed, "no one would ever say that of us Irish now, would they!" We all laughed.

"Do I hear a baby crying?" Martha asked. The wolfhound stood up and listened and then fell back again.

"What you hear is a baby shouting," I replied. "Our daughter is going through a shouting phase. As far as we can figure out, it's for the pure fun of it. When she's unhappy and needs her diaper changed or wants something to eat or is sick, then she cries. When she's feeling bored she shouts.

If you were to go up to her nursery now she'd keep on shouting. We trust Fiona. When there's something wrong with Nellie she knows it before we do."

"I'd like to see her before I go home if you don't mind."

"Nuala Anne McGrail not want to show off her red-haired, green-eyed daughter?" I asked.

Nuala laughed and bounded up the stairs.

"All of you have known one another since first grade?" I continued the discussion.

"I don't think so. Nick and I were baptized in the parish. Rog joined us in second grade. I think the others came later."

"I was surprised to learn that Doug Jurgens, the news director of Channel Three, was part of your group."

"He was and he wasn't. He was more of a loner than the rest of us. He moved in, I think, in seventh grade and never quite fit. He was a runner-up to Nick for salutatorian. They never got along too well as you might imagine. Nick was the hero of the school and Doug was an outsider."

An astonishing reversal in positions through the years. The outcast becomes a news director and the leader at school a down-at-the-heels reporter looking for one more chance.

"He really didn't owe Nick anything. It was awfully good of him to give Nick a chance on Channel Three. And Nick was quite good at first like he always was. Then he became angry again. At your wife. I have no idea why. I suspect there was some anger against the Irish from his days in high school, though I don't know whether that was the reason. I was horrified when I heard his first commentary. Maybe just before he died he really lost his mind."

"You were the valedictorian, of course?"

"Doesn't do me much good as a single mother wondering how she can pay for two college educations."

Nuala, who never bounded with Nelliecoyne in her arms, walked carefully back down the stairs, wolfhound in tow, with Nelliecoyne in her arms. Our daughter was still screaming and loving it. Fiona walked down the stairs like she were a queen-empress, proud of this screaming little redhead.

Nuala put Nellie on the floor and she promptly crawled over to the coffee table, reached up for it, pulled herself erect, and then flopped back onto her rear end much to her delight.

"What a beautiful little girl!" Martha Farmer exclaimed. "And very determined and very athletic. I bet she's a handful, a delightful handful."

"Och," said Nuala, "isn't she crawling already and won't she be walking in another month and you know what happens to people like that?"

"No," said Martha seriously, "I don't know what happens to people like that."

"They grow up to be total harridans altogether!"

"Nuala knows that from experience because her daughter is simply a clone, despite her red hair which she inherited from my side of the family."

We returned to the subject of Nick Farmer.

"And he had a nice family, did he now?" Nuala asked.

"I suppose that's how all the trouble began. No, he did not have a nice family. His father was a machinist and a sullen, angry man. Nick quit college because his father refused to help with the tuition. He hadn't gone to college. So he saw no reason why Nick should. It was time, he said, that Nick got out and earned his own money in payback to his parents for all he owed them."

"This was back in the 1950s?" I asked in surprise.

"Not exactly, this was growing up, that's when Nick was born. It was the 1970s when he was growing up and his dad made him quit college. He was a very domineering man and resentful. He avoided his neighbors and intimidated his wife completely. Nicholas hated him but he was also afraid of him and desperately wanted his respect."

"Which of course he never received."

"Not as far as I ever saw. His father was awful at our wedding. He didn't talk to me or my family but kept to himself at the ceremony and the banquet. I don't know why. I don't know what I ever did to him. He hated the Irish but we weren't Irish."

"Different social class, was it now?"

"He was born in Germany, and came over here as a prisoner of war. After the war he returned. Though he liked America better than Germany, he complained a lot about America too."

"He thought your family was too rich for his son?" I asked.

"I suppose so, but we weren't really that rich. My father owned a couple of restaurants that were quite successful and one absolutely wonderful bakery. There were no doctors or lawyers in our family."

"What was it like between your family and his family growing up with part of the German heritage but still cautious about asserting it after the two wars?" I continued.

"From what my grandfather said it was terrible during the First World War and the years after that. He stopped speaking German except occasionally at home. I know a little bit of German because my own mother and father spoke it sometimes. It's been useful in dealing with European clients. It wasn't something you wanted to reveal to people in the fifties and the sixties. By the time we were at high school in the seventies it didn't make any difference anymore. Still, probably there was a lot more German-related culture that we could have preserved but were afraid to. It's never been a problem for me or any of the other people I know. I didn't think it was a problem for Nicholas either. Maybe I was wrong. I was so wrong about so many things."

She removed a tissue from her purse and dabbed at her eyes.

"You think we should pay no attention to Roger?" Nuala asked, leading Martha back to her alleged reason for the visit.

"I can't understand why he told you those things. I don't know what good it will do."

"And then," Nuala said, "didn't he have to go and tell you he told us those things to make you worry?"

"As a matter of fact he did just that. As I said before, Rog was always a very strange man."

I shook hands with her. Nuala embraced her and promised they would get together soon. I doubted they would unless we were still pursuing a solution to the mystery.

Fiona escorted her to the door.

"Wasn't that an interesting conversation?"

"Nuala, what the hell is going on with these Germans from St. Gregory's?"

"Dermot Michael, they know something they don't want anyone else to know. They're trying to cover it up by pretending there's nothing to know. It's twisted all around altogether. You'd think they were Irish."

"So where does that leave us?"

"We know now for sure that Rog Conrad and Nicholas Farmer were rivals for Martha and Nicholas won. Roger has always thought that he was the better and would have made a better husband—which he probably would have."

"Does she know that Roger is still in love with her?"

"Of course she knows, Dermot Michael, women always know things like that!"

"Do you think his wife knows it?"

"I would be surprised if she didn't. She's probably worried now Nick is dead that Roger will drop her and go after Martha."

"Do you think he will?"

"Not until he's sure that Martha would accept him. There's not a chance in the world that would happen!"

"And you think that his death is somehow or the other connected with rivalry from the past?"

"I do, Dermot Michael, otherwise why would his wife and his alleged close friend come and talk to us about it. Aren't they trying to throw us off the scent?"

"Yet the things they told us would have put us on the scent."

"Sure, Dermot Michael, they'd put us on a

scent all right, but I'm thinking it's the wrong scent. And what was this about your men from the Balkans?"

"Our friends on the West Side tell us that it was a Balkan gang from Lakeview that was responsible for Nick's death. I passed it on to John Culhane."

"Isn't that the neighborhood right next to St. Gregory's?"

" 'Tis."

"Oh, my, Dermot Michael, the mystery gets thicker and thicker, doesn't it now?"

"It sure does, Nuala Ann, it sure does."

Now our determined daughter was trying to pull herself up next to the wolfhound. She clung to the dog's thick white hair and pulled. It didn't seem to bother Fiona. Nelliecoyne stood upright hanging onto the dog and once more fell back to the ground. This time her feelings were hurt. She began to cry in protest. Fiona backed off in surprise. What had she done to her little charge?

"Don't worry, Fiona," Nuala said, reassuring the huge dog with a hug as she picked up the baby from the floor. "It's not your fault. Our little terror here has suddenly discovered she's tired and wants to go to bed immediately. Dermot Michael, I'm going to put her down and then I'll come back and we can talk more about it."

It was then that the messenger arrived with the diary from Colleen Kavanagh.

21

Christmas Day, 1896.

*I have thrown away all my old diaries and
am beginning to keep a new one. It is settled
that I am going to become a married woman
right after Easter next year. March 15, 1897.*

*I don't want to become a married woman;
I'm too young to marry. I don't know what
wife means or what marriage means. I want
to learn more of both. Perhaps my father
should not have sent me to Cook County
Normal School. I didn't learn much there but
I did learn how much I don't know.*

I don't want to marry Tom Doolan. I don't

want to marry anybody but particularly I don't want to marry him. I don't hate him. I don't even dislike him. He's a nice enough man in a solemn, pretentious way. I am not in love with him and I will never be in love with him. I'm in love with Timmy Millan. Pa will never let me marry Timmy, a common laborer in the Yards.

My brothers told me I'm a spoiled little girl and maybe I am. Maybe Dad spoiled me deliberately so I could be used to win him social respectability. He actually insists I must marry Tom Doolan who, after his father's recent death, is the richest man in the parish. It will be a great achievement for a skilled meat cutter to marry his daughter off to what he thinks is wealth.

I would rebel if I could. But how do I rebel against the family? Dad has made up his mind. My brothers, who don't like me, think it's a wonderful idea and that Tom Doolan will force some sense into my head. My mother never disagrees with anything my father wants. So regardless of what I think I'll marry Tom Doolan on the Saturday after Easter next year.

I don't even know that Timmy Millan would want to marry me. He has a wonderful smile and he laughs a lot when we're together. But that doesn't mean he's in love the way I'm in love.

I'm so miserable I don't think anybody really loves me, my parents and my brothers not at all. Timmy I'm not sure about. Tom Doolan wants me but that's not the same as love.

I remember the first day he took me riding. He wanted to show me the big ditch they are building to reverse the flow of the Chicago River so it will not empty sewage into Lake Michigan anymore. He is on the committee responsible for the canal. His sister died in the last cholera epidemic.

It is a very big ditch. I did my best to seem completely uninterested in it. Then we rode back. He wanted to show me how thick Bubbly Creek is with refuse from the Yards, so thick that birds walk on it.

"That stuff goes into Lake Michigan when there's too much rain," he said as he lifted me off my horse. "We're going to stop that with the Sanitary District Canal."

The smell of the creek was disagreeable, even for someone who has grown up next to the Yards. It was even more disagreeable to find myself in his arms for even a moment. *He is a strong, powerful man. He held me like I was his plaything. I escaped as quickly as I could without losing my dignity.*

Everybody in the family is so proud of this huge diamond ring I'm wearing. I feel that it's more like a chain around my neck. Tom Doolan was very nice and polite, courteous, respectful, the perfect gentleman in his fabulous suit and shirt and waistcoat. I don't know what goes on inside his head, if anything. He is supposed to be a brilliant lawyer. But that would be said about the richest man in the parish anyway. But what he thinks about life, about God, about marriage, about a wife—I don't know any of these things and have a terrible feeling that I will never find out.

It is not a merry Christmas at all.

Wednesday, January 13, 1897.

I don't know why I'm keeping this diary. I don't make entries in it very often and I'm certain I'm not going to let anyone else read it. Maybe I'm keeping a diary so that years from now when I'm old and terribly unhappy I can look back and see how the unhappiness started.

We have already begun preparations for the marriage. Nobody cares what I think or what I want. Mother is completely in charge and she and Mrs. Doolan are fighting constantly—all very politely of course—but when they talk to one another their voices are filled with nastiness. My fiancé, my future husband, God help me, is very distant, reserved, and self-contained. He doesn't argue with his mother or my mother, he doesn't support me against them, he simply stays out of it. Maybe that's the only thing he can do, but I wish I could say that he was on my side. Will he ever be on my side in the course of the marriage? Thank God his mother doesn't go to the house and has her apartment downtown at the Palmer House. If I had to live in the same house as that nasty, mean woman I think I'd die.

I might die anyway. Sleeping in the same bed with a big, dark, hairy man like Tom Doolan. There's probably going to be even worse than that.

Father Dorney is very nice. I think he understands what's going on. But he wouldn't dream of interfering. Yet he tells me every day, every time I see him, what a wonderful man Tom is and how I should give myself a chance to get to know him.

The last time he said it I snapped at him, "I have a whole lifetime to get to know him."

"Ah, no, my dear," he said. "Many people are married for fifty years and never get to know one another. Getting to know someone else takes work and patience. And sensitivity to the fact that the other might be hurting even worse than you are."

I don't know what he meant by that. It sounded very wise, but then he's never been married, has he? And it doesn't seem to me that in that sort of hard work where you get to know the other one there is room for love.

Tuesday, February 16, 1897.

We decided that we are going to spend our wedding night at the Palmer House and then go to Los Angeles for our honeymoon. Tom had talked about taking a trip to Europe. But both his mother and my mother opposed that. They want to keep a close eye on us, very close, or perhaps I should say a close eye on me because they agree that I am an irresponsible scatterbrain and *that my moods as I approach the happiest day of my life are a sign that I have a lot of growing up to do.*

How do they know it's going to be the happiest day of my life? I don't feel happy now and I am not looking forward to the "happy" day. I think it's going to be an ugly day. I will be displayed for everybody to see as a beautiful virginal bride being given over by her father to her husband. They'll admire my good looks, whisper behind my back that I'm still childish, and think to themselves that I'm getting what I deserve.

I'll want to scream at them, scream, scream, scream, scream at my parents that I hate them, scream at Mrs. Doolan that she's a mean, old harpy, scream at Tom thinking he can buy me and that I don't love him and that I never will love him.

Will I do that? Probably not. I don't have the courage to do that. But I would love to.

I don't mind going to California, I've never been there—in fact I've never been west of Lyons Township. Or east of Lake Michigan. I would like to travel to Europe. Tom whispers in my ear that we will after we are married. I wonder it that's true.

He's telling people that we've decided on

Los Angeles. Perhaps to keep our family, our two mothers, out of the picture because they want us to go somewhere else, Niagara Falls. Everybody goes to Niagara Falls, and I don't like the idea of spending my wedding night in the same hotel where my mother-in-law has her suite. I will certainly have the feeling that she's peering through the keyhole to see what we're doing. As if I had any idea what we'd be doing!

Monday, March 1, 1897.

I'm absolutely furious.

My mother decided it was time to tell me about what men and women do after they're married. She made it sound perfectly hideous. Maybe it is. It certainly doesn't sound like fun. She seemed to think that I was somehow to blame because I didn't know the details. Who else is there to teach me the details except her? And she waited until it was too late or almost too late. I'm not as ignorant as she thinks I am. We did have a course in biology at Normal School and I understand how babies are made and where they come from—which is more than a lot of girls here in the parish do. I know what

Tom will do to me in bed. I have no idea what I will feel when he does it. I expect it will be painful and hurt. My mother told me that it was something that women have to put up with in order to have children and raise a family. I don't know whether I want to have children and I told her so.

She slapped my face and told me that I was a shameless hussy.

I don't understand why what I had said was shameless but it was probably a little rude.

She warned me that like most men my new husband would want to take off my clothes or have me take off my clothes. She said I ought not to let him do that. It is vulgar, disgusting, and totally unworthy of a Christian mother. She said I ought to be firm about that at the beginning of the marriage. No nudity, never. She said we should make love with the gaslight out in our room. And then she said but the man usually wants the lights on but that's because the man is a savage brute when it comes to lovemaking.

I'm tempted to walk into the hotel room with the lights on and undress immediately. That would show my mother how seriously I take her instructions. Of course, I would have to tell her I was going to do that or tell her afterward. No, it will be more fun to tell her beforehand just to see her reaction.

Maybe a woman must let her husband do whatever he wants to her in bed. Maybe it's disgusting and brutal and has nothing to do with love. I can't imagine what it would be like to undress in front of Tom Doolan. I wonder if he thinks I will. I wonder if he will try to make me do it. He'd better not, nobody makes me do anything.

Would you listen to that! My family is making me marry a man that I don't love and I said nobody's going to make me do anything.

March 7, 1897.

It's only one week plus one day 'til my wedding. I am the most miserable person in the world, I don't want to marry, I don't want to marry Tom Doolan. I just want to be left alone.

I saw Timmy Millan at Mass this morning. He was shy and sad and he admired my diamond ring and wished me all possible happiness. I thanked him quite politely. I was tempted to tell him that I would never *be happy and that the only one I wanted to marry was him. But that would have been foolish.*

Oh, Timmy, Timmy, Timmy! How much I love you.

March 10, 1897.

Tom Doolan kissed me good night, the first time ever. It was a very mild kiss. Nothing exciting but he certainly didn't force himself on me either.

"I will always treasure and respect you, Mary Louise," he said softly. "I'll treat you with reverence as if we are equals. We'll be partners, I won't be the boss and neither will you."

"Irishwomen are always the bosses!" I snapped at him.

He doesn't laugh much and when he does it's not for long. But he laughed.

"I think we're going to have a great time together, Mary Louise," he said.

"Incidentally," he said, helping me out of his Stanley Steamer, "why was your mother so furious with you this afternoon?"

I was tempted not to tell him and then I

thought what difference would it make. Maybe he would like to hear it.

"My mother has been giving me instructions lately about what men and women do to one another in marriage."

"Swell," he said grimly.

"She told me that you would be a brute like all men and that you would want to make love with the lights on and that you would want to see me naked and she said I should draw the line and never permit that because it was savage and unchristian and just giving in to a man's brutal instincts."

"Oh?" He smiled that small little smile of his under his thin mustache. "That sounds like a very interesting preparation for marriage."

"It sounded horrid to me. If that's what marriage is like I don't see why men and women marry. I told my mother that and she said they marry in order that they could have babies. And I said if that's why women marry that's not why men marry. Men marry because they want to possess us."

"I do want to possess you, Mary Louise, but not that way," Tom said, a light blush appearing on his face under the gaslight in front of his house.

"Well, Thomas Doolan, I don't know and I don't care. I didn't have much choice about this marriage as you know. It's all up to you anyway. It always has been."

"I'm sorry to hear that you feel you're being forced into the marriage, Mary Louise," he went on almost as solemnly as Father Dorney himself was when preaching at the noon Mass on Sunday, "I thought the arrangements were acceptable to you. I would be happy to cancel the wedding if it be your wish."

I suppose he thought he was being generous. He knows very well that my life won't be worth living if I try to cancel now.

"Too late, Tom. It was always too late."

He sighed. "If that is your wish."

"Tom, my wishes don't count! Haven't you seen enough of that as they prepared for the wedding?"

"Mary Louise, I am ashamed of myself for not defending you against my mother and your mother. I really am. I should have, I knew I should have, but I guess I was afraid of them all."

"I don't believe you're afraid of anything. You have too much money and too much power to fear anyone!"

"Would that were true, Mary Louise. Right now I'm just a little bit afraid of you."

"Well, maybe you should be."

"So you and your mother were arguing earlier about her premarital instructions which you found useless?"

He was talking just like a lawyer now.

"Yes, that's about it."

"And you said something outrageous?"

"You're learning a lot about me tonight, Thomas Doolan, though I'm not learning anything about you and probably never will. Yes, when people try to back me into a corner I say outrageous things. I will say outrageous things to you whether you like it or not."

"So I've been warned."

"They warned you that I am a spoiled little brat and that it is going to be up to you to make me grow up."

"Yes, Mary Louise, that's about what I've been told by both my mother and your mother."

"And you believe them?"

"I don't believe a single word they say, Mary Louise."

That comment took my breath away. "Really?"

"No, I don't believe a word of it. If you act childishly sometimes it's because they've forced you into a situation where you really would have to fall down and be dead for them or act childishly. I don't think you're childish."

He loves me and I didn't even like him. But he seemed to be a nicer man than I had expected.

"So what did you say to your mother that so infuriated her?"

"I probably shouldn't tell you."

In the back of my head, however, a voice was whispering you want to tell him.

"It is your decision."

I suspected that I would hear those words many times in the course of our marriage.

"Well, what I told her was that despite all the things she'd warned me against I would walk into our room at the Palmer House and immediately take off all my clothes!"

Thomas was startled. His eyes popped open and his mouth fell.

"Did you really?" he said in astonishment.

"Yes, I did really and I'm glad I said it."

"Mary Louise, I certainly will not hold you to that."

"I don't care whether you hold me to it or

not, I'll hold myself to it. If you like me naked, fine. If you don't like me then that's your problem. It's too late when we are married."

"I have no doubt at all," he said, putting his hand on my shoulder rather nervously, "that I will be overwhelmed by your beauty. . . . I must confess, Mary Louise, that the vision of that moment in the hotel room is going to haunt me every moment till then."

"Good enough for you. If you're a brute like my mother tells me that all men are, it serves you right."

"I don't think I'm a brute, Mary Louise, and I'll never be brutal to you."

My face gets very hot even as I write about this exchange. It was absolutely improper between a bride-to-be and her groom. It was probably sinful. My mother had told me that it was sinful even to think of such things and not to say them. I don't care. I'm going to do it just to see what happens. And then the first time I see her I will tell her I did it and will say it was wonderful, whether it was or not.

I'll show them all.

What do I think about my future husband after that conversation?

I think about what a friend of my father's

whispered in my ear the night of our engagement party.

"Sure," he said, "there's a lot worse around than Tom Doolan."

March 14, 1897.

Tomorrow is my wedding day and I am the most lonely, most miserable, most discouraged woman in all of the world. I don't want to marry him, absolutely do not want to marry him. He is a good man, I know that. He is even a nice man. I suspect he's truly a gentleman as well as intelligent. But it's not something I want to do. He offered last week to cancel it. I should have accepted that offer. No matter how furious my family would have been I would at least have been free. After tomorrow I will be bound to him until death do us part and I don't want that. I don't hate him but I hate the thought of being his wife and his being my husband. Dear God in heaven, if you exist, and tonight I'm not sure you do, please don't let this happen tomorrow. Please let Father Dorney announce to the whole congregation that on his own authority he is canceling the wedding. What if I went up to him before Mass *and said, "Father Dorney, I don't want to marry Thomas Doolan." He would laugh like he always does and then he would look in my eyes and he would say, "You mean that, Mary Louise, don't you?" and I would be crying and I would say, "Yes, Father Dorney, I do mean it. Please, please don't make me marry him."*

If I said those things Father Dorney would cancel the marriage. He's canceled other marriages when the same thing happened. I would be so humiliated, so ashamed everybody would stare at me next day at Mass and for the rest of my life. I would be humiliated, my parents would be humiliated, my rejected husband would be humiliated. Am I willing to pay that price for my freedom? I don't even have to answer the question. So tomorrow I will bind myself to Thomas Patrick Doolan.

March 22, 1897.

We are in Los Angeles. It is a lovely place, all sand and ocean and flowers. The train ride out was very interesting too. We had our own stateroom and it was very comfortable but not as comfortable as having your own bed. I enjoyed looking out the windows at the prairies and the mountains and the forests and deserts. How much fun it would be to see more about it. Thomas Doolan remarked that I seemed to be a good traveler. That I didn't complain much and I enjoyed it. "We will travel anywhere in the world, Mary Louise, anywhere you want."

"I'll hold you to that," I said.

Our first night on the train he offered to take the upper berth.

"Don't be ridiculous, Thomas Doolan. After all, we are husband and wife. There is little point in having a husband if you don't have him in bed with you."

He blushed. I love to make him blush. It is so easy to do. He is really quite delightful when he is embarrassed.

We are getting along reasonably well. He seems quite satisfied with me, which surprises me.

I am surprised to discover that it is amusing to be in the company of a man. I hated the very sight of my brothers because they were so crude and mean. My husband is neither crude nor mean. His male presence is pleasant, so different from that of both my brothers and other women.

He is very strong. He delights in lifting me off the ground and carrying me. Though I should be offended by his presumption, I rather enjoy it.

He also watches me very carefully, studying me as though I were a horse whose purchase he was considering or a law case he was working on. I fear I will lose all my secrets to him, that I will be quite transparent. That should worry me, but somehow it does not.

I still don't love him and I know I never will love him but I do like him. It is hard to find fault with him except that he is so solemn and so ponderous and so courteous.

And so intent on understanding every detail of me.

I suppose many brides on their honeymoon would agree with what my mother said—that husbands are brutes. Thomas Doolan is not a brute, he is, I hesitate to use the word, sweet. Solemnly sweet, ponderously sweet, but still sweet. There is so much reserve in him, so much hidden behind the courtesy. I don't think I will ever, ever come to know him. However, as the man said at my engagement party, there are a lot worse.

There are deep, deep fires within him. I do not understand those fires. Oddly, I do not dislike what little I see of them.

He has said certain things to me on our honeymoon which are either very filthy or very beautiful. Perhaps both. I am not troubled by them. I would not dare write them down, though it excites me even to think about them. I will not forget them. Not ever.

I did live up to my commitment when we walked into the Palmer House by the way. I guess he must have liked me. At least he didn't send me back.

"Mary Louise," he gasped, "you are so very, very beautiful."

That quite melted my heart.

My mother was completely and totally wrong about what happens between men and women in their bedrooms. I won't say that I'm accomplished at it and I probably will never be. But still it's nice.

Monday, May 3, 1897.

We're back home in Chicago now and in Thomas Doolan's house. I keep calling it "your house" and he insists that it is our house. It's not our house at all, it's really his mother's house in which she's letting me move with him until he gets tired of me.

That really isn't fair. He will never get tired of me. He said that today and somehow I believe him. He should get tired of me. I'm an ill-tempered, spoiled, diabolical bitch.

I've never written that word before. That's what I am, I'm a bitch.

I'll have to tell him that to see if he's shocked. Sometimes I think I do shock him. Well, too bad for him.

That's what I am just the same.

He wants me to redecorate the house. There were painters here today and I was making suggestions. Tom of course agreed with all my suggestions. Then his mother stormed into the house in fury because she'd seen the decorator's wagon in front.

"Don't you dare do anything to this house!" she snarled at me.

She was just like my own mother when she was mad at me. I wished the ground would open up and swallow my humiliation.

"Ma," said Thomas. "This is now our house, my house and my wife's. I have asked her to make plans for redecoration. Ah, I believe she has excellent taste. I have authorized her to go ahead with the decoration. I would be very pleased if you would not interfere."

I could hardly believe my ears. It was all solemn and polite and courteous, but he'd drawn the line between me and his mother.

She burst into tears and stormed out of the house.

"I dreaded that happening," he said to me.

I searched for a compliment.

"You did it very well, Thomas."

He glanced at me. "It's one of the few times in my life I've stood up to her. I suspect I will have to do that many times in the years ahead."

He was all so solemn and reasonable and lawyerlike. Not a hint of temper.

"Don't you have a temper at all, Thomas Doolan?"

He smiled his attractive little smile. "And if I do, Mary Louise Collins, you will never be the object of it, that I promise."

What could I say? So I said, "Thank you" and hugged him.

My own mother came over a couple of hours later and demanded to know what I thought I was doing to the house. "Who do you think you are?" she shouted at me. "What will people say?"

"They'll think I'm Mrs. Thomas Patrick Doolan," I said firmly. "If they don't like the way I decorate our house, then that is most unfortunate."

She continued shouting at me and I continued to ignore her. Tom came in from his office over in the Exchange Building on Halsted Street for lunch about that time.

He looked solemnly at my mother.

"Mrs. Collins, I respect and revere you as the mother of my wife. Nonetheless, I cannot in this house tolerate anyone abusing my wife. I will thank you never to shout that way at her again." Then Ma stormed out of the house.

"Well, Thomas Patrick Doolan," I said, "that wasn't bad for a beginning."

He laughed again, lightly and softly like he always laughs.

"If I wasn't so crazy in love with you, Mary Louise, I would never have dared to take on either one of those dragons."

I said something about him being a wonderful St. George.

He is a strange man. Fires burn beneath his courteous exterior. Frightening fires.

June 20, 1897.

I'm certain that I am pregnant. I have been sick the last couple of mornings and seem to have all the other signs of pregnancy. It was to be expected that I would have a child. That's what happens to people when they're married and they sleep in the same bed at night. They have children. I don't want to have a child. I am too young to have a child. I don't want to be saddled with the responsibility of a squalling little brat. Like everything else in my life it was not up to me. I suppose the baby will come sometime next March just around the anniversary of our wedding. My mother and father will be delighted, my brothers will laugh at me and say that I'm now going to find out how difficult life is. Mrs. Doolan will drool over her grandchild and want to take complete charge of her. My husband will smile his thin quiet little smile and, I think, be very pleased.

You can never tell what's going on inside his head. I suppose I should give up trying to find out. I know what goes on in his body when he looks at me. And I have to be content with that.

I do hope I'm not too much of a failure as a mother. We will have an extra maid to help us he has told me. That's not what I'm worried about.

I haven't informed him yet. He'll be very happy. Somehow or the other I want to hold it back for a while, keep my secret to myself like he keeps all his secrets to himself.

Tuesday, February 8, 1898.

I only have to wait another month the doctor says. I wish the baby would come tomorrow. I hate her, hate her, hate her, hate her! She's turned my body into a balloon. She's made me sick most of the time, she makes me awkward. I've fallen in the mud twice. I'm ashamed to go out for fear I will stumble and fall in the mud again. I hate her.

My husband says to me that it might not even be a girl. I tell him I know it's going to be a girl and I hate her. He smiles at me that same maddening little smile of his and says the day she comes you'll adore her.

"That's irrelevant!" I shout at him.

He has been very patient with me through this pregnancy. He's always patient. I wish sometimes he would shout at me or lose his temper or say something terrible. Then I wouldn't feel so guilty for being such a terrible person myself.

I do hope the baby that comes is healthy. I also hope that I survive at least long enough to get to know her. There was a time when I thought I would sooner die than be married. Sometimes I still feel that way. Yet I might almost say that I'd be happy if I wasn't so huge.

February 16, 1898.

Tom came home from his office in the Exchange Building today and collapsed into the big easy chair in our parlor.

"What's the matter, Thomas? You look like something terrible has happened."

"There's going to be a war, Mary Louise!"

"In Ireland?"

"No, with Spain. In Cuba and probably the Philippines and Puerto Rico. We will take over their whole empire. God knows we could do a better job at it than they do. However, I don't want to see our country ever become an empire like England."

"Why is there going to be a war?"

He sighed deeply. "They blew up the bat-

tleship Maine *in Havana harbor last night!
Hundreds of American sailors died!"*

"God rest them all!" I said, making the sign
of the cross.

"Yes indeed. God rest them all!"

"Who blew it up?"

"Nobody knows who blew it up. The Spaniards probably but I don't know how you ever
prove something like that. That madman
Theodore Roosevelt and the yellow journalists Hearst and Pulitzer will be determined
to get us into a war. A lot of young Americans of our age are going to die needlessly."

"We can't let them blow up our ships and
kill our sailors, can we, Thomas?"

"I suspect we could probably negotiate
our way out of it somehow if we were of a
mind to. Unfortunately, the American people
are not of the mind to negotiate. The Civil
War ended thirty-three years ago. Most people have forgotten what a terrible bloody
mess it was. Our country seems to wait a
generation before it gets into wars, until
we've forgotten the horrors of the last one."

I went over to the chair and sat on the
floor next to him with my arms around his
legs.

"You didn't used to think this way about

the war, did you, Thomas? You have a commission in the Irish Rifles. You belong to the Clan'a Gael and the Ancient Order of Hibernians. You support revolution in Ireland, don't you?"

"Yes, to all of those questions, Mary Louise. Yet, since I became a husband and almost a father I began to wonder about those things. I will resign my commission in the Rifles, that's certain. As to the Clan and the Hibernians, well, I can't leave as long as Father Dorney is under pressure. However, I'm not so sure that I'm going to give any more money for killing in Ireland. There has got to be some better way."

"Will the English ever give the Irish their freedom unless they take it?"

"I don't know, Mary Louise, I just don't know. Maybe not. Probably not. Maybe there has to be more bloodshed over there before Ireland emerges as the free nation that can take its place alongside the other nations of the world. Still, I personally don't think I will spend any more money on killing. I don't want blood on my hands, even if it is English blood."

"You won't be going to war, will you?" I asked, suddenly terrified at the prospect.

He patted my hand reassuringly. "You don't have to worry about that, Mary Louise. It's going to be a short war. There are many young fellows from Canaryville who know nothing about the last war and will be eager to sign up and run off for adventure and excitement. And all they will find, I'm afraid, is disease and death."

I ought not to have been surprised. Since I know very, very little about this man whom I married, and since he has disclosed almost none of himself to me, there is no way I can predict how he will react when something happens in the world outside our home. If I'd been asked beforehand what I thought he would do if the Spaniards blew up one of our ships, I would have said that he would be for marching not on Havana but on Madrid.

I hope my baby comes soon.

March 15, 1898.

Agnes Mary Elizabeth was born on our first wedding anniversary. That means we are going to have to have two parties on that day for the rest of our lives. I am very tired and very sore but very happy. She is an adorable little girl, looks more like her father than she does like me, and seems to be healthy in every way. Thomas Doolan was delighted.

July 13, 1898.

I have been sobbing all day, Timmy Millan, the love of my life, who dashed off to fight in Cuba the day the Maine blew up, died on San Juan Hill, not from a Spanish bullet but from disease. What a terrible end for such a young life! He was bright and quick and charming. Unlike my husband, he made me laugh. Now I will never see him again. Somehow I know I let him down. I shouldn't have married my husband, I should have waited for Timmy. I should have defied my parents. I didn't and now he is dead. If I had married him or even told him that I would marry him eventually, he would not have run off to Cuba, so it's all my fault.

My husband said to me when he found me in tears, "I am told that Timothy Millan died in Cuba."

I nodded.

"I am very sorry, Mary Louise. Very sorry."

He must know that I loved Timmy.

I don't want to go to the funeral mass. My husband says that he will go; whether I attend, he says, is my decision. I wonder what Father Dorney will say.

July 21, 1898.

My little Agnes is becoming so cute, she's not four months old and has a personality all of her own. She is a good baby. She sleeps at night. She makes very little fuss. As one of the maids said, "She's a pleasure to have in the house."

I don't know whether I'm a good mother or not. I spend a lot of time with her and take care of her. It's not right that the maids should act like a mother and so I try to be a good mother. Thomas says he thinks I'm a good mother. He would say that anyway.

The war with the Spaniards is over, Cuba is free and we've got the Philippine Islands and Puerto Rico. Thousands of Spaniards are dead and thousands of Americans, including the love of my life Timmy Millan. I don't know whether Thomas understands how much I was in love with Timmy and still am. If he does he says nothing. I wonder what he thinks. That's something I guess I will never know even about Timmy or about anyone else.

I do know, however, he absolutely adores our little Agnes.

October 11, 1898.

The fool Hibernians are having a cruise across the lake to Saugatuck on the weekend. I've never been to Saugatuck. I hear it's very nice. I don't want to go on a silly boat ride even if the weather is nice. Thomas says that we have to go because the Hibernians are raising money to help the people that are starving in Ireland.

"I don't believe it's for starving people," I said angrily. "I believe it's for more guns to kill policemen and English soldiers."

"I don't think so, Mary Louise. It looks like some sort of home rule is going to go through, if not this year or next year, certainly in the very early years of the next century. And then Ireland will be partially free and able to work its way peacefully to full freedom. The English know they can't hang on to Ireland much longer. The Land League wars have made it possible for Irish farmers

to own their own land at least for all practical purposes. The country is prosperous now. I don't think anyone wants a war."

"Then why do we have to go on the cruise? I don't want to take my baby out on that lake!"

"Because I'm still one of the leaders of the Hibernians. Though I'm not as active as I used to be, I owe it to Father Dorney to support the cause of Irish freedom. I owe it to my friends who belong to the Hibernians. My father was their leader for a long time."

"I remember," I said sadly. Sometimes Thomas seems to feel that his father—a nasty old man—is still alive and still watching him. If his father could hear the things Thomas says about war these days he would be horrified. I understand that Thomas must go on the excursion. I'm only sorry that my baby and I have to go with him.

He told me that it was my decision, as he always does. Perhaps I will decide not to go.

October 18, 1898.

I wish I were dead.

Really dead. I should kill myself. There is nothing more to live for.

October 21, 1898.

Father Dorney came over this morning to try to calm me down. I'm still hysterical. I tear at my clothes, I pull at my hair, I scream, I shout, I am a disgrace to my husband and to my family and to my parish and to my church. It was my fault poor Agnes died. If I only held on a little longer she would still be alive. I didn't, I didn't have the strength or courage to keep her in my arms. I've never had the strength or courage to do anything right.

October 31, 1898.

Father Dorney was back again today. Thank God that he doesn't say what most everyone else says, I must accept it, that I should pull myself together and get on with my life. I murdered my little daughter and I don't want to go on with life.

I'm not speaking to Thomas. I haven't spoken to him since the shipwreck. When I saw him on the beach still alive and I knew that our daughter was dead, I hit him in the face, I punched him in the stomach, I tore at his clothes, I screamed curses at him. He did not respond because he knew that he was responsible. If he had not made us go on the cruise our daughter would still be alive.

Tuesday, November 1, 1898.

I dream about it every night. I'm in the salon of the old ship, the band is playing. Thomas and I are dancing. He has become a very good dancer since he knows that I like to dance. Everybody is having a wonderful time. I have enjoyed the cruise. I loved Saugatuck. I'm all ready to cross the Atlantic. Someone comes round and says there is a terrible snowstorm outside. I don't believe him. There can't be a snowstorm in October, not even on Lake Michigan. The boat rocks more in the waves. Someone else says we're going to be a couple of hours late getting back into Chicago. That worries me for a little while. Thomas and I are having too much fun and our daughter is sleeping comfortably in our cabin. Every five minutes I go down to make sure she is all right.

Then there is a terrible noise as though we have been hit by a gigantic rock, the ship trembles and shakes, tilts over in both direc-

tions and then stops. People are screaming. I break away from Thomas and run to get the child. I don't know what happens next. I don't know what happens to him. I find her in our cabin and snatch her up. Then there is this awful explosion and fire bursting out of all sides of the ship. The wind is howling, the snow is beating against my skin and blinding my eyes, I'm screaming, I think Agnes is screaming too. There is so much screaming around us. Then the ship seems to fall out from under us and I'm in the water with my baby. The water is cold and the wind continues to howl, the waves wash over me, my clothes are dragging me down, I know I'm going to die. Then a man grabs my arm and pulls me to a piece of wood. Hang on to this he tells me. We are not far offshore.

The waves are bigger and I'm shivering all over. I know I'm going to die, I only hope that Agnes survives. I cling to her for dear life, I must not let her go no matter how weak I am or how cold my body is or how I'm shivering I must hold on to her. And then a big wave comes and it washes over us. The water flies into my mouth and my nose and down my throat into my lungs and stomach and I can't breathe, I cough and shout and scream, hang on for dear life to the piece of driftwood, and then finally I can breathe again. Only Agnes is no longer in my arms!

Another big wave sweeps over us and I no longer want to live. I let go of the little platform we were hanging on. The man grabs me and won't let me drown. Then amazingly we feel the sand of the beach beneath our feet and another big wave hits us and washes us up on the shore. I sit there for hours and hours and hours in the cold, wet and sick and in the depths of despair. I want so much to die.

Then it's morning, the sun comes out, the storm is gone, it even feels a little warm. I struggle to my feet and see Thomas coming towards me down the beach. He has Agnes in his arms, she is still alive, and we are both happy.

When I wake up from the dream, I think for many minutes it is really true, that our baby is still alive. Then I know better, she is dead and I am dead myself.

I might just as well be dead.

Tuesday, December 13, 1898.

I tell Thomas I want no Christmas tree, no candles, no plum pudding and no decorations, nothing. I don't want to celebrate Christmas this year or ever again, Christmas is a trick, a deception, I want no part of it.

He looks at me sadly and says what he so often says, "It's your decision, my dear."

How disgusted with me he must be, I'm acting like a woman who has no faith, a woman who does not believe in God, a woman who is a hypocrite every time she walks into church to pray. Maybe I'll get over it, maybe this terrible ache will go away. Maybe I'll be something like myself again. I can't imagine that happening. It would be better for me and for Thomas and for everybody else if I were dead.

Then I relent a little.

"Thomas, that doesn't mean you shouldn't celebrate Christmas."

"If you're not going to celebrate it, my dear, then neither am I."

At least I am talking to him again. I have not forgiven him, however. It's his fault he killed my daughter and he killed me.

Wednesday, December 21, 1898.

Father Dorney came over again today to see me. I'm astonished that the man pays any attention to me. He knows that I don't believe in anything. He knows that I hate God, he knows that I don't listen to his kind words. Yet he keeps coming, time after time after time. He promises me that he is going to bring a little present over on Christmas Day. I tell him not to bother, I don't believe in Christmas anymore. He just laughs and says, he'll come with his present anyway.

Sunday, Christmas Day, December 25.

I can't believe Father Dorney would be so heartless and cruel. I told him I never wanted to see him again, I slapped his face and ordered him out of my house. He was shocked. I don't think anyone has ever hit him since he was ordained a priest. He deserved to be hit for what he tried to do to me. I think Thomas was really angry at me, more angry than he has ever been. He did not, however, speak a word of anger.
Father Dorney brought over a baby girl for

us. It was a survivor of the wreck. No one had claimed it. It has neither mother nor father. He wanted us to raise it.

"I don't even know whether she's Catholic," he said to me, kindness radiating from his flashing blue eyes. "So I baptized her conditionally and called her Ellen, which was my mother's name. It's a form of St. Helena, who was the mother of St. Augustine."

"What am I supposed to do with it?" I said.

"Well, I thought you and Tom might take care of her and see that she gets a decent Catholic upbringing."

I looked at the child, I thought she was terribly ugly. Why did she live, and my beautiful Agnes die?

"I don't want a child!" I shouted hysterically. "I hate this little thing. I want my Agnes, if I can't have her back I don't want a baby to take her place."

"Now, my dear," Thomas said with his usual polite gentleness, "this little girl isn't supposed to be a substitute for Agnes. There will never be a substitute for Agnes. This is a child who needs a home and a family. Father is asking us to take care of her."

"Father can take her back to his rectory

and raise her there! I don't want her in my house!"

The little girl began to cry, probably because of my sobbing. I didn't change my mind, I knew what they were doing. They were trying to cheer me up by giving me another daughter, I didn't want another daughter, I didn't want a son, I wanted no more children.

"Maybe, Mary Louise," Father said carefully, "just maybe God wants you to help this little child have a decent life."

"God be damned!" I shouted at him. "Why didn't God want my little girl to grow up. Why has he sent me this ugly replacement for her!"

Thomas took a deep breath. "It's Christmastime, my dear, we can't turn this child away. Why don't you let me take her into the house. I'll be responsible for her. The maids will take care of her, you won't have to have anything to do with her."

"No!" I screamed. "I absolutely forbid that thing to come into my house."

Thomas turned to Father Dorney. "We'll take care of her, Father," he said, "leave her with me."

"If you take her into this house, I'll leave you!" I shouted.

Father Dorney hesitated, the child still in his arms.

"Thomas, maybe now isn't the time."

"It's Christmastime, Father. It's the time when we must give a home to somebody for whom there is no room in the inn. I'll be responsible for her."

He took the child out of Father Dorney's arms. I stormed upstairs to the guest bedroom in which I had been sleeping. I will kill that child before New Year's Day.

Monday, January 2, 1899.

The last year of the century. I don't know what that means to me. It was a cruel century. I hate it, I hate everything.

I have not killed Ellen. One night I went down to her nursery with a knife in my hand, I was going to slit her throat. When Thomas woke up in the morning he'd find his new love dead in her bed covered with her own blood.

I didn't do it and I suppose I'm glad of that. I'm not talking to Thomas, I'll never talk to him again unless he gets rid of this obnox-

ious and ugly child. He's trying to win me back by giving me a new baby to worry about and to love. He doesn't understand that I'm not capable of love anymore.

After Nuala had read the red leather notebook for a second time she handed it back to me.

"Where is the rest of it, Dermot Michael?"

"There is no rest of it, Nuala. This was all that came in the envelope."

"That terrible woman is keeping it from us!"

"Probably, but I don't know how we are going to get it away from her."

"It's such a terrible sad story, isn't it?"

Nuala had sobbed through the diary.

"That poor, poor mother."

"And the poor father too."

"The poor dear man. She was probably a very lovely young woman but so immature. Still, if I lost our Nellie that way I'd be every bit as bad, maybe even worse."

"We still don't know how the story ended."

Nuala Anne dabbed at her eyes.

"We do know a lot of things, Dermot." She reached for the picture of the Doolan kids that was on her desk. "We know they had four more children and we know that Ellen was raised as one of them, perhaps not even realizing that she was a kind of foster child. There is nothing in this picture, now is there, that suggests that she's something of an outcast? So most likely Mary Louise did fall in love with her. And if she wasn't the substitute for little Agnes, she was a wonderful girl child to have around the house."

"You just want to put a happy ending on the story, Nuala."

"Well, I think the story has to have a happy ending, Dermot Michael. Don't you, girl?"

She scratched the wolfhound's belly. Upstairs there was no sound at all from the nursery, an exhausted Nellie was sleeping soundly, neither wailing nor shouting.

"We know more than we knew before," Nuala went on. "We know that Thomas Doolan was no longer a fervent nationalist. We know that he didn't want to go on the cruise either. He did it out of a sense of duty. We know that he felt terrible guilt for what happened."

"And we know that he was an extremely patient man."

"Sure, didn't he love her something terrible, Dermot Michael, and himself so shy and reserved."

"Shy?"

"Certainly the poor man was shy! She must have terrified him from the very beginning and herself not knowing it at all, at all."

"No one will say that about your husband!"

"Not twice if I'm around!"

"Do you think the little girl was the child of the couple from Detroit that drowned?"

"She had to be, didn't she, Dermot Michael?"

"We still don't know what might have gone on between Thomas and the man from Detroit. We don't know what he went over to the dunes in midsummer after the wreck to search for. We don't know why you saw the ships out there last month and why Nellie went ballistic. We don't even know why she did the same thing when we drove by the house on South Emerald. So it doesn't seem that we're much closer to solving anything."

"We don't know the whole answer, Dermot. Let's hope that this Hogarty person has the rest of her great-grandmother's diary."

22

The next morning Mr. Forest picked us up promptly at nine-thirty. Nessa was in residence again keeping an eye on our daughter while Nuala and I set out for a couple of hours of exploration. My wife continued to carry the telephone with her and used it every half hour on the half hour.

"Well," she said as we settled down in the back of Mr. Forest's taxi. "At least we've got one problem a little better under control."

"I'm glad to hear that, Nuala Anne."

"Don't you want to know which problem it is?"

"Well, I guess I do if you want to tell me."

"Dermot Michael Coyne, you're just being deliberately difficult!"

"Who me?"

"Haven't we got the beginning now on solving the Nessa problem?"

"Do we now?"

"Yes, we do. Aren't she and Seamus coming over for dinner tomorrow night?"

"Was that wise?"

"They both know that the other is coming, so that might give them one more chance."

"Are we supposed to talk them into a reconciliation?"

"Dermot Michael Coyne, don't be an eejit all the time. Who is going to try to talk anybody into anything? Oh, no, that's not what I have in mind at all, at all."

"Well, what do you have in mind?"

"Won't the little Bishop be here?"

"You invited the little Bishop to dinner, with Nessa and Seamus?"

"Well, you and me too!"

I thought about it for a moment.

"Nuala Anne, that's just brilliant. The little Bishop won't talk a bit about reconciliation but when he's finished they will be reconciled!"

"Och, haven't you caught on now, Dermot

Michael," she said, inordinately pleased with herself. "I told you I was working on something."

Our first stop at ten o'clock was at the John Hancock Center where I had once lived and where I still kept the apartment and watched it appreciate each month. Sometimes Nuala and I used its swimming pool when, for one reason or another, we didn't want to go to the West Bank Club. I would have felt guilty about having a second home in the city if it wasn't earning me at least as much as common stock was earning.

We were not, however, going to the apartment. We were headed rather for the offices that front on the forty-third floor of CTC, Channel Three Chicago. We had an appointment with Doug Jurgens, who was the news director of Channel Three.

He looked like news directors are supposed to look, lean, distracted, nervous, and frightened. His edgy, dark brown eyes jumped nervously under his high forehead. His hairline had receded pretty far, his stomach had projected farther than it should, and he chewed gum even more vigorously than Michael Jordan.

"Come right in," he said with an attempt at geniality. "It's nice to meet you."

"To begin with, Mr. Jurgens," my wife said, "I'm not here to complain about those terrible things that poor Mr. Farmer said about me and me music. I believe that we should let the dead bury the dead."

Jurgens looked baffled. He'd heard the quote somewhere but he wasn't quite sure where it was from. Probably would have his researchers dig it up after we left.

"Well, I'm glad to hear that," he said with a sigh of relief. "I'm ready to apologize to you personally for what Nick said. He claimed he had evidence to back up any words but of course he didn't have any evidence."

"You still put him back on after he arranged his own assassination?"

"I did, and I shouldn't have. We were flooded with protests. He would have been off the following week anyway."

"You figured you owed him something because you worked on the school paper with him?"

"I really wasn't part of their crowd," Doug Jurgens said with a thoughtful frown. "We only moved into the neighborhood when I was going into my sophomore year in high school. Since St. Gregory's is right down the street and the tuition was cheap, my parents sent me there. It wasn't a bad place. I'm sure I got as good an education as I would have if I'd gone to Loyola or St. Ignatius. It's kind of hard to break into the crowd in a new school at that age, particularly a small school where everyone knows everyone else, I didn't feel much like an outcast. Since I wanted to go into broadcast journalism, I lobbied pretty heavily to get on the school newspaper. I had no idea why Johnny Quinn didn't want me. Perhaps because he thought there were too many Germans as it was. Nick seemed to side with him until Martha took my side. Then he seemed happy to have me on board. I can't say that I ever became as friendly with him as the others. I did admire him. He was an awfully gifted young man."

"Martha ran the show?" I asked.

"Dermot Michael," my wife interjected, "of course she did!"

"You're right, Ms. McGrail. Martha was a special kind of woman. Everybody in the school was in love with her, including me and, unless I'm mistaken, a couple of the priests."

"Sure, why wouldn't they be in love with her?"

"She was beautiful and fragile and smart and gentle and very determined. Absolutely irresistible!"

"And Nicholas Farmer won?" I asked.

"That's right," he said sadly. "That didn't surprise anybody then because he seemed far and away the best bet of the lot. No way you could foresee what would happen to him. . . . Hey, are you two investigating the question of who killed him?"

"We're kind of interested, as you well might imagine, Doug," I said as smoothly as I could. "We were accused of the first assassination attempt which he plotted himself. Though the cops don't think that we're behind the assassination attempt that worked, it's still something that's going to float around out there and perhaps embarrass our children unless we put it to rest now."

"Good idea," he said. "If you figure it out could we have an exclusive on it?"

"And why wouldn't we be giving you the exclusive? Sure, you were a friend of his and resent his killing even if you weren't such a close friend."

There was, I thought, a lapse of logic in that response.

"Roger Conrad has been talking to you, hasn't he?"

"Didn't he take us off to lunch after the funeral?"

"I don't know exactly what motivates Roger. He is an extremely successful journalist, makes tons of money. Somehow or the other there is always a little something uneasy about him. I'm not quite sure what it is, but he certainly likes to stir up trouble. . . . I think he's never really accepted defeat in the contest for Martha. Rog certainly doesn't like to lose."

"And you think he still wants her?"

"Yeah, I suspect he does. I don't see that he has much hope, however. Martha is a pretty straight-laced Catholic. She'd never have an affair with a divorced man, much less a married one. You never can tell what goes on in Roger's head . . . I suspect there's a trace of depression in him. He takes pills of some sort."

"Not enough in love to kill Nick, however?"

"No." Doug Jurgens considered his words

carefully. "I don't think so. Somehow I can't imagine Rog being involved in murder. Even his journalism is a bit soft. He's won prizes, but somehow the hard edge is missing. It's the color of his style and his ability to pry out the inside story that makes him a success. Maybe I resent that because I'm in television and we have only enough time for the hard edge. We don't have the leisure of a long article in the *Journal* or a book. Rog saw both sides of every question. He understood the oil companies and the Nigerian military. I can't see somebody who saw both sides of every question putting out a contract on poor Nick."

"Was Nick working on a big story for Channel Three?"

Doug Jurgens's eyes narrowed and he shifted position in his chair.

"I don't suppose there is any reason not to talk about it now. Yeah, he claimed that he had found something really big, prize-winning stuff. Nick always wanted prizes. It would knock my socks off, could blow the Chicago business community out of the water. It really was something terrific. Or so he said. He promised us if we gave him another shot at television exposure he'd give it to us."

"Did you believe him?" I asked.

"Not really. We'd all heard this many times before from Nick. I figured there was nothing much to lose. He always gets attention when he goes on the camera. He loses it after a couple of weeks. In the initial period he would boost our ratings at a small cost. Nicholas came cheap. And maybe, just maybe, you think, he's finally latched on to something big. Maybe it wasn't too late for him to turn his life around."

"Something with a flavor of the old days of St. Gregory's in it?"

A mask descended on Doug Jurgens's face.

"You guys have found out more than I thought you would find out. To tell you the truth, Nick hinted at that. I don't know what he meant. He was always trying to settle a grudge. There was no reason for a grudge against any of us who went to school with him because he was certainly a hero at school. Yet everyone who was in that newsroom in the old days is a success, except Nick. I'm a news director. Martha heads a successful market research firm. Robin is one of the best PR consultants in town. Johnny is a big investment banker down at First Cook County. Roger is a world-famous business reporter. Nick is still scrounging. I think that would stir up some resentment now, wouldn't you?"

"Was he trying to destroy someone?" I asked.

"That's what investigative reporters do, Mr. Coyne. They destroy people."

We thanked Doug Jurgens for being helpful and took our leave.

Nuala Anne called home, spoke a few minutes in Irish, and reported to me that our daughter was still shouting and still throwing herself up and then falling on her rear end. She showed no signs of giving up.

"You know what standing up means?"

"Woman, I do. It means that she's fixing to walk. Then we'll have our work cut out for us."

"We will, won't we, Dermot Michael. But sure won't it be fine to see her walking around."

There, I thought to myself, speaks the mother of her first child. On second thought, however, my wife would be as delighted when our fifth or sixth child started to walk.

It was a brisk autumn day and we had some time so we strolled down Michigan Avenue and then turned on Monroe Street to walk over to the Trader's Inn.

"Well, Dermot Michael, that was interesting now, wasn't it?"

"Wasn't it now, Nuala Anne?"

"Your man knows more than he is saying."

"So do they all—Roger Conrad, Martha Grimm Farmer. I'm sure if we talked to Robin Cleary and Johnny Quinn they'll all tell us a lot but they won't tell us anything we really need to know."

"They're all trying to put us on the wrong scent, Dermot Michael."

"And what's the right scent, Nuala Anne?"

"The right scent, unless I'm wrong altogether—and you know, Dermot, that I'm never wrong altogether—someone was involved in something that revealed a character trait back in the years when they were at high school together. Your man found out something about one of them. He remembered what happened in high school and that confirmed his suspicions. Whatever it was, there's a link between the present and past—but isn't there always?"

"And in this one there's more hints floating

around in that neo-Neanderthal vestige of yours."

The little Bishop had once said that "arguably" psychic sensitivity was a throwback to an earlier stage of evolution in our species when, much more poorly equipped with voice boxes, humans had developed an ability to communicate by reading psychic vibrations. The fact that it is now agreed that we are not descended from Neanderthals did not bother the little Bishop.

"We are patently descended from an earlier species," he said, eyes flicking rapidly behind his Coke-bottle rimless glasses, "who would not have as sophisticated speech abilities as we have. Certainly the evolutionary process at that time would have selected the people who were psychically sensitive. Obviously that change persists in our species even today, and is probably a lot more common than we realize."

Who was I to disagree?

At one-thirty in the afternoon, Trader's Inn, around the corner from the world's largest commodity exchange, attracts milling throngs of high-powered and noisy traders eager for a bite to eat and a couple of drinks to calm their jagged nerves. The atmosphere is of a men's locker room—obscenity and forced geniality—and the maturity of a children's playground.

The Hegartys were two of a kind. A couple of years older than I am, medium size, outspoken, energetic, jumpy, charming, and, like all good traders, just a little crazy. Ellen was a redhead like my grandmother and like my daughter—pretty, opinionated, and very much in charge of the family. Liam was your typical black Irishman. Dark hair, dark skin, dark mustache, and deep, deep blue eyes that didn't miss a thing. They would either make a fortune together or go broke together. Kill each other perhaps, but as the saying goes, they would never divorce.

"So you are interested in my grandmother," Ellen asked as soon as we found ourselves a table and ordered beer and ham and cheese sandwiches.

"We're really interested in your great-grandmother. They both were remarkable women it seems," I responded.

"My grandmother Ellen was an astonishing woman," Ellen Hegarty said enthusiastically. "She was an Ellen and my mother is Ellen and I'm Ellen too. Everybody in the family simply adored her. I only knew her for the first eleven or twelve years of my life, but she made an enormous impression on me. She was handsome and intelligent and vigorous and determined and funny and just plain wonderful. Any family party where Ellen showed up was bound to be a success."

"Did she ever talk," Nuala asked, "about what it was like growing up in St. Gabriel's back at the turn of the century?"

Ellen Hegarty talked in rapid, enthusiastic, convulsive paragraphs.

"Did she ever! Grandma Ellen couldn't talk enough about that subject. It sounds like an incredible place. Like Bubbly Creek, a branch of a fork on the south branch of the Chicago River which carried so much waste that they said it would compare to the waste from a city of one million people. It bubbled because there was so much crap and corruption that you could walk on it. One story was that a bubble once consumed a whole boat. I don't think that's true but Grandmother loved to tell the story. And stories about the Dumps over on Damen Avenue, where poor people used to come and collect Christmas trees after the season was over so they could save them for the next Christmas and clothes and furniture and all kinds of other things, and the infant mortality rate in the houses around the Dumps was ten times above the city average."

"Your grandmother didn't live there, did she?"

"Oh no, she lived on Emerald Avenue in St. Gabe's when, as she liked to say, the shanty Irish were about to become the lace curtain Irish. Her parents, Tommy and Mary Louise Doolan, were lace curtain. However, they had very strong social concerns. They were involved in cleaning up the Dumps and filling in part of Bubbly Creek and trying to diminish the smoke and the fire and the noise in the Yards. Her father was a lawyer whose practice involved the Yards. He was so good at it, however, that he was able to talk a lot of the packers into cleaning things up. A really forceful and remarkable man. Ellen worshiped him and her mother too. I suppose that's why she was the woman she was. She was powerfully loved as a kid and she powerfully loved other human beings throughout her life. I hope a little bit of it is passed on to her grandchildren."

"You may have noticed," her husband joined in, "there is a lot of the old lady in my wife."

"Why, Liam, such a nice compliment!"

"Don't husbands reserve their compliments now," Nuala Anne observed, "for when there are guests around to be impressed with the gentlemen they are!"

We laughed, Liam and I uneasily.

"You wouldn't be seeing much of your cousin out on the South Side, would you now, Ellen?"

"As little as possible, she was so embarrassed by the fact that she'd spent a little bit of time Back of the Yards that she's never recovered from it. She is the worst snob I have ever met, an absolutely insufferable snob. She has wormed herself into key positions on a number of important boards and now she's wearing out her welcome. It won't be long now before she gets dumped on some new and unsuspecting boards."

This was a surprisingly bitter outburst for a young woman who seemed to have a sanguine personality.

"You'll have to excuse my wife on the subject of our cousin Colleen," Liam explained. "Colleen drives her up the wall. She thinks she is not only superior to her ancestors who lived Back of the Yards, but she is also superior to all us West Siders who live in civilized places like River Forest and Oak Brook."

"Och, sure, how could anyone make that mistake!"

We all laughed again. Ellen Hegarty relaxed a bit.

"What made you ask about Cousin Colleen?"

"She gave us a diary in a red leather notebook which Mary Louise Collins Doolan began to keep on the day of her engagement. It ends in 1899. And we need to know more about what happened after that."

"You have read her notebook?" Ellen asked.

"We have," Nuala replied. "Would you ever have some of the later editions of it?"

"Yes, as a matter of fact I think I do. There is a lot of Great-grandmother's things up in our attic, in a chest in which Grandmother put them. She told me many times that someday the historians would come looking for it. I haven't looked through it much. But there is at least one of the red leather books up there. I glanced at it, and it seemed to be in Great-grandmother Mary Louise's script. I was too busy to explore."

"I should think that the Chicago Historical

Society would be very interested indeed in it now," I said. "Your great-grandparents and your grandparents were obviously important people in the development of the City of Chicago. Those records and other relics could just be priceless information."

"Tax deductible?" Liam asked brightly.

"Liam!" his wife warned him. "You shouldn't say things like that. It's all right to think them but you shouldn't say them. You can never tell who has a wire on for the feds in this place."

It seemed obvious that Ellen had only the vaguest notion of life in Chicago at the end of the last century—about what I knew before those two ghosts ships appeared off Grand Beach.

"St. Gabe's wasn't exactly in Back o' the Yards," I said. "Back o' the Yards, strictly speaking, is the south and west of what used to be the Union Stockyards while St. Gabe's is east of it. It was an older community and more established than the others. The Irish who lived there fought their way into the middle class, before the other immigrants made it. It wasn't exactly a comfortable place to live, there were open sewers and muddy streets and hunger and poverty and disease, even when your great-grandparents were living at 47th and Emerald."

"Was the stench as bad as they say it was?"

"Some people fainted when they smelled it for the first time on a hot day. The South Side Irish used to say that's what put the color in our cheeks. It didn't do that, but it did put money in their pocketbooks and purses as they struggled out of the mud and the filth into the American dream, such as it is."

"Are the Irish still out there?" Liam asked. "There are a bunch of traders from a place they call Canaryville. Is that the neighborhood?"

"It was meant to be an insult because grackles used to live there. As the Irish have been known to do, they turned it into a compliment and the whole neighborhood proudly became Canaryville."

"These guys are really proud of their neighborhood," Liam agreed, "and they're pretty rough customers."

"Would you ever let us look at that diary? Me husband belongs to the Chicago Historical Society and they might be very in-

terested in having it. And aren't we fasci-
nated altogether by their story. We'll give it
back to you and the volume we have."

"Fair enough," Ellen Hegarty agreed
briskly to the trade. "I'd like to read them together if I get time from this job and from
kids around the house. Maybe we'll have
some more of those red leather notebooks
in the chest."

While we were sitting at the table eating
a scoop of chocolate ice cream, an enormous man with silver hair and a red face
and a huge belly blundered into the dining
room. He was about my height—six-three—
and probably outweighed me by a hundred
pounds, almost all of it in fat. His face was
pushed into a furious scowl, one I suspected
was his usual facial expression. He was
trailed by a sleek, well-decorated, well-
dressed woman in a black leather suit with
a miniskirt. She glared at the crowd with a
hungry feline face, a cat ready to pounce. A
gorilla and a panther.

"Who's that guy?" I asked Liam Hegarty.

"Oh, that's Johnny Quinn, he's a real jerk.
He messes around in some of the money
markets, mostly Eurodollars. He's a vice
president of some sort or the other at First

Cook County, one of their allegedly smart investment guys. I hear he's in real trouble with the funds that he's managing and that the feds are all over him. He always looks that angry."

"The woman is his wife," Ellen told us, "Robin Cleary. Poison."

Johnny Quinn and Robin Cleary. Fancy that!

They headed right to our table as I thought they might. How did they know we were here? Doug Jurgens call them?

"You, you're Coyne?"

Johnny Quinn shoved my arm.

"That's my name, Dermot Michael Coyne at your service."

"Listen, you fucking bastard," he bellowed, grabbing my shoulders and shaking me. "You fuck off! You've got no right to fuck around in my life and my past. Leave me and my wife alone or I'll fucking kill you, you hear me?"

"Like you killed Nick Farmer?"

He shoved me again. "Keep those fucking ideas to yourself, you hear? I don't need somebody like you fucking around in my life."

"I can understand that with the FBI investigating your financial dealings."

"Dermot!" Nuala barked. She didn't want a fight. Women never do, well almost never.

Neither did I, at least not one that I started. Johnny Quinn was going to have to floor me before I fought back. Then I'd have a hundred witnesses saying that I fought in self-defense.

"Mr. Quinn," I said pleasantly, "my wife is a sensitive young woman from the County Galway. I don't appreciate hearing that kind of language in her presence."

Nuala laughed. So did the Hegartys.

Quinn pulled me out of my chair and shook me. That was a mistake, because now he saw that I was as tall as he was and much more solid.

"You take your hands off me, sir, or I will land one punch to your fat belly and you will explode like the balloon of flesh that you are."

"Dermot Michael!" my wife shouted.

"Don't worry, Nuala, I don't beat up on fat men or little children, especially when they are combined in one moronic person."

He backed off, apparently intimidated by my size and demeanor. I was astonished. I don't intimidate very many people. I noted in the back of my head that Johnny Quinn was easy to intimidate.

"If you do anything to our reputation we'll sue!" Robin Cleary hissed.

"Go ahead and sue," I replied. "My lawyers will be better than your lawyers. However, I have no reason to want to do anything to your reputation. I'm trying to find out who killed Nick Farmer so that lingering suspicion won't be held against me and my family."

"Don't confuse us with that crazy bunch. They are no good, they are fakers," she snarled. "They've always been fakers. They were faking things back at St. Gregory's. That's why Johnny and I broke away from them. We can't stand fakers."

I almost said that it takes one to know one. However, the warning light in my wife's eyes silenced me.

They turned on their heels, the leopard and the gorilla, and strolled out of Trader's Inn. Now wasn't that interesting?

"Isn't Ellen a darlin' little thing, Dermot Michael?" my wife asked as we walked back up the Magnificent Mile. "And didn't she love her grandmother something terrible? And her having all them wonderful things in the chest in her attic. Isn't it surprising that she's never looked at them?

"I wonder if Ellen Doolan ever realized that she was not a Doolan child? Maybe we ought to try to keep that a secret."

"You can depend on it, Nuala, that Ellen and Liam will never go up there to take a look at the notebook. They are too busy with their family and their careers and other important things. She will never read her great-grandmother's diaries!"

"Not very likely. We Chicagoans really don't care much about our past. We would rather not think about what our ancestors went through."

"Maybe that's because you only had a couple of generations of history and ourselves a couple of thousand years!"

"Probably. . . . You think they know that Ellen was a foster child? Do you think that Ellen knew? Do you think she read her mother's diaries after her mother was dead?"

My wife hesitated.

"I think she probably did and that it didn't bother her at all. . . . And what would you be

thinking about your friends Johnny Quinn
and Robin Cleary?"

"I think they have a lot to hide."

"Wasn't I thinking the same thing! And
they making fools out of themselves in public!"

"They would have been perfect targets for
Nick Farmer—rich, successful, and Irish."

"I wonder," she murmured as she slipped
into the deep silence in which she communicates with . . . well, with whatever she
communicates with.

23

"The popes are not, by and large, an attractive lot," the little Bishop commented as he destroyed altogether my fettuccine Alfredo.

Nessa and Seamus looked up in surprise.

"They tell us the Pope is the Vicar of Christ, don't they?" Nessa demanded. "Doesn't God choose each one of them."

The Bishop looked in some surprise at his empty wineglass but waived aside my proffered bottle of Niersteiner.

"Then God has chosen murderers, simonists, blasphemers, womanizers, adulators, fornicators, liars, thieves, poisoners, spendthrifts, drunks, gluttons, incompetents, men who have kept slaves and harems, men who have committed incest, men who have drunk toasts to the devil, men who have bought and sold ecclesiastical office, men who wasted money and lives, men whose only desire was to enhance their own power and the wealth of their families, vicious men, mean men, arrogant men, cruel men."

"All of them?"

"Oh, no"—the Bishop waved his hand—"as Eamon Duffy says in his book and TV series, *Saints and Sinners*, there were a lot of good men in between. Even a few wise administrators. Not all the sinners were bad administrators and not all the saints were good administrators. Occasionally there has been a saint who was also a good administrator. On the average, the Popes have been a good deal better than your typical European emperor or monarch of the last two millennia. My point is that if the Lord wanted perfect men sitting on the throne of the Fisherman, he would not have turned the job over to human beings."

"They never told us that in school," Seamus said thoughtfully. "They never told us that there was so much evil in the Church."

"A mistake for which we are paying." The Bishop shook his head sadly. "No thanks, Dermot. Your fettuccine would do honor to Alfredo himself. However, two helpings is quite sufficient. . . . From Peter on down, Popes have been flawed humans. At least Peter had the grace to apologize, which most of the others have not. So we have some Catholics, all too many I fear, who worship the Pope and not God. There is no room in the Catholic heritage for personality worship."

"So why stay in the Church, me lord?" Seamus asked.

"Because it is the only Church we have and because we do not make the mistake of equating the virtue or the wisdom of our leaders with the wisdom and grace of the heritage which embraces us. Why do you stay in, Seamus?"

"Well"—he hesitated, trying to put his thoughts together—"because of the Mass and the parish back home and the parish priest and my family and Christmas and Easter and First Communions and May Crownings and the angels and the saints and Mary especially and the Souls in Purgatory and because the Church tries to take care of the poor and the hungry, though often it makes a mess of it, much as I am doing now."

"I don't think you're making a mess of it at all, at all," Nessa said fervently.

"You'd answer the question the same way, Nessa?" the Bishop asked.

"Yes, me lord."

"Call me Blackie. . . . Now with the two of you agreeing about the Church, don't we have the voice of the faithful?" he sighed contentedly, feeling that his work was done.

Which it probably was.

"What I like about the Church," Nessa said, "is that it always forgives you."

"Hadn't it better." Nuala could contain herself no longer. "Isn't that what your man preached when he was here with us?"

"It never lets us go, even when we try to get away," Seamus agreed.

"Once a Catholic, always a Catholic," I permitted myself to intrude.

"It can't let you go, you see," the Bishop said, attacking my cherry cobbler. "Because you are the Church, not just we poor priests and bishops. All of you. We need bishops and priests to have a church. And we need lay folk to have a church. Neither can make it without the other. We've always had a grand bunch of laity from Ireland. . . . Yes, Dermot, a little more whipped cream won't hurt."

Thus we had done the job on our young friends, older than either me wife or meself, without a word being said about their silly quarrel.

Nuala beamed triumphantly.

The second volume of Mary Louise's diary arrived right after our guests left.

24

March 15, 1899.

Today is the anniversary of my marriage and the birth of my daughter. I am no longer hysterical. I have not been hysterical for a month and a half. I suppose that is good, I am acting mature. I haven't forgiven anyone, neither myself nor my husband, nor the Hibernians, nor Father Dorney, nor God. The estrangement between my husband and myself is complete. It will be so for the rest of our lives. I hope my own life is not a long one. It would be better if he were free. The little girl continues to live in what he once called my house, adored by the servants and spoiled by my husband. I no longer become furious at the sight of her. I continue to avoid her on all possible occasions. She's a very seductive little person, winning everybody over with her smiles and her beauty. She will not, however, win me. I do not want a substitute child, in fact I do not want any children. I feel oppressed by her presence in the house. I no longer scream at her. She is not to be blamed for what happened to my own daughter and for what other people have done to me by bringing her into the house.

April 15, 1899.

My husband has decided that he must have a birthday party for his daughter Ellen. We have no idea of when she was born. It seems likely that she is a few weeks younger than my beloved Agnes. Therefore he has chosen April 15 for her birthday, a month to the day after Agnes's birthday. Which is cruel. I suppose he didn't realize the coincidence. I absolutely refused to come to the party. Why should I? She's not my daughter, I don't want her in my house.

July 4, 1899.

It is unbearably hot here in Canaryville. My husband has taken his daughter and some of the servants to a new house he has bought at Lake Geneva. I am sure it is hot there too. As he says, there is not the smell and the smoke of the stockyards and life is more informal. I hope they have a delightful time. I will not miss them. I refused to go to Lake Geneva because I thought it would be inappropriate, as inappropriate as taking off my black mourning clothes, which I never intend to do.

August 30, 1899.

My husband has gone back to Michigan City again for the second time searching for whatever it is he's been searching for. I now realize that there was something more involved in that cruise to Saugatuck than just an autumn weekend. He did something there on the trip or obtained something that *was extremely important. I wonder if he organized the trip behind the scenes so that whatever exchange took place in Saugatuck or on the Lake coming back could occur. He is spending a lot of money searching for something in the sand and the dunes along the lakeshore. Though he has the money to spend, he has never been reckless or foolhardy with money. To be fair to him, however, he's always been generous to me. I want nothing from him now, however.*

If I knew what the mystery was behind the clues it would not bring Agnes back nor would it change my attitude towards my husband. He did not need to insist that his wife and child accompany him on the voyage. Therefore, he was responsible for her death and my loss. I am responsible too. I didn't hold her tightly enough while we were floating on the waters after the ship went down. I wouldn't have had to hold her tightly if he had not made us come on the trip.

Am I being fair to him?

Why should I worry about fairness, has God been fair to me!

However, when he asked me if I wanted to go on the trip to Saugatuck and I argued against it at that time of the year he did tell me it was my decision. He always tells me things are my decision.

I hate him for that. Why does he shift so much responsibility to me? Why am I the one who has to make the decisions? It is not fair.

October 3, 1899.

The child is irresistible. I do not like her, I do not want her in my house. I do not accept her as a member of my family. Nonetheless, when she walks over to me with her funny little walk and looks up at me with her wondrous blue eyes and calls me "Mummy" I cannot help myself. I pick her up and hold her in my arms. My embrace is not too affectionate. I do not want her to think she has been accepted. Nonetheless she curls in my arms very contentedly. Since I'm going to have to live with her for many years to come, I must at least be civil to her. I must pretend that she is welcome. I don't know what this pretense will do to her or to me or to my husband. One must do the best in the circumstances in which one finds oneself.

December 1, 1899.

Our poor little Ellen is terribly sick. Somehow she has caught pneumonia. She has a high fever, her doctor is not optimistic. I am weeping all the time. As much as I do not want her in the house, I also do not want to lose her. My husband is terribly distraught. He blames himself for taking her out to make snowballs last week. My feeling is that if you are going to catch pneumonia you can get it anywhere. At least it's not diphtheria or typhoid fever. The doctor says the crisis will come in a day or two. I pray to God he grants the poor little child health and long life. She is not responsible for anything. Rather she is a victim just like I am.

December 3, 1899.

Our poor Ellen is in crisis now. She may be dead by morning. Or she may have surmounted the fever. The doctor does not think she will survive, she is too young and too frail. I have never thought of her as frail. Perhaps that is because I only notice her smile.

We have suffered so many losses, I pray to God that this will not be one more.

December 7, 1899.

Ellen is still alive. The doctor says that she is recovering. Although she will be weak for some time, she certainly will be able to celebrate Christmas.

I had forbidden her father even to think of Christmas. What can I do now? I suppose they have to have Christmas. It doesn't mean that I have to be part of it.

When I go into the room to see her, she holds out her arms to me and repeats over and over again, "Mummy, Mummy, Mummy." I must restrain my heart lest I fall in love with her.

December 25, 1899.

Christmas Day. We went to Mass at St. Gabriel's and wished everyone merry Christmas. People told me how well I looked. They admired my smart new gray dress. Perhaps they wanted to tell me that it was time that I gave up my mourning clothes and went on with life. It is so easy to say that one should go on with life. Those that say it have not had the life torn out of their hearts.

Christmas was pleasant at our home. My mother and father and my husband's mother came to dinner. They were very cautious with me. Perhaps my hysteria on past occasions warned them away from my temper. I hope so. I hope they are cautious with me for the rest of my life.

They also seemed to have been enchanted by Ellen who is, I must say, a very skillful enchantress. Nobody says a word about our poor lost Agnes.

Will I mourn forever? How can I not mourn forever?

Father Dorney said this morning to me it was good to see me looking so well and now that we're about to start a new century I should consider smiling again.

"What do I have to smile about?"

I snapped at him. I tell myself that I have not forgiven him for being part of the plot that brought that child into our house.

"You have to smile, Mary Louise," he said to me, with a laugh, "because it's in your very nature to smile. You have the best smile in St. Gabriel's. You will not be able to deprive us of it much longer."

What a terrible thing to say!

Nobody ever told me before I had the best smile in St. Gabriel's.

I asked my husband after our mothers had gone home whether he thought Father Dorney was right.

"Father Dorney is always right," he said. "Everyone knows you have the best smile in the parish."

This upsets me. Now suddenly I find yet another obligation imposed on me. My freedom has been taken away from me so often. Now they are trying to deprive me of my freedom not to smile.

January 2, 1900.

I returned to our marriage bed last night.

It was an impulsive act. I realize now that it was irrational, that I should not have done it. In the moment, after the celebration of the beginning of a new century that my husband had organized, I seem to have lost control of myself. Perhaps I had consumed too much champagne. Maybe I wanted to be in bed with a man. Without searching for a reason or understanding what I was doing I simply walked into the room in my nightdress. He was, much to my surprise, very happy to see me. He asked no questions, he offered no recriminations, he did not mention the beginning of the new century or suggest a new beginning in our marriage.

He simply said, "Mary Louise, you are so very, very beautiful."

I have enough vanity left to be influenced by such a remark. In fact, for the second time in our life together those words quite melted my heart.

I thought my heart would never melt again.

Recklessly, shamelessly, I threw aside my gown.

Today I am filled with remorse and mortification. I have been false to poor Agnes's memory. I should not have permitted a renewal of our marriage. Indeed, I am firmly determined not to share the same bed with him tonight.

Despite that statement of determination I know that I will. Perhaps it is the only sensible thing. A man and a woman living in the same house can hardly avoid one another indefinitely. Even if there is no love and very little affection, even if rage and grief clutch at my heart, it is absurd to pretend that we are not husband and wife.

Later.

I am anxious, frightened, and curious.

At noon, Tom came home from his office for dinner as he often does. It is bitter cold outside and the snow is falling. Yet another blizzard which makes the lives of the poor even more miserable.

We said very little over the dinner table.

As he rose to return to the office, he said, quite softly, "Is it your intention to share my bed again tonight, my dear?"

I was flustered by the candor of the question, especially in the dining room where the servants might have heard it.

"I think it was the champagne last night," I said grudgingly.

His face was grim, his fist clenched white, his eyes burning brightly.

"It is your decision, my dear. However, I must warn you that if you make the decision to join me again, I shall never again permit you to leave."

All I could say before he was gone was a meek, "Oh."

I spent some of my time this afternoon making sure that the servants had warm clothes and blankets. They looked at me strangely. It has been a long time since I showed any concern for them. They surely know that my husband and I slept in the same bed last night.

It is the fire that was in his eyes which terrifies and intrigues me. What will he do to me?

January 3, 1900.

Last night I put aside the book I was reading and unsteadily climbed the stairs. Tom, whose eyes were more fiery at supper than at dinner, followed, a large and foreboding male presence behind me. I imagined his fingers tearing at my clothes, his hands digging into my body. No, I would not tolerate disgusting male passion. My heart beat wildly. My limbs were unsteady.

"I shall sleep in my own room," I said, trying to sound confident.

"It is your decision, my dear."

I do not have to say, however, that I turned into the room with our marriage bed. He chuckled softly.

I will not describe what happened, save to say that now I know the fires which burn within him. They consumed me last night, utterly and completely. I was but a piece of straw riding on those waves of fire.

"I trust I did not hurt you or frighten you, Mary Louise?" he asked weakly much later in the night, as we lay exhausted and covered with perspiration, despite the blizzard outside.

"Don't be absurd," I said, with as much dignity as I could muster. "You never would hurt me. You didn't give me time to be frightened. . . . And, Thomas Patrick Doolan, you need not be concerned about my departing from this bed ever again."

"I am happy to hear that."

"I have one question."

"Ah?"

"Do you propose that we engage in this kind of behavior every night?"

He chuckled.

"Not every night, Mary Louise, but often enough."

After that we slept in each other's arms. I was certain that I was loved with a love that, like God's, would never end.

We are, I believe, now fully married. Perhaps one must overcome tragedy with passion to be fully married.

I try to adapt myself to being happy. I re-

fuse to give way for the euphoria that is building up inside of me. I do not see how I can resist. I learn much about human nature. We get over our grief. They are still part of us, but we get over them and we do go on with life. People who told me that I should get on with my life appeared heartless and insensitive. However, they were right. I am now in the process of getting on with my life. As much as I hate it, happiness seems to be lurking for me just around the corner of 46th and Emerald. I cannot escape from it much longer. Nor can I escape from him. Amazingly, I do not want to.

April 15, 1900.

It is our darling child's second birthday. She smeared the birthday cake all over herself and then all over me and her father. She is a very pleasing child. And also very smart. She's talking in whole sentences now and humming along when we sing. She is convinced that I am her mother. I wonder if we ever should tell her any different. We don't know, we will never know who her mother and father were. She is in every respect now our child. And so I must begin to think of

*myself as her mother. This is no longer dif-
ficult. As a matter of fact it is easy, I do it
without thinking. Our Ellen has captured my
heart. In the process and despite my resistance she has put its broken pieces back
together again. I will always love her for that
and for everything else that she is and will
become. I will love her because, though I
didn't want her in the first place, she is now
my daughter.*

*July 4, 1900.
Lake Geneva, Wisconsin.*

*Our entire family is here this year for the
summer months. Tom has been able to ar-
range the responsibilities of his law practice
so that he need only spend three days a
week in Chicago. He rides back and forth on
the train to Williams Bay. It is a splendid
place. I love to be here and I know I'll miss
it when I go home. I think I'm pregnant again
though this time it does not seem that I will
be quite so sick. I haven't told Thomas because I want to be sure. I never wanted to
have another child, the heartache of losing
a child was too horrible. Then, whether I*

wanted it or not, another child was included into my life. Now that I may give birth to yet another child I find that I am delighted. It was a terrible risk to have a child. We Doolans cannot help ourselves. We want children just the same. I pray to God that I will be a good mother for this new child as I am trying to be a good mother for our dear little Ellen. I have even got into the habit of thanking God every day for Ellen, not as a substitute for Agnes but as a great blessing in my life.

My mother and father and my mother-in-law were here with us several days last week. It was intolerable. They complained about the inconvenience, about the house, about the cooking, about the servants, about everything they could see. I completely ignored them. My husband, poor man, simply nodded politely. He would whisper into my ear later, "Don't pay any attention to them, we're not going to change a thing."

"They resent my happiness," I said bitterly.

He guided my arm to him, "As always, my dear, I believe you are right."

I still have my quick tongue. I told the two

of them one afternoon as I was strolling along the lakeside that Tom and I swam almost every night, Indian style, in the lake. Of course we don't do that. They were horrified. They both told me I was an evil sinful woman, that I had no modesty, that I was a disgrace, and that I would corrupt my children with such behavior.

God forgive me for it, but I was delighted by their reaction. Perhaps they will not come here again.

Now I will have to tell Tom what I said. Perhaps the prospect would interest him.

I confess it certainly interests me.

July 18, 1900.

"You told them what!" Tom exploded in surprise and dismay.

"I told them that we swim Indian style in the lake almost every night. I said it just to make them angry, they are always picking at me and our marriage. I thought that would keep them away for a while."

Tom's face was red but he was not angry. I had embarrassed him—which I love to do.

"Mary Louise," he said, "you are an astonishing woman."

"If you say so."

"Oh," he said, "I say so. I would love to have been there to see the expressions on their faces."

"The expression just now on your face is interesting too," I said. "I have embarrassed you again. You know how much I like that."

"Well," he said cautiously, "what time to-night?"

I took a very deep breath and said, "Oh, Tommy, would eleven o'clock do?"

May 30, 1907.
Galway, Ireland, The Great Southern Hotel.

We have just crossed the country by train. Our hotel, a sumptuous and elegant place, is above the train station. We are taking a day off to rest from our trip. I thought it might be time to reflect. I have decided to jot down a few more thoughts in this old red leather notebook.

So long it has been since I kept this diary and so many things happened. Tom and Johnny are our two new and wonderful boy children. Our Ellen, now nine years old, has appointed herself an assistant mother to help me take care of these little hellions. She's got them charmed too. I wonder if there is anyone who is immune to Ellen's charm, the priests, the sisters of the school, the people on the streets, the servants, everyone is delighted by her.

As naturally so am I.

Sometimes, not very often but sometimes, I wonder what her parents were like. The charm has to be natural, she was born with it. In the family we've helped her to grow and develop. Her charm was there the first night that poor Father Dorney brought her into our house.

I cannot believe how terrible I was that year. Tom has often said that we won't discuss that interlude in our life. What was there to discuss? I was a fool, something I often am, and he's been an extraordinarily patient husband.

He's still a mystery, still impossible to figure out, still big and handsome and aloof and reserved. What goes on inside his soul escapes me completely. I want to know who he really is. I wanted to know that when we married but one way or the other it didn't seem to be necessary. Now that we have been married for ten years and are taking a second honeymoon here in Europe, I tell myself that I must find out who he is. I cannot live with this man towards whom my affections are so intense and still be a stranger. I must ask him on this trip to Ireland who and what he really is.

Thomas and I have discovered that both our families had come from the poorest part of the poorest county in Ireland. My family is from Ballyhaunis and his from Castlebar. The poverty of people there is just unbelievable. Even the poorest foreigners in Canaryville have proper places to live instead of the stone and thatched cottages. And even the poorest people in St. Gabriel's have a much better life than the people here. Small wonder that our ancestors emigrated to Chicago. Thomas says these people would not be poor if it were not for centuries of English oppression. That has to be true. But neither he nor I are willing to spend much money in the cause of violent nationalism. He admits to me that somebody has to rebel and kill English soldiers. But he doesn't want the blood to be on our hands. There is a conflict in these sentiments. I don't think there is anything we can do about it.

June 2.
Connemara.

Tom and I are staying several nights at a small hotel, out on this barren, desolate but incredibly beautiful peninsula. Last night I finally asked him the question. The result was an interlude in our marriage that I would not have believed possible.

"Thomas Patrick Doolan," I said to him as we lay together in bed, "who are you?"

"Pardon, my dear?"

"I said, who are you?"

My heart was beating fast, I was taking a big chance by trying to break through the wall of his reserve. The chance was worth taking and anyway, what loss could we suffer?

"When I married you, you were a stranger, an aloof but kindly stranger. Now ten years later you are still a stranger, a stranger in whose bed I sleep and who is always pleasant, kind, and considerate to me, who puts up with all my intolerable failings, and who tells me at least once a day that something is my decision. I am tired, Thomas Patrick Doolan, of living with a stranger."

I expected that he would dismiss my

question as foolish, the kind of question only a woman would ask.

"I'm your husband."

"I know that. What I want to know is, who is my husband?"

There was complete silence for a few moments.

"You still think I'm a stranger?"

"Well, in some ways certainly not, but in some ways, yes, you still are a stranger. You are a man who hides almost everything to himself, behind that polite reserved exterior. It's fine in the courtroom and it's wonderful when you are negotiating with business partners or those awful packing barons about cleaning up the mess they have made. It's not a good way to be with your wife."

"I'm sorry," he said with a catch in his voice.

"There is nothing to be sorry about," I replied. "I should have asked this question a long time ago. It's not your fault that you are so aloof, it's my fault for not telling you how much it troubles me."

"Do you love me?"

"Do I love you? Thomas Patrick Doolan! What do you think? Haven't I said that often

enough, haven't I acted that way often enough? Didn't what we just did together show how much I love you?"

"You told me before we were married that you did not love me."

"I was a silly, frivolous, immature child, Tommy. I found you a lot more attractive than I was willing to admit to myself. Haven't I told you often enough since then that I love you?"

"I know you have, Mary Louise. I thought perhaps you were simply going through the routine that you thought was appropriate for husband and wife. If I've learned one thing about you in our years together it is that you are a practical person. You do whatever is necessary in the circumstances even if it's distasteful. And you say whatever needs to be said even though your heart really isn't in it."

"I must admit that I've never thought of myself that way."

"I'm not being critical," he went on. "Rather, I admire your ability to adjust and to be in harmony with every possible situation, I wonder, however, to what extent I'm just one more possible situation?"

"You listen to me, Tommy Doolan, I

haven't been pretending, you're not a possible situation. I've loved you all along, I loved you even when I didn't think I loved you. I will always love you. You're a wonderful, wonderful husband. I could never ask for a better husband. I'm not just being tolerant of you, even if sometimes I seem to act that way. When you have been gone to the office all day and come in at the end of the day looking tired and sometimes discouraged, I become weak all over in my love for you. Is that enough?"

He drew me into his arms.

"It is more than enough, my dear. Sometimes I have thought to myself that that's your way and that you do feel powerful love for me. Yet I've never really been sure."

"Are you sure now?"

"I'm sure now, Mary Louise."

"You've turned the conversation back on me. We are not lying here in bed discussing me, we're discussing you."

"I will concede to the court that I am a hidden man. I do not speak often of my feelings or my emotions, of my joys or my sorrows. I quite agree with you that that is a mistake. One of your good traits as a mother that I admire greatly is your ability to let our

children talk of their feelings. I understand that this is not fashionable child rearing practice. I think it's by far the better way."

I've never even been aware that I've done that. Maybe I was the kind of person who couldn't do anything else.

"Thank you."

"It's my father. He's been dead these fifteen years now and I feel he's still watching everything I do."

I had thought that. I didn't say it, however. I let him go on.

"He said often that I was not a real man. My mother had spoiled me rotten. He said I would never survive in the practice of law because I was too soft. He said I would be a poor husband, because I was not tough enough to keep a woman in line."

"Did he keep your mother in line?"

"No. He thought he did. He thought he was the boss. As you must realize, he wasn't."

"You have done very well in the world, Thomas. You're a good lawyer and the best husband ever. Your father was wrong."

"I've never been sure."

"Well, you can be sure now."

He drew me to himself and hugged me very tightly.

"It's hard to explain, Mary Louise my love, since the day I first saw you I've wanted you. I've always been afraid of losing you. There were several times early in our marriage when I thought I would lose you. I suppose I've been afraid that if I told you how many terrors there are in my life I might lose you. I now realize that's silly. It will be difficult for me but I promise you that I will do everything I can to drop the wall between us."

"Well, Thomas Patrick Doolan, you can depend on it I'm going to claw at that wall."

"You have my permission," he said with a light laugh. "I'm not going to change completely, Mary Louise, but I think I am now, after ten years, confident enough in love that I'll be able to share a lot more of myself with you."

It was stiff and formal, but it was enough. I clung to him in near adoration.

"Oftentimes," he said, "I simply don't know what to make of you, you astonish me, you delight me, you baffle me, but, Mary Louise, you are never dull!"

"That's a great compliment," I said, kissing

him, and then kissing him again and again
and again. "I hope I always surprise you."

He sighed, and then I realized that he was
crying. Tom Doolan, the man without emotion, was crying as his wife just did. So I kept
on kissing him.

"Why do you weep, my dear?"

"Why does a baby cry when it's born?"

June 1, 1907.
London.

"What were you looking for when you tried
to salvage the ship off Michigan City?"

My husband and I were walking on the
Strand, arm in arm like young lovers. Suddenly that question had popped into my
mind and because our relationship is changing, however slowly, I felt I had to ask him.

He was quiet for a little while.

"Tommy?"

"Oh, Mary Louise, I heard the question. I
need time to think of how to answer it."

"You will answer it, however."

He hugged me fiercely. It was embarrassing on a street in London but I didn't care.

"I am now finding myself in a phase in my

life when there are questions that I have to answer."

"That is correct, Thomas."

"There were no elaborate plans when the cruise was planned. It was straightforward. The Ancient Order of Hibernians needed to raise money as I told you then. I didn't want to go but I felt that out of loyalty I had to. On the other side of the lake I encountered a man and a woman with a child. Presumably the child was Ellen and the man and woman were her parents, they were even younger than we were. They had just arrived from Ireland and they had been searching for me because they wanted to give me something. They had heard about the cruise to Saugatuck and felt it would be better to find me there than to come to St. Gabriel's, which was, I hardly need tell you, seething at that time with Irish nationalism. He gave me a box. It was not a large box, oh maybe twelve inches square. He wanted me to take it home and to keep it for an unspecified amount of time until he or someone else came back and asked for the package that I had received. It was carefully wrapped. And closely sealed. I sensed that there was some sort of metal container inside it. Yet it was not heavy enough to be gold."

"You didn't find the box?"

"No, I didn't find the damn thing. Yet I am convinced that it is out there somewhere. Perhaps someday someone will find it. That young man and his wife risked their lives to get the box to me. If he hadn't tried to reach me on the ship, he and his wife would be still alive and their daughter would have her real parents."

"We're her parents now, Thomas."

"You know what I mean. . . . It seemed to him to be a wise way to deliver the box. It was much better than his showing up at my office in the Exchange Building where you can't tell who might be watching. Both of them were terrified. Apparently he had stolen whatever was in the box from people who were going to sell it to get money for arms. Perhaps his days were numbered anyway. Nonetheless, I feel responsible for what happened to him."

"How did he know you would be on the cruise?"

"His people, whoever they are, must have allies in Chicago. They heard about our cruise and somehow got word to him. . . .

They were so very young, Mary Louise, so very young."

"You're too hard on yourself, Thomas."

"Sometimes I know that, Mary Louise. I'm not really responsible for their deaths or for the death of little Agnes. Yet if I had made a couple of different decisions, they would all still be alive."

"I wasn't much help to you in those days, was I?" He shrugged his shoulders.

"We had different ways of crying, Mary Louise. I understood how you felt. I couldn't tell you how I felt. Moreover, in those days I thought I'd better keep the secret of the man from Detroit."

"Did he speak of his little girl as 'Ellen'?"

"I think so. We're not certain that our Ellen really is his daughter. I thought Ellen might be a nice name to call her."

"It's such a dear name I'm glad he chose it."

"It's more dear because of the person that bears the name, I think, than just the name itself."

I agreed with him.

"I'm sorry for how bad I was during that year. Please forgive me."

"I was not angry at you, Mary Louise. I

520 ANDREW M. GREELEY

knew that you would get over it and would be my wonderful wife again."

"You're not going to hide from me any-more, Tommy, are you?"

"I'll be careful, Mary Louise, I'll try not to hide. I will depend on you to prevent me from doing that."

"You knew about Timmy Millan, of course?"

"I understood before we married that you had a crush at one time on him. I thought that was over. I didn't realize until after we were married how deeply you felt. I'm sorry that he died when he did. From everything I knew about him he was a wonderful man."

"He has gone, Thomas. Just like our little Agnes. The two of them are looking down on us and taking care of us."

"So we must believe, Mary Louise, so we must believe."

25

Nuala sobbed. I felt salt in my eyes too.

"Dermot Michael, what a beautiful story!"

"We really don't know the end of it, Nuala. They're still in their early thirties in the story and are going to live thirty more years."

"Well, maybe there are diaries all around someplace. It would be interesting to see how herself reacted to all the changes that must go on in the world. Still, the story really ends there. The story we're interested in. Now we know what the mystery was. All we have to do is to find the box."

That's all. No problem.

"How are we going to find the box?"

"Isn't that obvious, Dermot Michael. Aren't we going to go down to Grand Beach and isn't your daughter going to find it for us?"

"How is Nellie going to do that?"

"Isn't she going to crawl around on the dune and when she starts to cry and shout, then we know that's where we have to dig."

"You're going to use my daughter as a divining rod?"

"Dermot Michael, this psychic business is no fun. If you're going to have it I think we might as well use it once in a while to do something good for people."

26

The next morning Nuala asked if I would ever let her borrow the Benz for a couple of hours. She had left milk and baby food in the fridge for herself.

"Sure," I said, not looking up from my keyboard. The new novel was now moving at breakneck speed.

I didn't ask her where she was going with it. If she wanted to tell me, she would. Doubtless she expected me to ask.

"Would you ever mind if I went out to see Maybelline?"

"It's your decision, my dear!"

She thought that was pretty funny.

Fiona was disappointed that she wasn't permitted to accompany her chief.

"Your job," I told her, "is to take care of Nelliecoyne."

Reluctantly she traipsed up the stairs.

I fed the child, burped her, and changed her diaper. She made enough fuss about the feeding and burping to let me know I wasn't doing it right. Since it was not time for her next nap, I brought her down to my office and put her on the floor. I stationed the wolfhound at the door.

"Don't let her out of here, Fiona."

The child displayed no interest in crawling out of my office. Her intent rather was to disrupt it as much as possible.

Finally a key turned in the front door. Fiona barked and dashed to the door. Nelliecoyne charged after her. I followed in the show position.

"Och, isn't it a grand welcome committee? Yes, Fiona, me darlin', I love you too. Nelliecoyne, you look neglected. Hasn't your daddy been taking care of you?"

"He has too."

She kissed me with more vigor than the situation demanded.

"You didn't change her diaper?"

"Woman, I did!"

"You didn't feed her?"

"Woman, I did."

"You didn't burp her?"

"Woman, I did."

"Isn't that grand! I don't suppose you made a fruit salad for me?"

"Woman, I did."

"Did you really! Dermot Michael Coyne, aren't you the sweetest husband in all the world!"

"Woman, I am!"

My wife put our daughter to bed. She was sleeping almost before her head hit the pillow.

"Didn't you tire her out, Dermot Michael?"

"She tired herself out."

"Crawl around your office, did she?"

"She did."

"Well, where's me fruit salad? I'm perishing with the hunger."

We settled down to the fruit salad and a "small glass" of white wine.

"Don't I need it after that terrible place? Dermot, promise me that when I go crazy you won't put me in such a terrible place!"

"I promise, though I doubt that you'll ever

go crazy. Besides, how would I know the difference!"

"Brat!" she protested.

"How's Maybelline?"

"Tranquil."

"Valium?"

"No, one of the newer mood-stabilizing drugs—Depakote. And lots of it. I'm thinking . . . why didn't anyone notice she was manic?"

"Perhaps because she was always that way."

"Well, now I'm her new best friend. We're great buddies, so I suppose that's a good thing."

"What our Jewish friends call a mitzvah."

She sighed, the virtuous sigh of a woman who has done a good work.

"Would you ever do two favors for me, Dermot Michael?"

"That many!"

"The first one is to call Martha Farmer for me and ask if she has time to talk to me."

I looked up the number of NewFacts, her firm, and called her. Of course, she had a few minutes for my wife.

Nuala motioned for me to stay on the phone.

They chatted about children for a few moments. Martha said that hers were "as good as could be expected" under the strain of the last several days.

Then Nuala got down to business.

"Was there ever a scandal back in the days when you and your friends were working on the high school paper?"

Martha hesitated, perhaps wondering what was behind the question.

Then she answered, "It wasn't really a scandal. One of us submitted a story for the paper about an experience over at Rosehill Cemetery. It was wonderfully written and very scary. A parent called and said the story couldn't be true because it had mixed up the locations of certain graves. We replied that actually it was fictional and said that in the next issue. A lot of kids in the school were disappointed because it was such a wonderful ghost story."

"Who wrote the story?"

Martha didn't hesitate this time. She answered candidly.

Nuala went on to other questions about Chicago high schools, which were not of immediate interest to us, but which provided a way for her to ease out of the conversation.

So that was the way of it.

My next call was to John Culhane.

"John, do you have a record of the books and papers which were on Nick Farmer's desk when your men searched his apartment?"

"Sure, Dermot. Let me see. Hey, there's a lot of books on one subject. . . ."

"Nigeria!" Nuala said with a whoop of triumph. "I knew it. Roger Conrad wrote a prize-winning book on Nigeria. Nick Farmer remembered that he had once submitted a fake story to the high school paper years ago. He suspected that the Nigeria book was a little too good to be true. He was trying to prove it and destroy Conrad."

"After all of the stories this year about journalistic fakes! Was the book a fake?"

"I don't know for sure. Farmer thought it was. He was trying to prove it. Conrad found out, maybe from Doug Jurgens. He couldn't face the disgrace. So there's probably some fakery in it. Find someone at the University of Chicago and ask them what they think."

Culhane was silent for a moment.

"It would be a motive for murder, though it would be hard to prove. We'll roll up Zog and his crowd of Balkan commandos in a day or two. I suspect that some of them will tell us."

"You could ask Conrad himself, poor man."

"We will certainly do that. . . . Good work, Nuala Anne."

"Thank you."

She sighed after we had hung up.

"It couldn't be Martha, because she still loved her husband. Anyway, she's not a big enough player to bother with. Why would Doug Jurgens kill him? News directors are not exactly virtuous men. Still how would you rebuild your career by exposing one of them? No, he had to be after a big fish. Roger Conrad was the only big fish."

"Robin Cleary and Johnny Quinn?"

"No money there. Your FBI was already after them. Besides, they're too dumb to be killers. Then I remember what they said about fakes. Martha told us that Roger had submitted a story when they were in high school which was a brilliantly written fake. They saved him, probably because she persuaded Nick to say it was intended to be fiction. Nick remembered. When Roger's book on Nigeria was such a success, Nick was furious with envy. Then perhaps he realized that Roger was not what Doug Jurgens called a 'hard-edged' reporter, a little too lazy to take the chances the book must have involved. He set out to destroy Roger."

"How did Roger find out? From Martha?"

"Nick wouldn't have told her because she wouldn't have approved. We'll never know for sure. As I said, perhaps Doug hinted to him about it."

"It all figures," I admitted, astonished at how clearly Nuala "saw" things when she turned on whatever dimensions of herself that are dedicated to "seeing."

"They're all such fools," she said bitterly. "None of it had to happen. Why would Roger run the risk of a huge fake? Someone would have found out eventually, especially in this time when fakes are popping up all over the place. Why would Nick need to destroy an old friend? Why would Doug let himself get involved? Was a story worth that much? Poor people."

"Poor people indeed, Nuala Anne."

"Martha is an innocent, Dermot Michael, a sweet, lovely innocent who needs a nice husband to protect her from her innocence. We'll have to find one for her."

Naturally.

"We have solved both mysteries."

"And I need a nap."

"Alone?"

"Don't be silly, Dermot Michael Coyne."

There was, unfortunately, one possibility which Nuala and I had not taken into account.

27

We were sitting in the first floor of our house when the Balkan gang shot their way in. We were watching the PBS series on the Pope of which the Bishop had spoken at our dinner with Nessa and Seamus. Nelliecoyne was sleeping peacefully on the couch. The wolfhound was curled up beside her. Nuala and I, arm in arm, were watching the fascinating story. Suddenly automatic weapons fire tore apart our front door. Three men in black ski masks came bursting in. One of them had an automatic weapon and the other two had dangerous-looking knives. While the man with the automatic weapon covered us, one of the knife bearers snatched Nellie off the couch. He must not have noticed the wolfhound or he must not have thought she was important. Instantly Fiona jumped on him, knocked him to the floor, and grasped his throat with her teeth. He dropped Nelliecoyne as he fell. Nuala dove from the couch and rolled over with the baby in her arms. The man with the automatic weapon moved it back and forth as if he was going to kill the lot of us. The wolfhound's attack surprised him. Thus I had time to jump on him, diverting the weapon into the air. The burst of gunfire ripped into the ceiling of the room. The other man with the knife closed in on me. I kicked the man with the gun, yanked it out of his hand, and swung it towards the attacker who was now only a few feet away from me. I hesitated to begin firing for fear the ricocheting bullets might hurt somebody. Besides, I had no idea how to work an automatic weapon.

Then the man whom Fiona had pinned to the floor sank his knife into her side. Blood poured from her side and stained her white fur. The knife wielder had made a terrible mistake. Fiona tore out his throat. His blood gurgled out. The man advancing towards me stopped in horror. Even gangsters are shocked when somebody dies such a horrible death. I swung the barrel of the automatic weapon and hit him in the face and now it was his turn to scream. The man from whom I'd taken the weapon jumped on me.

At that point I wouldn't have given any of us much of a chance to survive. I had not reckoned with Nuala's canogi stick. She hit the two remaining invaders on the back of the head with it. A sharp bark of wood hitting bone exploded. Both of them slumped to the bloody floor. Fiona was yelping with pain. Nelliecoyne was screaming.

Then the reinforcements arrived, two of Mike Casey's Reliables arrived with drawn guns.

"Dermot!" Nuala said, clutching our daughter to her breast. "Fiona is going to bleed to death!"

"Not if I can help it!" I said, which is an appropriate line for John Wayne in a situation like that.

At that point I heard the sirens of the uniformed police of the Sixth District arriving on the scene. I grabbed a pillow and stuck it into the wound on Fiona's side to stop the flow of blood. One of Mike Casey's staff said, "I know where you can find a veterinarian! Let's get her into the car!"

So I carried the bleeding dog to the surveillance car and we sped over to Clark Street. I didn't think Fiona was going to make it. She'd made no attempt to resist being carried away, most unlikely behavior for any dog, especially a wolfhound.

She weighed 130 pounds but somehow she didn't seem that heavy as I carried her out to the car.

"It will be all right, girl, it will be all right," I reassured her. Or perhaps I was only reassuring myself.

Somebody must have called the veterinarian before we got there because she was waiting for us.

"Good heavens!" she shouted. "What have they done to this beautiful dog?"

"A guy stuck a knife in her as she jumped him because he had seized the little girl the dog was protecting."

The vet had us put her on the operating table and quickly injected something. Fiona's eyes looked glassy. I was afraid she was going to die right there.

"It's an artery," said the doctor, "she's lost a lot of blood. I'll rig up a transfusion."

I didn't know they had transfusions for dogs.

"You stopped the flow of blood, sir," she said to me, "now let's see what we can do about stitching her up."

Fiona's large brown eyes were sad. She looked at me pleadingly as though begging me to keep her alive.

"Don't be afraid, girl," I said, "it's going to be all right, it's going to be all right."

"Good dog," the vet said as she worked feverishly. "Very good dog."

Fiona whimpered in return.

"It was a close one," the young woman finally told us as she stitched up the hole in Fiona's side. "I think she's going to make it, aren't you, good doggie?"

"Fiona," I said, "good dog, very good dog."

Fiona responded with a weakened bark.

We moved into our apartment at the Hancock Center late that night until the mess at our house was cleaned up. Nelliecoyne was fretful, displeased, upset, as well she might have been. I suggested that we might not want to return. Nuala Anne would have none of it.

"Wouldn't that upset Letitia?"

"Nuala Anne, Letitia Walsh Murray is in heaven. Nothing upsets them there!"

"How do you know?"

Then she took her daughter in her arms and sang to her.

"Dread spirits of the Blackwater,
Clan Coyne's wild bahn si,
Bring no ill to him or us,
My helpless babe and me.
And Holy Mary pitying us,
To heaven for grace does sue,
Sing hush a bye loo, lo loo lo lan,
Hushabye loo lo loo."

The next day my daughter and my wife and I, the former two much more relaxed than I, drove up to the veterinarian's.

Fiona's cage looked like a hospital room. She lay on her side with a couple of IVs hanging above her. The vet had tied her down and sedated her lest she pull on the stitches and the IVs. She looked up at us and whimpered.

"Good dog." The vet caressed her forehead. "This dog is a very special patient."

"She's an Irish female," I said, "they have their ways."

Nelliecoyne, with the doctor's help, touched the good dog's huge snout. Nuala and I petted her. She made a noise like a purr of satisfaction.

"She'll be up and around in a day or two," the vet told us. "She's one very lucky dog. You saved her life, sir, when you applied that compress."

"Didn't she save all of our lives?"

On our next visit, Fiona was up and about, a little shaky on her feet. The veterinarian's two kids, early primary school, were fussing over her. Fiona was eating up their attention. Faithless bitch.

At the end of the week, after we had returned to Southport Avenue, we brought her home. No running for a couple of weeks. She immediately went on a patrol of the house to make sure that the smells hadn't changed since she had left. Then she barked happily and insisted on kissing all three of us.

"Sure, Fiona," Nuala said as she hugged the massive pooch, "what would we do without you."

The Chicago cops had rolled up the Balkan gang at the very time three of their members were trying to kill us. On a contract put out by Roger Conrad. Martha Grimm, meaning no harm, had mentioned to him as a curiosity our interest in the faked article of their high school years. He knew that we were on to the same story as Nicholas had been investigating. When the police went to his office to arrest him the following morning, they found that he had hung himself. Doug Jurgens admitted to the police that Nick had given him hints that he was working on an exposé of Conrad's prize-winning book on Nigeria. He argued that he had not thought that Nick could ever deliver such a story. Nor did he think that Roger was the kind of man who would put out a contract on anyone. In his depressed mood he would not. However, according to his doctor, in his manic mood he would do almost anything. He had not taken his medication for several weeks.

"Two women without husbands," Nuala said with a sigh. "Why do men have to be such fools. . . . Not all men, Dermot Michael, just some of them."

"Conrad was afraid of disgrace."

" 'Tis no excuse, poor dear man. God rest him, and Nicholas too. And that poor man that Fiona killed."

Indeed.

They would all go on her nightly prayer list.

Nuala insisted that we visit Bubbly Creek, a place which I had steadfastly avoided all my life because of rumors that blacks who had been killed in the 1919 race riot had been thrown into its polluted depths. However, as we gazed at it from the parking lot of the Riverside Shopping Center on Ashland Avenue just south of Archer (Mr. Dooley's Archery Road) it seemed quite harmless, even peaceful, in the late October afternoon sunlight. Two canoeists paddled by as we watched.

"Should they be doing that?" herself asked me.

"So long as they don't try to swim or fall in. None of the larger craft use it anymore, so it's a nice place to canoe."

"Uhm . . . you know, Dermot, this is the place where for the first time she admitted to herself that she found him physically attractive, though she wouldn't have used those words."

"If you say so, Nuala Anne."

" 'Tis true. The whole story started here."

She sighed her loudest West of Ireland sigh. Sometimes that sigh is melancholy. But not always.

28

It was not a bad day for November, temperatures in the upper fifties. George the Priest, Nuala, the little Bishop, Nelliecoyne, and myself were at my parents' house at Grand Beach. I thought the project was utterly mad. I don't know what George the Priest thought. The little Bishop probably thought it was delightful. He arranged himself on a deck chair, pulled out of storage just for him to survey the whole situation. He seemed quite confident that Nelliecoyne would unearth the buried treasure.

Nuala's idea was simple enough. When we had experienced the vibrations in October, that was a sign we were supposed to find the magic box. It seemed to me most unlikely that the box would be in our dune. One hundred years had passed. The winds and the waves had come and gone. Our dune undoubtedly had been shaped and re-shaped many times before the house was built back in 1917. The landscaping had changed, the shape of the dune had changed, the beach had changed, it would be pure luck if the box was there at all. More likely it was somewhere out under the sand-bars on the Lake.

My fey daughter was dressed warmly in a black and red Chicago Bulls warm-up suit, including a matching ski cap which, as far as I know, the Bulls never wore for a game. In fact I don't think even Dennis Rodman, aka Rodzilla, ever wore one.

And, oh yes, the wolfhound was there too, parading around as though she owned the dune and the beach and the Lake and the City of Chicago many miles away invisible in the distance.

So, after a cup of coffee and a dozen rai-sin Danish purchased at the Village Bake Shop in New Buffalo (the best such rolls in the North American world, according to the little Bishop, who ate three of them), we went to work. Nuala put Nelliecoyne on the lawn in front of the house. Characteristically, she decided she didn't want to crawl. Rather, she rolled over, sat up, and made faces at the little Bishop. Naturally, he made faces back.

"Nelliecoyne," Nuala insisted, "we're here to work, not to flirt with the poor man."

So it was decided that if she didn't want to crawl we would just pick her up and carry her across the lawn and down the steps of the dune and out along the beach, now utterly abandoned beneath the naked trees that leaned over us like watchmen in a graveyard.

We walked up and down the beach, Nellie in Nuala's arms, waiting for something to happen. Nothing did.

It was, I said to myself, an absolutely crazy notion, nobody is going to find a box from the missing ship after a hundred years and one month simply by carrying a possibly fey child up and down a dune and around on the beach.

After an hour and a half of fruitless search, it was time for lunch. We went back to the house and fed Nellie with baby food, much of which she endeavored to throw at the little Bishop with appropriate screams of glee. The rest of us settled for Swiss cheese burgers from Redamak's.

"Isn't the little brat going to sleep now," Nuala asked. "But she can't go to sleep until she finds the buried treasure for us, can she?"

"She's your daughter, Nuala," said George the Priest.

"You are absolutely certain, Nuala Anne, the treasure is there?" the little Bishop asked.

"Well, Your Reverence, not to say absolutely certain. It's not like some of those other things that I'm really certain about."

"I don't know anything at all about this," I said, though no one had asked for my opinion. "However, if my daughter wants to sleep, we may as well let her sleep. She's not going to be any good to us if she isn't wide awake."

Nuala went upstairs to take a nap with her, and the little Bishop, George the Priest, and I went for a walk on the dune.

"This is absolutely the craziest thing I've ever done in all my life," I told them.

"Little Bro, I wouldn't mess with those two

women in your life for all the money in the world. If Nuala says there's a treasure around here someplace, I'm not going to disagree with her."

"It can do no harm," the little Bishop said wisely, "for us to continue to look."

So after Nelliecoyne woke up and I changed her diaper and put the Bulls uniform back on her, we sallied forth once again.

Incidentally, Nuala isn't the one responsible for the Chicago athletic team's clothes her daughter wears. She does admit, however, that they're darlin' altogether.

We had hardly locked the door of the house when she began to scream just as she had on those mysterious Indian summer nights.

"She knows something is close," Nuala said, confident that her predictions were correct.

"Why didn't she scream when she came out of the house in the morning?"

"Dermot Michael, you ought to know by now that this business of picking up vibrations doesn't follow any logical rules."

"I'm not sure I like the idea of my daughter being a divining rod."

"Your wife is a divining rod too," Nuala insisted. "So let's just see what happens when we put her on the ground."

The ground in November was too cold for that. But what did I know?

Though wailing fiercely, Nellie began to crawl across the dry brown grass of our front yard. I could never see why we had to have a lawn on the top of the dune. Dune grass would have been more natural. My father said the lawn was there when we got it and anyway we might just as well keep it up.

The logic of the argument escaped me, like I said, however, what did I know!

"We lost a lot of the dune in the storm in '72," George said. "Most of this is fill."

"You mean this isn't the original dune?"

"I don't think so," said George. "It was twenty-six years ago and I don't remember all the details, but I think we hauled a lot of sand and dirt in here."

So Nellie crawled vigorously across the lawn and then headed right for the edge of the dune. Did she know she was supposed to be a human divining rod?

What do babies know anyway?

They know how to drive their parents crazy, that's what they know.

Nuala snatched the child up just as she reached the stairs going to the beach. Very slowly and carefully we walked down the stairs again. Then at the very edge of the deck which was just a few feet above the beach, Nellie went ballistic.

"It's nearby, Dermot, I know it's nearby."

She walked back and forth along the platform a couple of times and then settled on one spot where Nellie's cries were loud enough to be heard across the Lake in Chicago.

"It's right below here, Dermot," Nuala insisted. "I know it's right underneath this deck and down in the sand. I don't know how it got there but it's there."

Then, astonishingly, our child stopped wailing and snuggled into her mother's arms. It was as though whatever she was supposed to do had been done and now she could relax.

She didn't need a lullaby. Nuala sang one anyway.

"Astonishing," George said. "Absolutely astonishing."

"Uh-huh."

"Arguably," the little Bishop added.

I removed from a pocket of my Bulls

denim jacket a large indelible marker I had been carrying with me for just such an eventuality and painted a great red "X" on the deck.

"What do we do now?" I asked.

"Isn't it obvious, Little Bro," said the priest. "We get a contractor to come out here and he'll move the deck and dig beneath it, right on this spot."

"How are we going to explain this to Mom and Dad?"

"Sure, Dermot Michael, won't that be easy? Won't I tell them that I'm convinced that there's buried treasure underneath the sand, a kind of Holy Grail?"

"Oh."

That's what she told them and they might have thought that all of us were crazy. However, my parents being the kind of people that they were had no objection so long as we put everything back.

Joe Anderson, our contractor, was a bit concerned about the possible intervention of the Army Corps of Engineers or the Michigan Department of Natural Resources. I reassured him that it would be a one-day task and the sand would be replaced at the end of the day. So, at the end of November, six weeks after the two ships had mysteriously appeared in the Indian summer evening, we were back with the same crew, Nelliecoyne snug in her mother's arms, Fiona as lordly as ever. Mr. Anderson and his two sons had maneuvered a front loader into position on the beach. Very carefully they removed the boards of the deck and then began to clear the sand beneath the red spot on the deck, sand which had washed in during the March storm. Some storms stole beach and dune, others restored them.

I'm sure they thought we were crazy. So did I.

We were all bundled up because even though the sun was shining, it was a cold November morning. This morning Nelliecoyne was wearing a Chicago Bears sweatshirt and was wrapped protectively in an orange and blue blanket. Her mother also wore a Chicago Bears sweatshirt and her usual jeans.

They must have lifted fifteen or twenty loads of sand and dumped it behind the sea wall. Nothing but sand.

"I think we are getting close to the clay," Joe Anderson warned us.

"Clay?" Nuala exclaimed in dismay.

550 ANDREW M. GREELEY

"The base at the bottom of the Lake, underneath the sand, is clay, ma'am."

Nelliecoyne slept in Nuala's arms. Fiona, curled up on the beach, watched us with an air of tolerance at the human follies. Periodically I threw a stick into the water and she chased it, utterly unperturbed by the fifty-two-degree temperature of the water.

Then they hit something that was not sand. It crunched as though it were fragile. The workers grabbed shovels and began to move the sand away from whatever it was they hit. Sure enough, it was wood, wreckage of some sort.

"Something that probably washed in with the sandbars during the big storm in March," Anderson said.

"We had better be careful now," I warned everyone. "We have an archaeological find here."

The wood might have at one time been part of a ship's cabin. Or so it looked to us who were expecting a cabin.

I wondered how we would explain our "dig" to the Department of Natural Resources. I decided that we'd better not. Next summer we'd tell them that there was a lot of driftwood on the new beach which the

March storms the previous year had piled up on the beach. They could dig if they wanted to. If there really was a treasure in the rubble, they would want to claim it.

Suddenly, Nuala shoved Nellie into my arms and jumped into the rubble. She kicked through the sand and shoved it away. Fiona bounded in after her and joined in the fun.

Nuala burrowed into the sand, shoving her head and the upper part of her body into it as if she were some sort of burrowing creature. Then, she pulled herself out of the sand and held above her head triumphantly a small box, just as Thomas Doolan had described it to his wife in London ninety-one years ago. Fiona barked loudly in celebration.

Nelliecoyne stirred in my arms, distracted from her nap. She opened her eyes, considered the situation, thought better of it, and went back to sleep.

"See, Dermot Michael, didn't I tell you we'd find it now?"

"Woman, you did."

"You are a wise woman, Nuala Anne," the little Bishop said.

"Maybe we ought not to open it," George

the Priest said. "Maybe we ought to find an archaeologist."

"Och, Your Reverence, you're just as daft as your brother. Aren't *we* supposed to open it now?"

That was easier said than done. We had to get one of our big screwdrivers and plunge the screwdriver into the lid of the box to pry it open.

Inside were several cloths, old and dark and moldy.

Nuala tore off the wrapping and finally came to the buried treasure, stolen from violent revolutionaries in Ireland over a hundred years ago so they couldn't try to turn it into money for more violence.

"Would you look at it! Isn't it the most beautiful thing you've ever seen?"

"The Ardagh Chalice!" George gasped.

It looked to be a tarnished drinking goblet, studded with stones. But what would I know?

"I think not," the Bishop said, examining the treasure which Nuala Anne had thrust eagerly into his hands. "It's small like the Ardagh Cup, but unless I am mistaken, it may well be older and it is certainly more richly covered in jewels. Presumably those who had discovered it were going to remove the jewels and sell them."

That was that. We had discovered a precious relic of Irish antiquity for which a man and a woman and a child had died a hundred years ago, a Holy Grail that my daughter, with some assistance from my wife, had discovered again. Just as Tom Doolan had predicted ninety-one years ago.

"What will we do with it?" I asked.

"Well, what else can we do with it?" my wife replied. "Aren't we going to give it back to the people of Ireland who have owned it all along."

And so we did at Christmastime when we brought Nelliecoyne to the land of her origins. We paid a discreet visit to the National Museum. The chalice (or grail as I always called it) had disappeared during Cromwell's depredations. There were rumors that it had surfaced at the end of the last century. The curators asked no questions. The find was reported the next day in *The Irish Times*. There were no hints about who found it.

" 'Tis a lovely chalice, Dermot Michael, isn't it?" herself said as we walked across Stephen's Green to have lunch at The Commons in the basement of the house where

Newman had been rector, Hopkins a teacher, and Joyce a student.

" 'Tis," I agreed, as I was supposed to.

"No matter how beautiful, not worth risking the lives of three people."

"It wasn't the chalice, Nuala Anne. It was a winter storm that came too early, an old boat, and a dangerously irresponsible captain. Ellen's parents were young and romantic and convinced that they were immortal. They were caught in an accident, just like the plane crashes that kill many innocent young people."

"Aren't they all happy that the chalice has been returned? Even happier in heaven now?"

"I'm sure they are."

"Och, Dermot Michael, aren't you the most brilliant husband in all the world!"

I wasn't and I'm not. But you take praise wherever you can find it. That I was a brilliant husband and a brilliant father became the theme of our visit.

YOU'RE BEGINNING TO BELIEVE THAT BULL-SHIT.

"What matters is that she believes it."

FOR HOW LONG?

The new disc was an instant hit. I made progress on my novel. The Christmas TV program had sky-high ratings. We heard on good authority that Nessa would receive a ring at Christmas. Maybelline was quiet and smiling at our family Christmas party the Sunday before Christmas (and the day before we left for Ireland). She and Nuala were together for a good part of the time. Nelliecoyne stole the show by toddling around the party. She shouted gleefully after every successful step. Nuala had taken both Maybelline and Martha Grimm under her wing. The lines of tension around her eyes diminished. More and more she enjoyed her daughter and less and less did she worry about her. We gave the Mary Louise diaries to the Chicago Historical Society. With a few tears from my wife, we deposited Fiona with Cindy's family. She made friends instantly with Cindy's kids and pretended not to notice us when we were leaving.

Nelliecoyne won the hearts of everyone she met in Ireland. Naturally. Especially since she was cautiously experimenting with walking.

When Irish eyes are smiling, sure they'll

steal your heart away, especially when they are the green eyes of a little girl with red hair who has just learned to walk and whose smile is as almost as big as her mother's.

NOTE

In the text of this story I have acknowledged my debit to Louise Wade and Thomas Jablonski for telling me the real story of the "Jungle" and exorcising the versions of both Upton Sinclair and my predecessors at the University of Chicago.

There are scores of books about Great Lakes shipping and shipwrecks. They are available from Northern Lights Bookstore—*www.norlights.com*. Two that were especially useful were *"A Fully Accredited Ocean": Essays on the Great Lakes* edited by Victoria Brehm and *Great Lakes Shipwrecks and Survivals* by William A. Ratigan.

A beautiful book of photographs and prints is *Ladies of the Lake* by James Clary. There is an especially wonderful drawing of the graceful *David Dows,* a five-masted barkentine on which the *Charles C. Campbell* is based. The largest sailing boat ever to appear on the Great Lakes, the ship was launched in 1881 and sank in the ice off Whiting, Indiana, in late November of 1889. She did ram and sink a ship but no lives were lost.

Although Chicago was the busiest port in the world in 1870 and the fourth busiest (after New York, London, and Hamburg) at the turn of the century, there, alas, is no comprehensive history of shipping into Chicago.

The shipwreck on which the story is based was the ramming of the *Lady Elgin* off Winnetka, Illinois, by the schooner *Augusta* in the summer of 1860. God rest those that died in the wreck and all those who have died on these terrible inland oceans.

I am indebted to Robert Hornaday for the story of the wreck discovered in the dune forty years ago at Grand Beach and to John and Richard Daley for background about the Yards and Canaryville. Seamus Heaney and Nóirín Ní Rrian found Irish lullabies for me.

None of the people in the story exist outside my imagination.

Will there be more people in the Coyne family, when next we meet them? Well, isn't that up to God?

AG
Grand Beach
Summer 1998